DANIEL CROGAN

ALLOWAY" CROGAN

PRIVATE EYE, c.1951

tur

WITHDRAWN

ALEXANDER CROGAN

RET AGENT, c.1964

BENJAMIN

GUNFIGH

8

JUN

i+

2012

JOSEP

DIAMOND
MINER, c.1893

ETER CROGAN

LEGIONNAIRE, c.1912

CROGAN'S
LOYALTY

*This book is dedicated to Woody, Howie, and Chingy,
who became my brothers when I married their sister, and
Ryan, who joined their ranks when he married mine.*

CROGAN'S LOYALTY

by

Chris Schweizer

· ·

book design by
Keith Wood

edited by
James Lucas Jones and **Jill Beaton**

AN ONI PRESS PUBLICATION

Published by Oni Press, Inc.

JOE NOZEMACK, publisher

JAMES LUCAS JONES, editor in chief

KEITH WOOD, art director

CORY CASONI, marketing director

GEORGE ROHAC, operations director

JILL BEATON, editor

CHARLIE CHU, editor

TROY LOOK, digital prepress lead

ONI PRESS, INC.
1305 SE Martin Luther King Jr. Blvd.
Suite A
Portland, OR 97214
USA

www.onipress.com
www.curiousoldlibrary.com

First edition: June 2012
Library of Congress Control Number: 2011943514

ISBN: 978-1-934964-40-8

1 3 5 7 9 10 8 6 4 2

Printed in China at 1010 Printing International Limited.

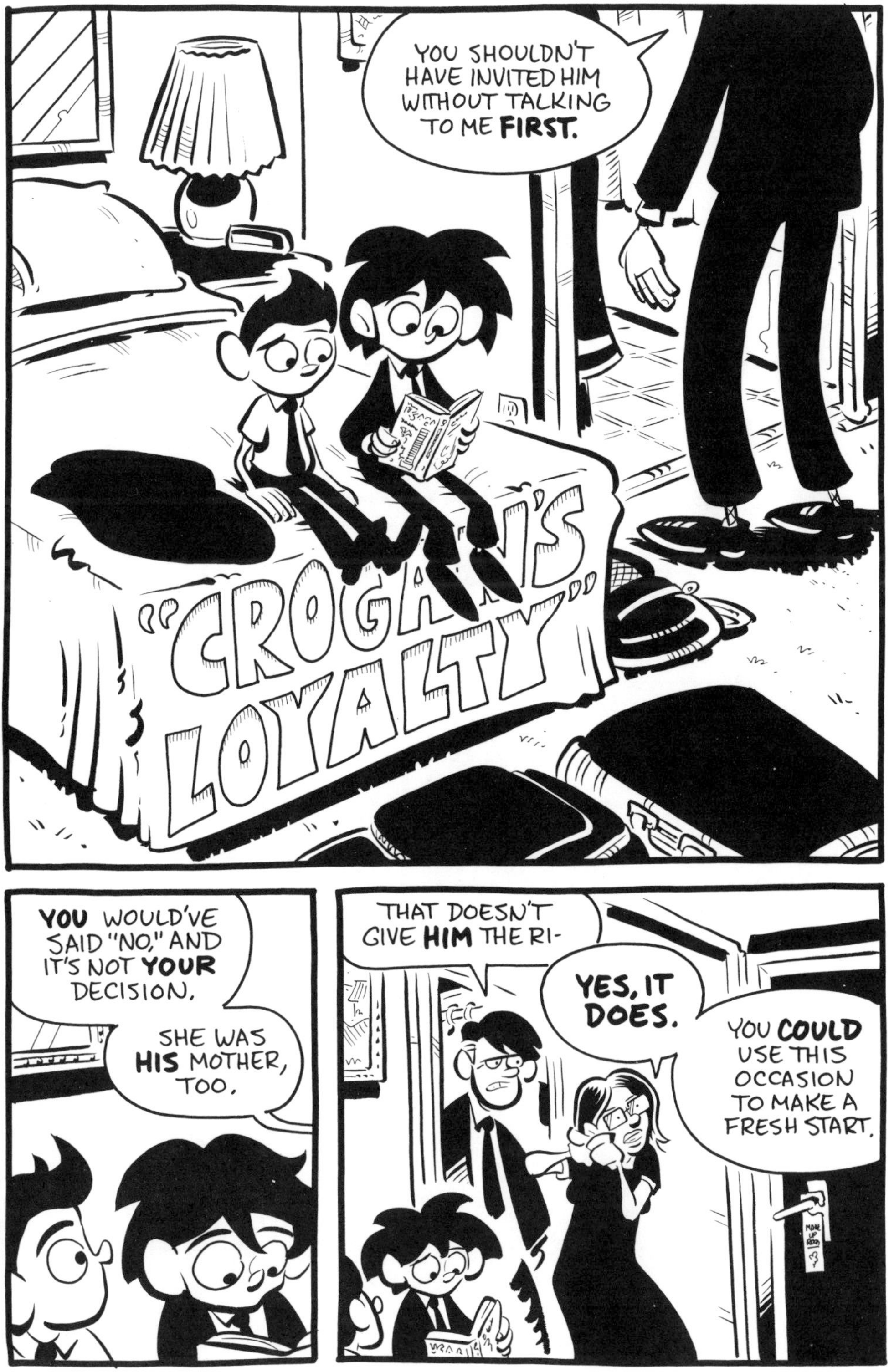
YOU SHOULDN'T HAVE INVITED HIM WITHOUT TALKING TO ME **FIRST.**
"CROGAN'S LOYALTY"
YOU WOULD'VE SAID "NO," AND IT'S NOT **YOUR** DECISION.
SHE WAS **HIS** MOTHER, TOO.
THAT DOESN'T GIVE **HIM** THE RI-
YES, IT DOES.
YOU **COULD** USE THIS OCCASION TO MAKE A FRESH START.

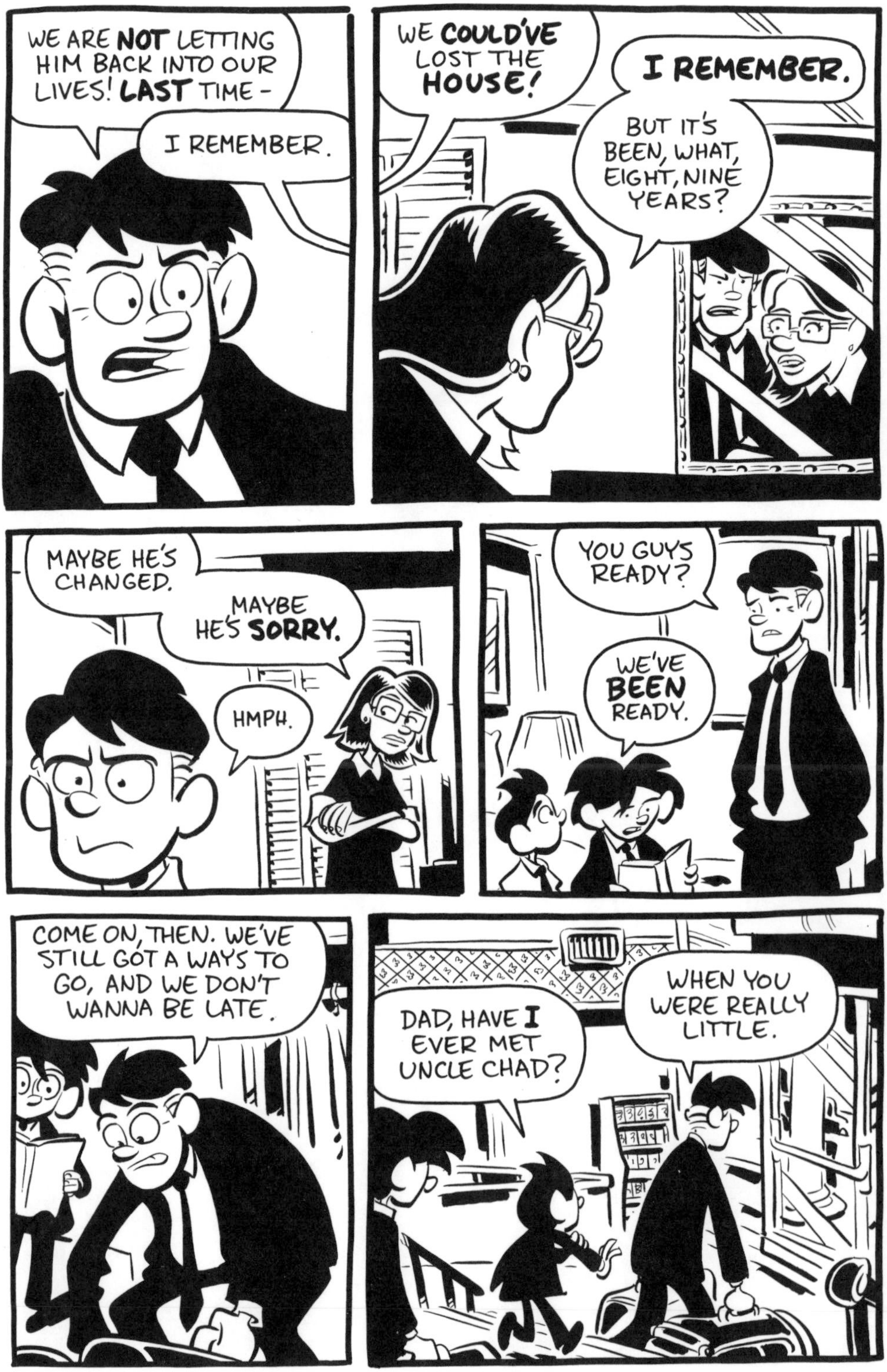
WE ARE **NOT** LETTING HIM BACK INTO OUR LIVES! **LAST** TIME -
I REMEMBER.
WE **COULD'VE** LOST THE **HOUSE**!
I REMEMBER.
BUT IT'S BEEN, WHAT, EIGHT, NINE YEARS?
MAYBE HE'S CHANGED.
MAYBE HE'S **SORRY**.
HMPH.
YOU GUYS READY?
WE'VE **BEEN** READY.
COME ON, THEN. WE'VE STILL GOT A WAYS TO GO, AND WE DON'T WANNA BE LATE.
DAD, HAVE **I** EVER MET UNCLE CHAD?
WHEN YOU WERE REALLY LITTLE.

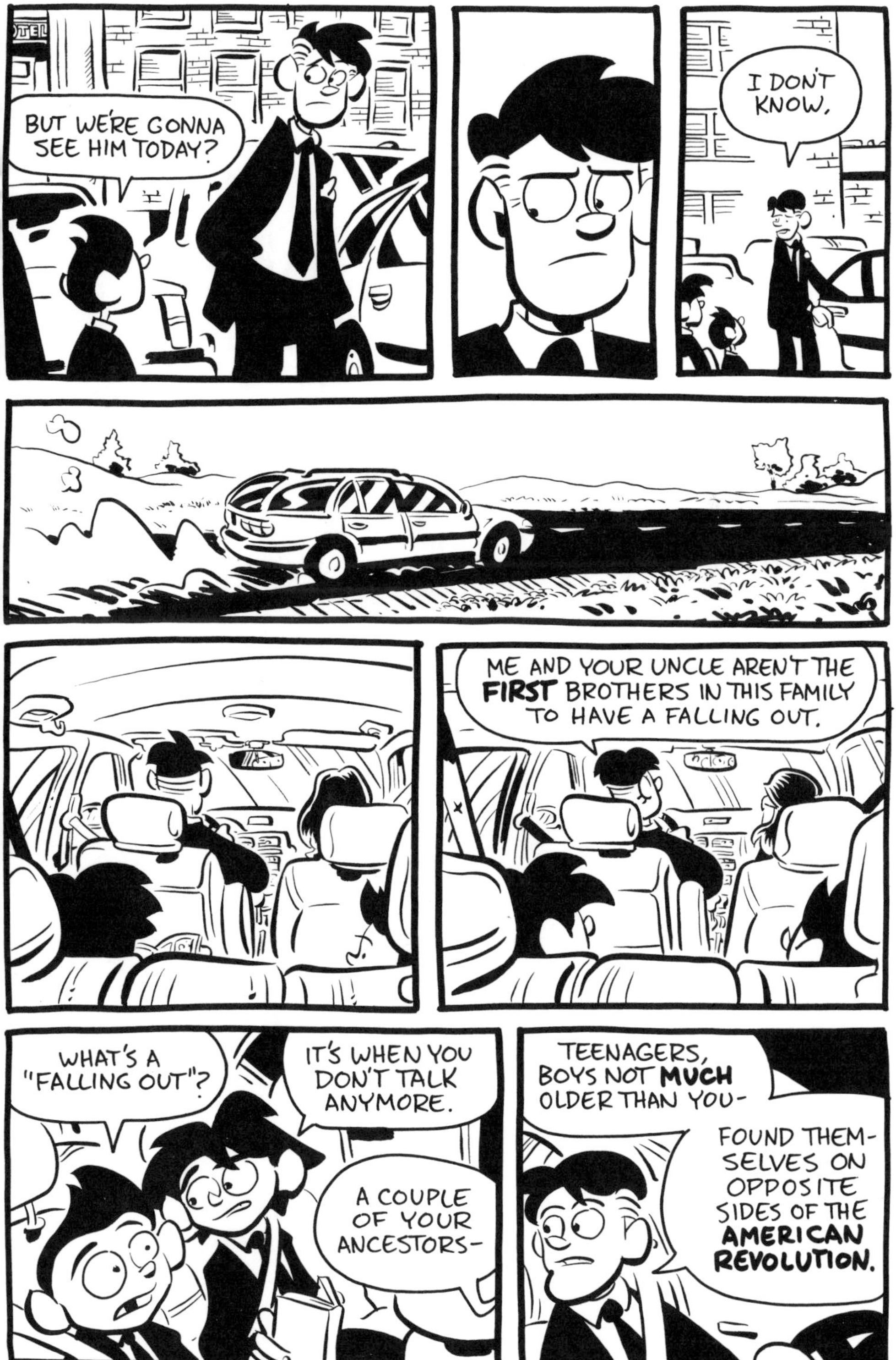
BUT WE'RE GONNA SEE HIM TODAY?
I DON'T KNOW.
ME AND YOUR UNCLE AREN'T THE **FIRST** BROTHERS IN THIS FAMILY TO HAVE A FALLING OUT.
WHAT'S A "FALLING OUT"?
IT'S WHEN YOU DON'T TALK ANYMORE.
A COUPLE OF YOUR ANCESTORS-
TEENAGERS, BOYS NOT **MUCH** OLDER THAN YOU-
FOUND THEMSELVES ON OPPOSITE SIDES OF THE **AMERICAN REVOLUTION.**

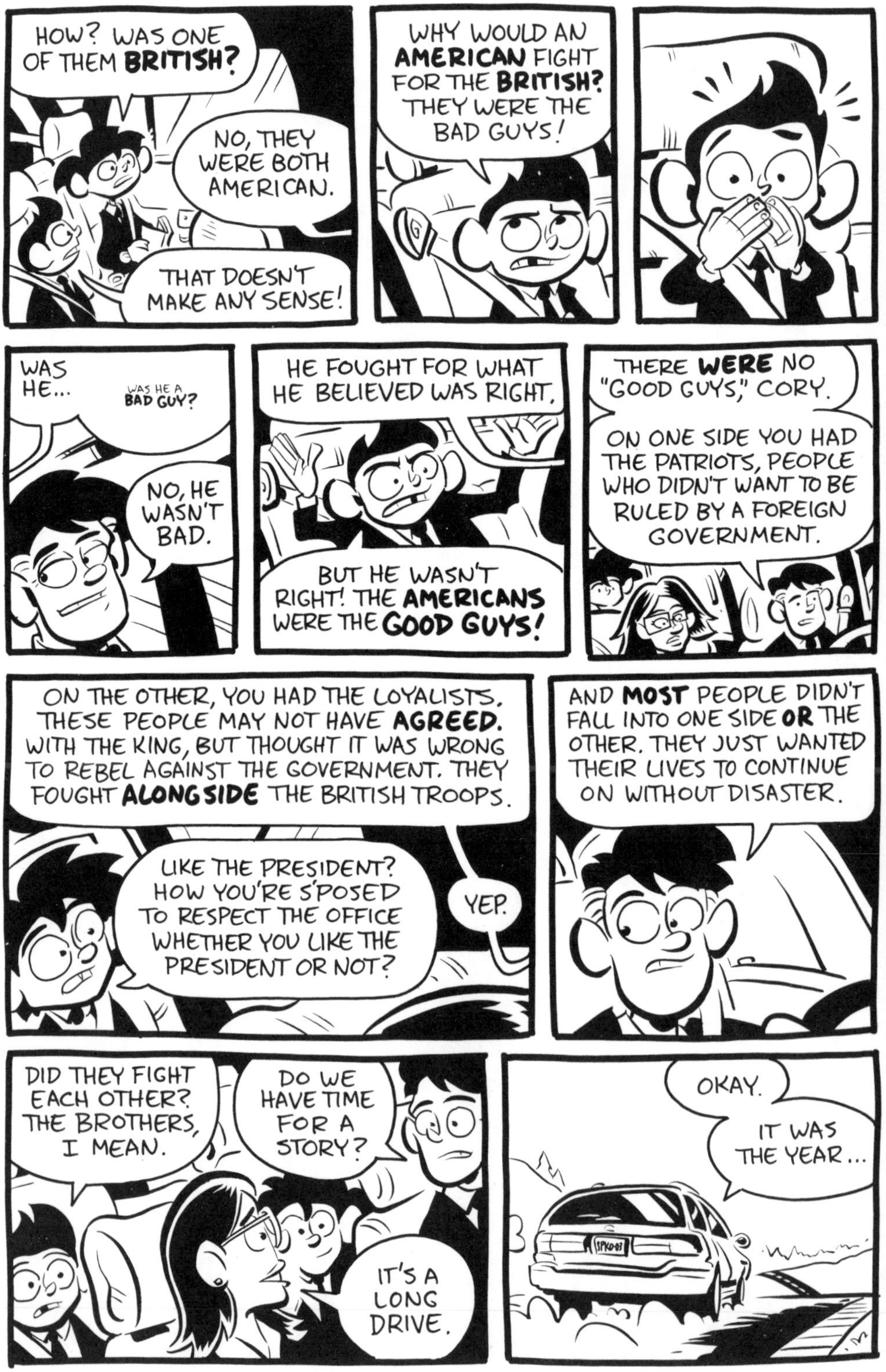
HOW? WAS ONE OF THEM BRITISH?
NO, THEY WERE BOTH AMERICAN.
THAT DOESN'T MAKE ANY SENSE!
WHY WOULD AN AMERICAN FIGHT FOR THE BRITISH? THEY WERE THE BAD GUYS!
WAS HE...
WAS HE A BAD GUY?
NO, HE WASN'T BAD.
HE FOUGHT FOR WHAT HE BELIEVED WAS RIGHT.
BUT HE WASN'T RIGHT! THE AMERICANS WERE THE GOOD GUYS!
THERE WERE NO "GOOD GUYS," CORY.
ON ONE SIDE YOU HAD THE PATRIOTS, PEOPLE WHO DIDN'T WANT TO BE RULED BY A FOREIGN GOVERNMENT.
ON THE OTHER, YOU HAD THE LOYALISTS. THESE PEOPLE MAY NOT HAVE AGREED. WITH THE KING, BUT THOUGHT IT WAS WRONG TO REBEL AGAINST THE GOVERNMENT. THEY FOUGHT ALONGSIDE THE BRITISH TROOPS.
LIKE THE PRESIDENT? HOW YOU'RE S'POSED TO RESPECT THE OFFICE WHETHER YOU LIKE THE PRESIDENT OR NOT?
YEP.
AND MOST PEOPLE DIDN'T FALL INTO ONE SIDE OR THE OTHER. THEY JUST WANTED THEIR LIVES TO CONTINUE ON WITHOUT DISASTER.
DID THEY FIGHT EACH OTHER? THE BROTHERS, I MEAN.
DO WE HAVE TIME FOR A STORY?
IT'S A LONG DRIVE.
OKAY.
IT WAS THE YEAR...

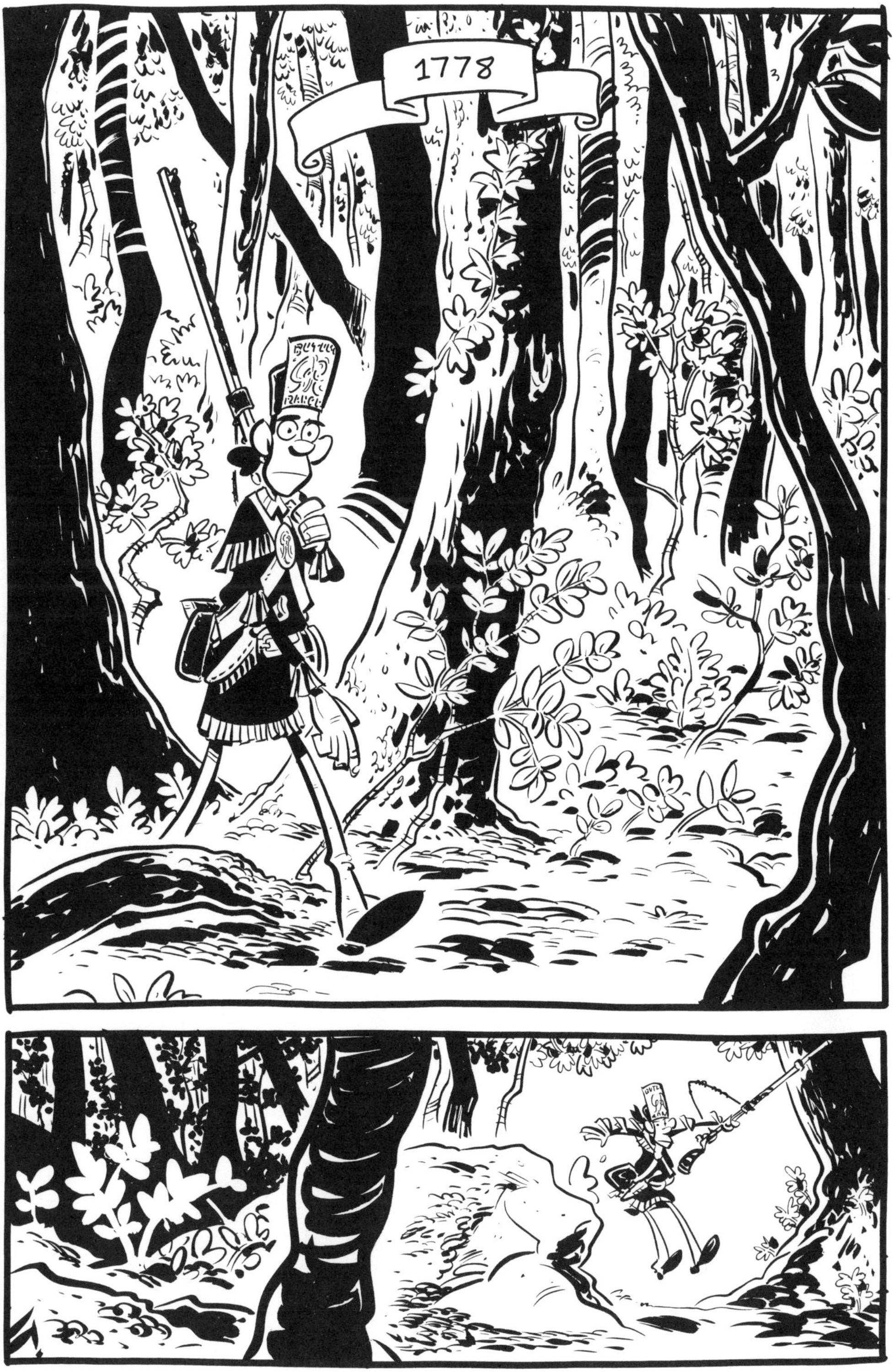
1778

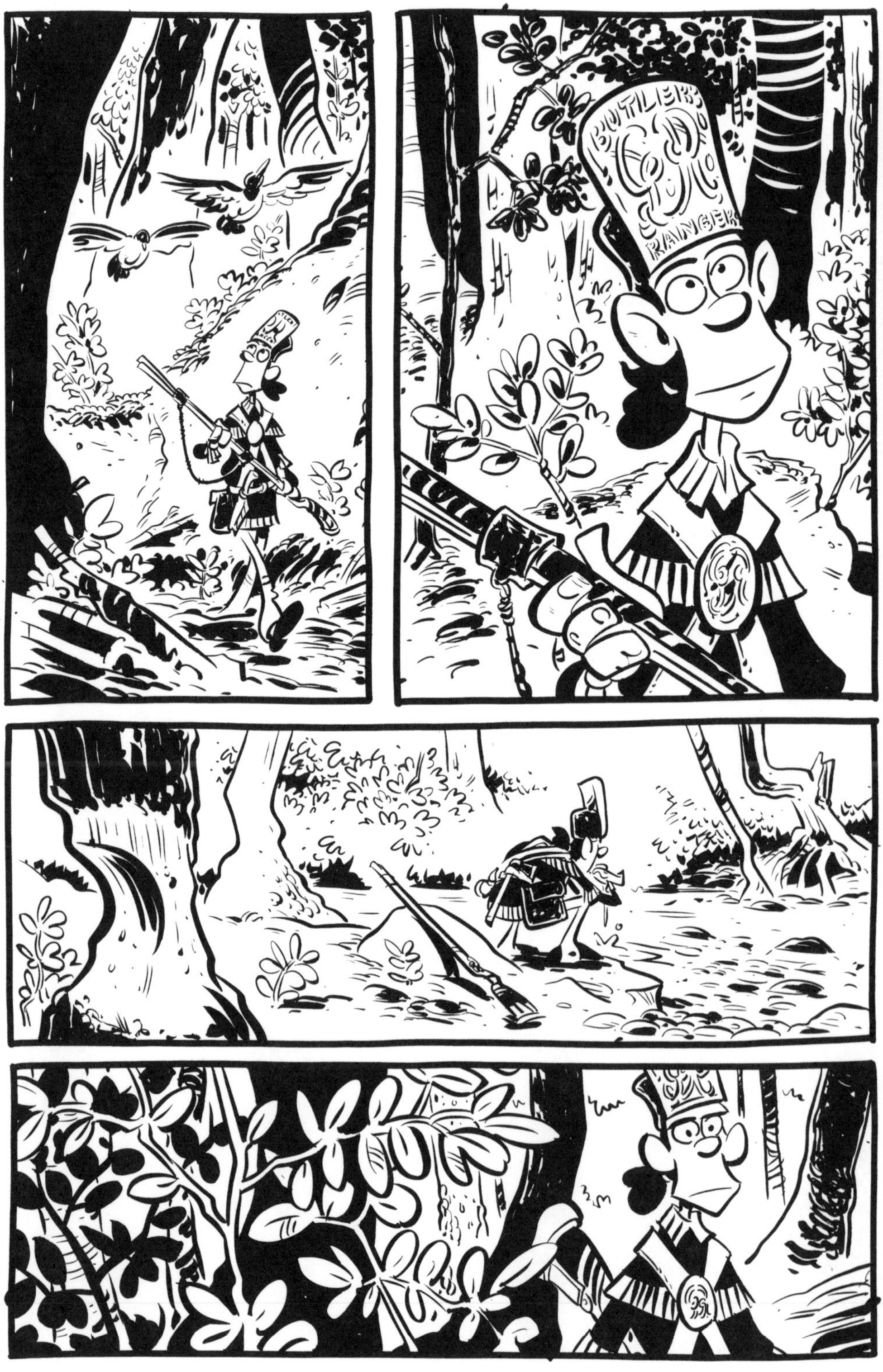
BUTLER'S
RANGER

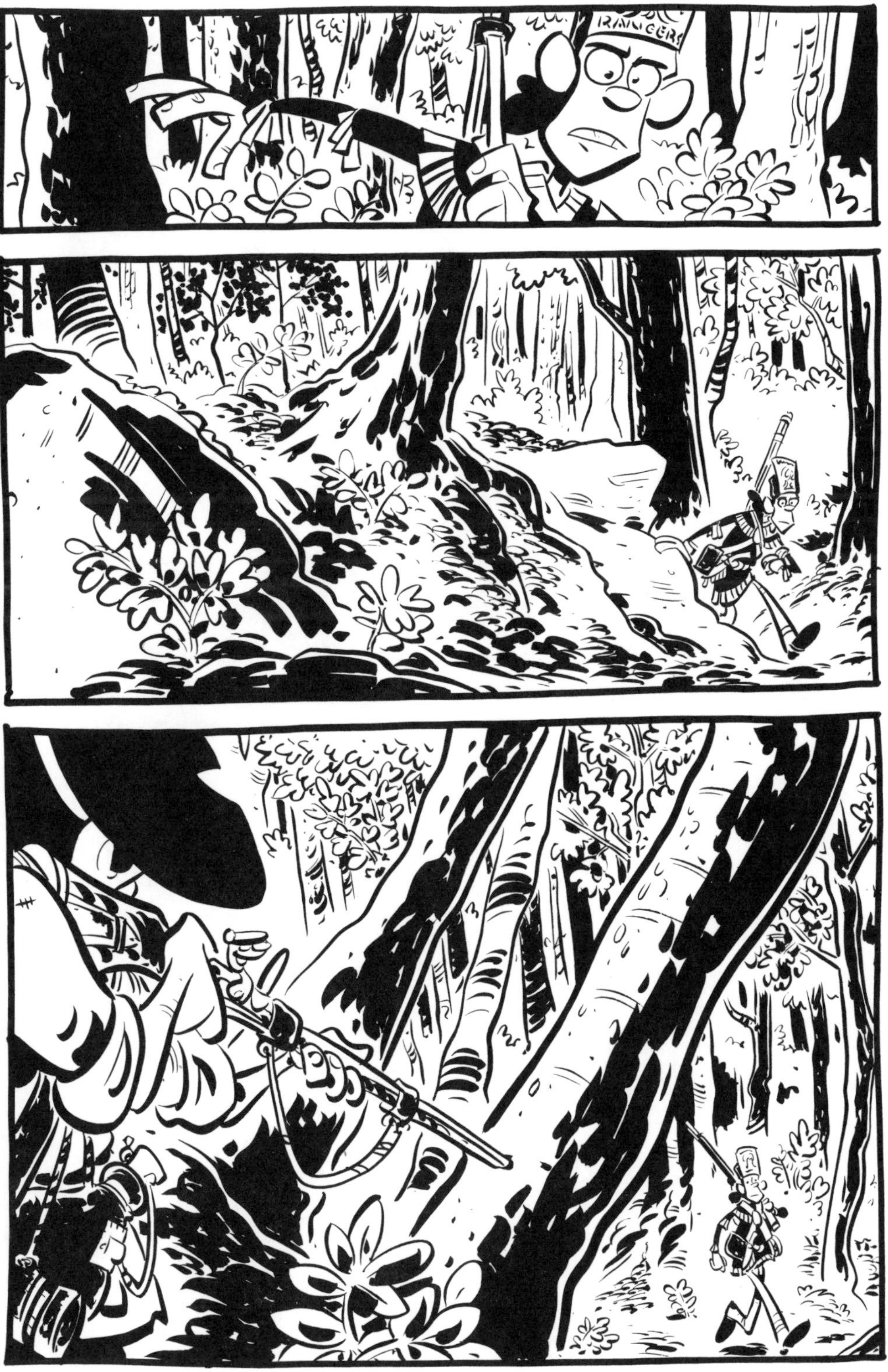
RANGERS

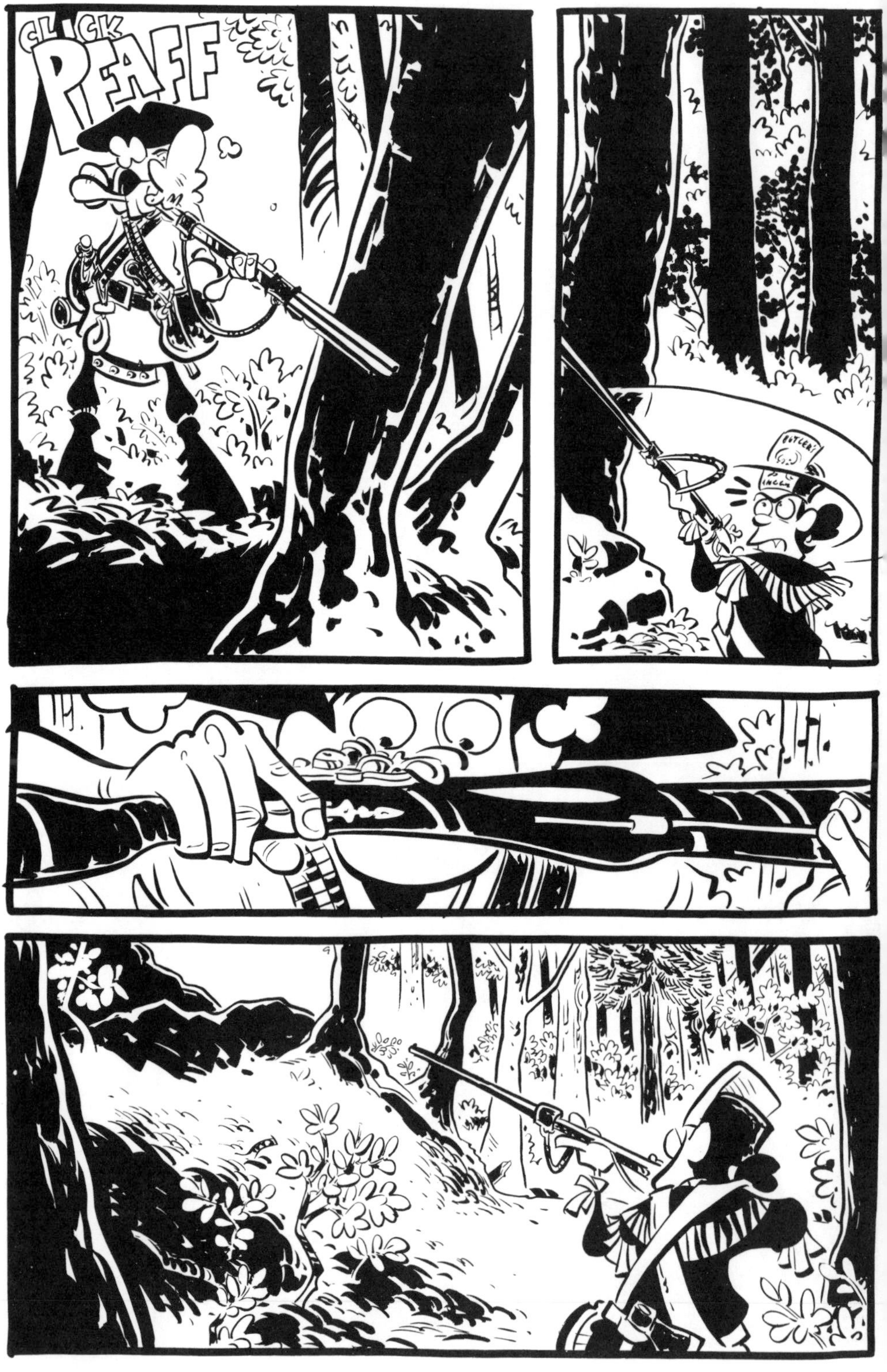
CLICK
PFAFF

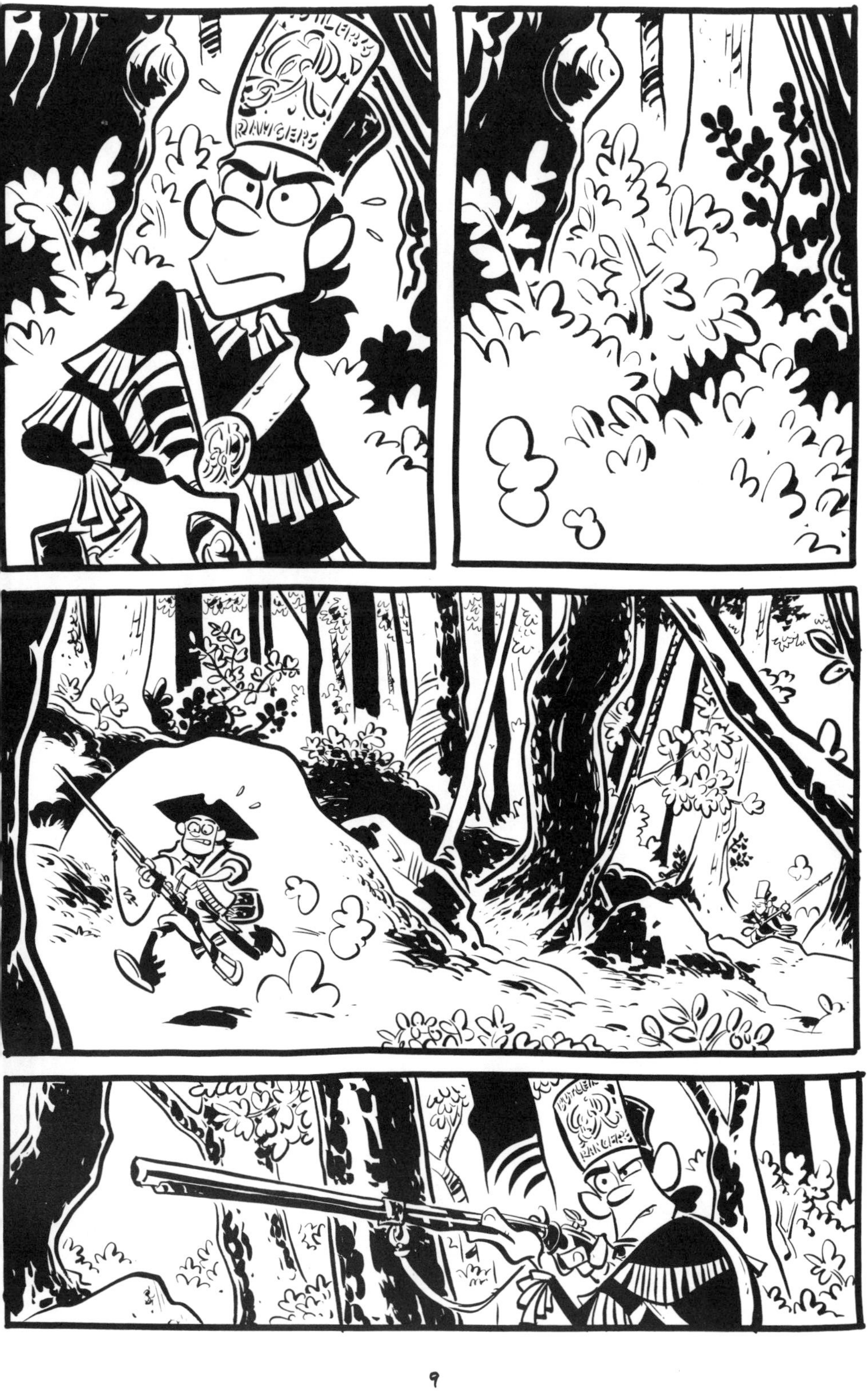
RANGERS
RANGERS

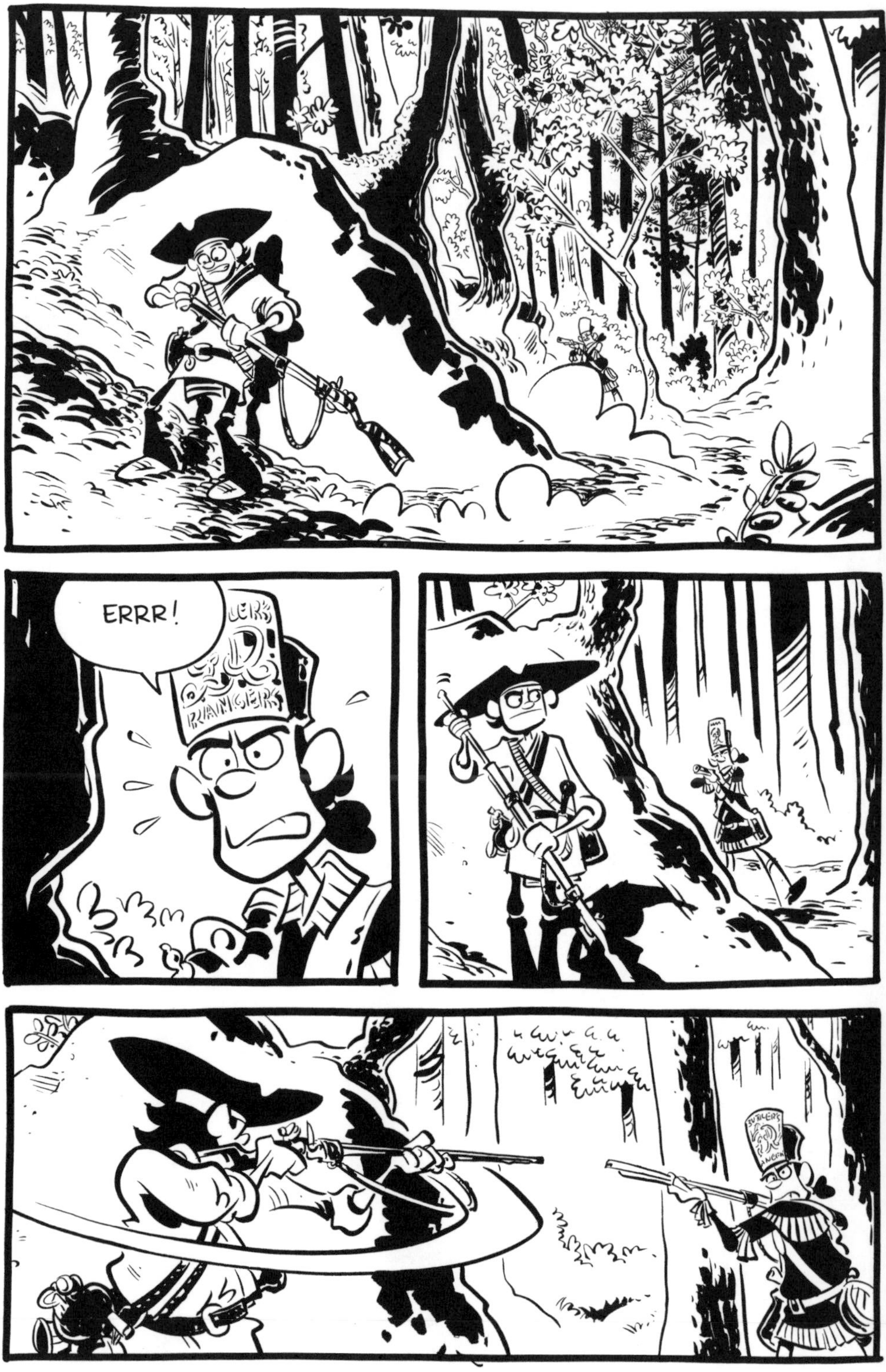
ERRR!

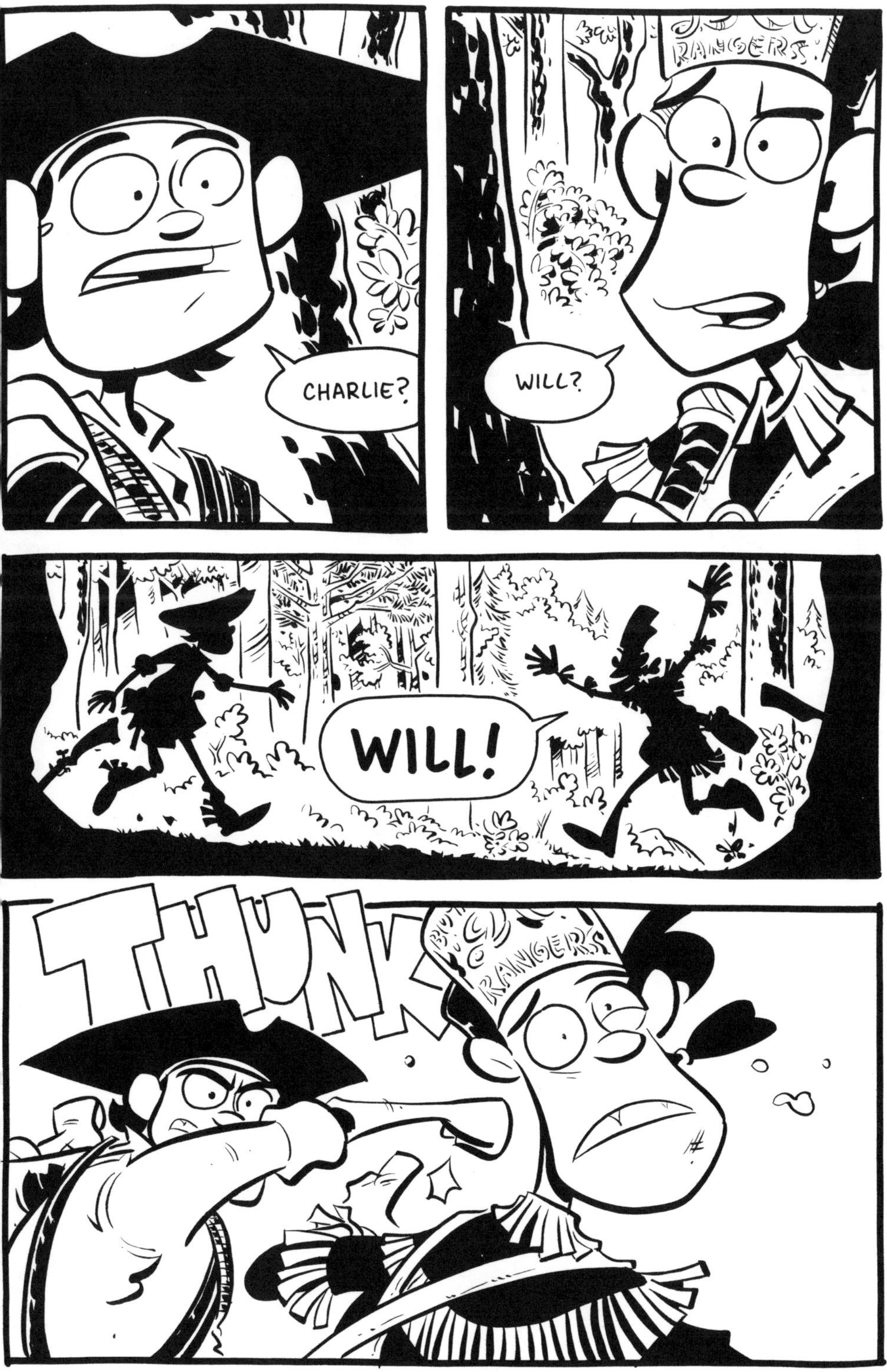
CHARLIE?
RANGERS
WILL?
WILL!
THUNK
RANGERS

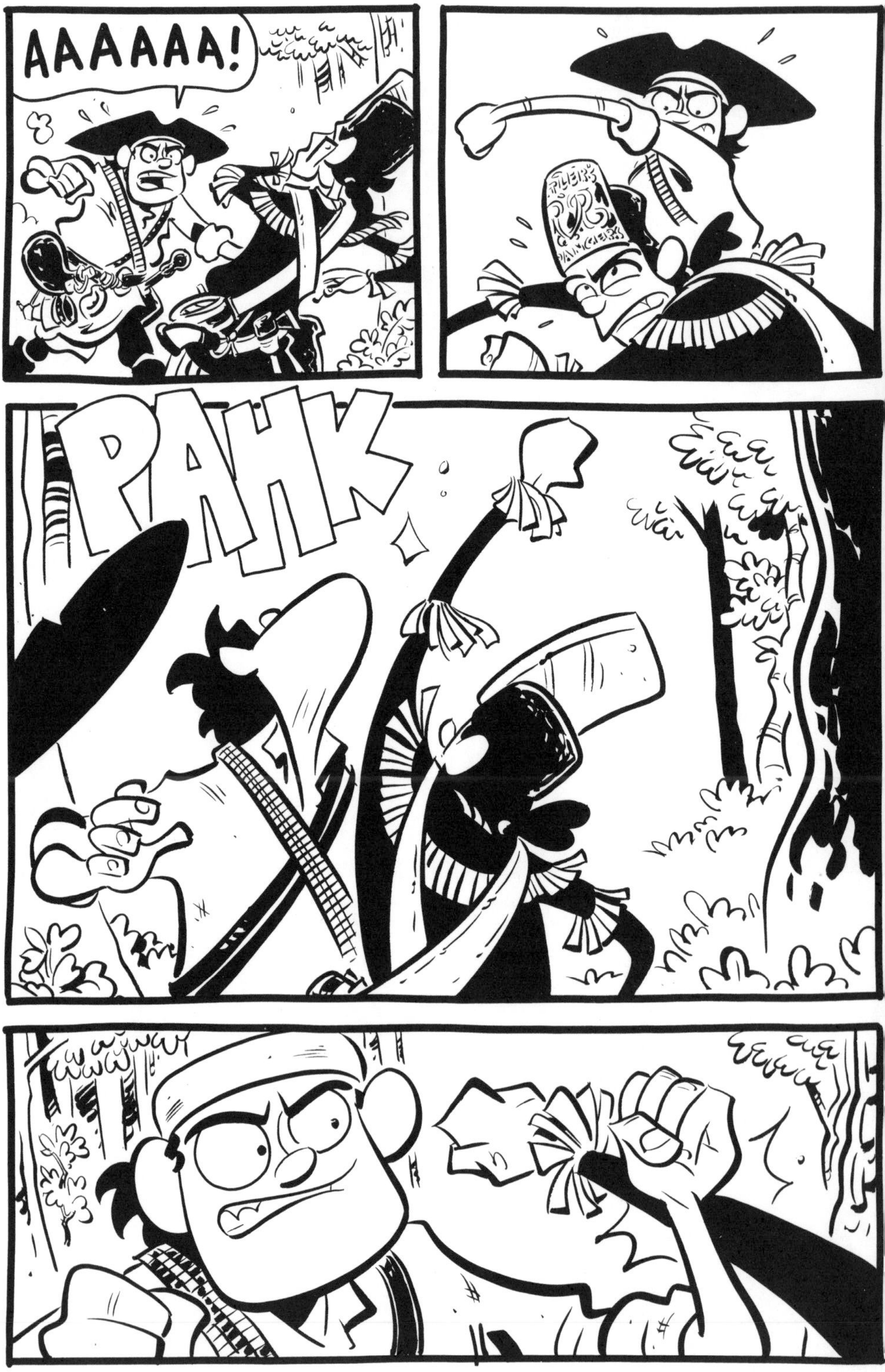
AAAAAA!
PAHK

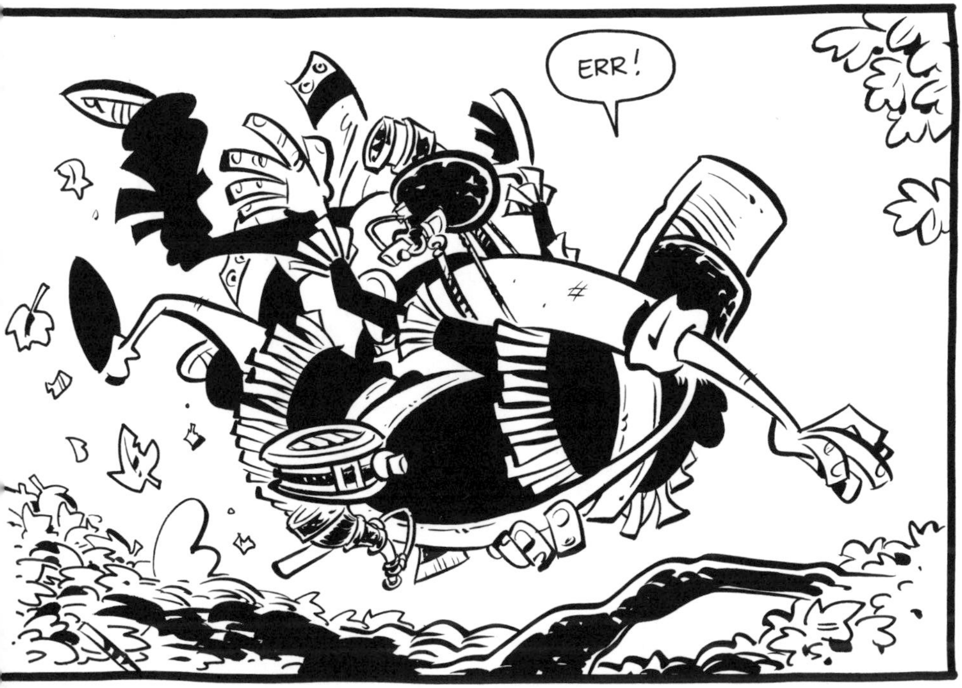
ERR!

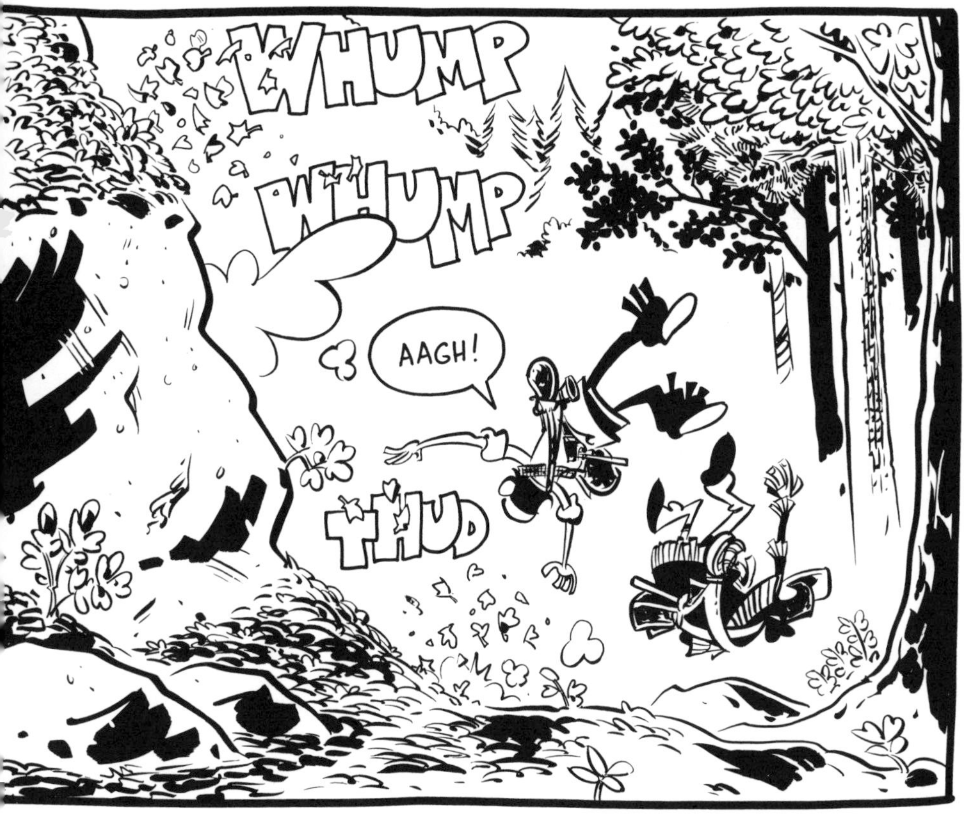
WHUMP
WHUMP
AAGH!
THUD

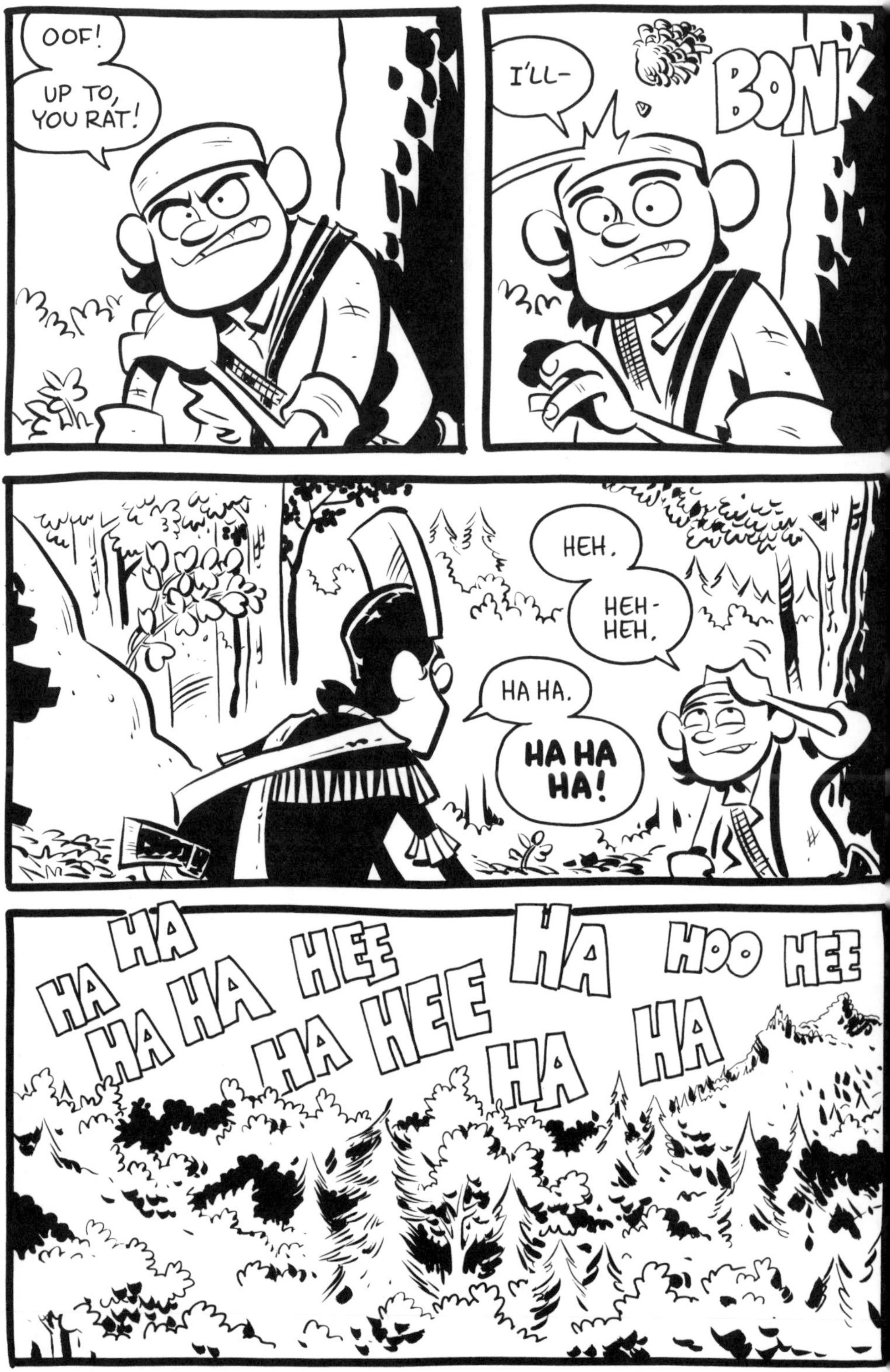
OOF!
UP TO, YOU RAT!
I'LL-
BONK
HEH.
HEH-HEH.
HA HA.
HA HA HA!
HA HA HA HA HEE HA HEE HA HOO HEE HA HA

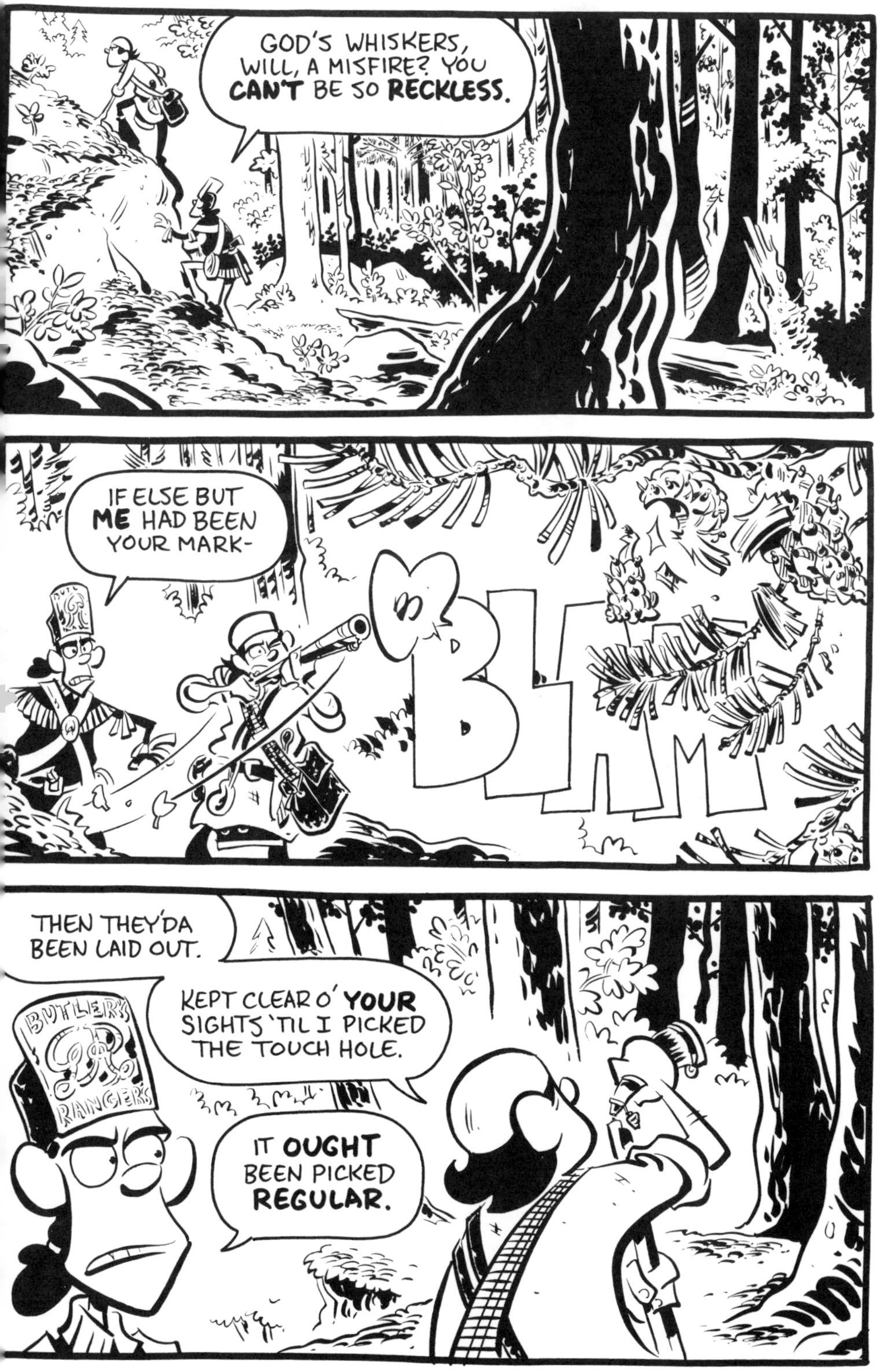
GOD'S WHISKERS, WILL, A MISFIRE? YOU **CAN'T** BE SO **RECKLESS**.
IF ELSE BUT **ME** HAD BEEN YOUR MARK-
BLAM
THEN THEY'DA BEEN LAID OUT.
BUTLER'S RANGERS
KEPT CLEAR O' **YOUR** SIGHTS 'TIL I PICKED THE TOUCH HOLE.
IT **OUGHT** BEEN PICKED **REGULAR**.

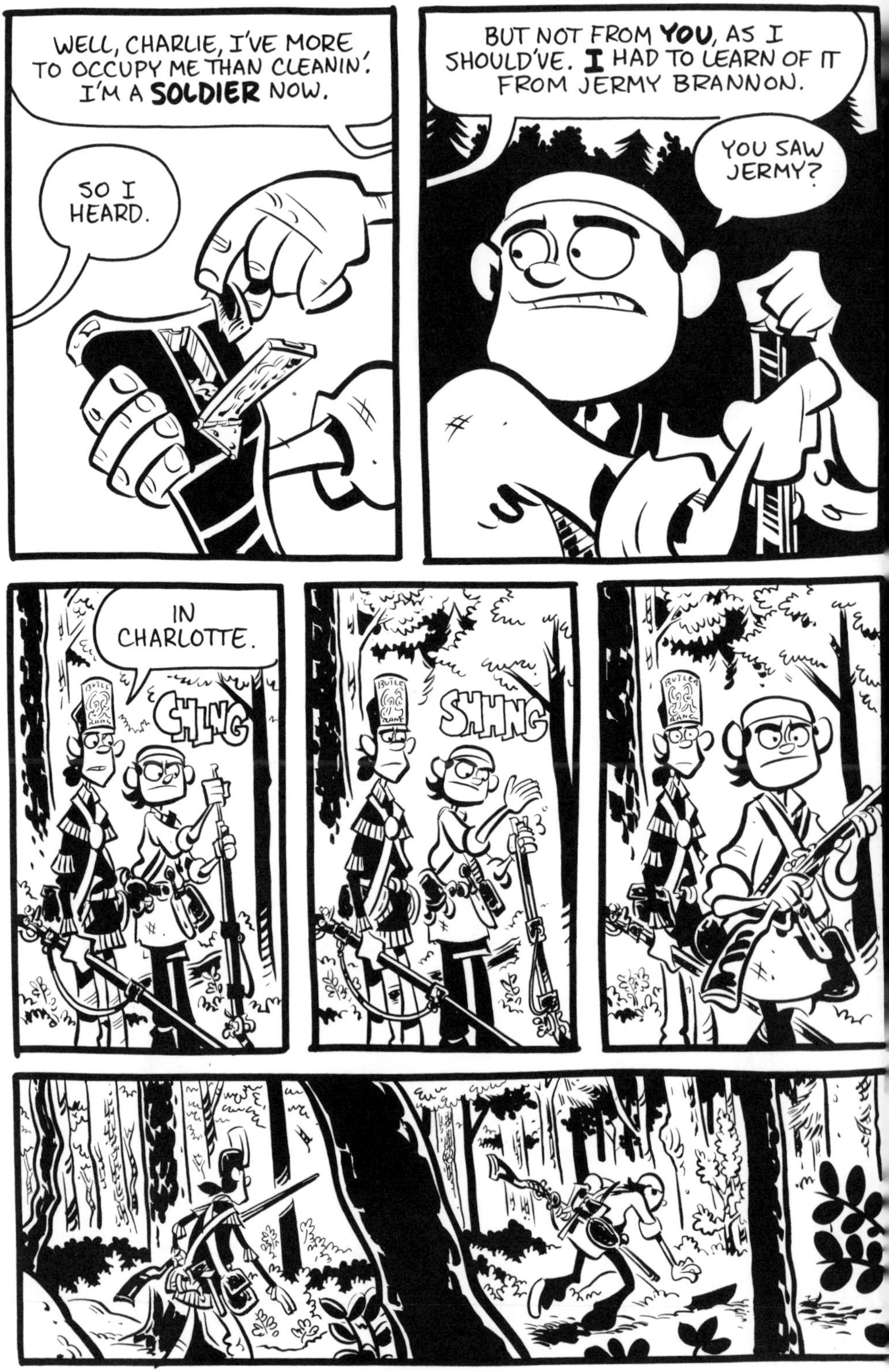
WELL, CHARLIE, I'VE MORE TO OCCUPY ME THAN CLEANIN'. I'M A **SOLDIER** NOW.
SO I HEARD.
BUT NOT FROM **YOU**, AS I SHOULD'VE. **I** HAD TO LEARN OF IT FROM JERMY BRANNON.
YOU SAW JERMY?
IN CHARLOTTE.
CHING
SHING

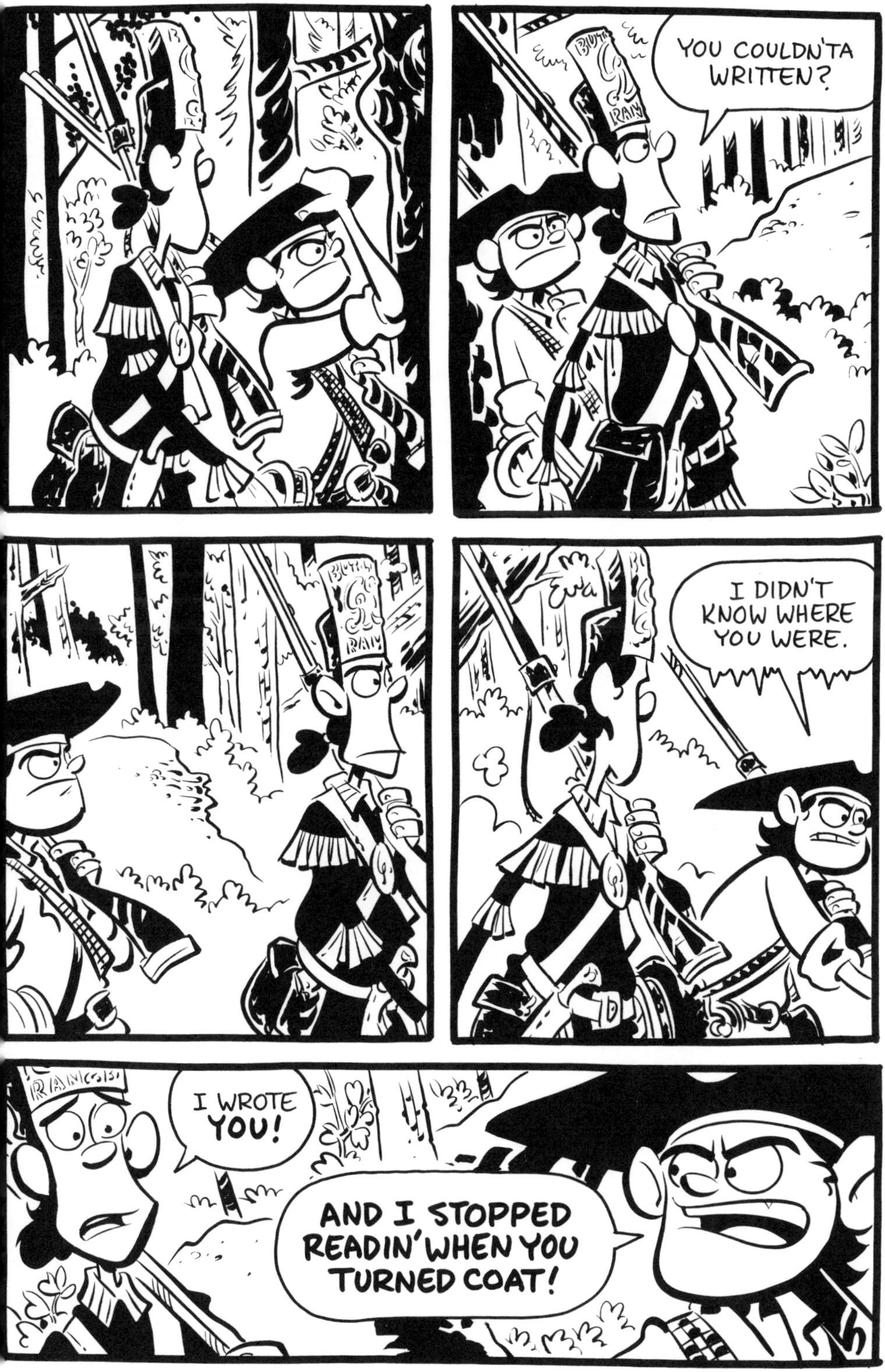
YOU COULDN'TA WRITTEN?
I DIDN'T KNOW WHERE YOU WERE.
I WROTE YOU!
AND I STOPPED READIN' WHEN YOU TURNED COAT!

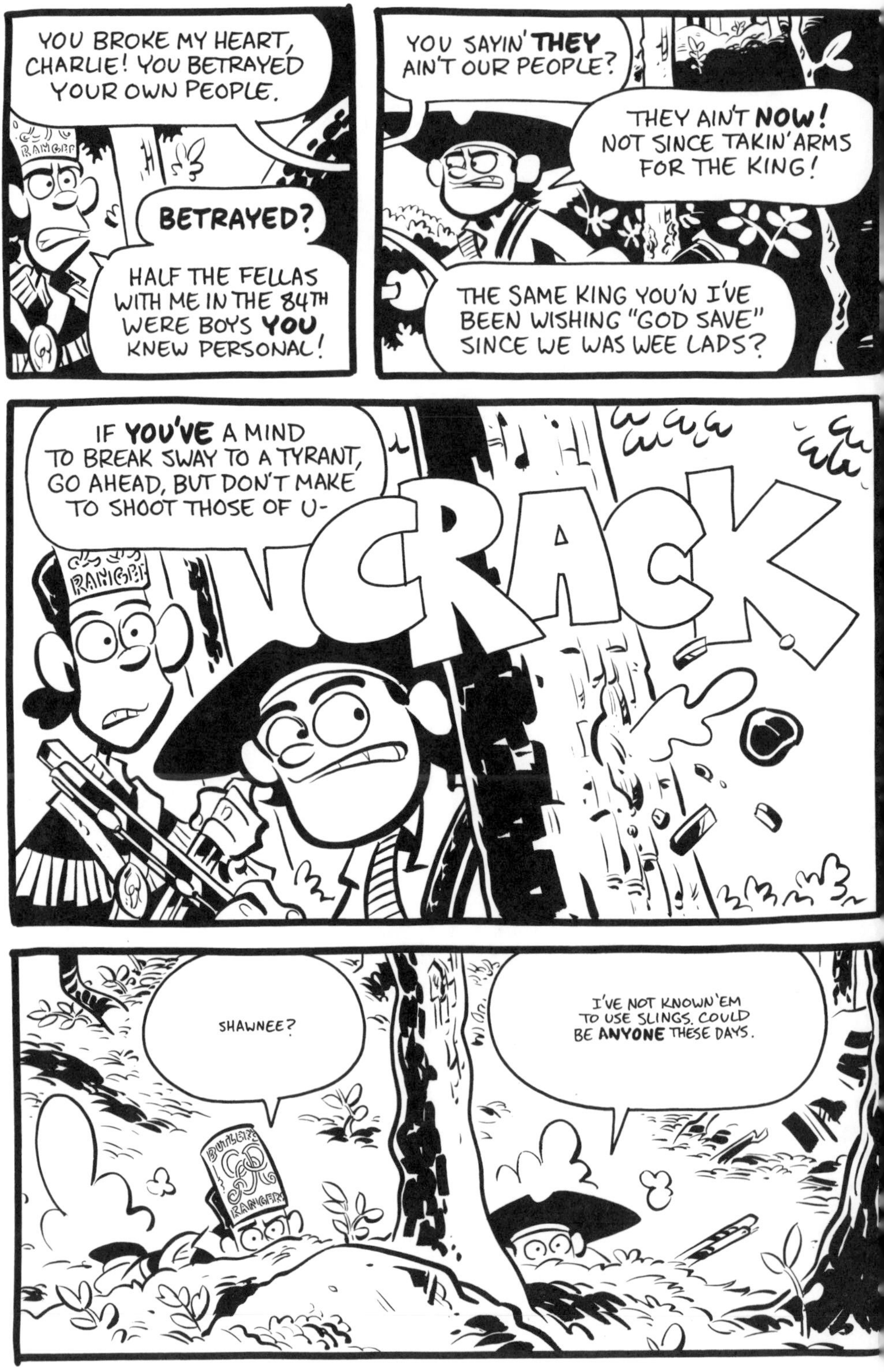
YOU BROKE MY HEART, CHARLIE! YOU BETRAYED YOUR OWN PEOPLE.
BETRAYED?
HALF THE FELLAS WITH ME IN THE 84TH WERE BOYS YOU KNEW PERSONAL!
YOU SAYIN' THEY AIN'T OUR PEOPLE?
THEY AIN'T NOW! NOT SINCE TAKIN' ARMS FOR THE KING!
THE SAME KING YOU'N I'VE BEEN WISHING "GOD SAVE" SINCE WE WAS WEE LADS?
IF YOU'VE A MIND TO BREAK SWAY TO A TYRANT, GO AHEAD, BUT DON'T MAKE TO SHOOT THOSE OF U-
CRACK
SHAWNEE?
I'VE NOT KNOWN 'EM TO USE SLINGS. COULD BE ANYONE THESE DAYS.

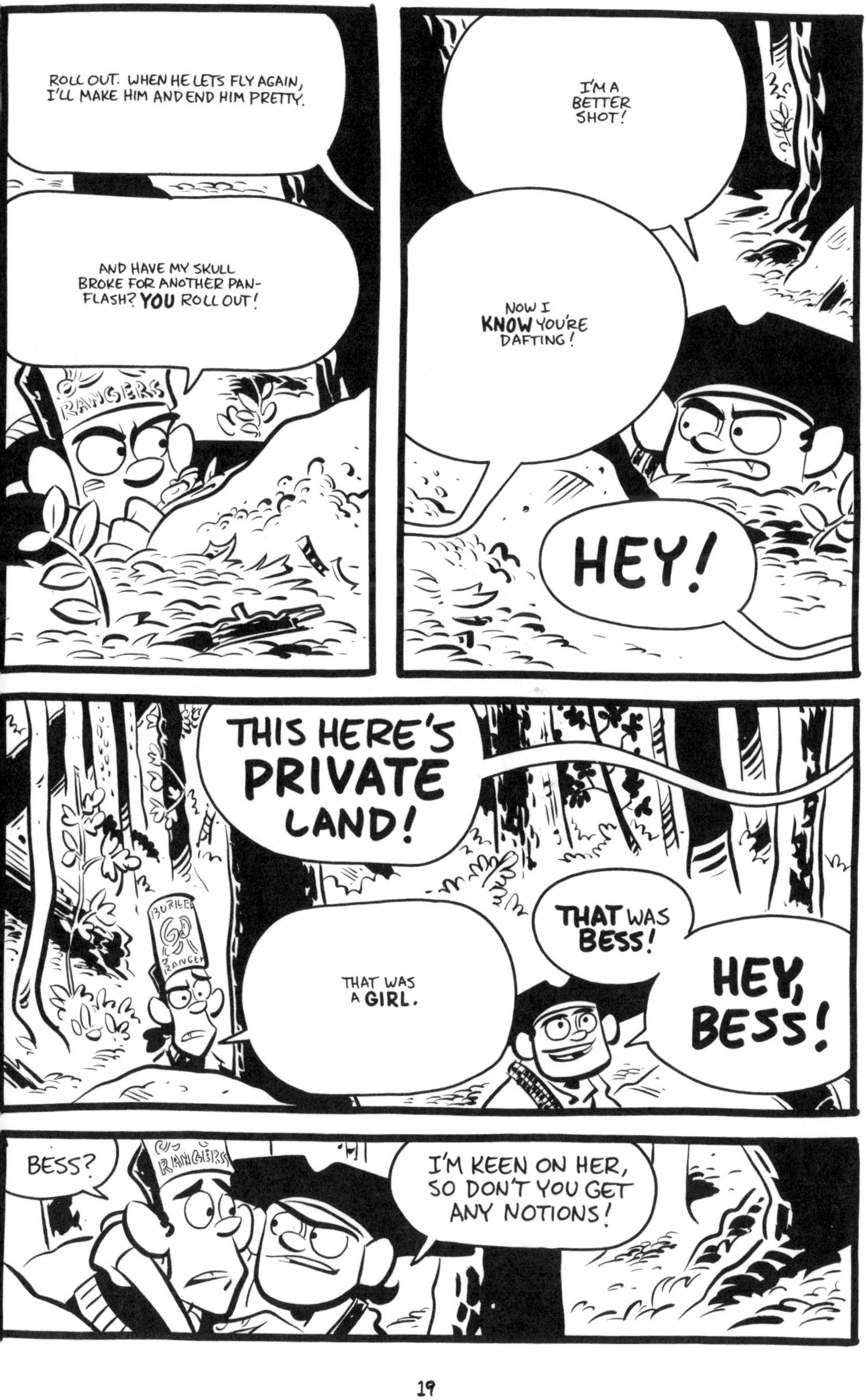
ROLL OUT. WHEN HE LETS FLY AGAIN, I'LL MAKE HIM AND END HIM PRETTY.
AND HAVE MY SKULL BROKE FOR ANOTHER PAN-FLASH? YOU ROLL OUT!
I'M A BETTER SHOT!
NOW I KNOW YOU'RE DAFTING!
HEY!
THIS HERE'S PRIVATE LAND!
THAT WAS A GIRL.
THAT WAS BESS!
HEY, BESS!
BESS?
I'M KEEN ON HER, SO DON'T YOU GET ANY NOTIONS!

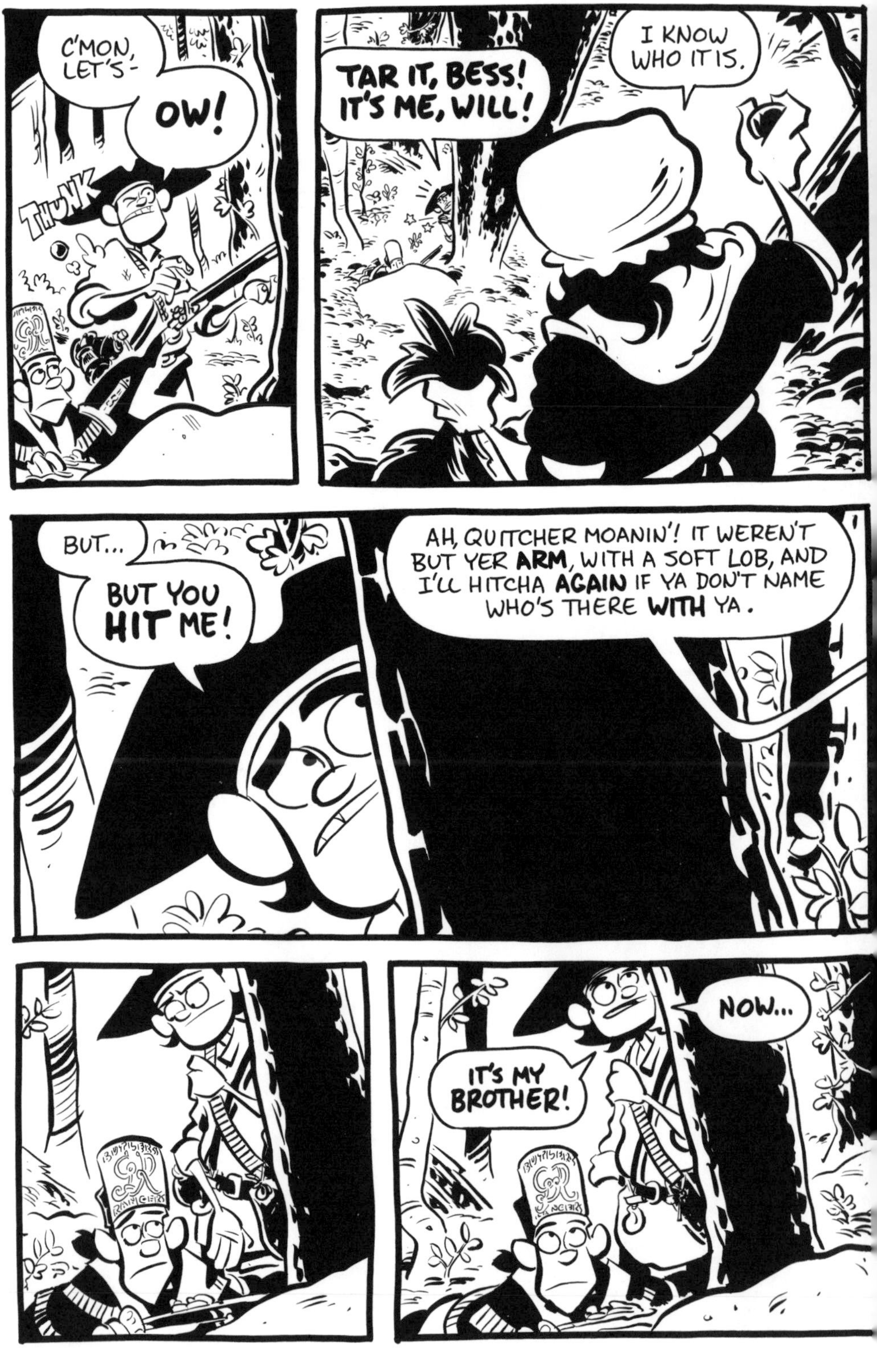
C'MON, LET'S-
OW!
THUNK
TAR IT, BESS! IT'S ME, WILL!
I KNOW WHO IT IS.
BUT...
BUT YOU HIT ME!
AH, QUITCHER MOANIN'! IT WEREN'T BUT YER ARM, WITH A SOFT LOB, AND I'LL HITCHA AGAIN IF YA DON'T NAME WHO'S THERE WITH YA.
NOW...
IT'S MY BROTHER!

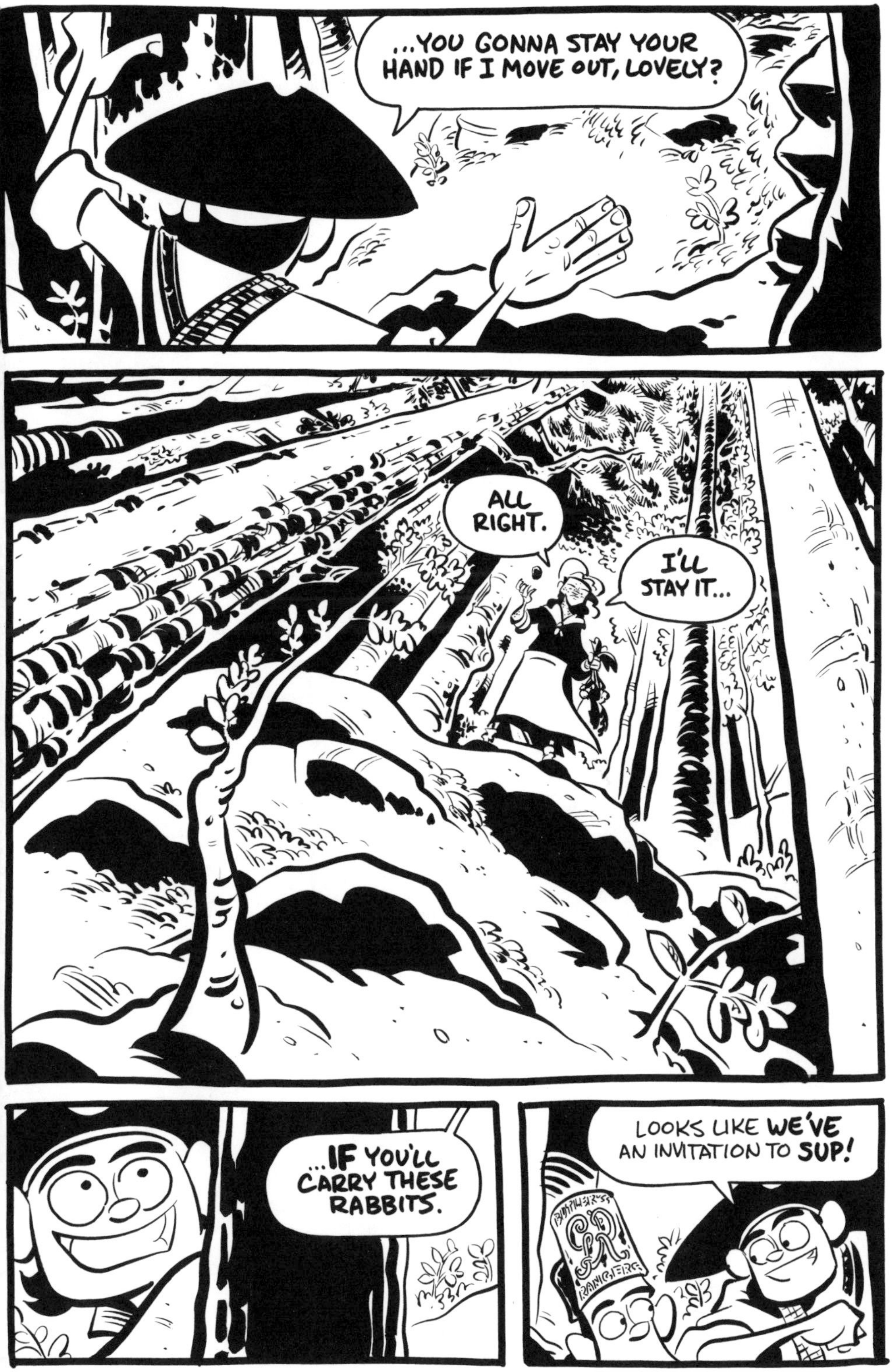
...YOU GONNA STAY YOUR HAND IF I MOVE OUT, LOVELY?
ALL RIGHT.
I'LL STAY IT...
...IF YOU'LL CARRY THESE RABBITS.
LOOKS LIKE WE'VE AN INVITATION TO SUP!

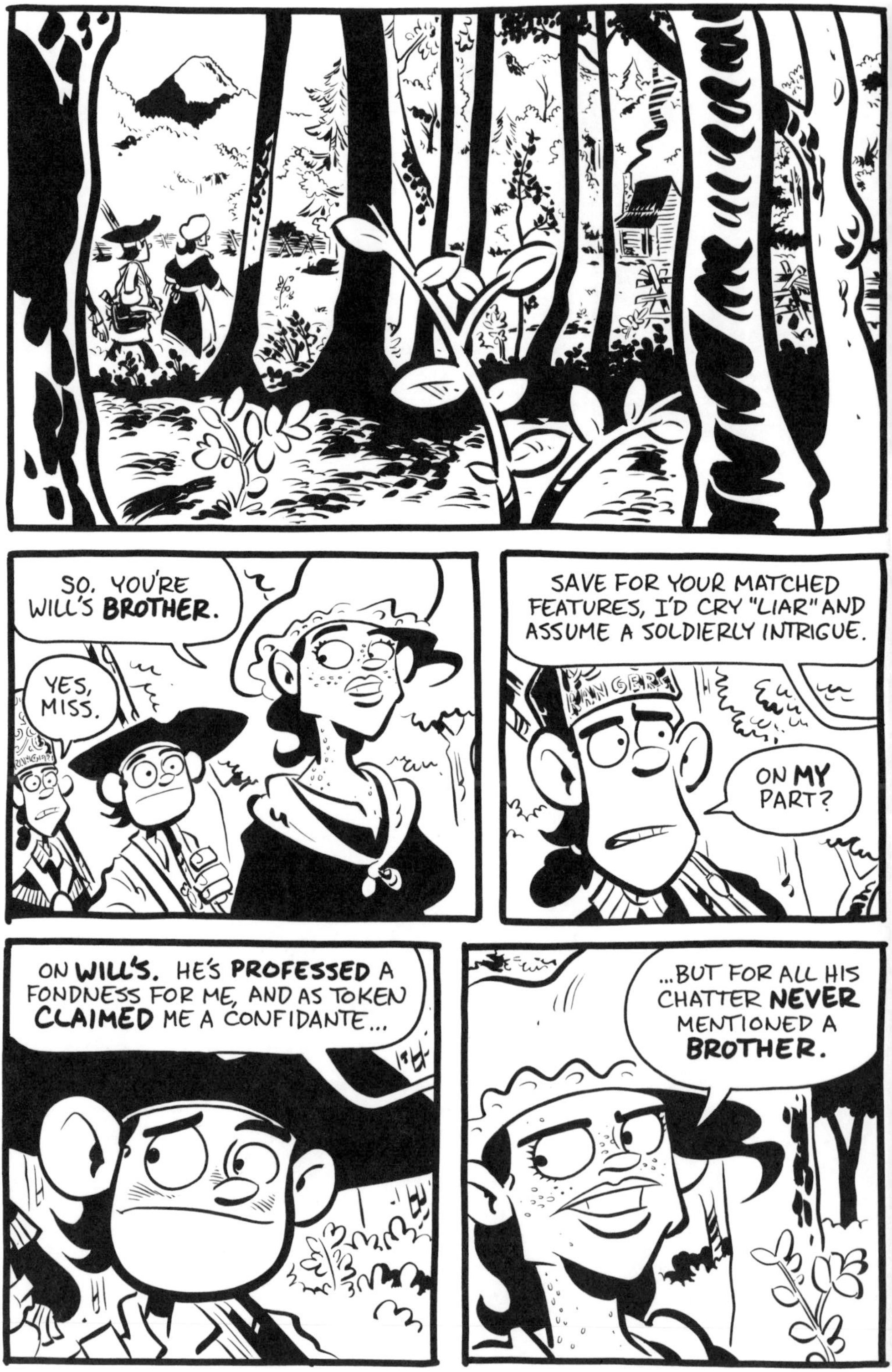
SO. YOU'RE WILL'S **BROTHER**.
YES, MISS.
SAVE FOR YOUR MATCHED FEATURES, I'D CRY "LIAR" AND ASSUME A SOLDIERLY INTRIGUE.
ON **MY** PART?
ON **WILL'S**. HE'S **PROFESSED** A FONDNESS FOR ME, AND AS TOKEN **CLAIMED** ME A CONFIDANTE...
...BUT FOR ALL HIS CHATTER **NEVER** MENTIONED A **BROTHER**.

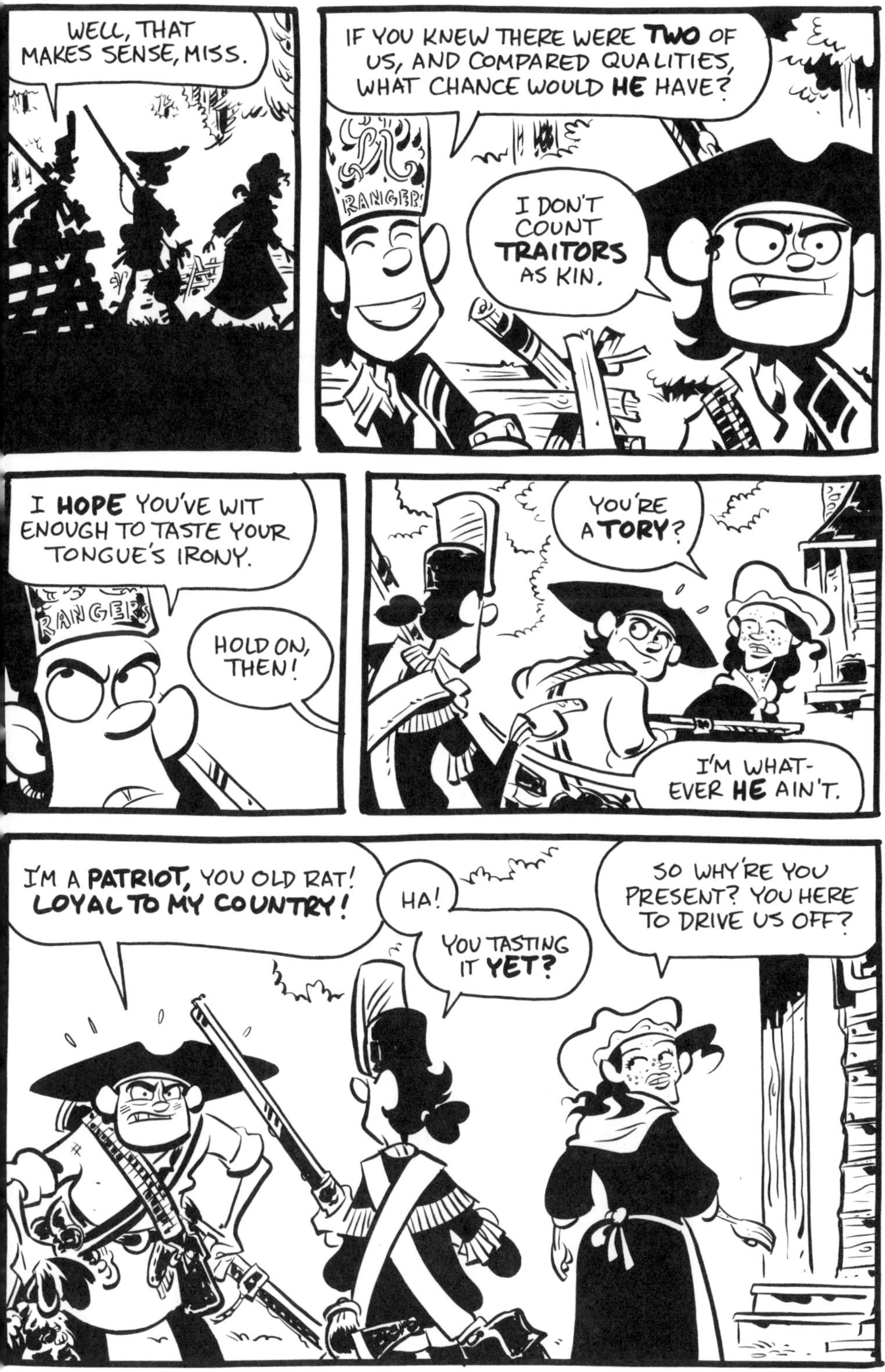
WELL, THAT MAKES SENSE, MISS.
IF YOU KNEW THERE WERE **TWO** OF US, AND COMPARED QUALITIES, WHAT CHANCE WOULD **HE** HAVE?
RANGERS
I DON'T COUNT **TRAITORS** AS KIN.
I **HOPE** YOU'VE WIT ENOUGH TO TASTE YOUR TONGUE'S IRONY.
RANGERS
HOLD ON, THEN!
YOU'RE A **TORY**?
I'M WHATEVER **HE** AIN'T.
I'M A **PATRIOT**, YOU OLD RAT! **LOYAL TO MY COUNTRY**!
HA!
YOU TASTING IT **YET**?
SO WHY'RE YOU PRESENT? YOU HERE TO DRIVE US OFF?

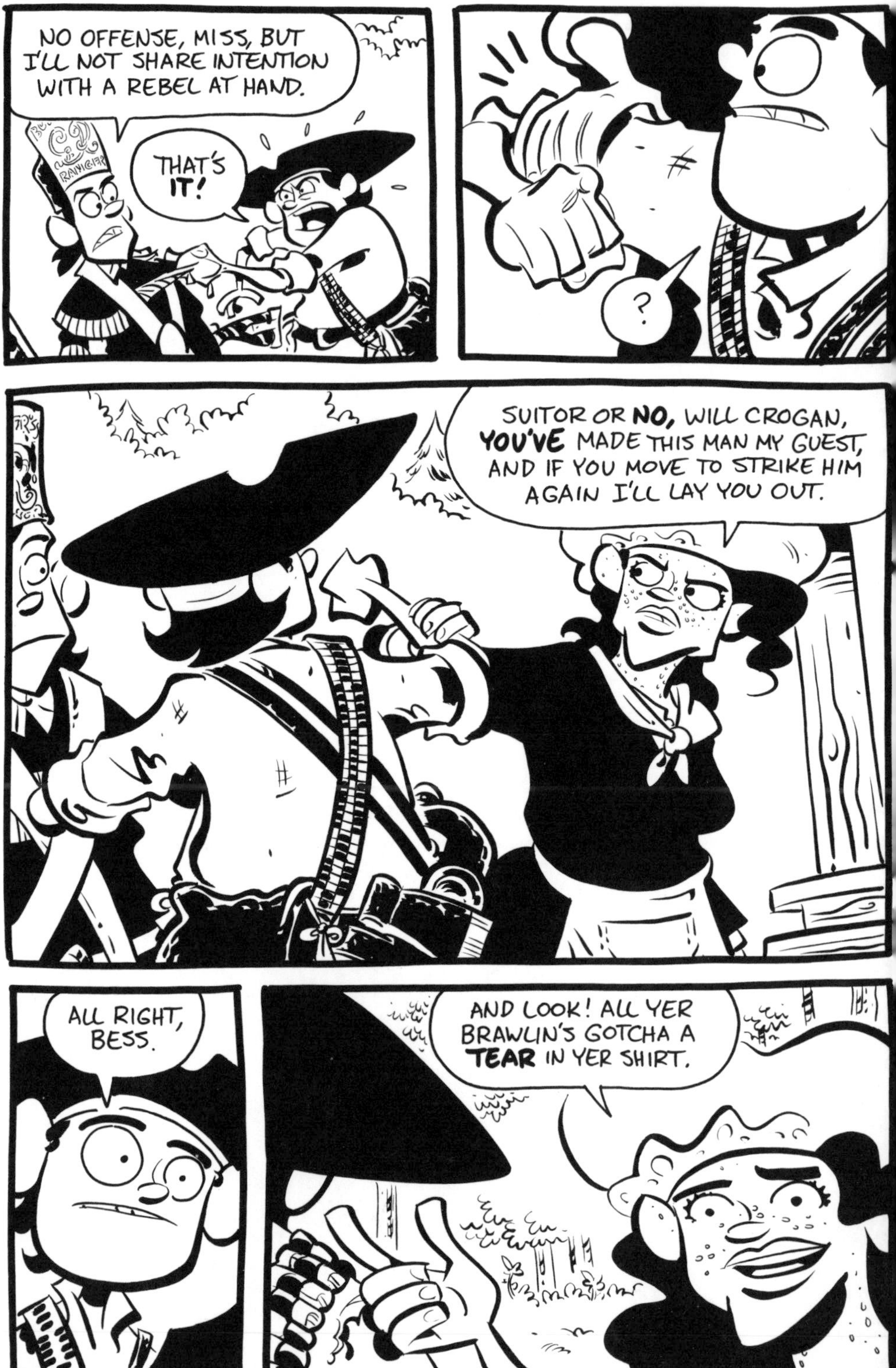
NO OFFENSE, MISS, BUT I'LL NOT SHARE INTENTION WITH A REBEL AT HAND.
THAT'S IT!
?
SUITOR OR NO, WILL CROGAN, YOU'VE MADE THIS MAN MY GUEST, AND IF YOU MOVE TO STRIKE HIM AGAIN I'LL LAY YOU OUT.
ALL RIGHT, BESS.
AND LOOK! ALL YER BRAWLIN'S GOTCHA A TEAR IN YER SHIRT.

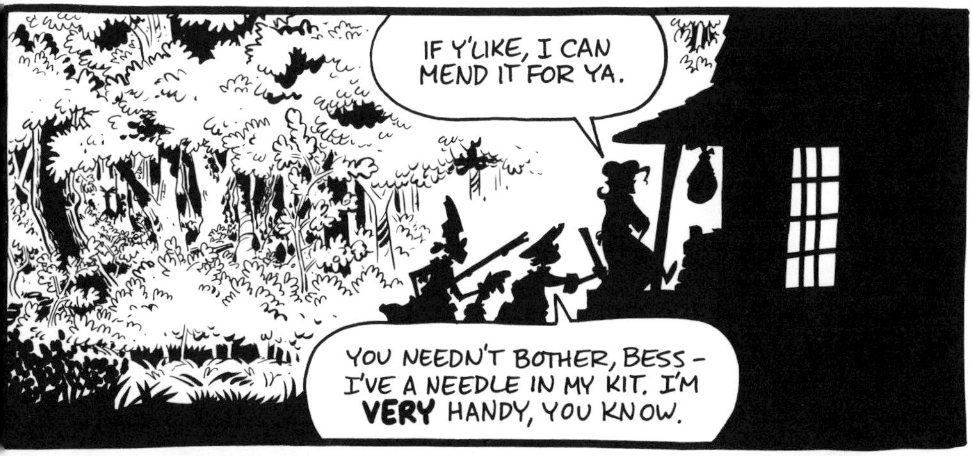
IF Y'LIKE, I CAN MEND IT FOR YA.
YOU NEEDN'T BOTHER, BESS - I'VE A NEEDLE IN MY KIT. I'M **VERY** HANDY, YOU KNOW.

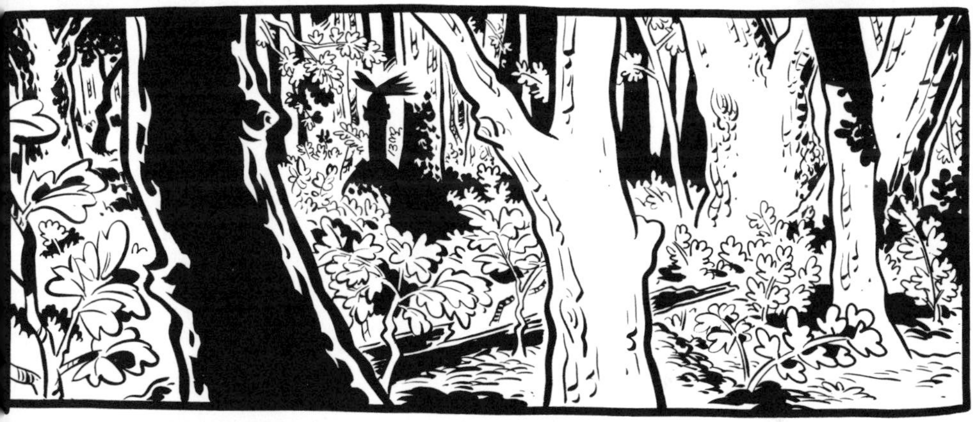

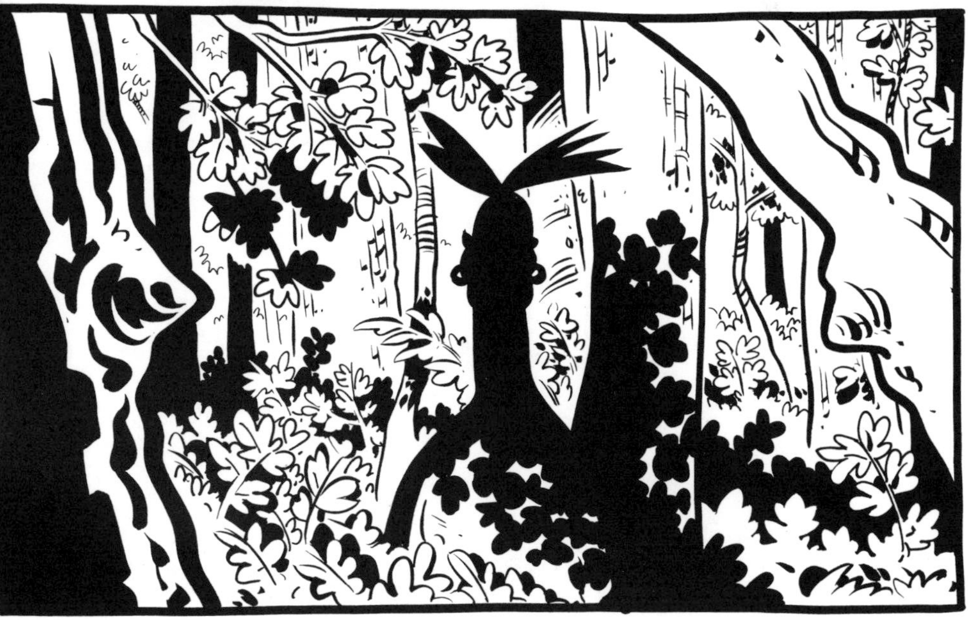

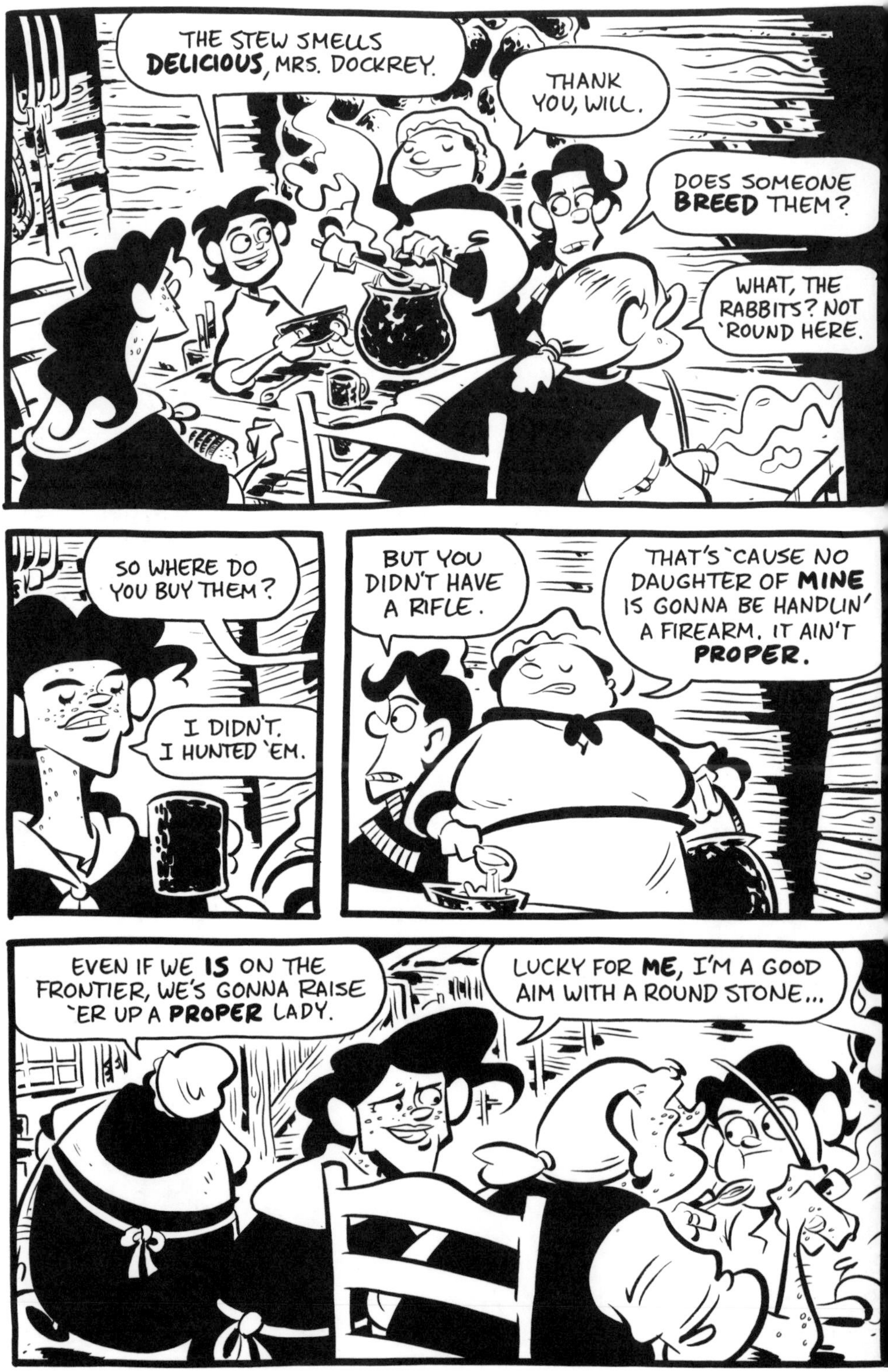
THE STEW SMELLS DELICIOUS, MRS. DOCKREY.
THANK YOU, WILL.
DOES SOMEONE BREED THEM?
WHAT, THE RABBITS? NOT 'ROUND HERE.
SO WHERE DO YOU BUY THEM?
I DIDN'T. I HUNTED 'EM.
BUT YOU DIDN'T HAVE A RIFLE.
THAT'S 'CAUSE NO DAUGHTER OF MINE IS GONNA BE HANDLIN' A FIREARM. IT AIN'T PROPER.
EVEN IF WE IS ON THE FRONTIER, WE'S GONNA RAISE 'ER UP A PROPER LADY.
LUCKY FOR ME, I'M A GOOD AIM WITH A ROUND STONE...

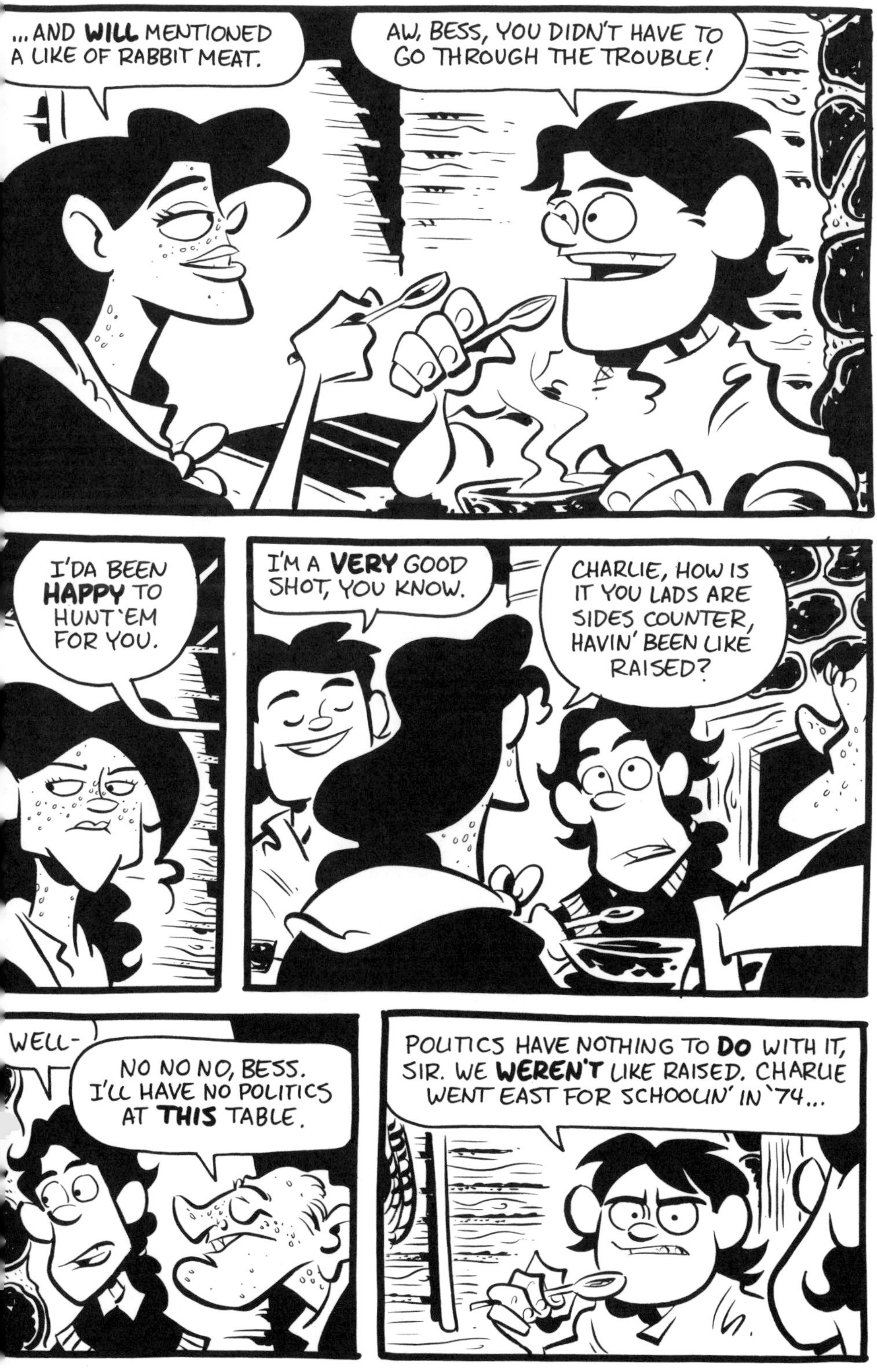
...AND WILL MENTIONED A LIKE OF RABBIT MEAT.
AW, BESS, YOU DIDN'T HAVE TO GO THROUGH THE TROUBLE!
I'DA BEEN HAPPY TO HUNT 'EM FOR YOU.
I'M A VERY GOOD SHOT, YOU KNOW.
CHARLIE, HOW IS IT YOU LADS ARE SIDES COUNTER, HAVIN' BEEN LIKE RAISED?
WELL-
NO NO NO, BESS. I'LL HAVE NO POLITICS AT THIS TABLE.
POLITICS HAVE NOTHING TO DO WITH IT, SIR. WE WEREN'T LIKE RAISED. CHARLIE WENT EAST FOR SCHOOLIN' IN '74...

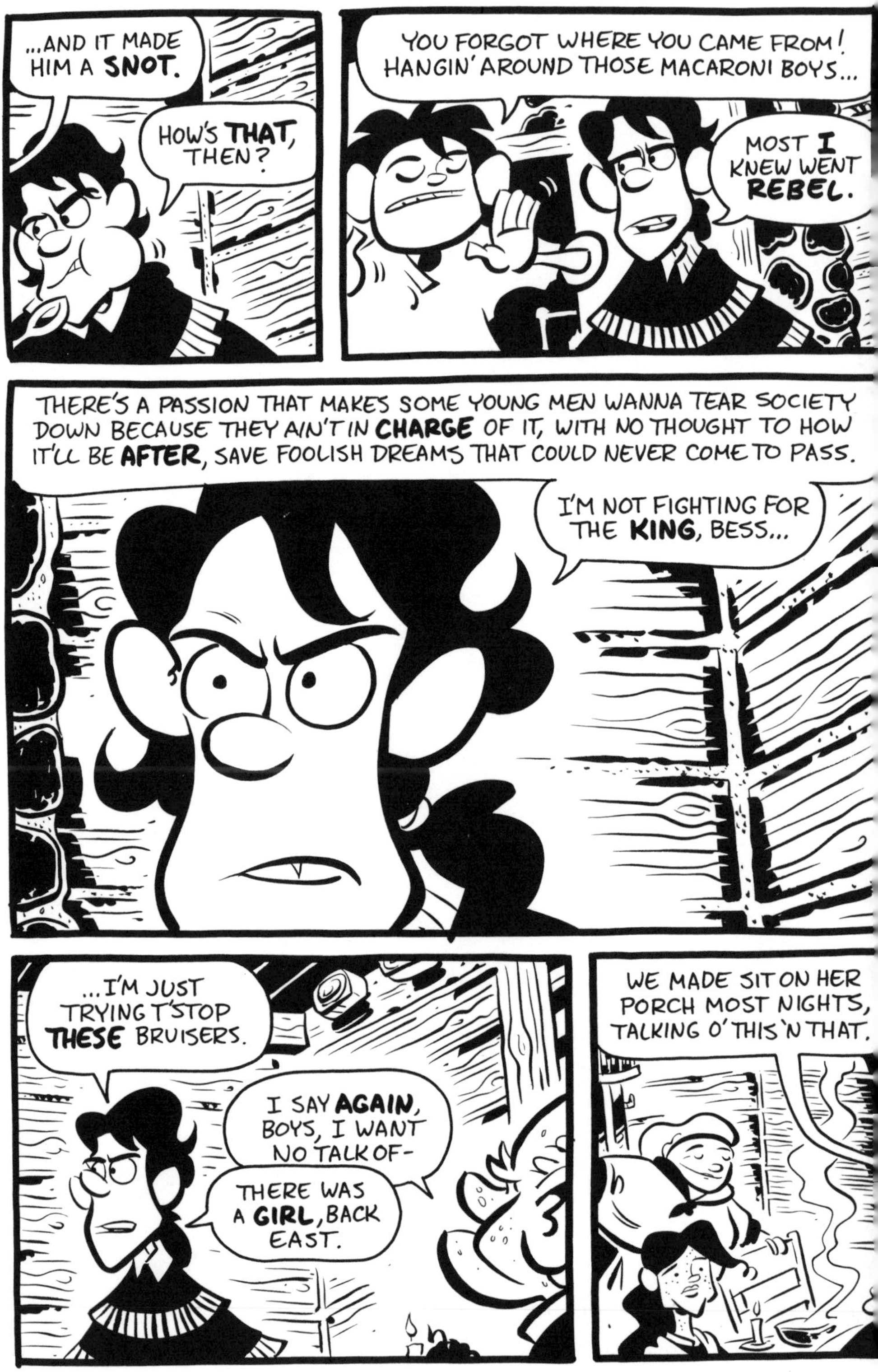
...AND IT MADE HIM A SNOT.
HOW'S THAT, THEN?
YOU FORGOT WHERE YOU CAME FROM! HANGIN' AROUND THOSE MACARONI BOYS...
MOST I KNEW WENT REBEL.
THERE'S A PASSION THAT MAKES SOME YOUNG MEN WANNA TEAR SOCIETY DOWN BECAUSE THEY AIN'T IN CHARGE OF IT, WITH NO THOUGHT TO HOW IT'LL BE AFTER, SAVE FOOLISH DREAMS THAT COULD NEVER COME TO PASS.
I'M NOT FIGHTING FOR THE KING, BESS...
...I'M JUST TRYING T'STOP THESE BRUISERS.
I SAY AGAIN, BOYS, I WANT NO TALK OF-
THERE WAS A GIRL, BACK EAST.
WE MADE SIT ON HER PORCH MOST NIGHTS, TALKING O' THIS 'N THAT.

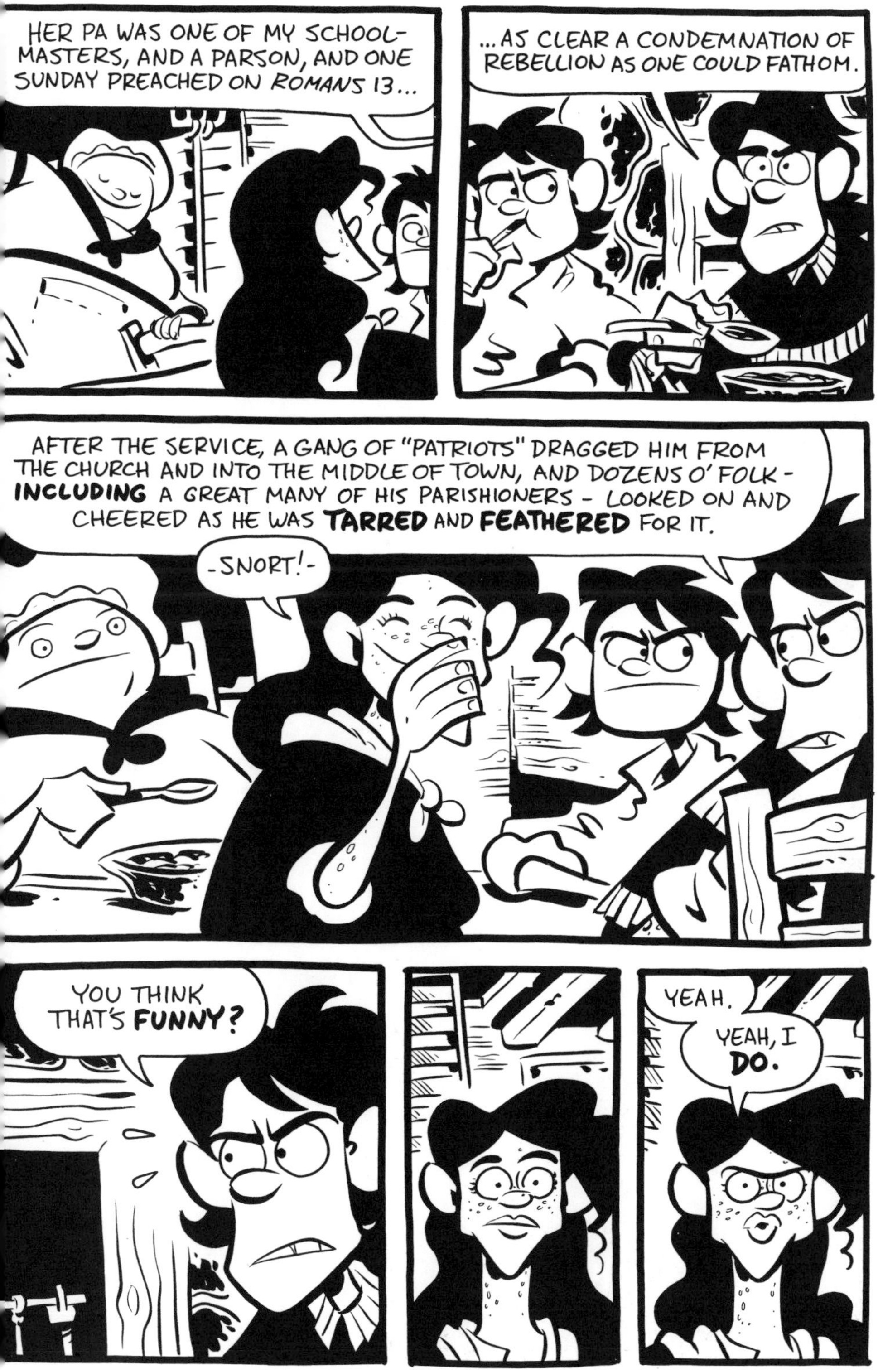
HER PA WAS ONE OF MY SCHOOLMASTERS, AND A PARSON, AND ONE SUNDAY PREACHED ON *ROMANS* 13...
...AS CLEAR A CONDEMNATION OF REBELLION AS ONE COULD FATHOM.
AFTER THE SERVICE, A GANG OF "PATRIOTS" DRAGGED HIM FROM THE CHURCH AND INTO THE MIDDLE OF TOWN, AND DOZENS O' FOLK - **INCLUDING** A GREAT MANY OF HIS PARISHIONERS - LOOKED ON AND CHEERED AS HE WAS **TARRED** AND **FEATHERED** FOR IT.
-SNORT!-
YOU THINK THAT'S **FUNNY**?
YEAH.
YEAH, I **DO**.

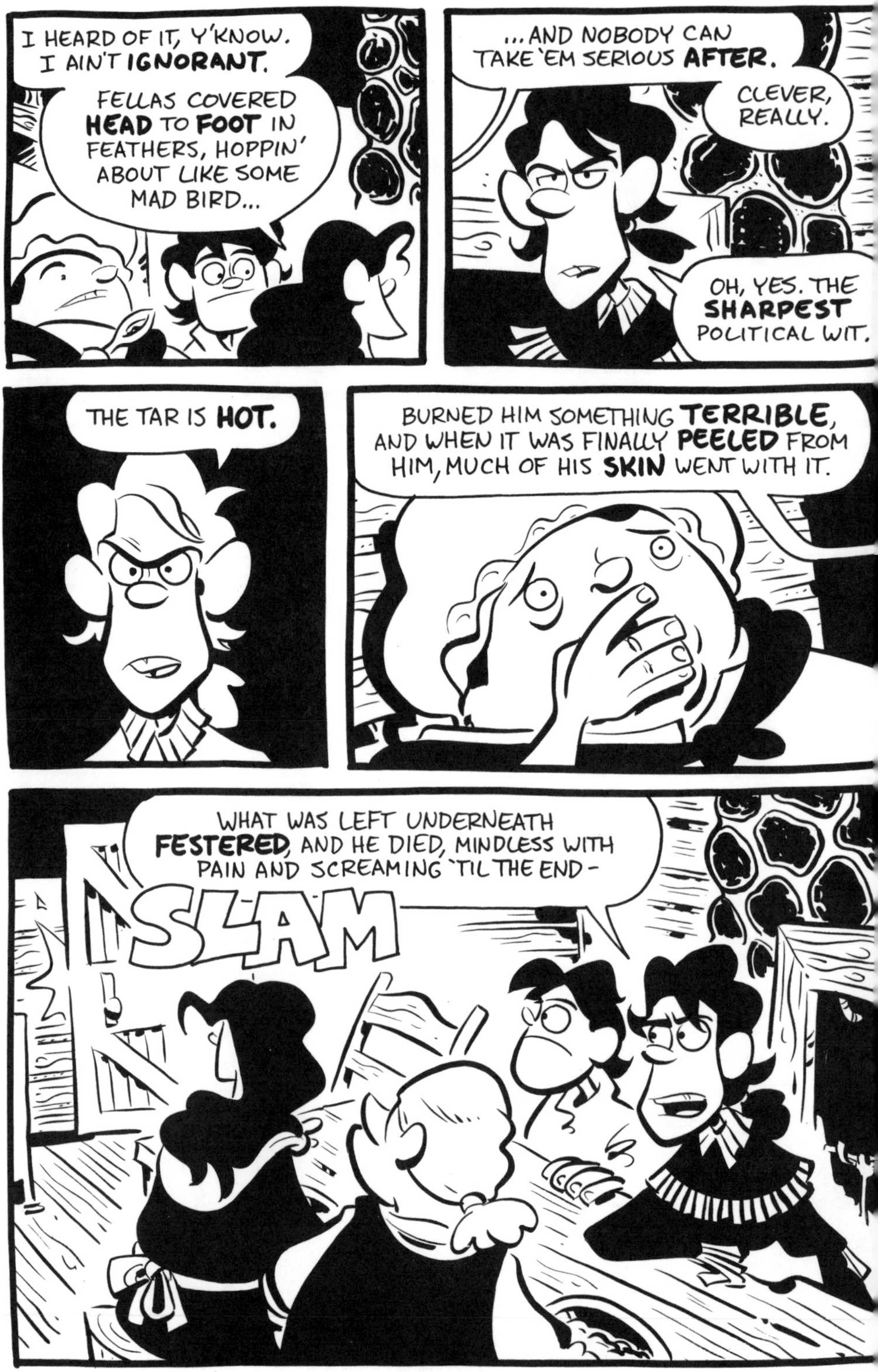
I HEARD OF IT, Y'KNOW. I AIN'T IGNORANT.
FELLAS COVERED HEAD TO FOOT IN FEATHERS, HOPPIN' ABOUT LIKE SOME MAD BIRD...
...AND NOBODY CAN TAKE 'EM SERIOUS AFTER.
CLEVER, REALLY.
OH, YES. THE SHARPEST POLITICAL WIT.
THE TAR IS HOT.
BURNED HIM SOMETHING TERRIBLE, AND WHEN IT WAS FINALLY PEELED FROM HIM, MUCH OF HIS SKIN WENT WITH IT.
WHAT WAS LEFT UNDERNEATH FESTERED, AND HE DIED, MINDLESS WITH PAIN AND SCREAMING 'TIL THE END-
SLAM

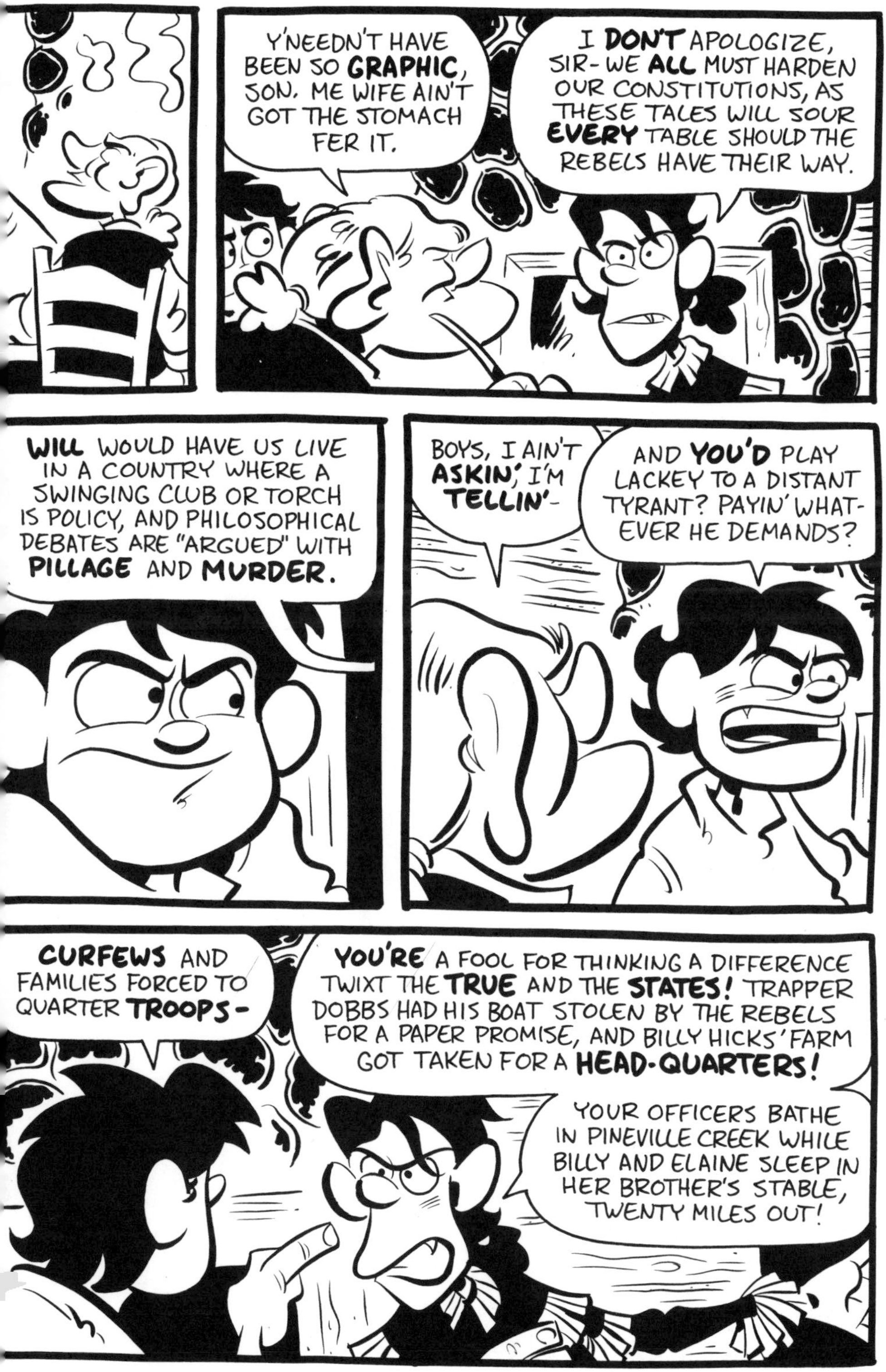
Y'NEEDN'T HAVE BEEN SO GRAPHIC, SON. ME WIFE AIN'T GOT THE STOMACH FER IT.
I DON'T APOLOGIZE, SIR- WE ALL MUST HARDEN OUR CONSTITUTIONS, AS THESE TALES WILL SOUR EVERY TABLE SHOULD THE REBELS HAVE THEIR WAY.
WILL WOULD HAVE US LIVE IN A COUNTRY WHERE A SWINGING CLUB OR TORCH IS POLICY, AND PHILOSOPHICAL DEBATES ARE "ARGUED" WITH PILLAGE AND MURDER.
BOYS, I AIN'T ASKIN', I'M TELLIN'-
AND YOU'D PLAY LACKEY TO A DISTANT TYRANT? PAYIN' WHAT-EVER HE DEMANDS?
CURFEWS AND FAMILIES FORCED TO QUARTER TROOPS-
YOU'RE A FOOL FOR THINKING A DIFFERENCE TWIXT THE TRUE AND THE STATES! TRAPPER DOBBS HAD HIS BOAT STOLEN BY THE REBELS FOR A PAPER PROMISE, AND BILLY HICKS' FARM GOT TAKEN FOR A HEAD-QUARTERS!
YOUR OFFICERS BATHE IN PINEVILLE CREEK WHILE BILLY AND ELAINE SLEEP IN HER BROTHER'S STABLE, TWENTY MILES OUT!

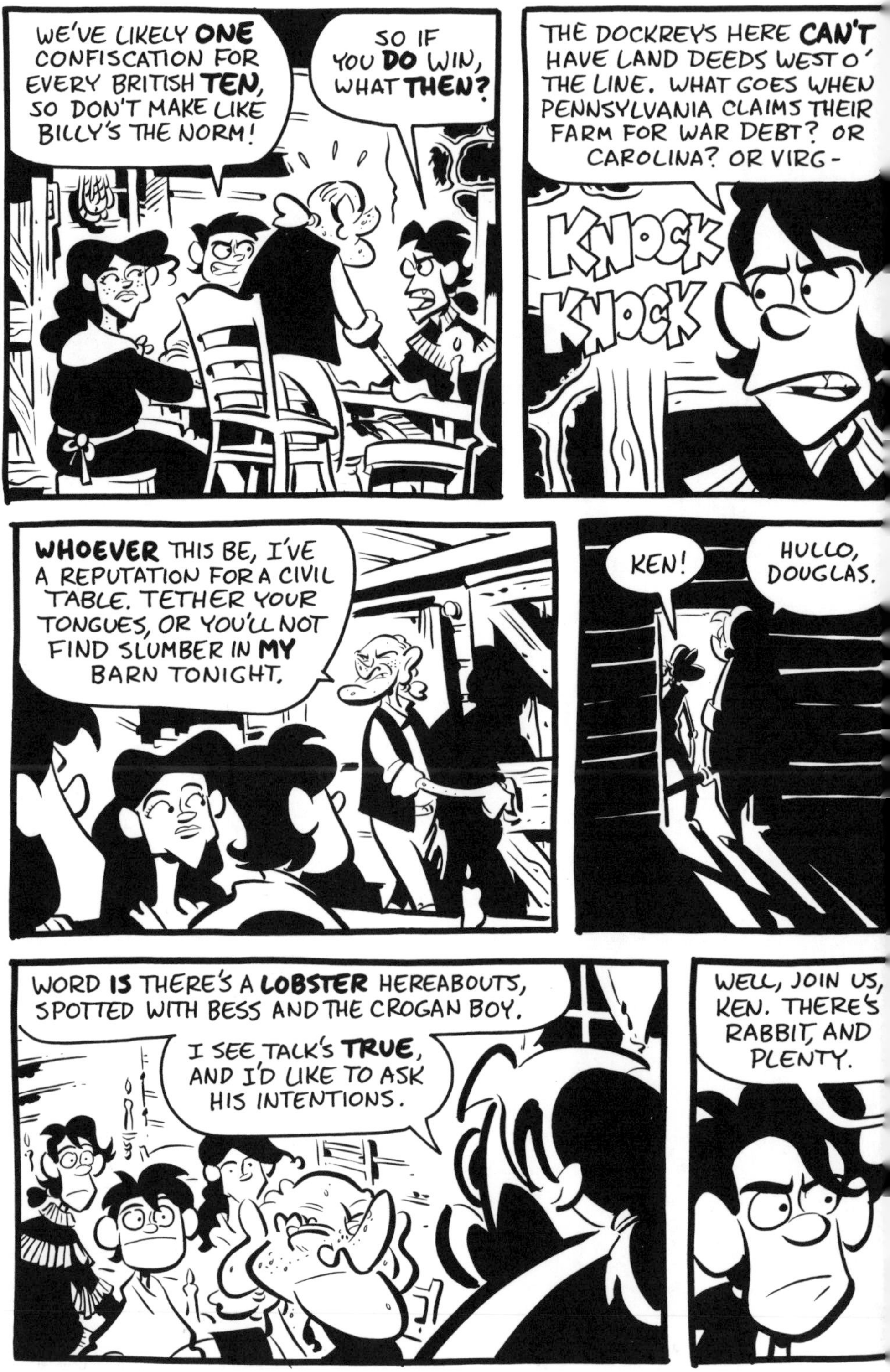
WE'VE LIKELY ONE CONFISCATION FOR EVERY BRITISH TEN, SO DON'T MAKE LIKE BILLY'S THE NORM!
SO IF YOU DO WIN, WHAT THEN?
THE DOCKREYS HERE CAN'T HAVE LAND DEEDS WEST O' THE LINE. WHAT GOES WHEN PENNSYLVANIA CLAIMS THEIR FARM FOR WAR DEBT? OR CAROLINA? OR VIRG-
KNOCK KNOCK
WHOEVER THIS BE, I'VE A REPUTATION FOR A CIVIL TABLE. TETHER YOUR TONGUES, OR YOU'LL NOT FIND SLUMBER IN MY BARN TONIGHT.
KEN!
HULLO, DOUGLAS.
WORD IS THERE'S A LOBSTER HEREABOUTS, SPOTTED WITH BESS AND THE CROGAN BOY.
I SEE TALK'S TRUE, AND I'D LIKE TO ASK HIS INTENTIONS.
WELL, JOIN US, KEN. THERE'S RABBIT, AND PLENTY.

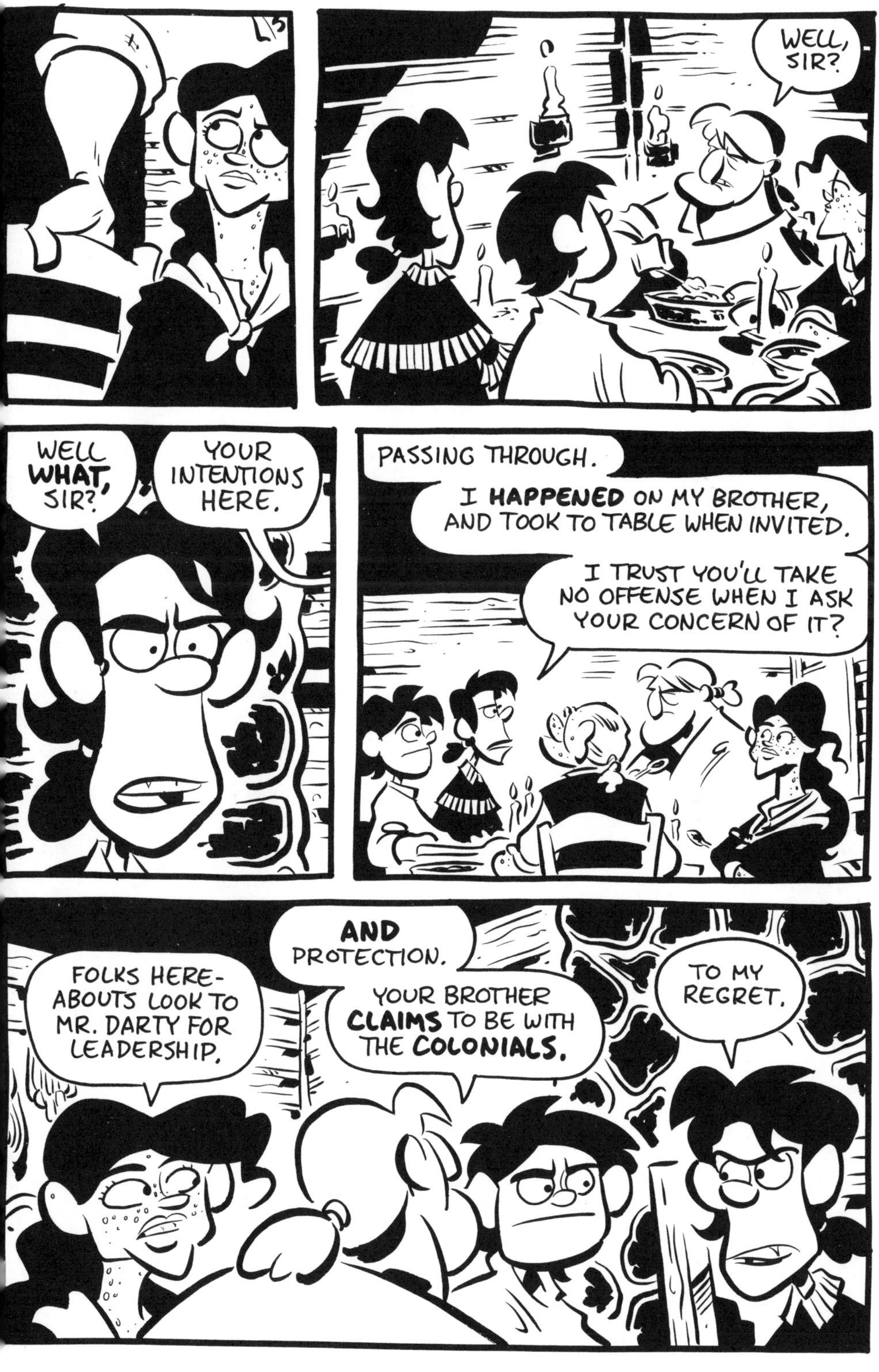
WELL, SIR?
WELL WHAT, SIR?
YOUR INTENTIONS HERE.
PASSING THROUGH.
I HAPPENED ON MY BROTHER, AND TOOK TO TABLE WHEN INVITED.
I TRUST YOU'LL TAKE NO OFFENSE WHEN I ASK YOUR CONCERN OF IT?
FOLKS HERE-ABOUTS LOOK TO MR. DARTY FOR LEADERSHIP.
AND PROTECTION.
YOUR BROTHER CLAIMS TO BE WITH THE COLONIALS.
TO MY REGRET.

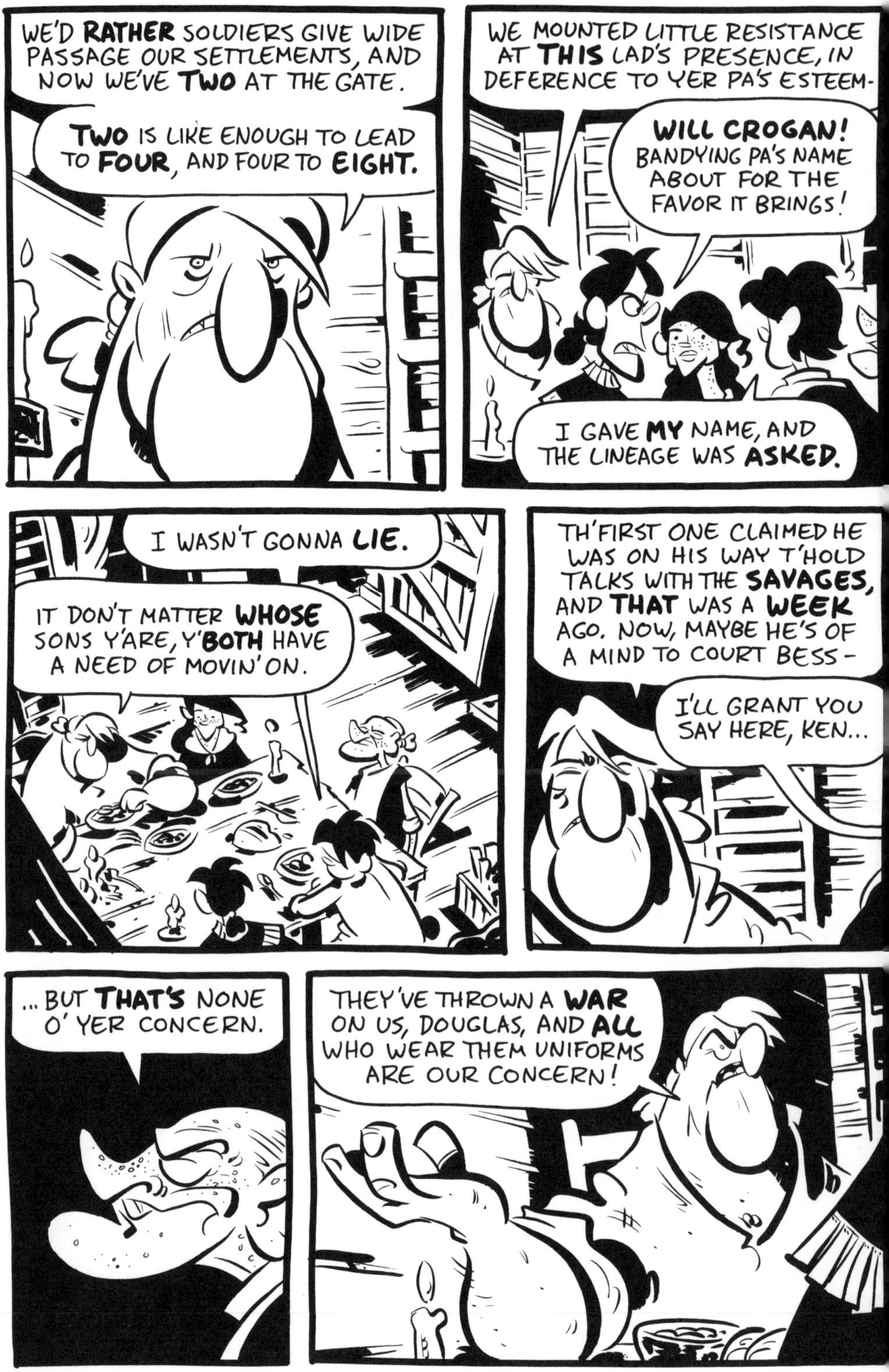
WE'D RATHER SOLDIERS GIVE WIDE PASSAGE OUR SETTLEMENTS, AND NOW WE'VE TWO AT THE GATE.
TWO IS LIKE ENOUGH TO LEAD TO FOUR, AND FOUR TO EIGHT.
WE MOUNTED LITTLE RESISTANCE AT THIS LAD'S PRESENCE, IN DEFERENCE TO YER PA'S ESTEEM-
WILL CROGAN! BANDYING PA'S NAME ABOUT FOR THE FAVOR IT BRINGS!
I GAVE MY NAME, AND THE LINEAGE WAS ASKED.
I WASN'T GONNA LIE.
IT DON'T MATTER WHOSE SONS Y'ARE, Y'BOTH HAVE A NEED OF MOVIN' ON.
TH'FIRST ONE CLAIMED HE WAS ON HIS WAY T'HOLD TALKS WITH THE SAVAGES, AND THAT WAS A WEEK AGO. NOW, MAYBE HE'S OF A MIND TO COURT BESS-
I'LL GRANT YOU SAY HERE, KEN...
... BUT THAT'S NONE O' YER CONCERN.
THEY'VE THROWN A WAR ON US, DOUGLAS, AND ALL WHO WEAR THEM UNIFORMS ARE OUR CONCERN!

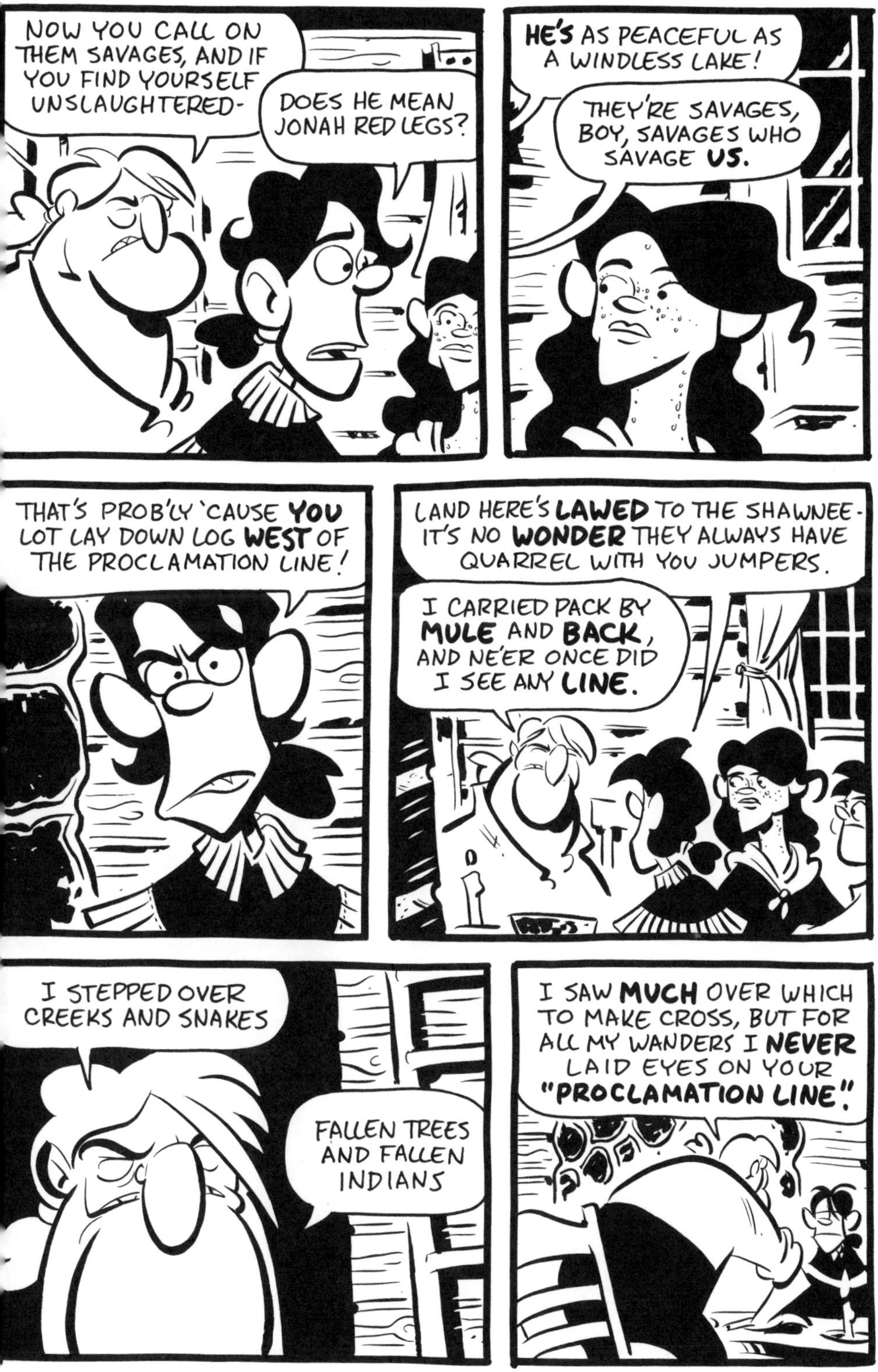
NOW YOU CALL ON THEM SAVAGES, AND IF YOU FIND YOURSELF UNSLAUGHTERED-
DOES HE MEAN JONAH RED LEGS?
HE'S AS PEACEFUL AS A WINDLESS LAKE!
THEY'RE SAVAGES, BOY, SAVAGES WHO SAVAGE US.
THAT'S PROB'LY 'CAUSE YOU LOT LAY DOWN LOG WEST OF THE PROCLAMATION LINE!
LAND HERE'S LAWED TO THE SHAWNEE-IT'S NO WONDER THEY ALWAYS HAVE QUARREL WITH YOU JUMPERS.
I CARRIED PACK BY MULE AND BACK, AND NE'ER ONCE DID I SEE ANY LINE.
I STEPPED OVER CREEKS AND SNAKES
FALLEN TREES AND FALLEN INDIANS
I SAW MUCH OVER WHICH TO MAKE CROSS, BUT FOR ALL MY WANDERS I NEVER LAID EYES ON YOUR "PROCLAMATION LINE".

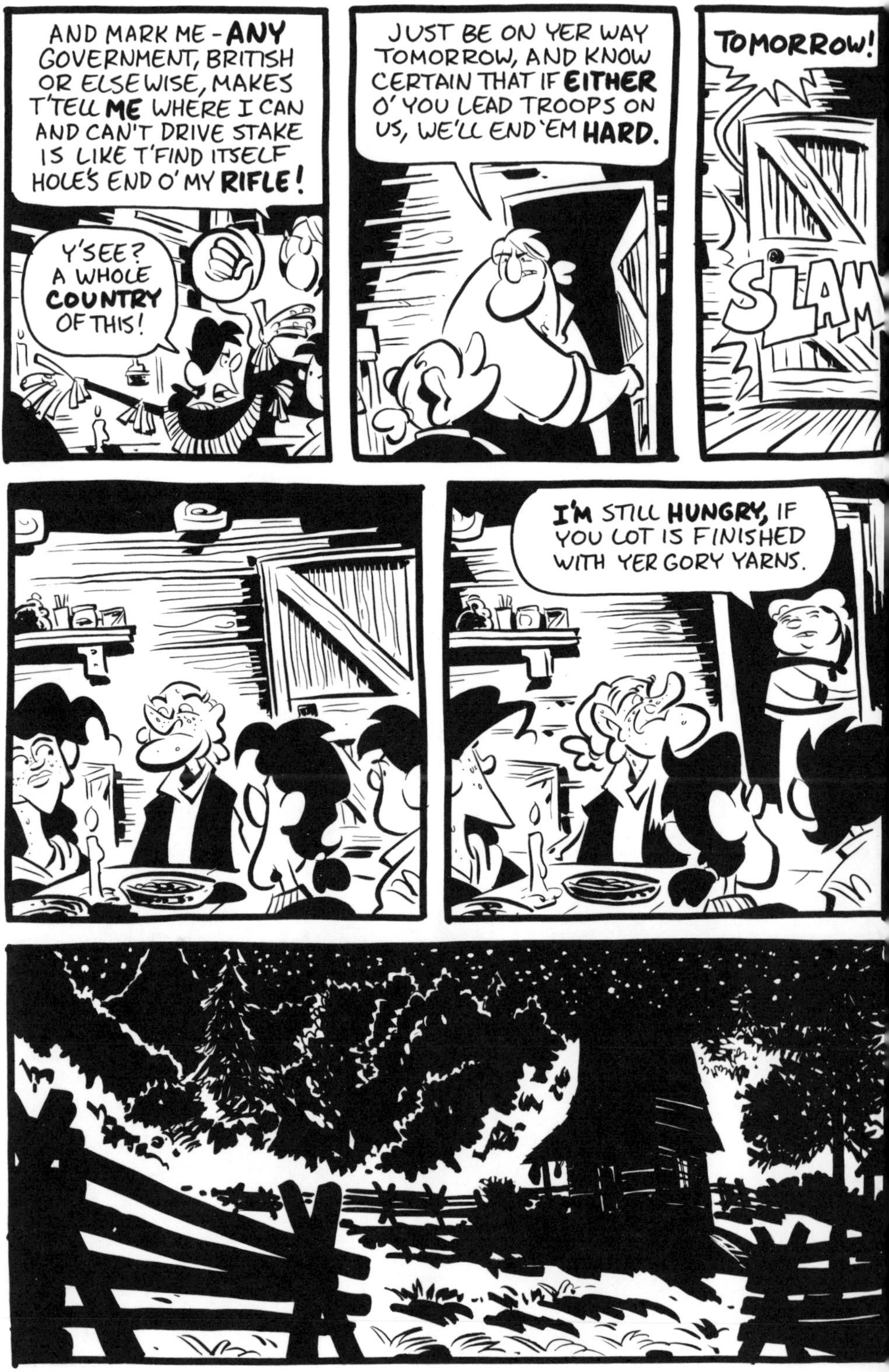
AND MARK ME - ANY GOVERNMENT, BRITISH OR ELSEWISE, MAKES T'TELL ME WHERE I CAN AND CAN'T DRIVE STAKE IS LIKE T'FIND ITSELF HOLE'S END O' MY RIFLE!
Y'SEE? A WHOLE COUNTRY OF THIS!
JUST BE ON YER WAY TOMORROW, AND KNOW CERTAIN THAT IF EITHER O' YOU LEAD TROOPS ON US, WE'LL END 'EM HARD.
TOMORROW!
I'M STILL HUNGRY, IF YOU LOT IS FINISHED WITH YER GORY YARNS.

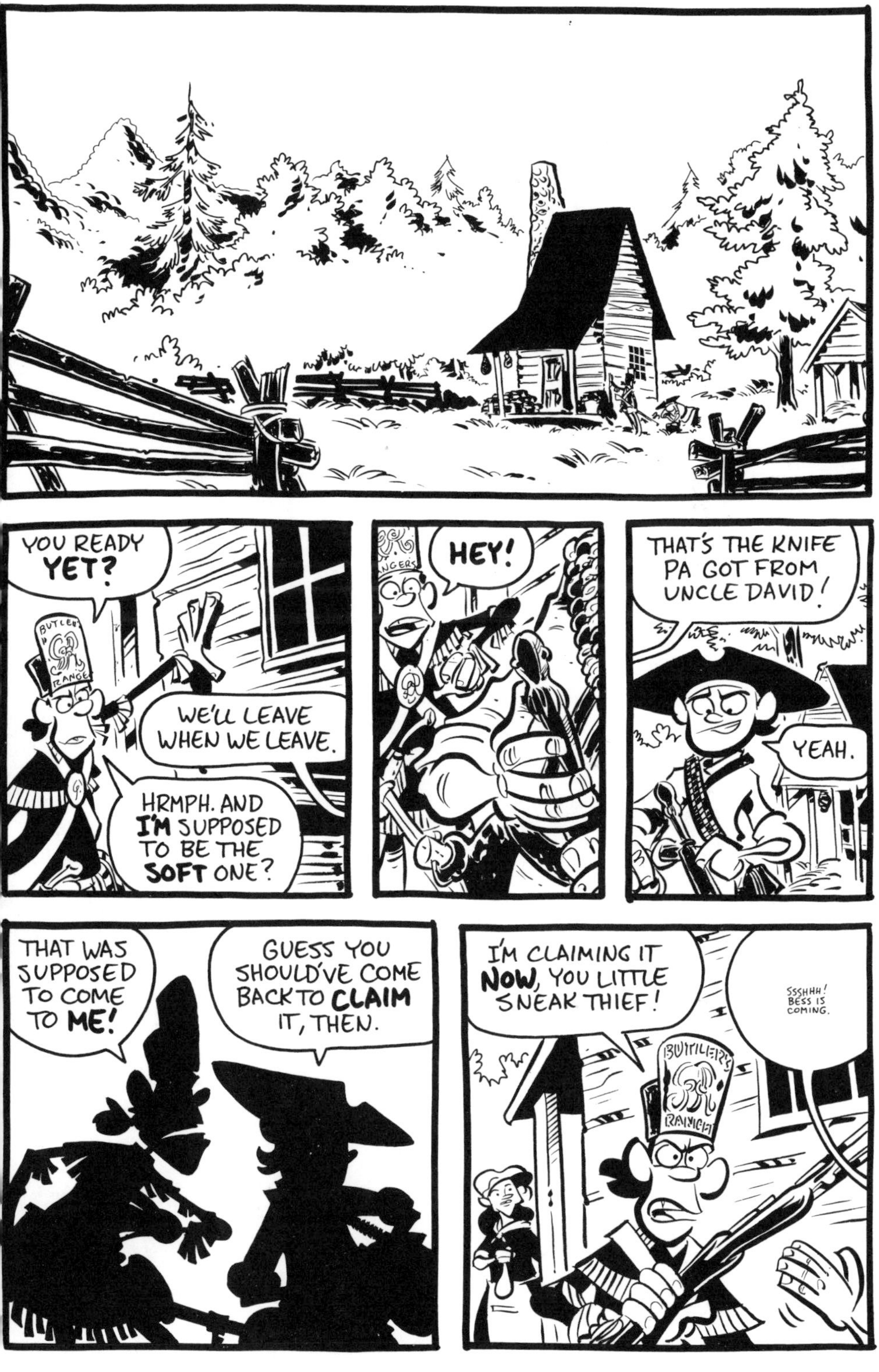
YOU READY YET?
WE'LL LEAVE WHEN WE LEAVE.
HRMPH. AND I'M SUPPOSED TO BE THE SOFT ONE?
HEY!
THAT'S THE KNIFE PA GOT FROM UNCLE DAVID!
YEAH.
THAT WAS SUPPOSED TO COME TO ME!
GUESS YOU SHOULD'VE COME BACK TO CLAIM IT, THEN.
I'M CLAIMING IT NOW, YOU LITTLE SNEAK THIEF!
SSSHHH! BESS IS COMING.

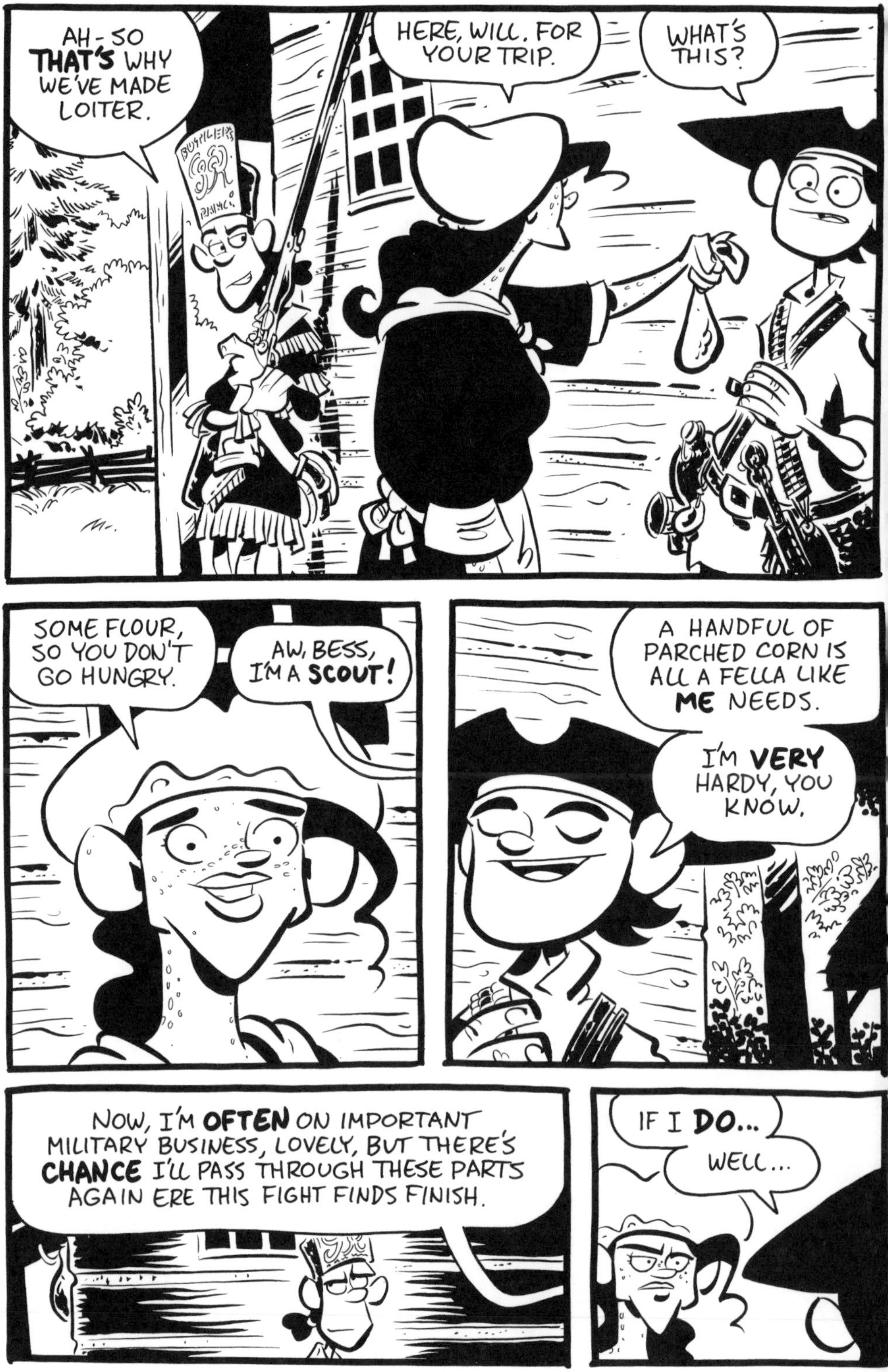
AH - SO **THAT'S** WHY WE'VE MADE LOITER.
HERE, WILL. FOR YOUR TRIP.
WHAT'S THIS?
SOME FLOUR, SO YOU DON'T GO HUNGRY.
AW, BESS, I'M A **SCOUT**!
A HANDFUL OF PARCHED CORN IS ALL A FELLA LIKE **ME** NEEDS.
I'M **VERY** HARDY, YOU KNOW.
NOW, I'M **OFTEN** ON IMPORTANT MILITARY BUSINESS, LOVELY, BUT THERE'S **CHANCE** I'LL PASS THROUGH THESE PARTS AGAIN ERE THIS FIGHT FINDS FINISH.
IF I **DO...**
WELL...

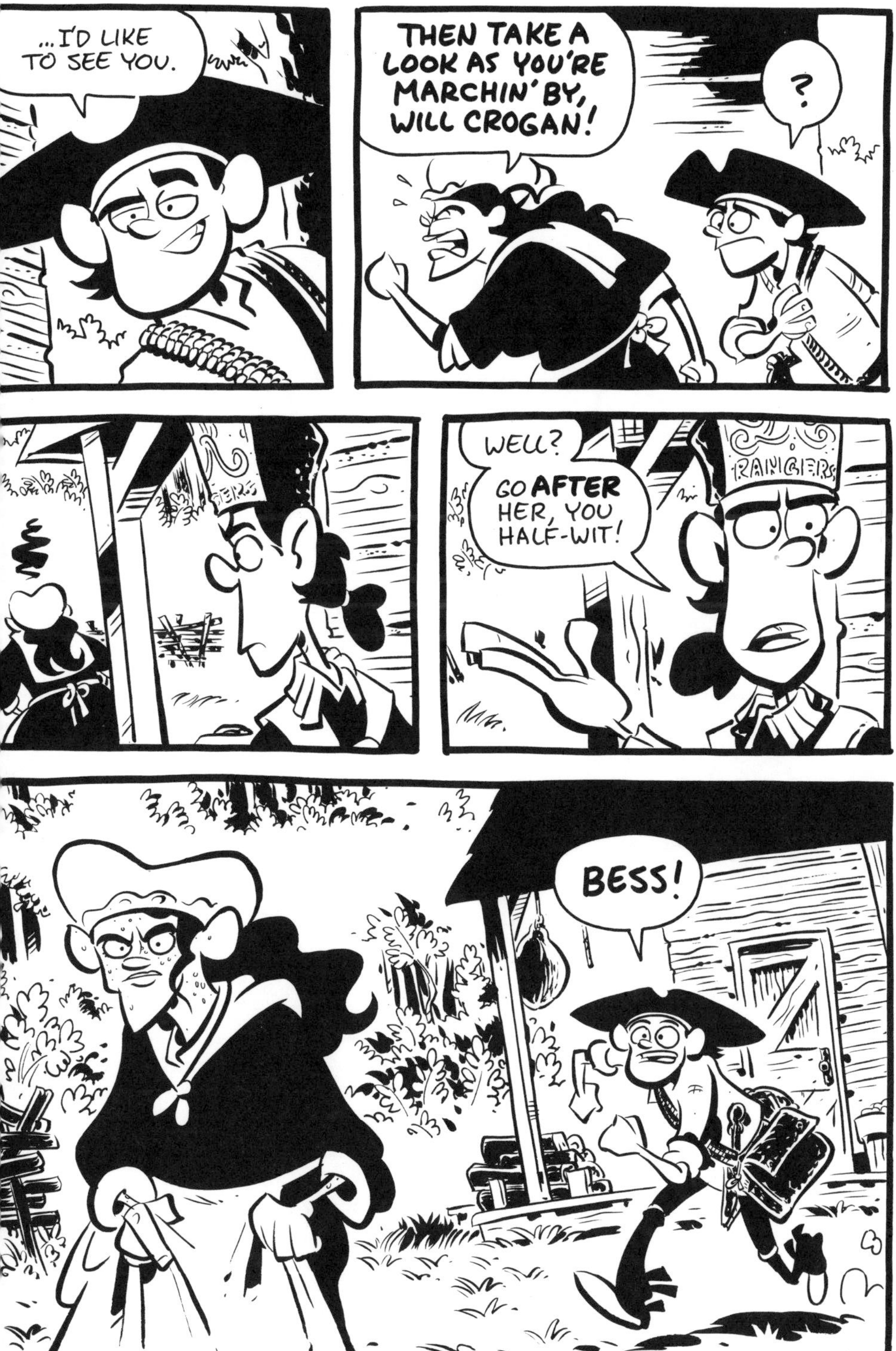
...I'D LIKE TO SEE YOU.
THEN TAKE A LOOK AS YOU'RE MARCHIN' BY, WILL CROGAN!
?
WELL?
GO **AFTER** HER, YOU HALF-WIT!
RANGERS
BESS!

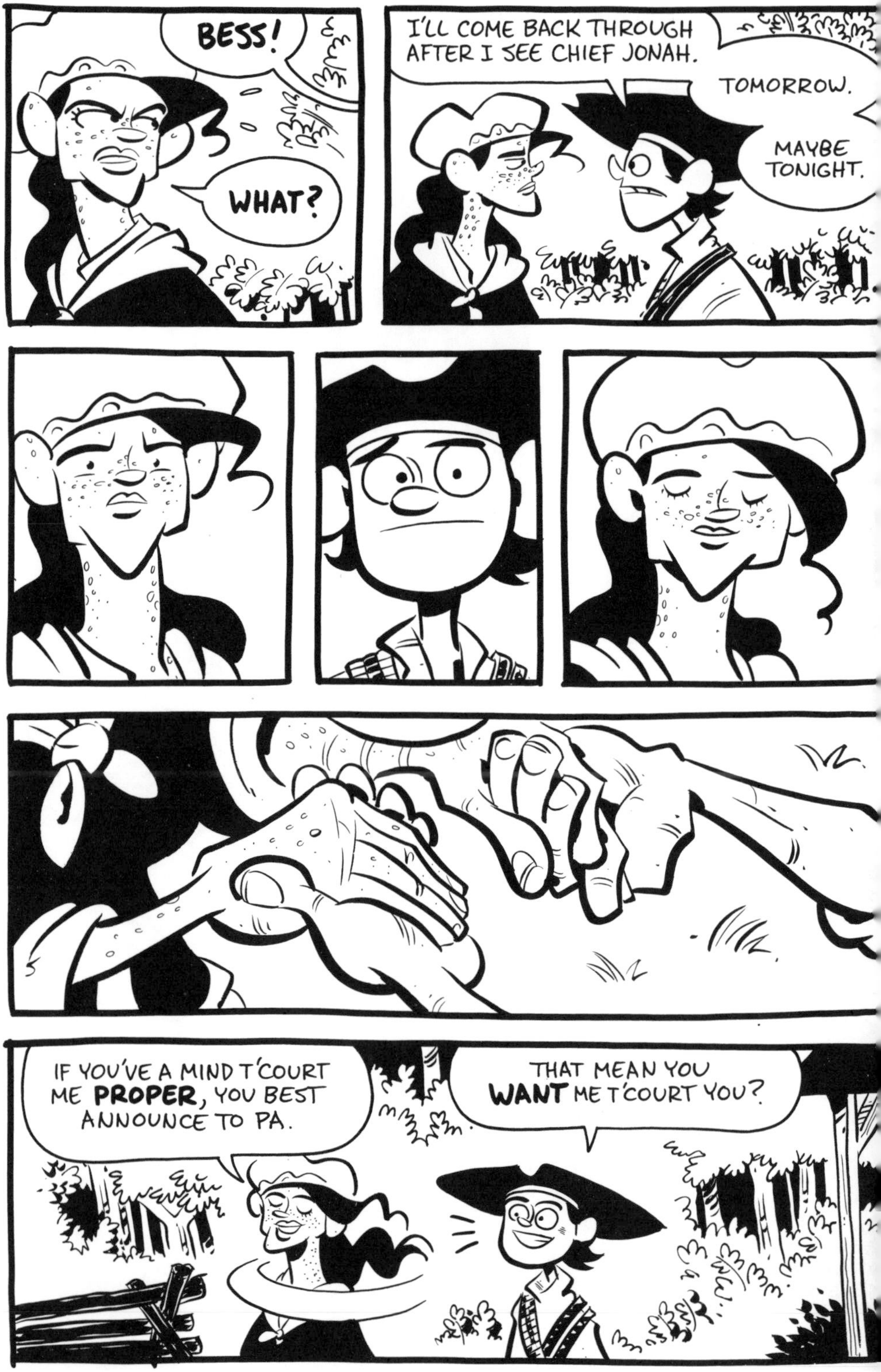
BESS!
WHAT?
I'LL COME BACK THROUGH AFTER I SEE CHIEF JONAH.
TOMORROW.
MAYBE TONIGHT.
IF YOU'VE A MIND T'COURT ME PROPER, YOU BEST ANNOUNCE TO PA.
THAT MEAN YOU WANT ME T'COURT YOU?

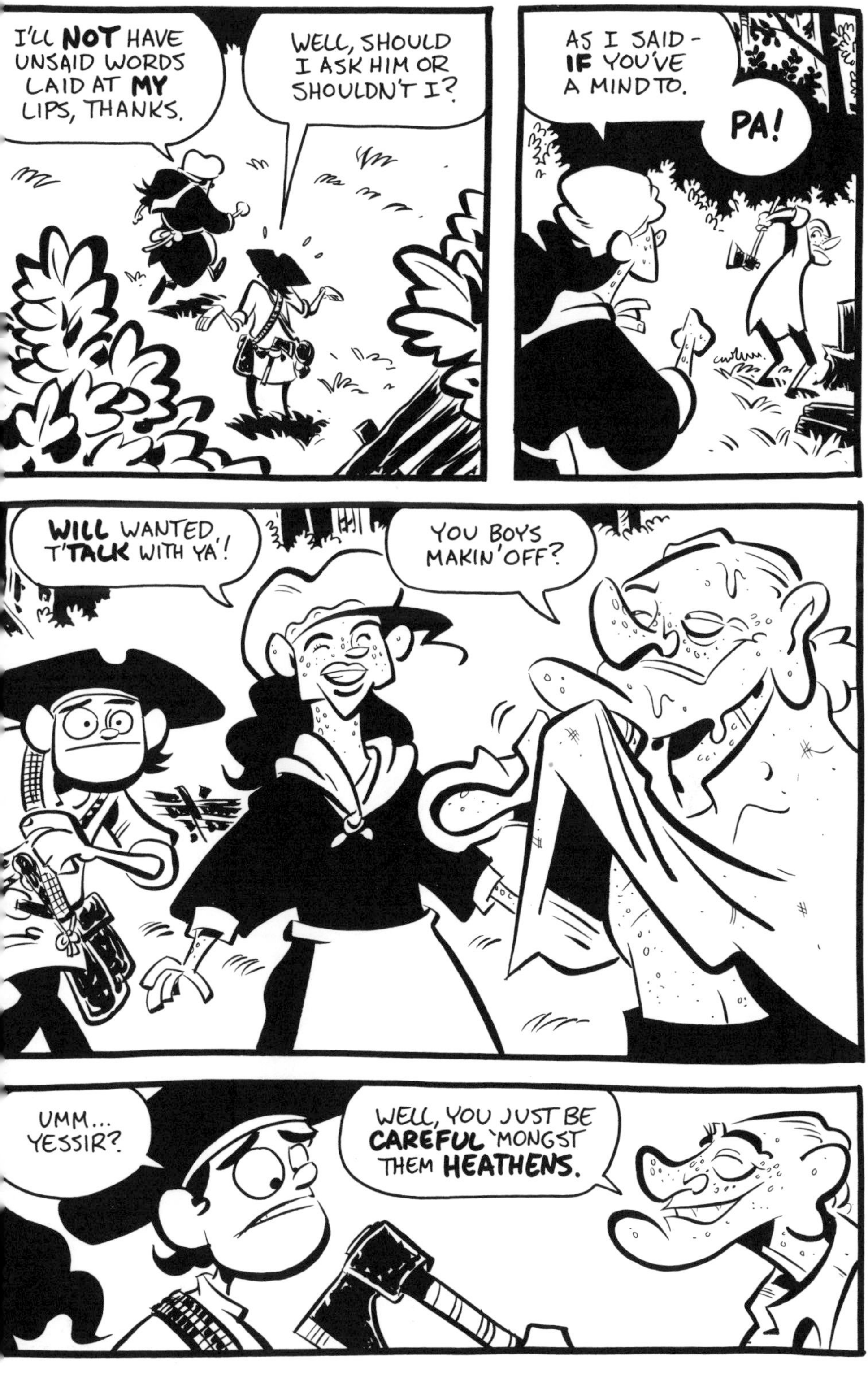
I'LL **NOT** HAVE UNSAID WORDS LAID AT **MY** LIPS, THANKS.
WELL, SHOULD I ASK HIM OR SHOULDN'T I?
AS I SAID - **IF** YOU'VE A MIND TO.
PA!
WILL WANTED T'**TALK** WITH YA'!
YOU BOYS MAKIN' OFF?
UMM... YESSIR?
WELL, YOU JUST BE **CAREFUL** `MONGST THEM **HEATHENS**.

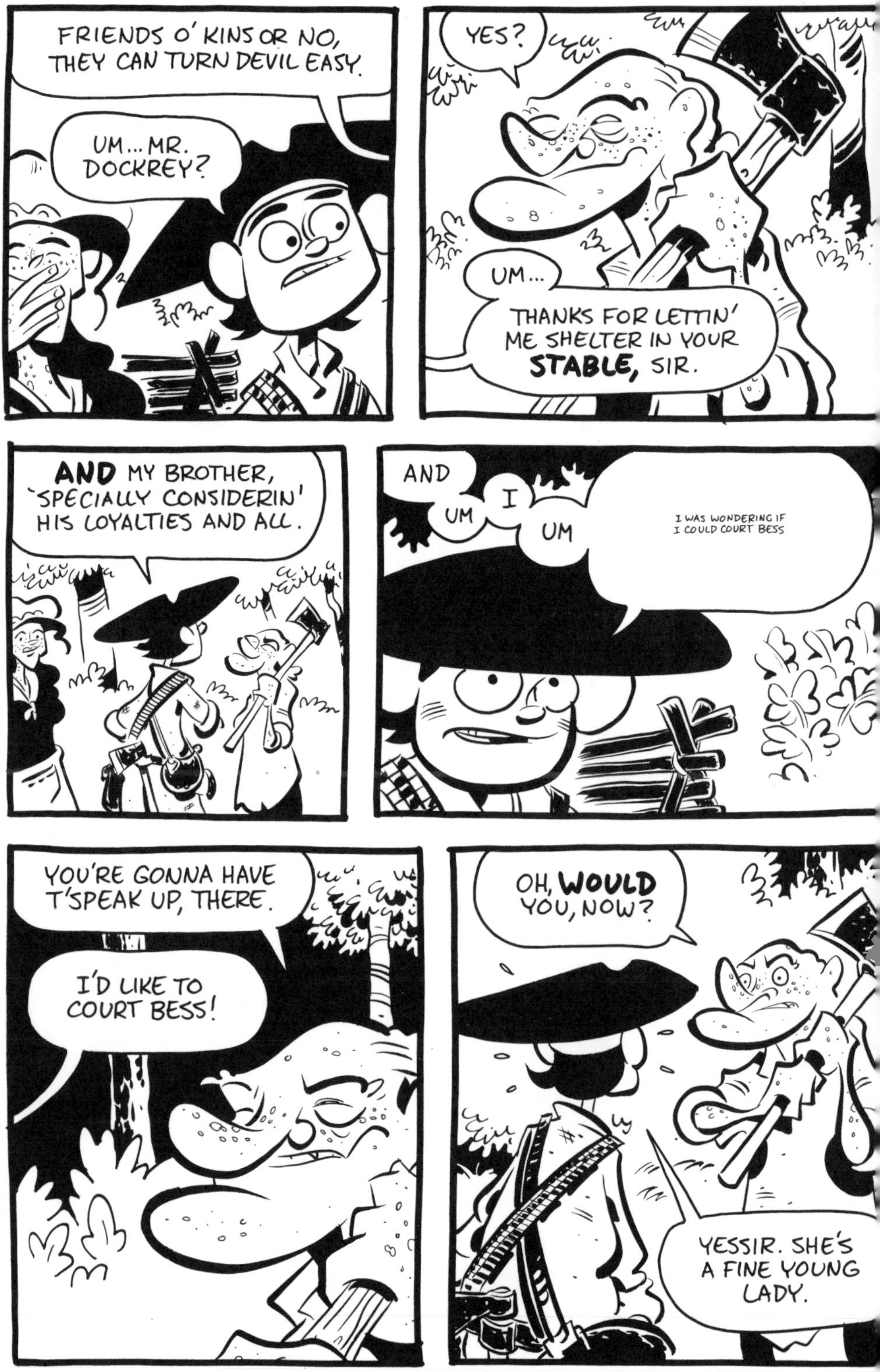
FRIENDS O' KINS OR NO, THEY CAN TURN DEVIL EASY.
UM... MR. DOCKREY?
YES?
UM...
THANKS FOR LETTIN' ME SHELTER IN YOUR STABLE, SIR.
AND MY BROTHER, 'SPECIALLY CONSIDERIN' HIS LOYALTIES AND ALL.
AND
UM
I
UM
I WAS WONDERING IF I COULD COURT BESS
YOU'RE GONNA HAVE T'SPEAK UP, THERE.
I'D LIKE TO COURT BESS!
OH, WOULD YOU, NOW?
YESSIR. SHE'S A FINE YOUNG LADY.

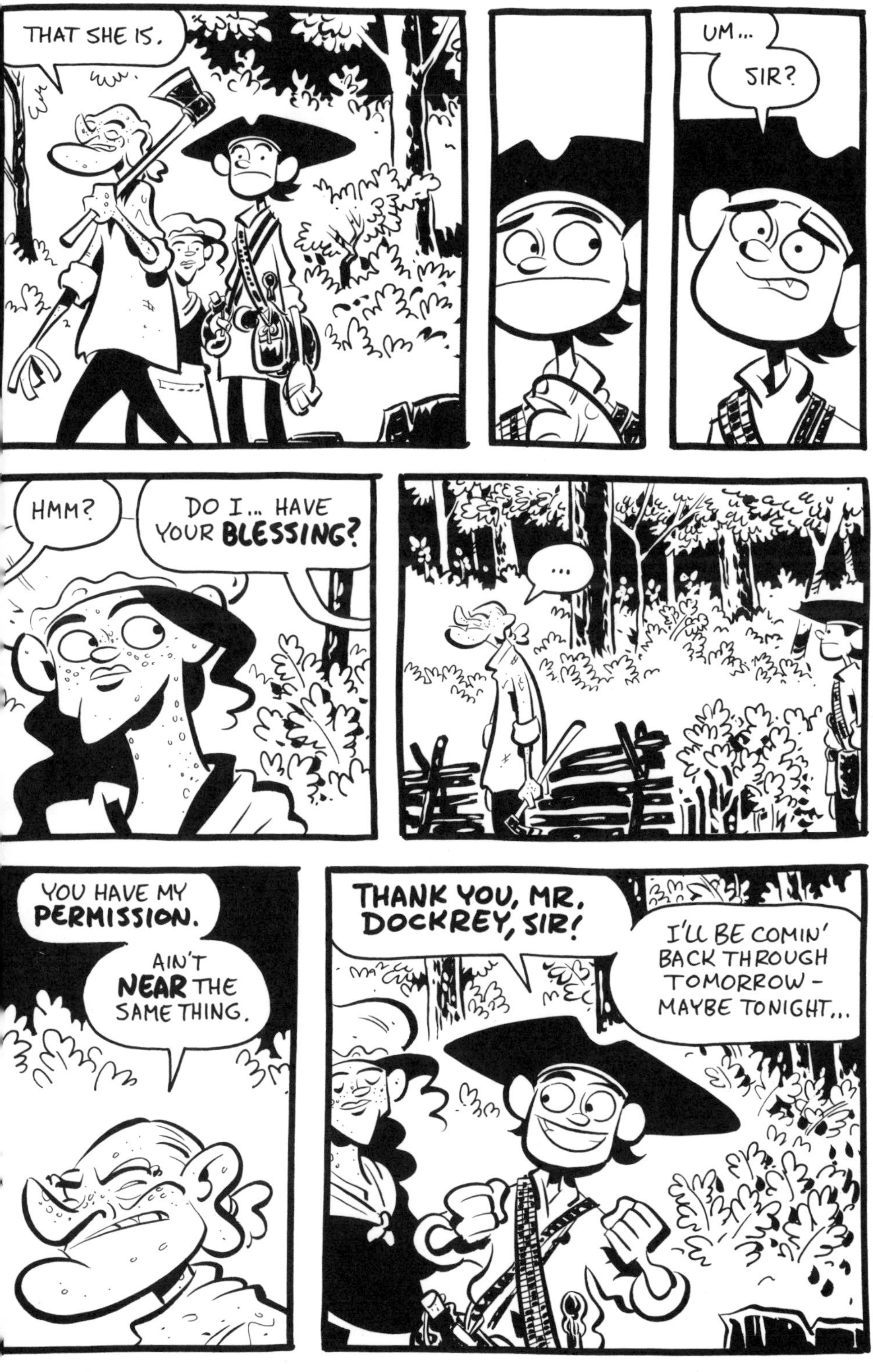
THAT SHE IS.
UM...
SIR?
HMM?
DO I... HAVE YOUR BLESSING?
...
YOU HAVE MY PERMISSION.
AIN'T NEAR THE SAME THING.
THANK YOU, MR. DOCKREY, SIR!
I'LL BE COMIN' BACK THROUGH TOMORROW - MAYBE TONIGHT...

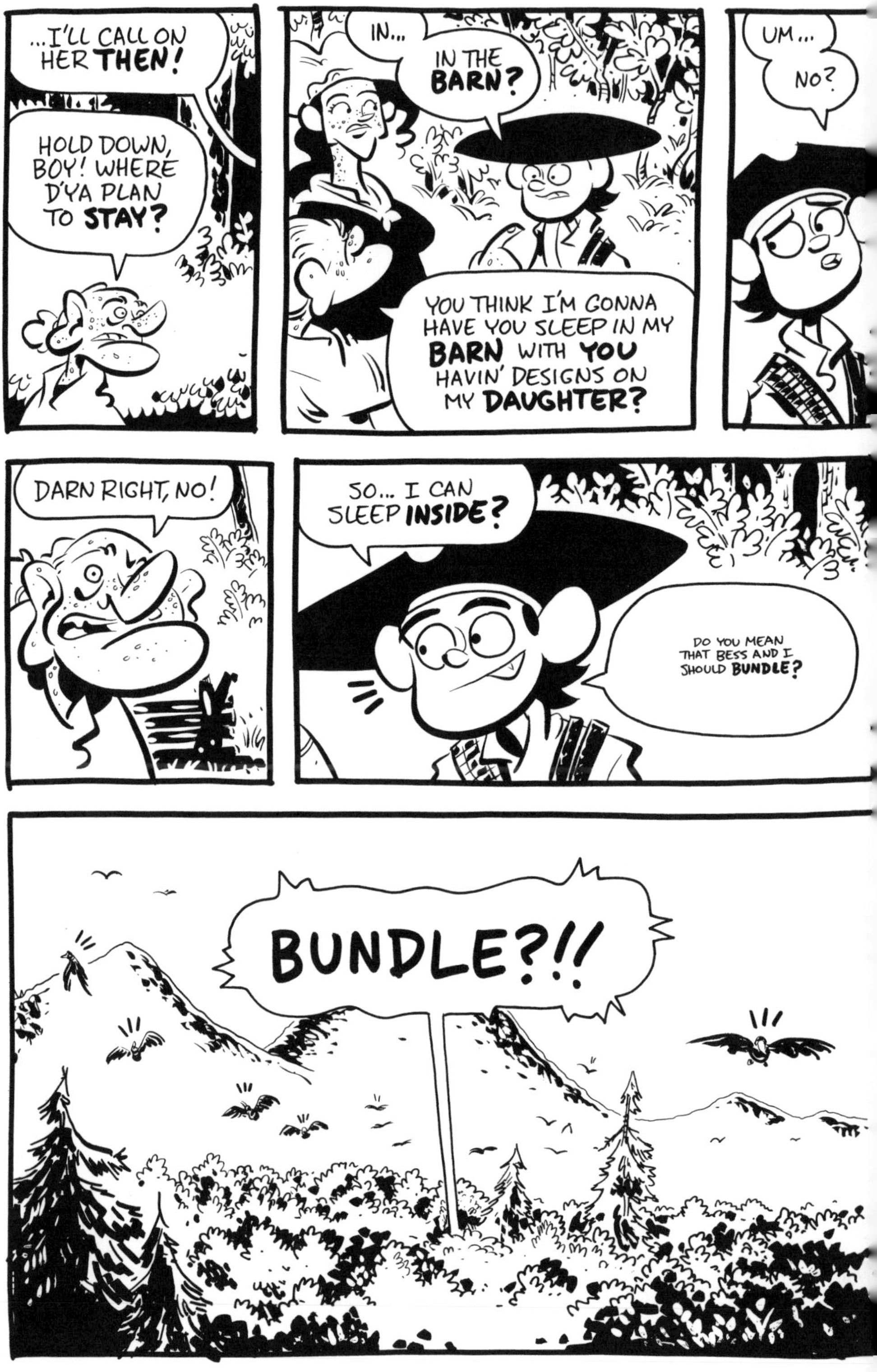
...I'LL CALL ON HER **THEN**!
HOLD DOWN, BOY! WHERE D'YA PLAN TO **STAY**?
IN...
IN THE **BARN**?
YOU THINK I'M GONNA HAVE YOU SLEEP IN MY **BARN** WITH **YOU** HAVIN' DESIGNS ON MY **DAUGHTER**?
UM...
NO?
DARN RIGHT, NO!
SO... I CAN SLEEP **INSIDE**?
DO YOU MEAN THAT BESS AND I SHOULD **BUNDLE**?
BUNDLE?!!

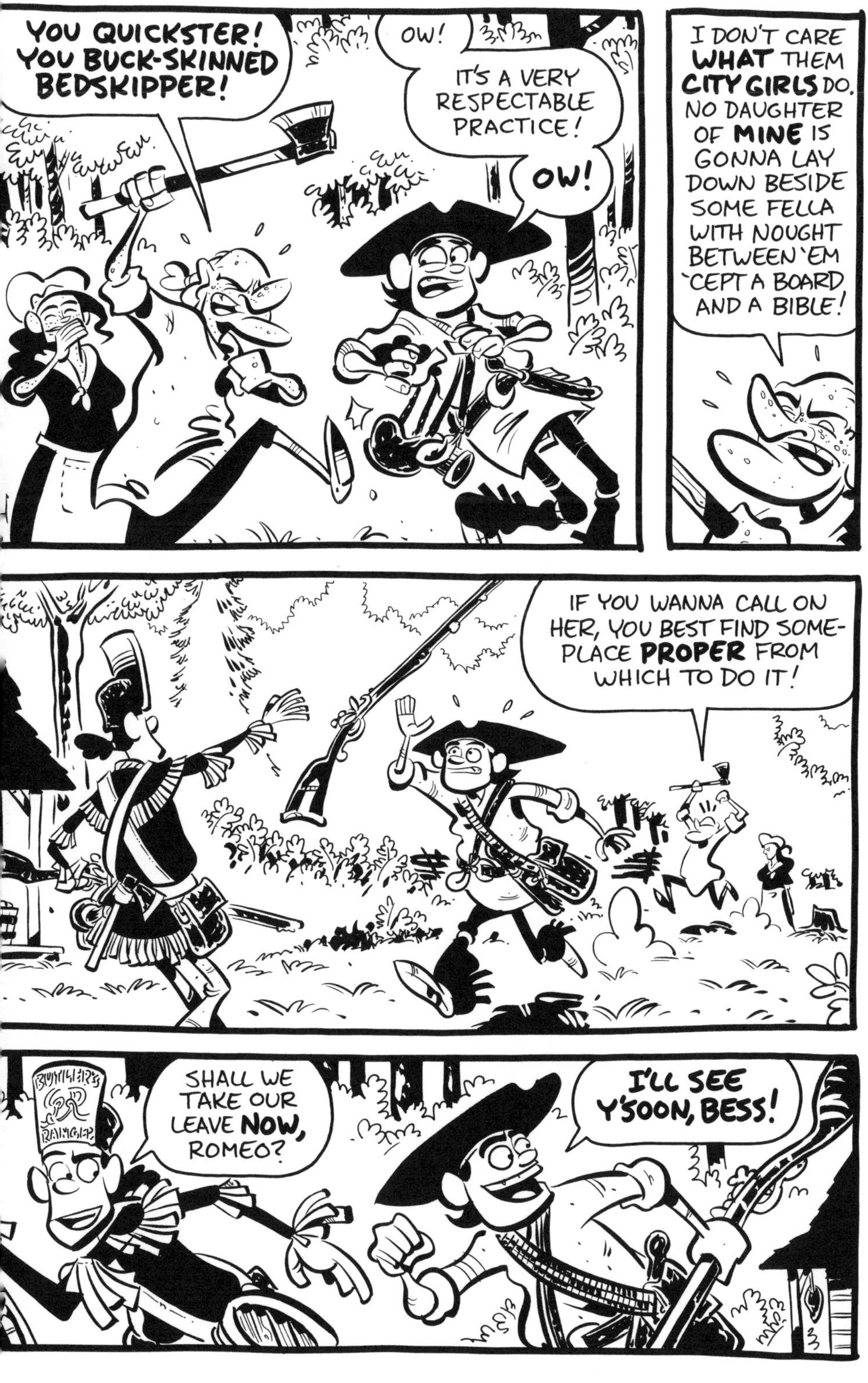
YOU QUICKSTER! YOU BUCK-SKINNED BEDSKIPPER!
OW!
IT'S A VERY RESPECTABLE PRACTICE!
OW!
I DON'T CARE WHAT THEM CITY GIRLS DO. NO DAUGHTER OF MINE IS GONNA LAY DOWN BESIDE SOME FELLA WITH NOUGHT BETWEEN 'EM 'CEPT A BOARD AND A BIBLE!
IF YOU WANNA CALL ON HER, YOU BEST FIND SOME-PLACE PROPER FROM WHICH TO DO IT!
SHALL WE TAKE OUR LEAVE NOW, ROMEO?
I'LL SEE Y'SOON, BESS!

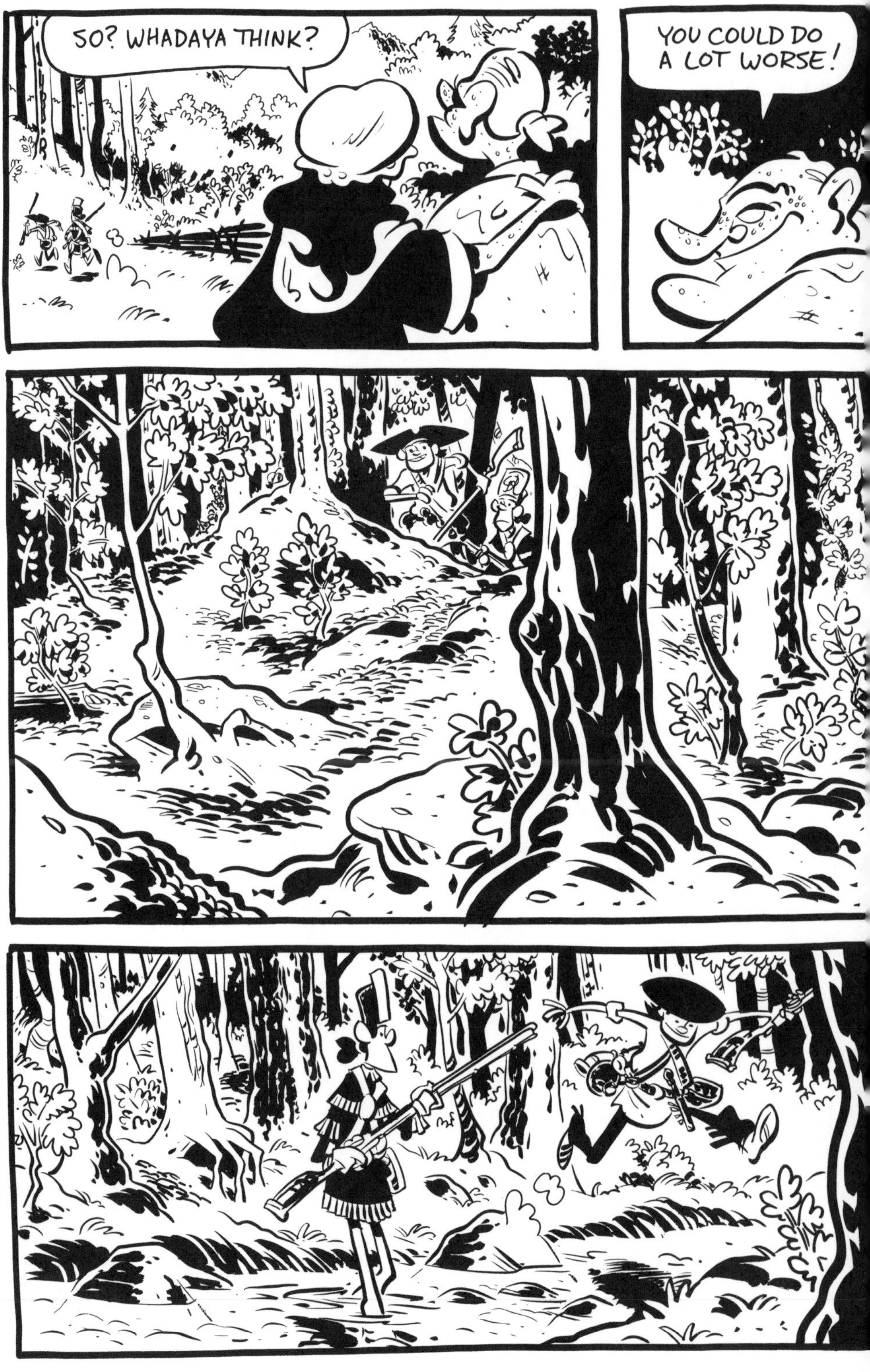
SO? WHADAYA THINK?
YOU COULD DO A LOT WORSE!

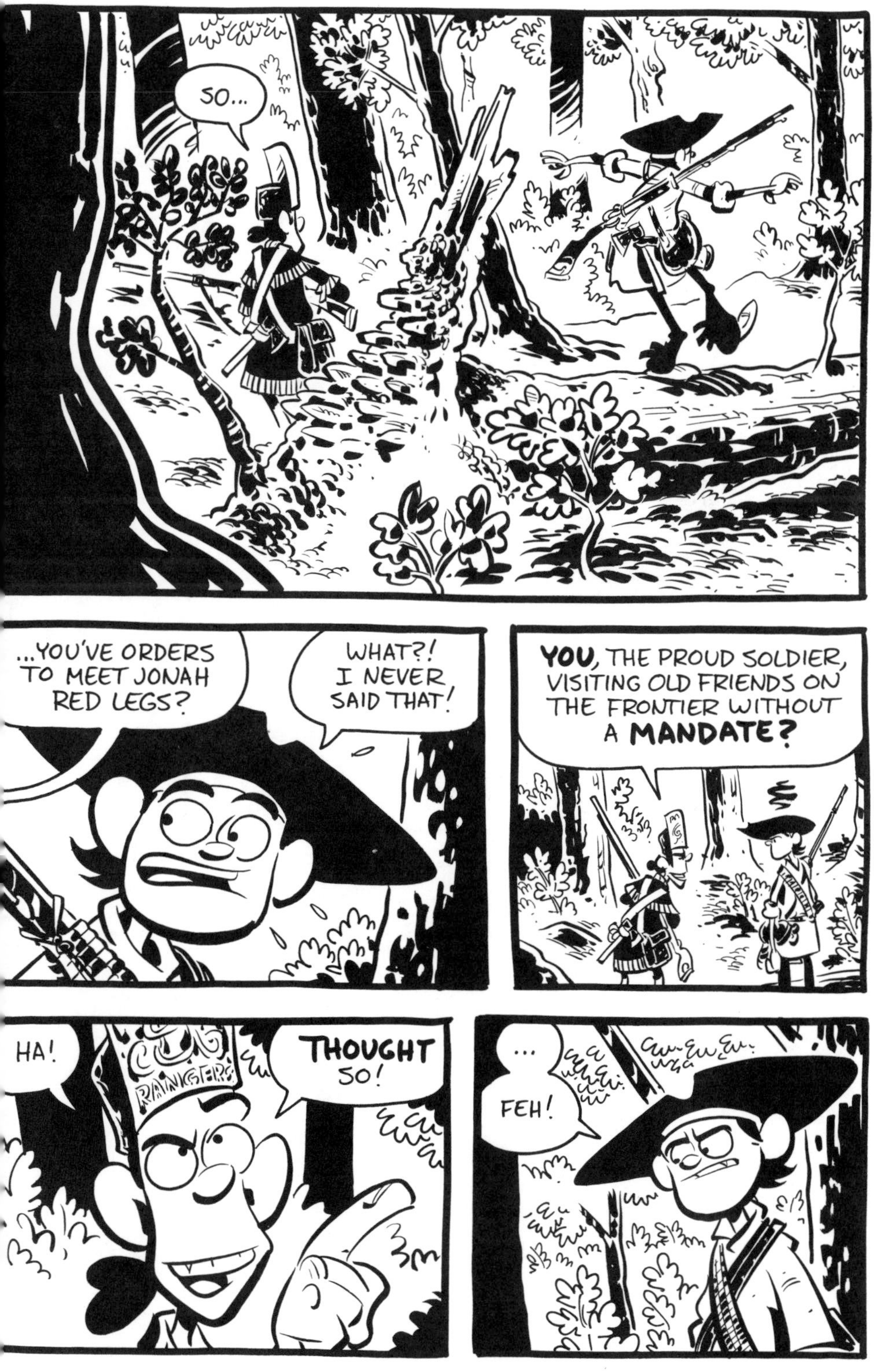
SO...
...YOU'VE ORDERS TO MEET JONAH RED LEGS?
WHAT?! I NEVER SAID THAT!
YOU, THE PROUD SOLDIER, VISITING OLD FRIENDS ON THE FRONTIER WITHOUT A MANDATE?
HA!
THOUGHT SO!
RANGERS
...
FEH!

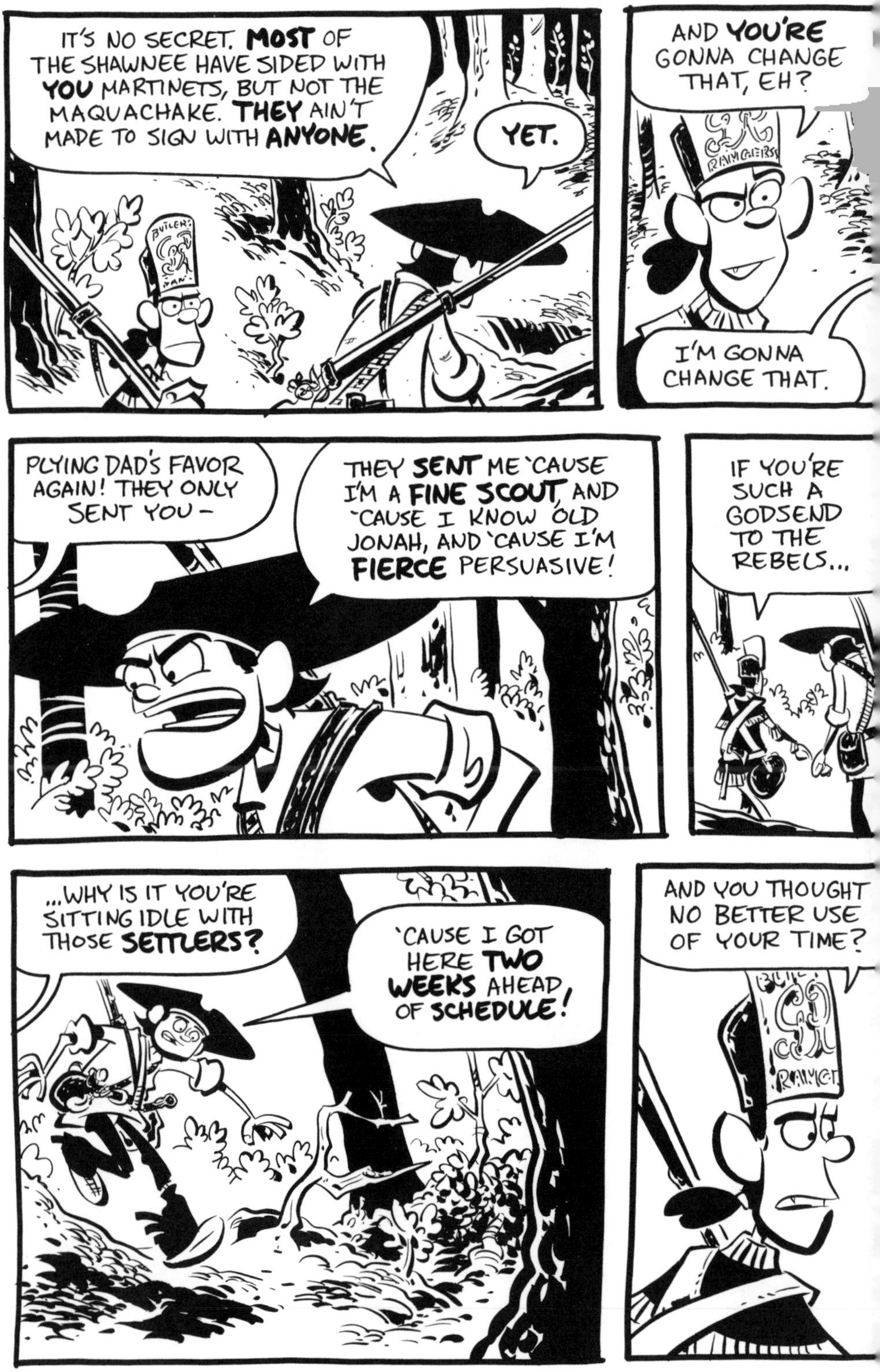
IT'S NO SECRET. MOST OF THE SHAWNEE HAVE SIDED WITH YOU MARTINETS, BUT NOT THE MAQUACHAKE. THEY AIN'T MADE TO SIGN WITH ANYONE.
YET.
AND YOU'RE GONNA CHANGE THAT, EH?
I'M GONNA CHANGE THAT.
PLYING DAD'S FAVOR AGAIN! THEY ONLY SENT YOU-
THEY SENT ME 'CAUSE I'M A FINE SCOUT, AND 'CAUSE I KNOW OLD JONAH, AND 'CAUSE I'M FIERCE PERSUASIVE!
IF YOU'RE SUCH A GODSEND TO THE REBELS...
...WHY IS IT YOU'RE SITTING IDLE WITH THOSE SETTLERS?
'CAUSE I GOT HERE TWO WEEKS AHEAD OF SCHEDULE!
AND YOU THOUGHT NO BETTER USE OF YOUR TIME?

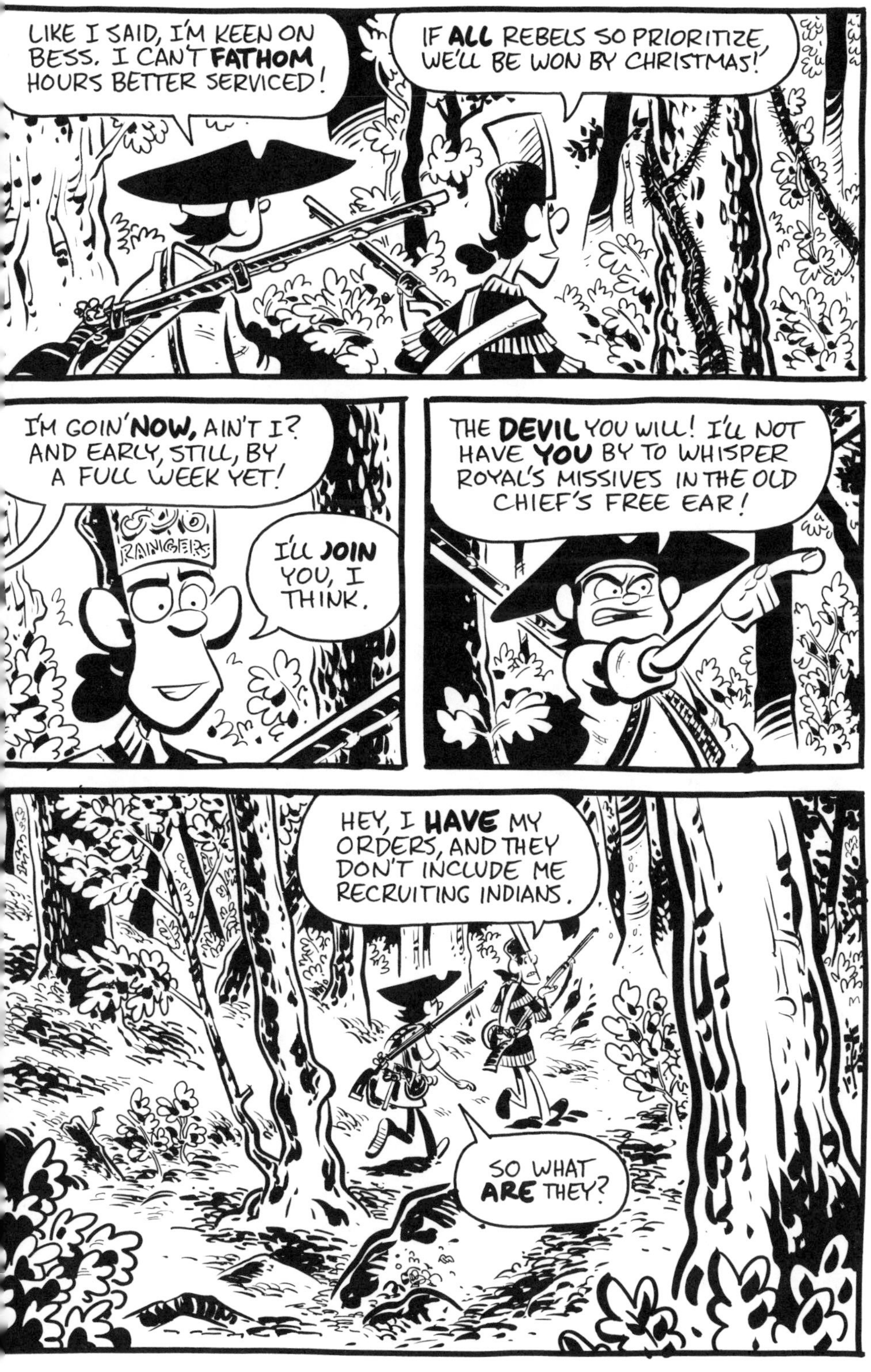
LIKE I SAID, I'M KEEN ON BESS. I CAN'T **FATHOM** HOURS BETTER SERVICED!
IF **ALL** REBELS SO PRIORITIZE, WE'LL BE WON BY CHRISTMAS!
RANGERS
I'M GOIN' **NOW**, AIN'T I? AND EARLY, STILL, BY A FULL WEEK YET!
I'LL **JOIN** YOU, I THINK.
THE **DEVIL** YOU WILL! I'LL NOT HAVE **YOU** BY TO WHISPER ROYAL'S MISSIVES IN THE OLD CHIEF'S FREE EAR!
HEY, I **HAVE** MY ORDERS, AND THEY DON'T INCLUDE ME RECRUITING INDIANS.
SO WHAT **ARE** THEY?

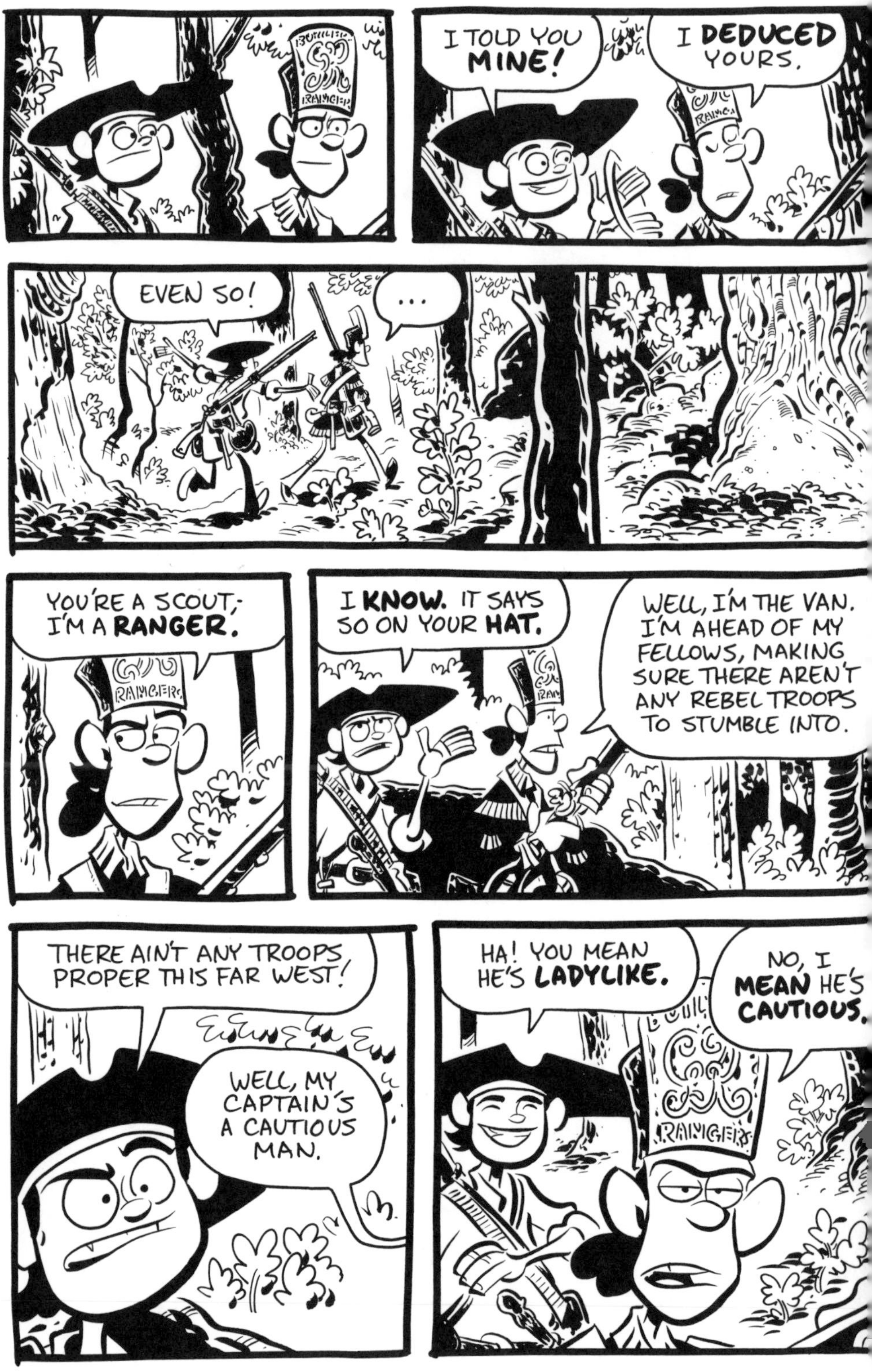
RANGER
I TOLD YOU MINE!
I DEDUCED YOURS.
EVEN SO!
...
YOU'RE A SCOUT; I'M A RANGER.
RANGER
I KNOW. IT SAYS SO ON YOUR HAT.
WELL, I'M THE VAN. I'M AHEAD OF MY FELLOWS, MAKING SURE THERE AREN'T ANY REBEL TROOPS TO STUMBLE INTO.
THERE AIN'T ANY TROOPS PROPER THIS FAR WEST!
WELL, MY CAPTAIN'S A CAUTIOUS MAN.
HA! YOU MEAN HE'S LADYLIKE.
NO, I MEAN HE'S CAUTIOUS.
RANGERS

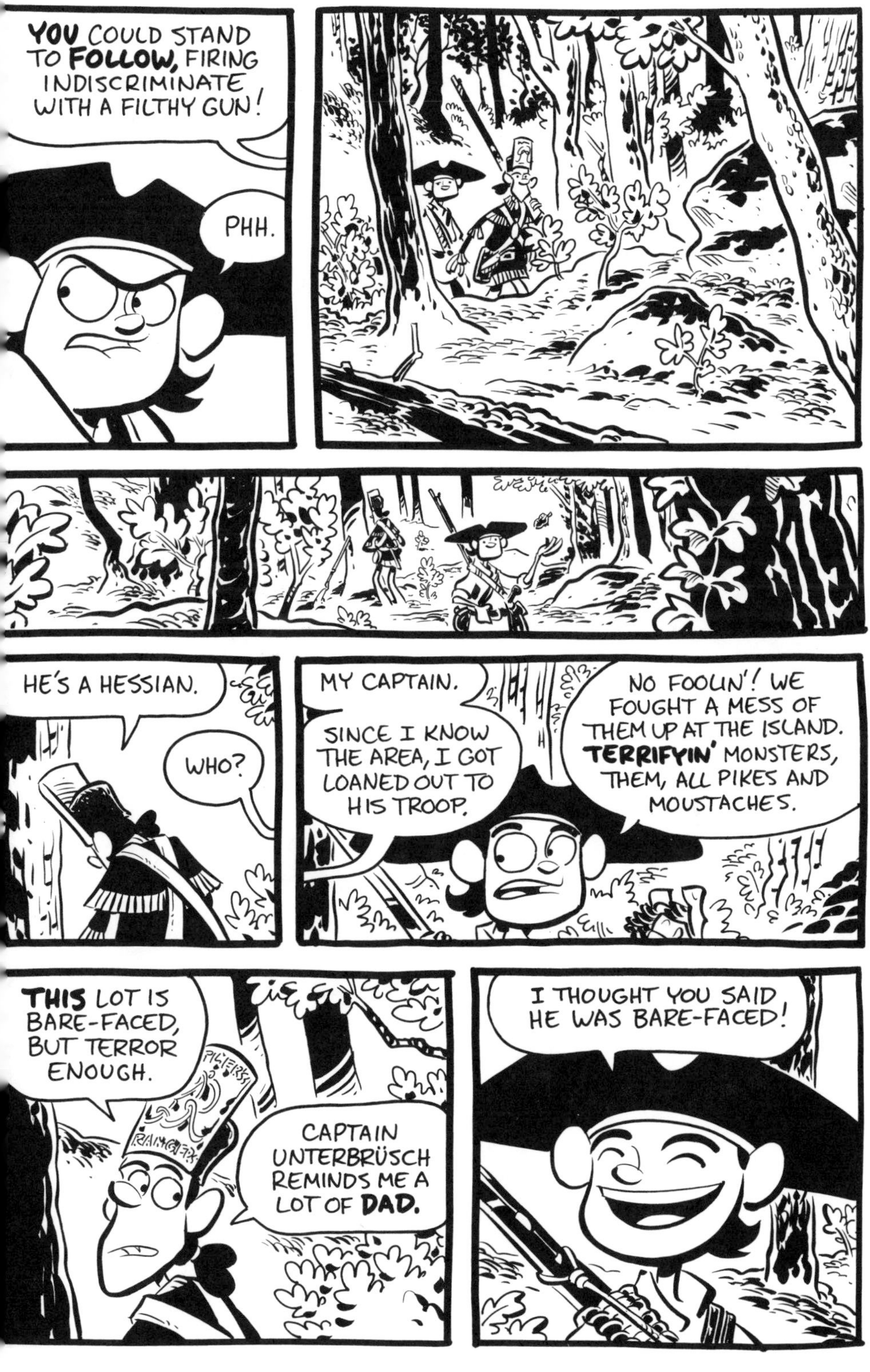
YOU COULD STAND TO FOLLOW, FIRING INDISCRIMINATE WITH A FILTHY GUN!
PHH.
HE'S A HESSIAN.
WHO?
MY CAPTAIN.
SINCE I KNOW THE AREA, I GOT LOANED OUT TO HIS TROOP.
NO FOOLIN'! WE FOUGHT A MESS OF THEM UP AT THE ISLAND. TERRIFYIN' MONSTERS, THEM, ALL PIKES AND MOUSTACHES.
THIS LOT IS BARE-FACED, BUT TERROR ENOUGH.
CAPTAIN UNTERBRÜSCH REMINDS ME A LOT OF DAD.
I THOUGHT YOU SAID HE WAS BARE-FACED!

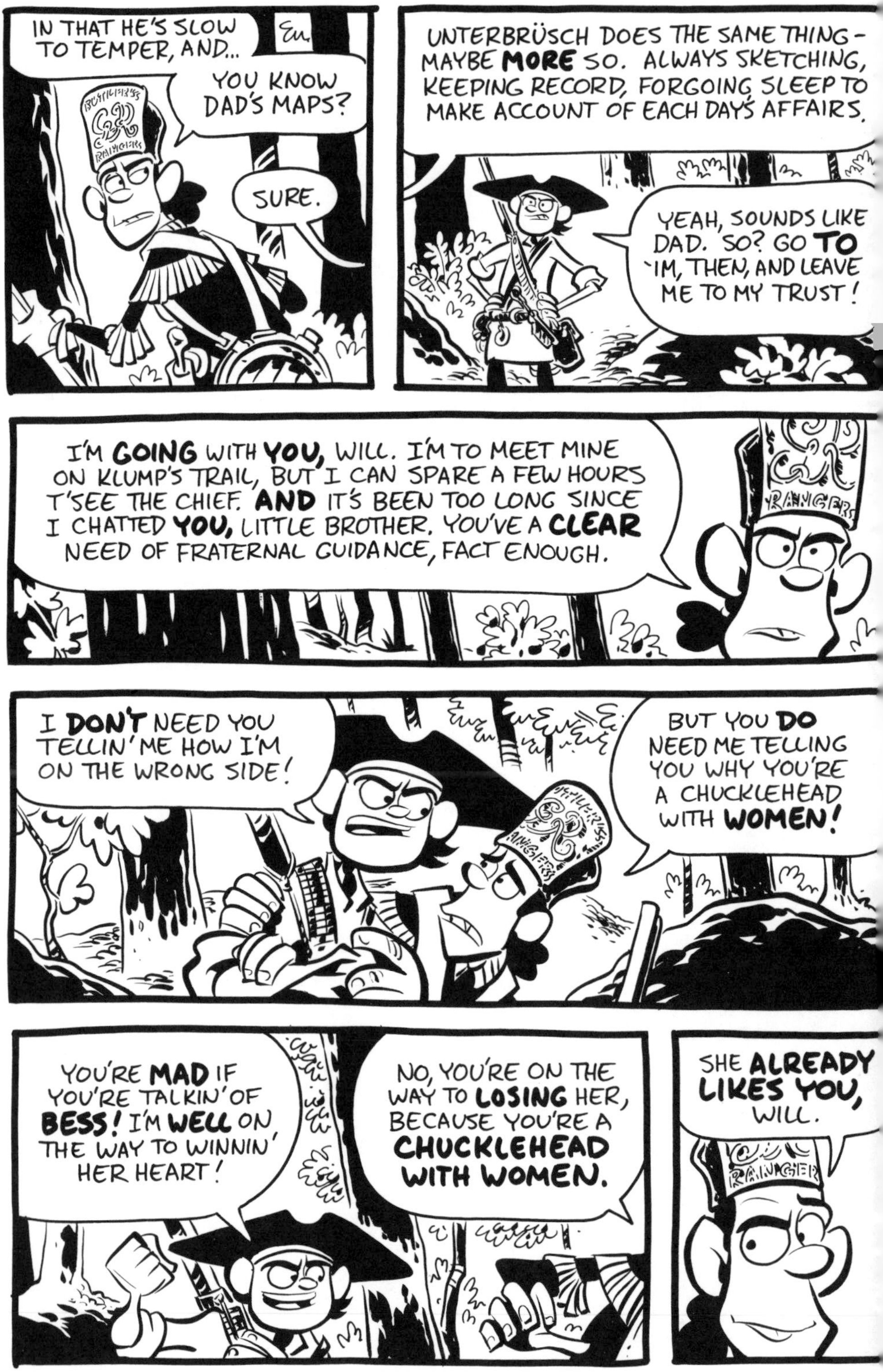
IN THAT HE'S SLOW TO TEMPER, AND...
YOU KNOW DAD'S MAPS?
SURE.
UNTERBRÜSCH DOES THE SAME THING - MAYBE **MORE** SO. ALWAYS SKETCHING, KEEPING RECORD, FORGOING SLEEP TO MAKE ACCOUNT OF EACH DAY'S AFFAIRS.
YEAH, SOUNDS LIKE DAD. SO? GO **TO** 'IM, THEN, AND LEAVE ME TO MY TRUST!
I'M **GOING** WITH **YOU,** WILL. I'M TO MEET MINE ON KLUMP'S TRAIL, BUT I CAN SPARE A FEW HOURS T'SEE THE CHIEF. **AND** IT'S BEEN TOO LONG SINCE I CHATTED **YOU,** LITTLE BROTHER. YOU'VE A **CLEAR** NEED OF FRATERNAL GUIDANCE, FACT ENOUGH.
I **DON'T** NEED YOU TELLIN' ME HOW I'M ON THE WRONG SIDE!
BUT YOU **DO** NEED ME TELLING YOU WHY YOU'RE A CHUCKLEHEAD WITH **WOMEN!**
YOU'RE **MAD** IF YOU'RE TALKIN' OF **BESS!** I'M **WELL** ON THE WAY TO WINNIN' HER HEART!
NO, YOU'RE ON THE WAY TO **LOSING** HER, BECAUSE YOU'RE A **CHUCKLEHEAD WITH WOMEN.**
SHE **ALREADY LIKES YOU,** WILL.

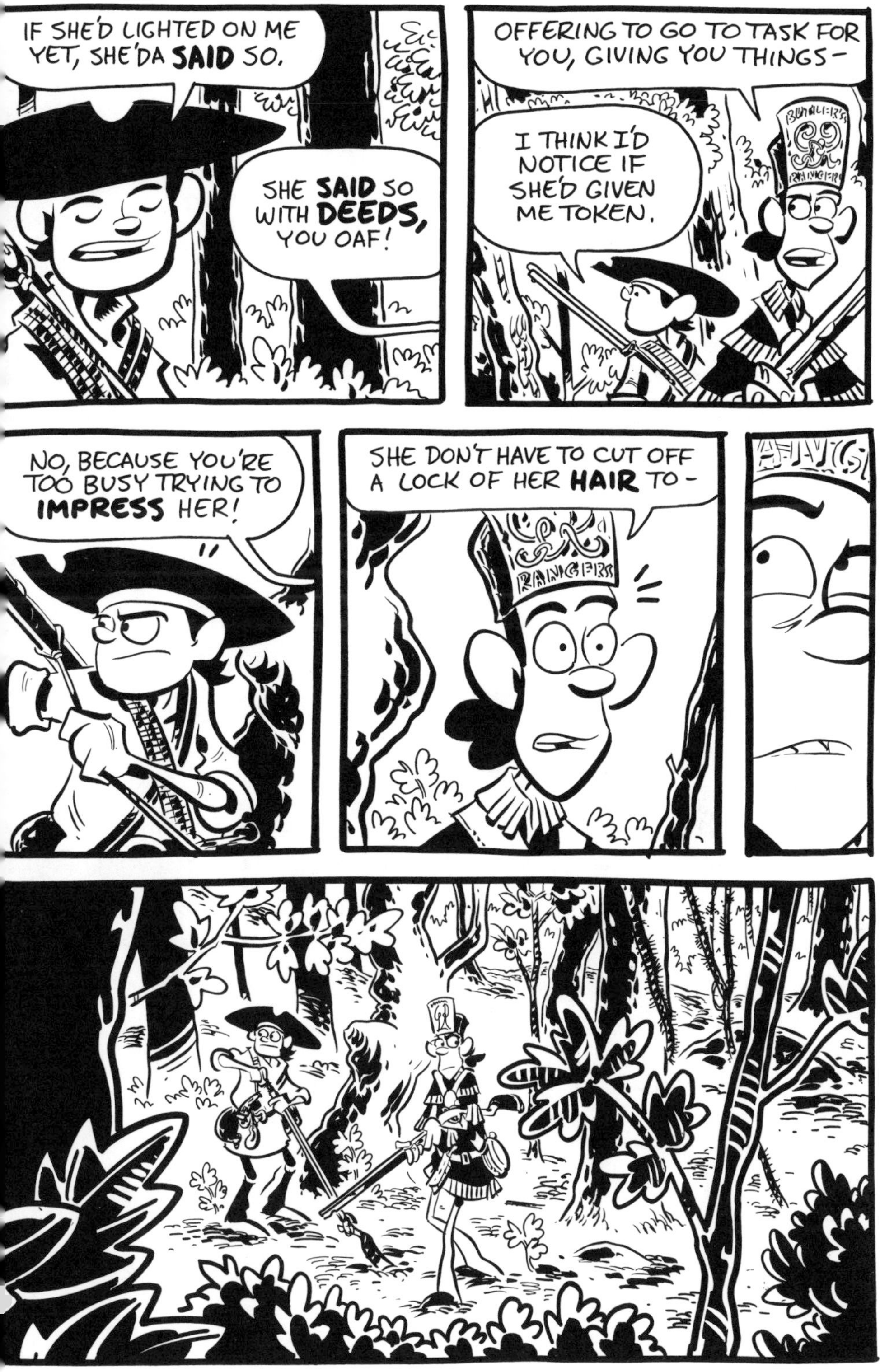
IF SHE'D LIGHTED ON ME YET, SHE'DA SAID SO.
SHE SAID SO WITH DEEDS, YOU OAF!
OFFERING TO GO TO TASK FOR YOU, GIVING YOU THINGS-
I THINK I'D NOTICE IF SHE'D GIVEN ME TOKEN.
NO, BECAUSE YOU'RE TOO BUSY TRYING TO IMPRESS HER!
SHE DON'T HAVE TO CUT OFF A LOCK OF HER HAIR TO-

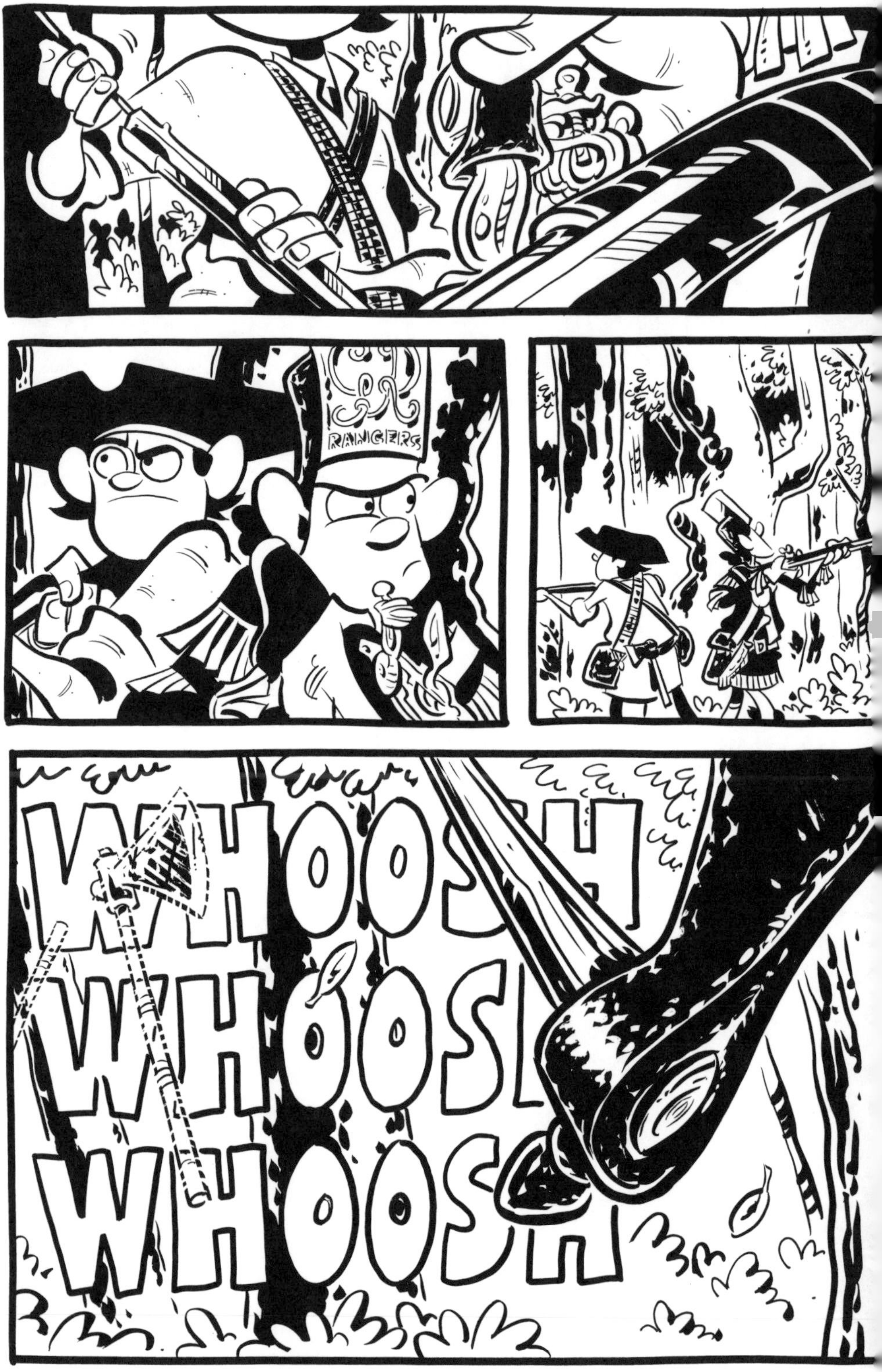
RANGERS
WHOOSH
WHOOSH
WHOOSH

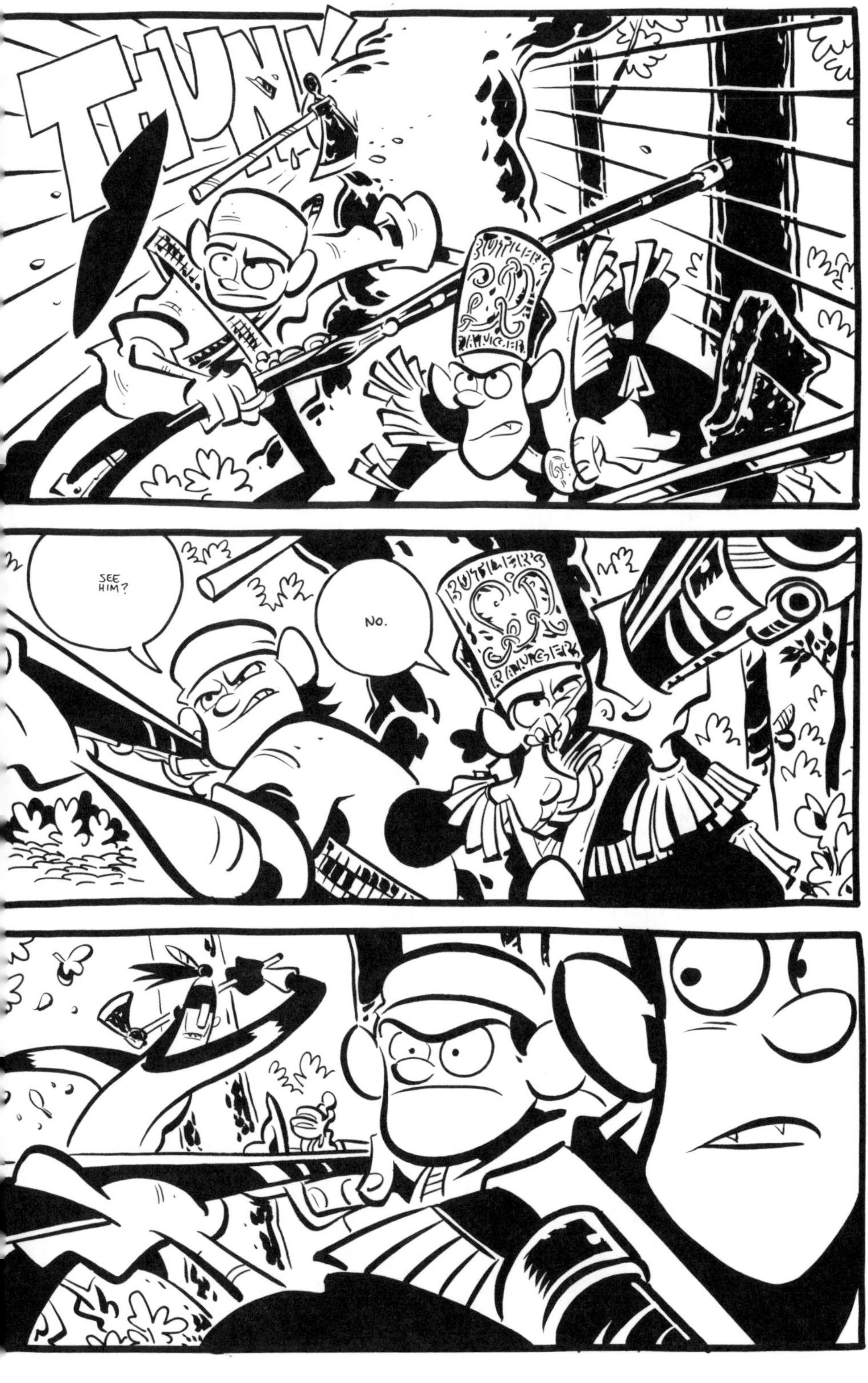
THUNK!
BUTLER'S RANGERS
SEE HIM?
NO.

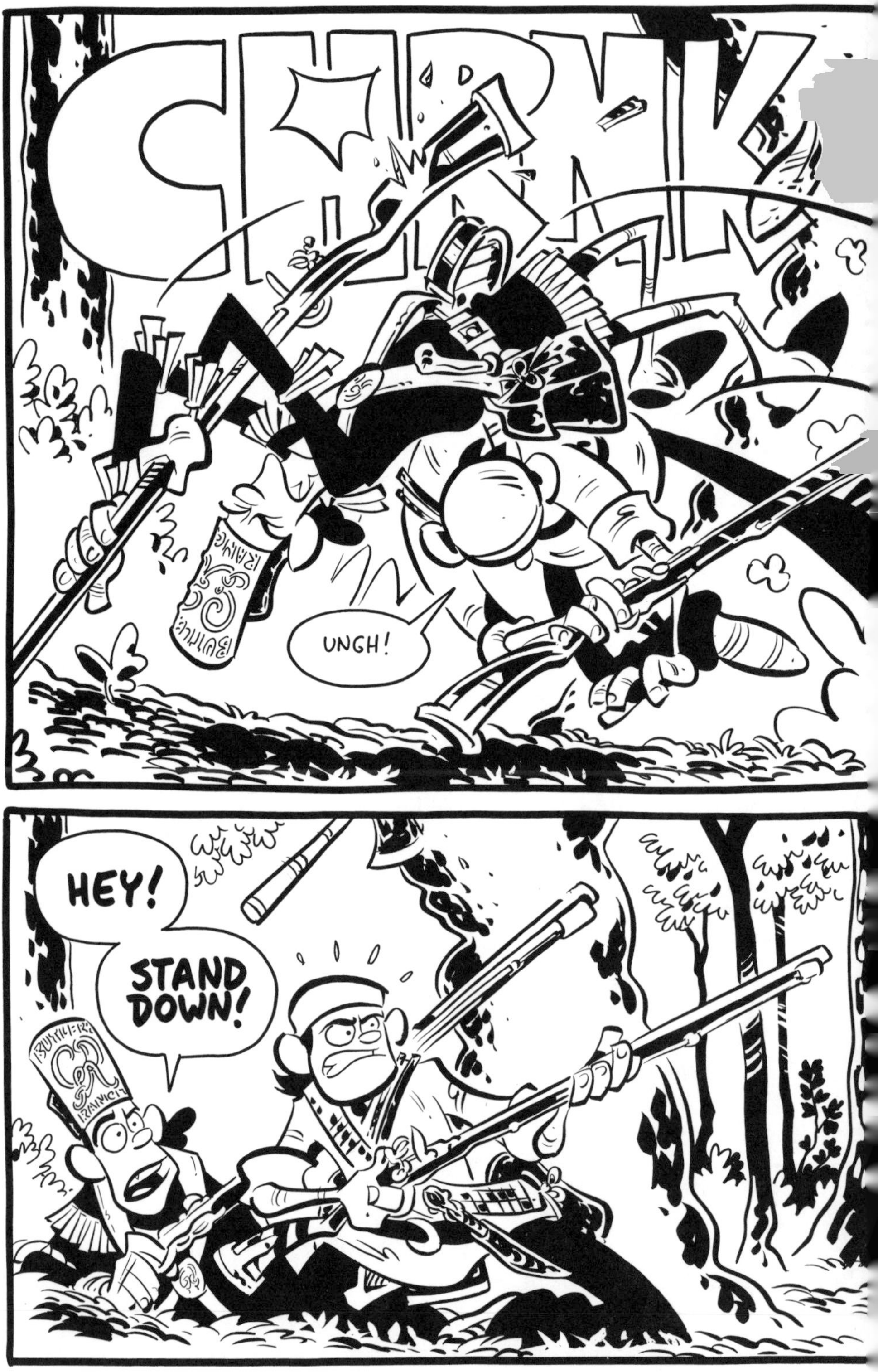
CHRNK
UNGH!
HEY!
STAND DOWN!

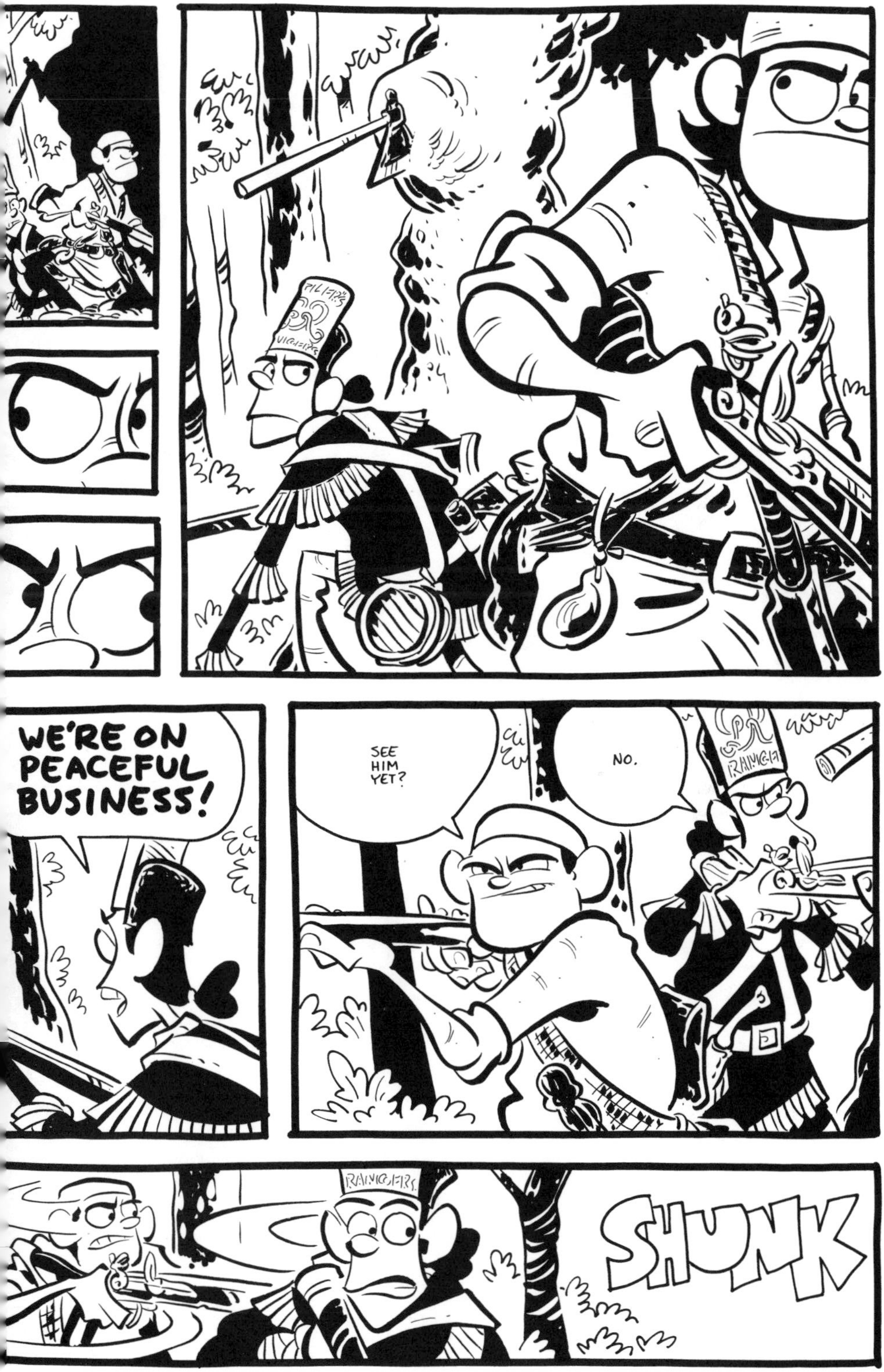
WE'RE ON PEACEFUL BUSINESS!
SEE HIM YET?
NO.
SHUNK

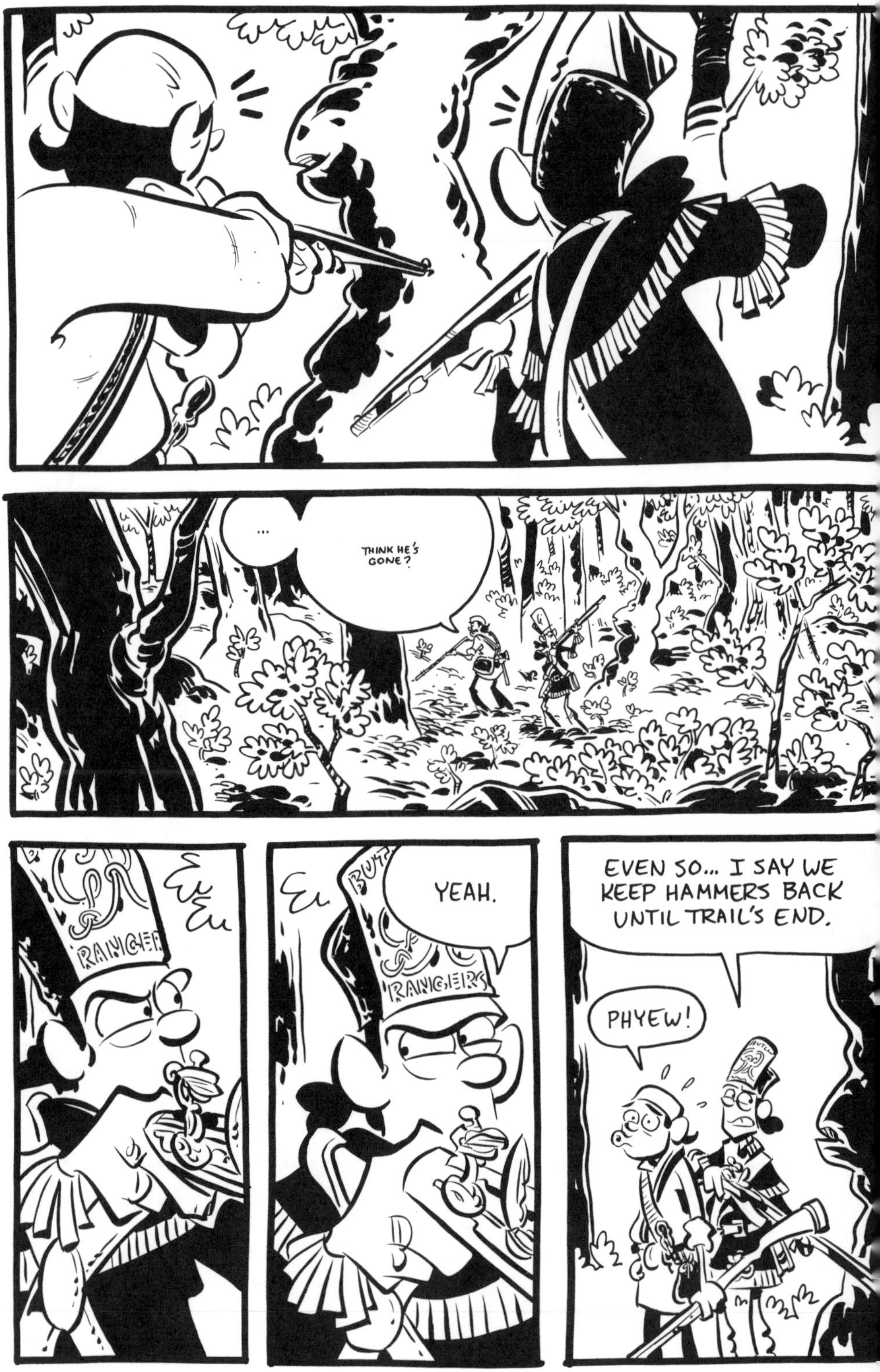
...
THINK HE'S GONE?
RANGERS
YEAH.
EVEN SO... I SAY WE KEEP HAMMERS BACK UNTIL TRAIL'S END.
PHYEW!

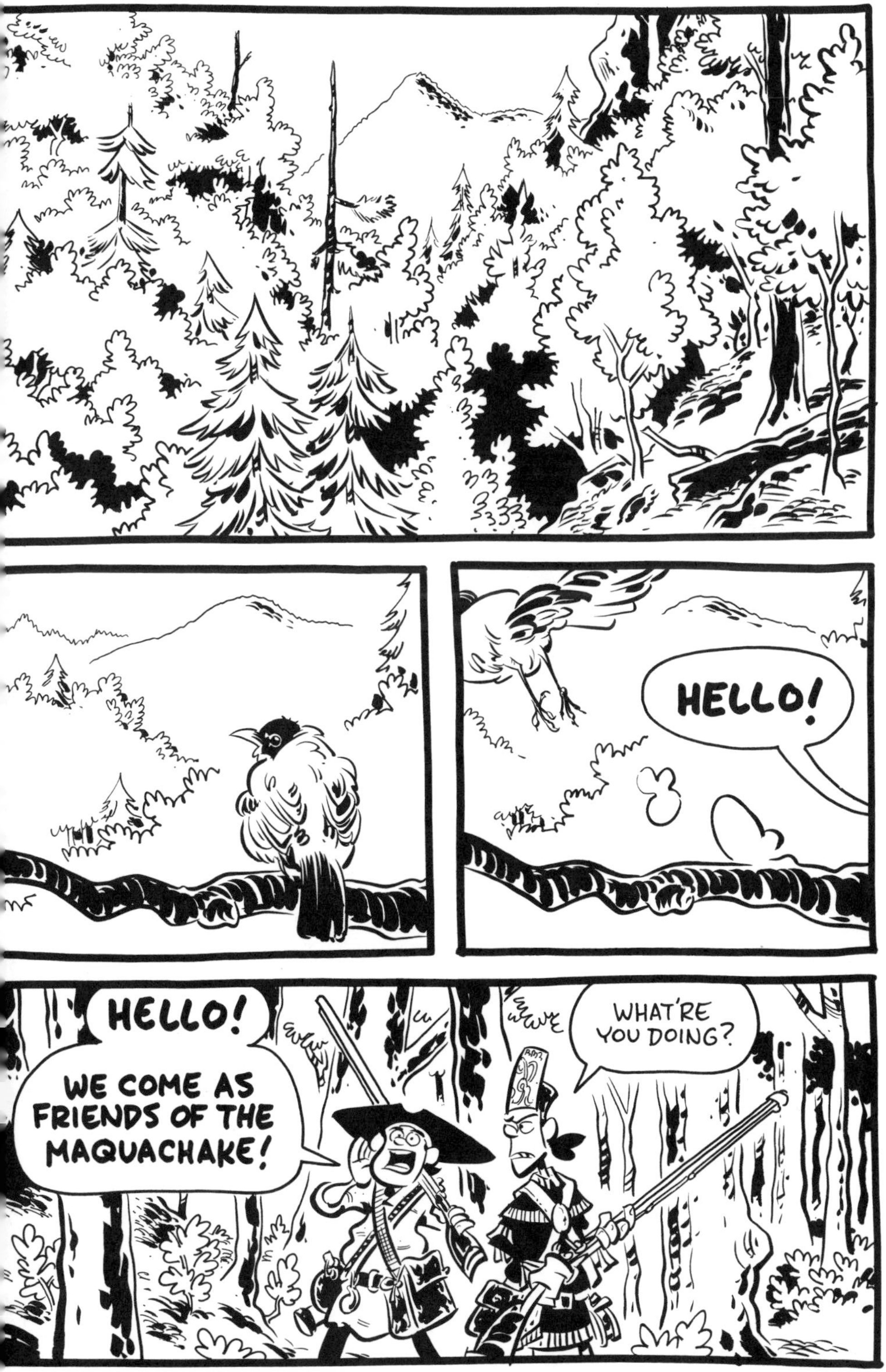
HELLO!
HELLO!
WE COME AS FRIENDS OF THE MAQUACHAKE!
WHAT'RE YOU DOING?

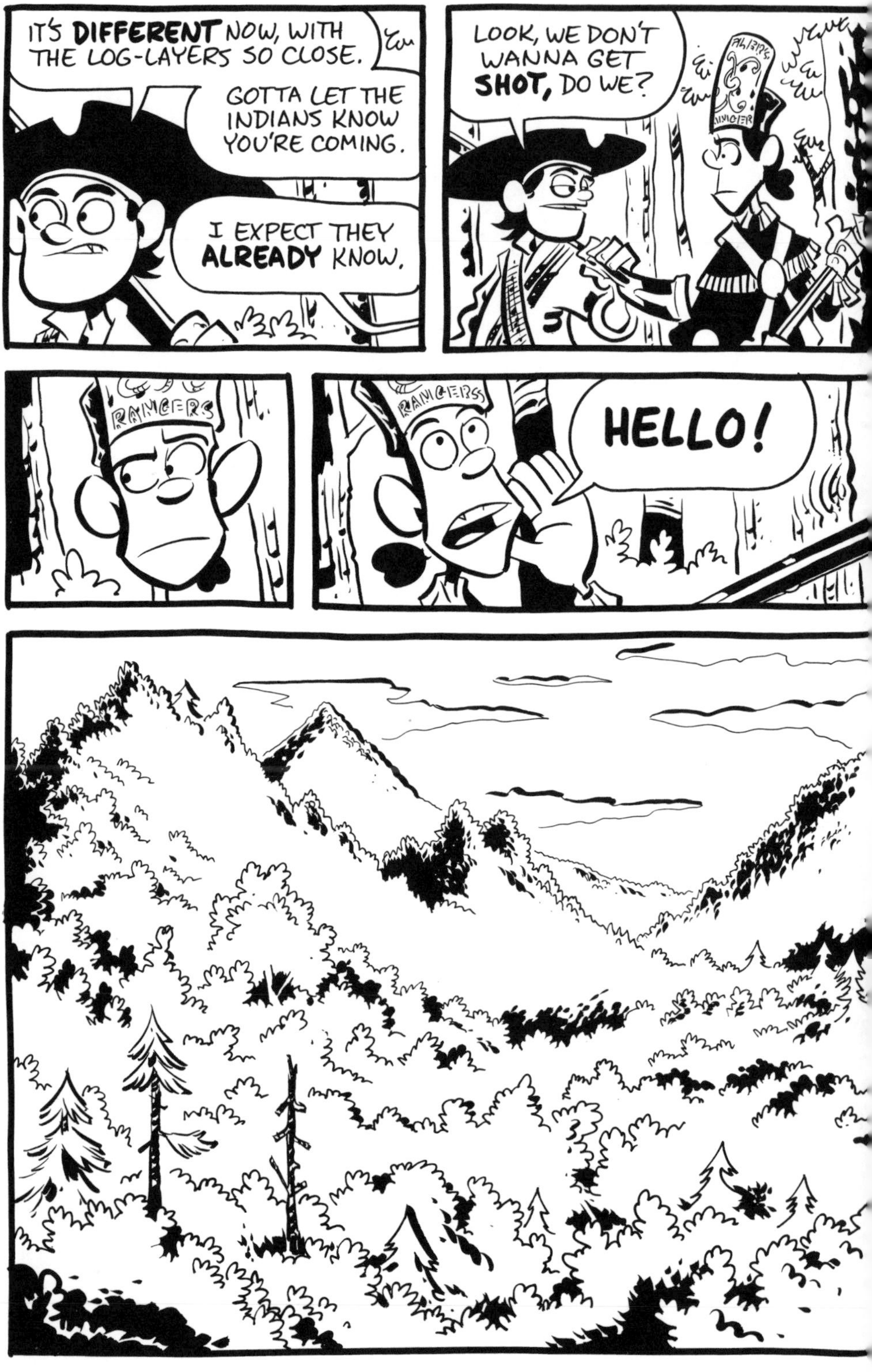
IT'S DIFFERENT NOW, WITH THE LOG-LAYERS SO CLOSE.
GOTTA LET THE INDIANS KNOW YOU'RE COMING.
I EXPECT THEY ALREADY KNOW.
LOOK, WE DON'T WANNA GET SHOT, DO WE?
RANGERS
RANGERS
HELLO!

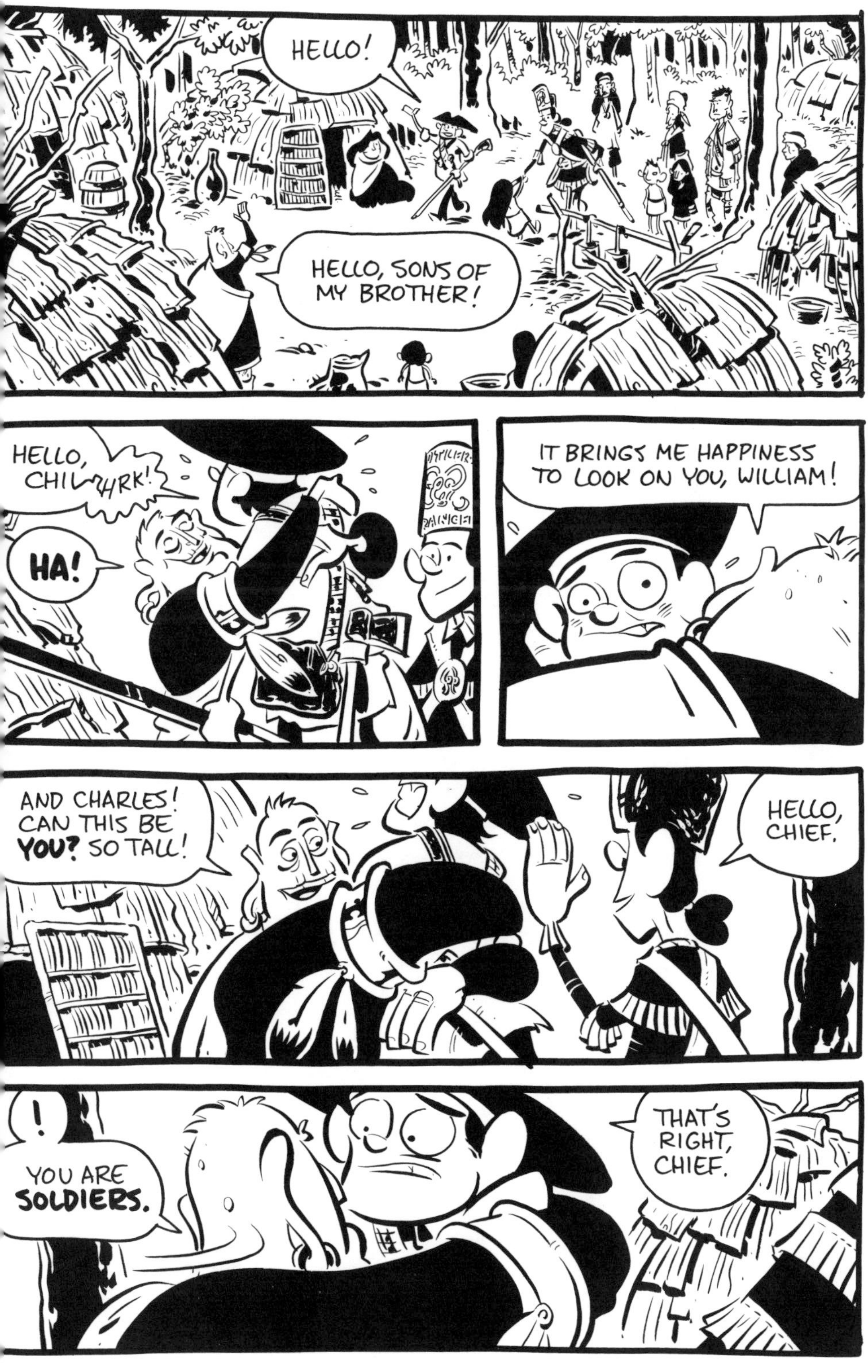
HELLO!
HELLO, SONS OF MY BROTHER!
HELLO, CHIL— HRK!
HA!
IT BRINGS ME HAPPINESS TO LOOK ON YOU, WILLIAM!
AND CHARLES! CAN THIS BE **YOU?** SO TALL!
HELLO, CHIEF.
!
YOU ARE **SOLDIERS.**
THAT'S RIGHT, CHIEF.

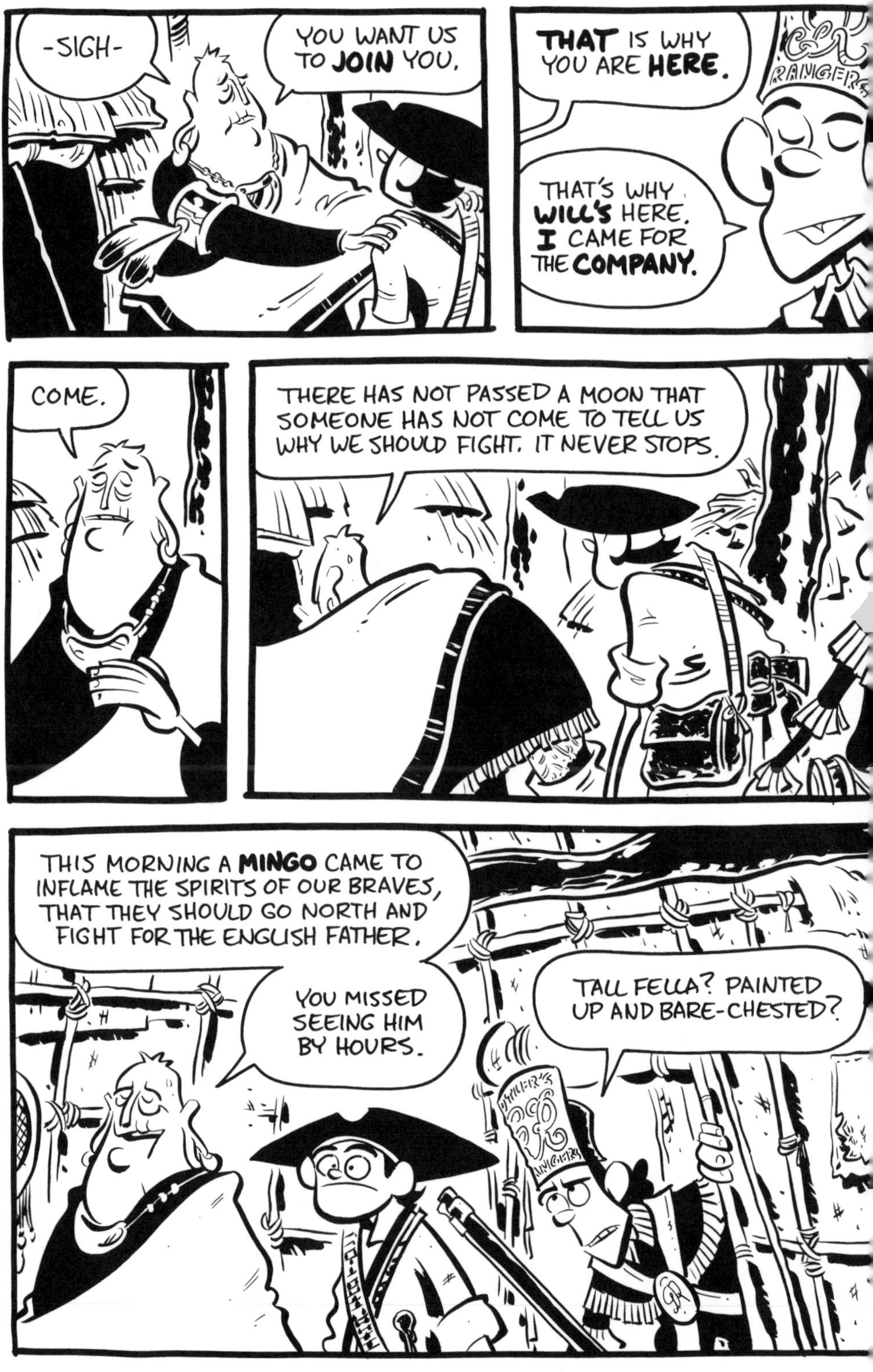
-SIGH-
YOU WANT US TO **JOIN** YOU.
THAT IS WHY YOU ARE **HERE**.
THAT'S WHY **WILL'S** HERE. **I** CAME FOR THE **COMPANY**.
RANGERS
COME.
THERE HAS NOT PASSED A MOON THAT SOMEONE HAS NOT COME TO TELL US WHY WE SHOULD FIGHT. IT NEVER STOPS.
THIS MORNING A **MINGO** CAME TO INFLAME THE SPIRITS OF OUR BRAVES, THAT THEY SHOULD GO NORTH AND FIGHT FOR THE ENGLISH FATHER.
YOU MISSED SEEING HIM BY HOURS.
TALL FELLA? PAINTED UP AND BARE-CHESTED?

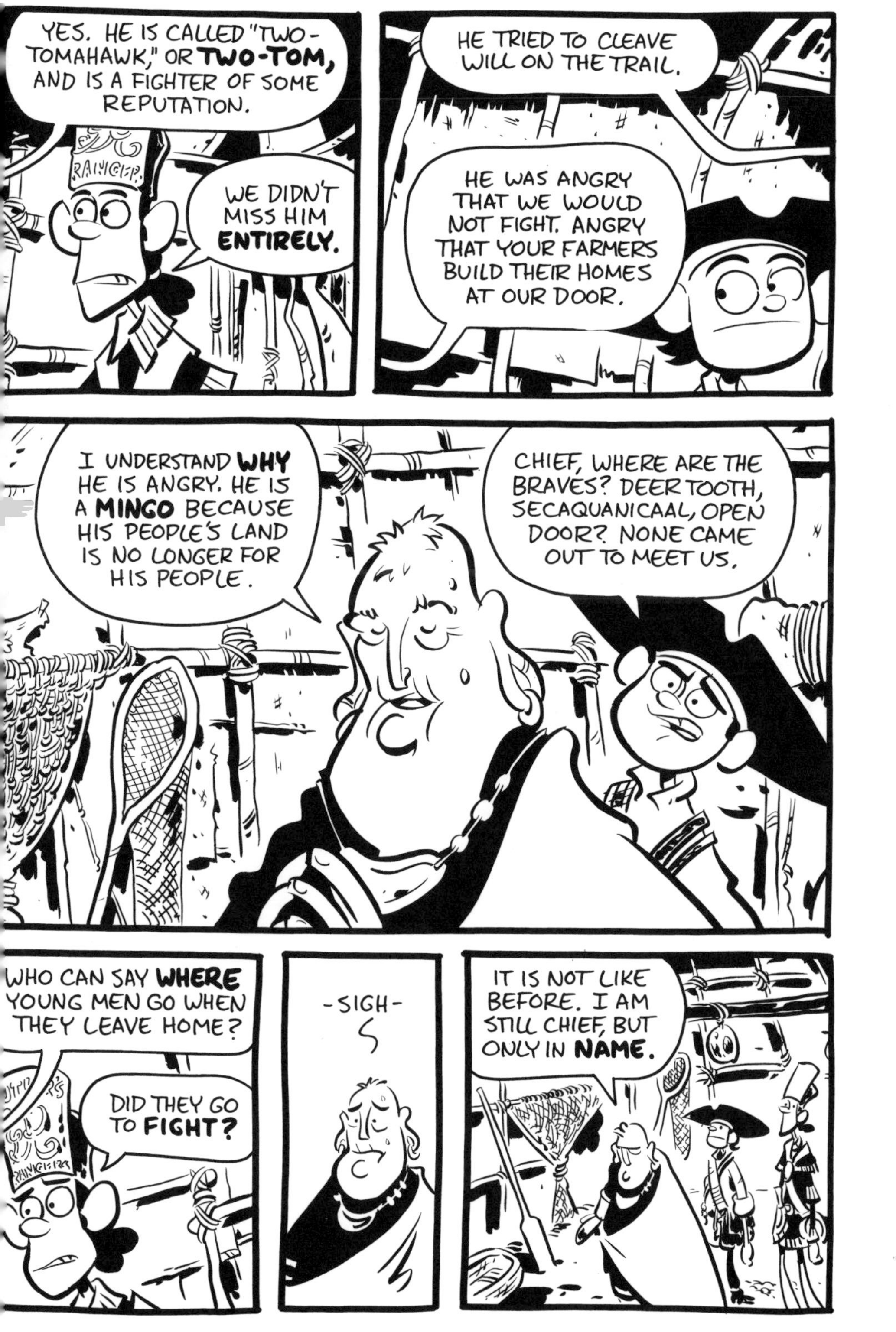
YES. HE IS CALLED "TWO-TOMAHAWK," OR **TWO-TOM,** AND IS A FIGHTER OF SOME REPUTATION.
WE DIDN'T MISS HIM **ENTIRELY.**
HE TRIED TO CLEAVE WILL ON THE TRAIL.
HE WAS ANGRY THAT WE WOULD NOT FIGHT. ANGRY THAT YOUR FARMERS BUILD THEIR HOMES AT OUR DOOR.
I UNDERSTAND **WHY** HE IS ANGRY. HE IS A **MINGO** BECAUSE HIS PEOPLE'S LAND IS NO LONGER FOR HIS PEOPLE.
CHIEF, WHERE ARE THE BRAVES? DEER TOOTH, SECAQUANICAAL, OPEN DOOR? NONE CAME OUT TO MEET US.
WHO CAN SAY **WHERE** YOUNG MEN GO WHEN THEY LEAVE HOME?
DID THEY GO TO **FIGHT?**
-SIGH-
IT IS NOT LIKE BEFORE. I AM STILL CHIEF, BUT ONLY IN **NAME.**

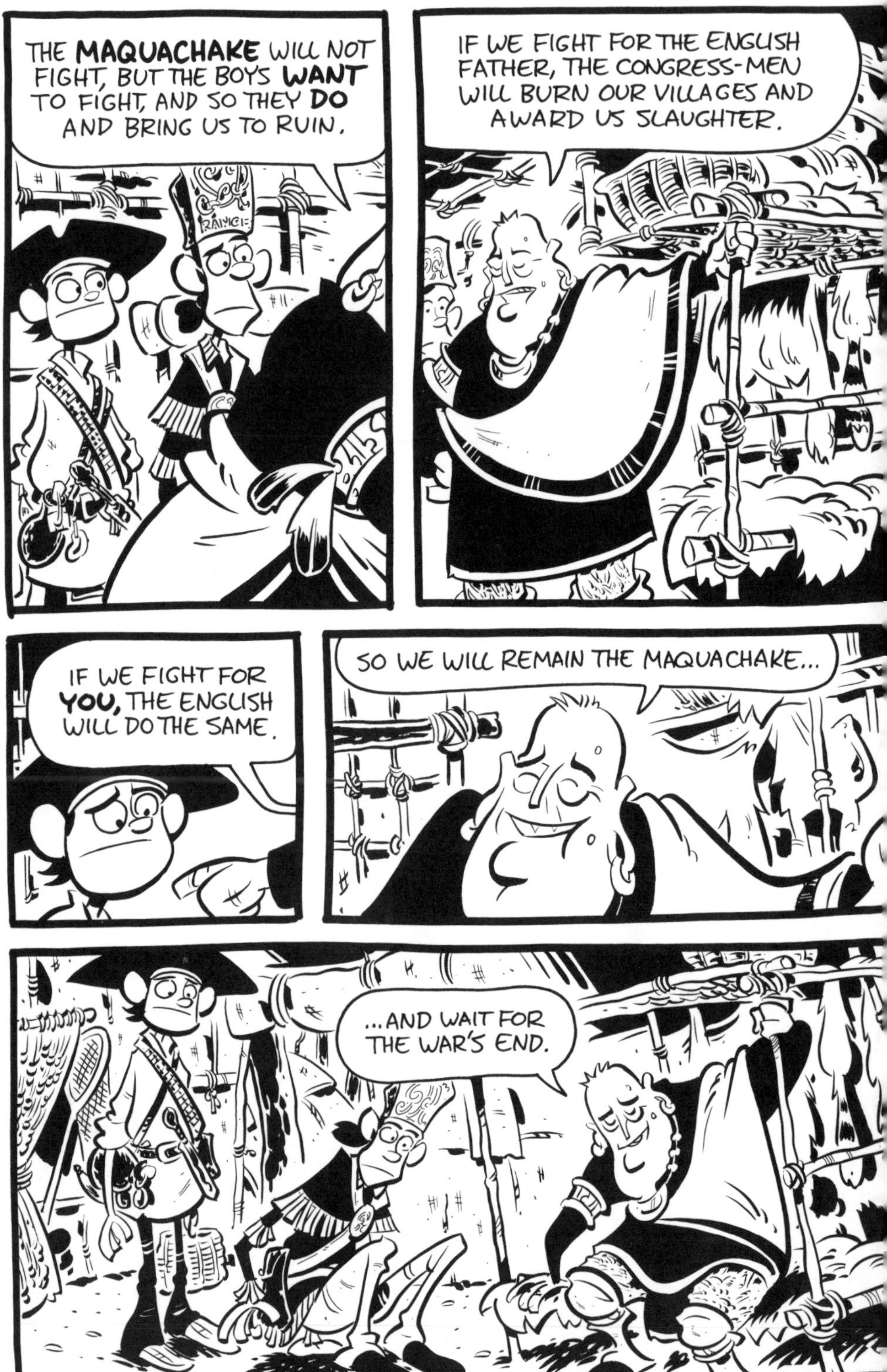
THE **MAQUACHAKE** WILL NOT FIGHT, BUT THE BOYS **WANT** TO FIGHT, AND SO THEY **DO** AND BRING US TO RUIN.
IF WE FIGHT FOR THE ENGLISH FATHER, THE CONGRESS-MEN WILL BURN OUR VILLAGES AND AWARD US SLAUGHTER.
IF WE FIGHT FOR **YOU,** THE ENGLISH WILL DO THE SAME.
SO WE WILL REMAIN THE MAQUACHAKE...
...AND WAIT FOR THE WAR'S END.

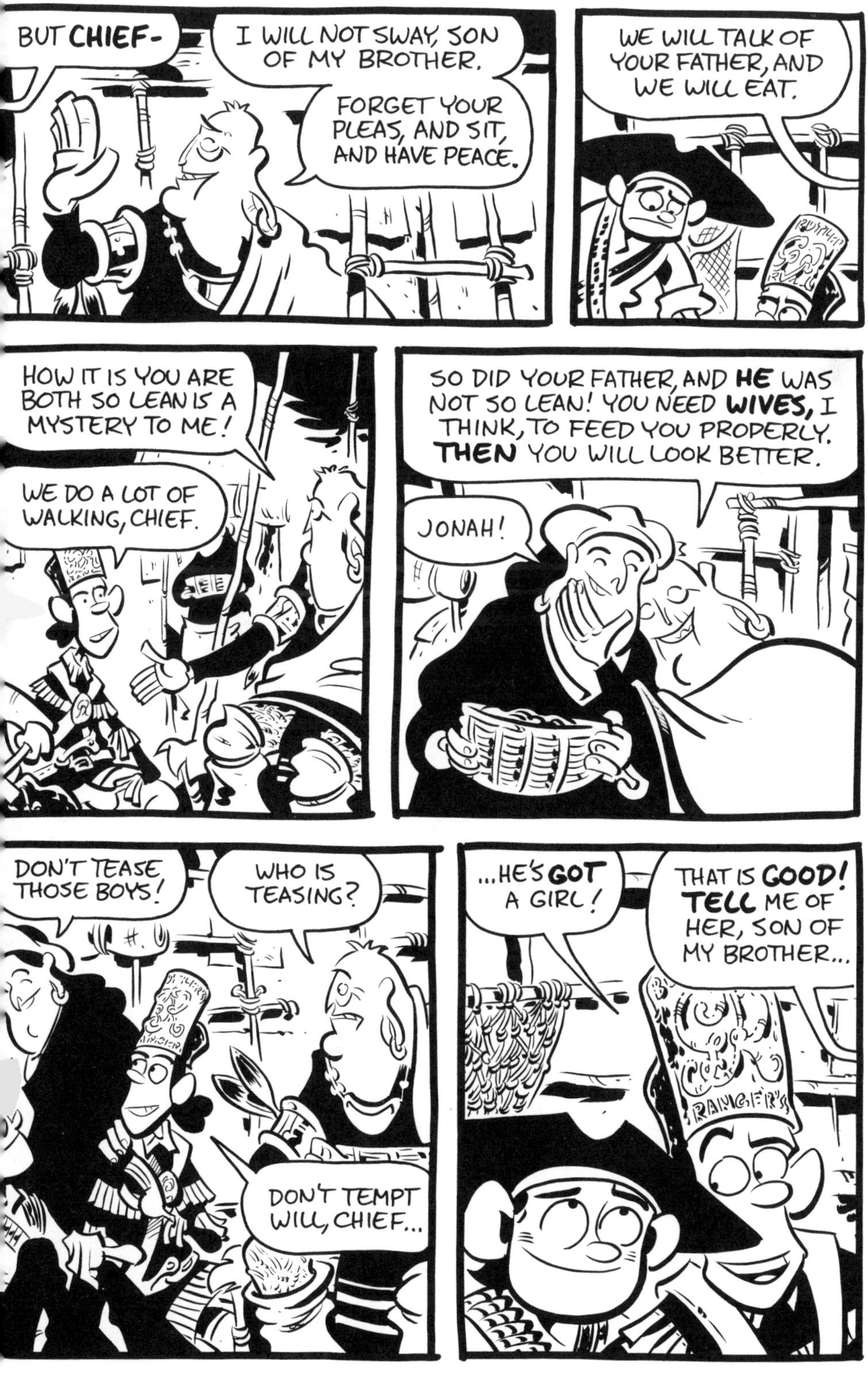
BUT CHIEF-
I WILL NOT SWAY, SON OF MY BROTHER.
FORGET YOUR PLEAS, AND SIT, AND HAVE PEACE.
WE WILL TALK OF YOUR FATHER, AND WE WILL EAT.
HOW IT IS YOU ARE BOTH SO LEAN IS A MYSTERY TO ME!
WE DO A LOT OF WALKING, CHIEF.
SO DID YOUR FATHER, AND HE WAS NOT SO LEAN! YOU NEED WIVES, I THINK, TO FEED YOU PROPERLY. THEN YOU WILL LOOK BETTER.
JONAH!
DON'T TEASE THOSE BOYS!
WHO IS TEASING?
DON'T TEMPT WILL, CHIEF...
...HE'S GOT A GIRL!
THAT IS GOOD! TELL ME OF HER, SON OF MY BROTHER...
RANGER'S

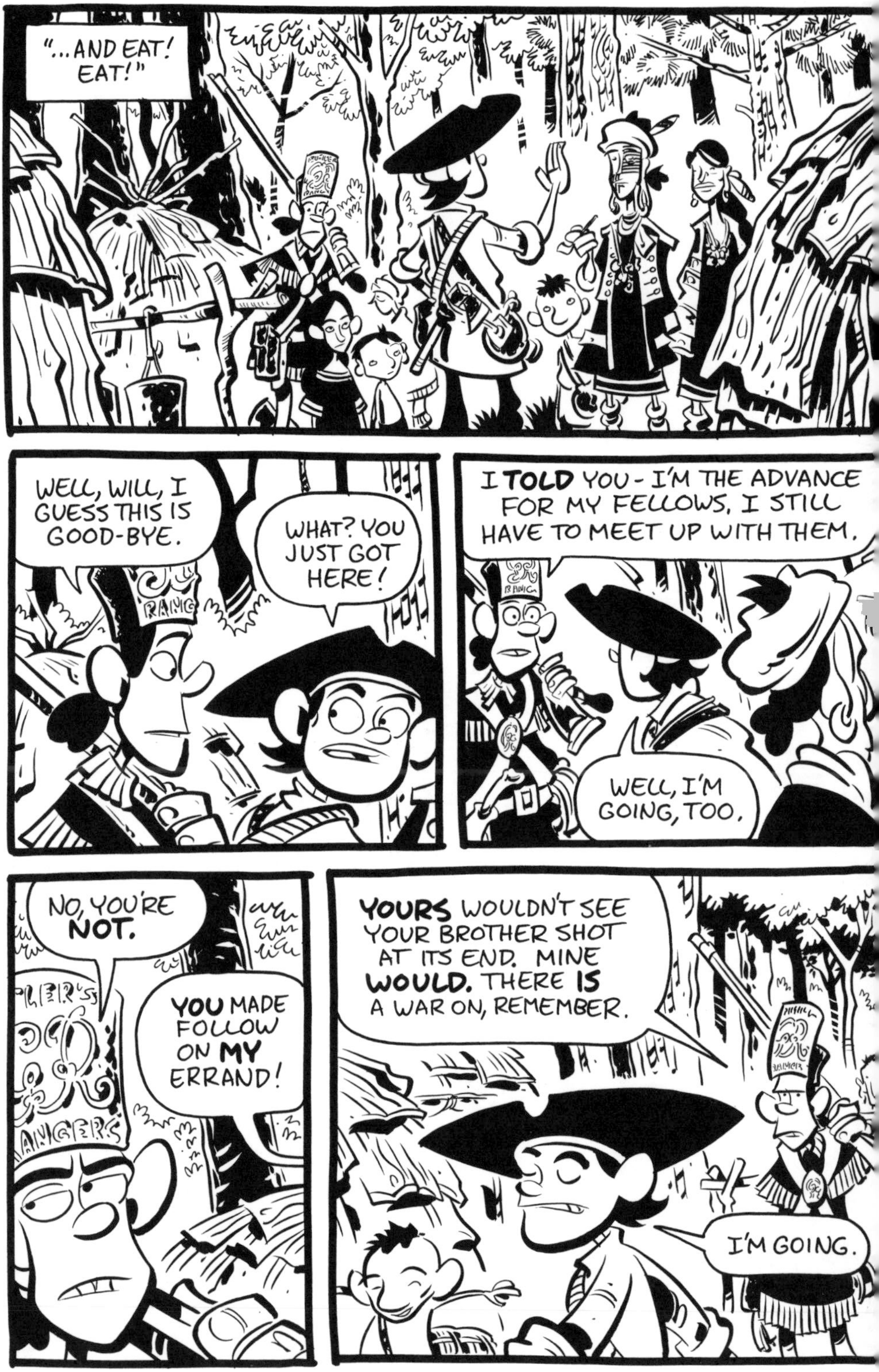
"...AND EAT! EAT!"
WELL, WILL, I GUESS THIS IS GOOD-BYE.
WHAT? YOU JUST GOT HERE!
I TOLD YOU - I'M THE ADVANCE FOR MY FELLOWS. I STILL HAVE TO MEET UP WITH THEM.
WELL, I'M GOING, TOO.
NO, YOU'RE NOT.
YOU MADE FOLLOW ON MY ERRAND!
YOURS WOULDN'T SEE YOUR BROTHER SHOT AT ITS END. MINE WOULD. THERE IS A WAR ON, REMEMBER.
I'M GOING.

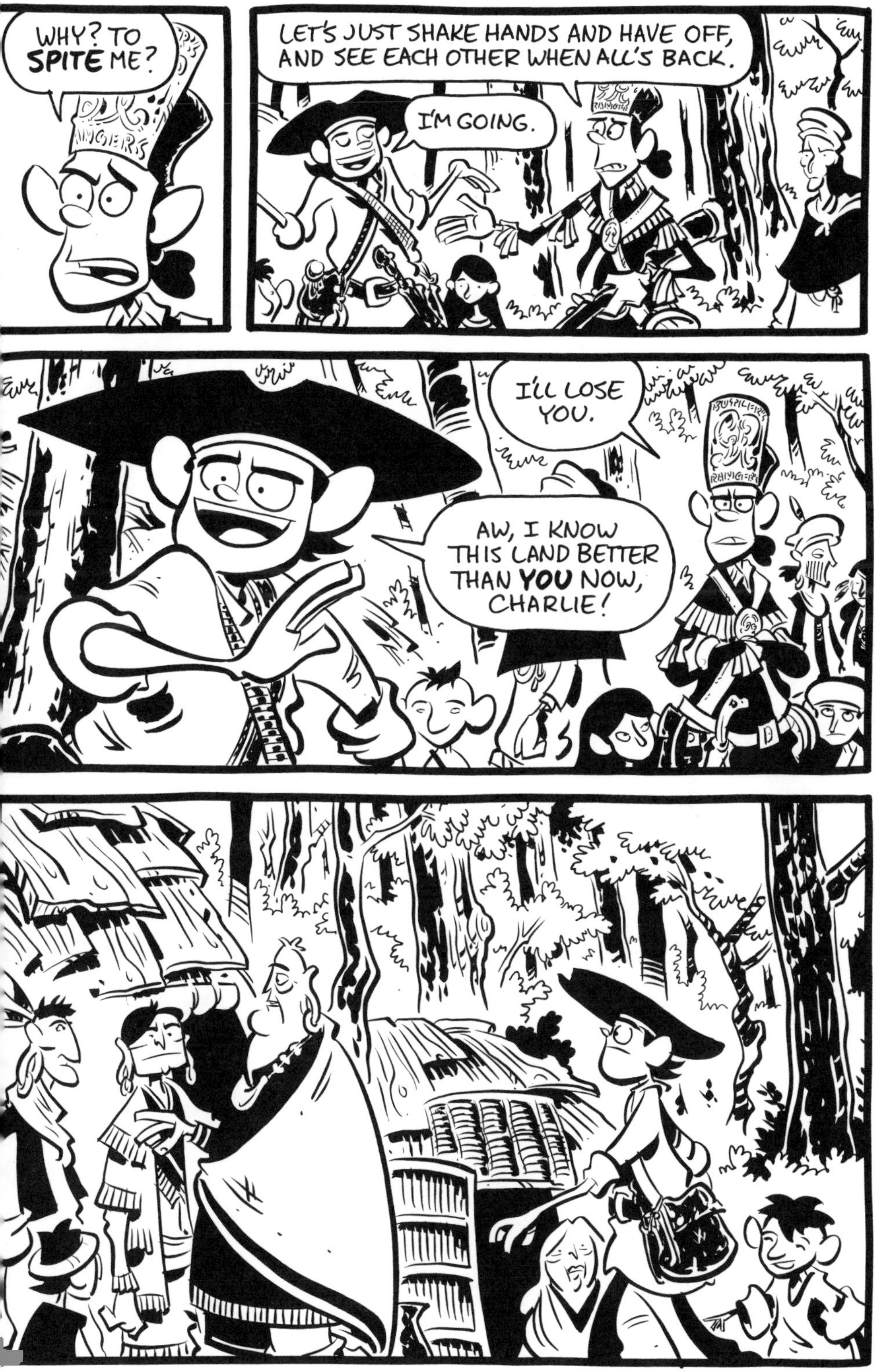
WHY? TO SPITE ME?
LET'S JUST SHAKE HANDS AND HAVE OFF, AND SEE EACH OTHER WHEN ALL'S BACK.
I'M GOING.
I'LL LOSE YOU.
AW, I KNOW THIS LAND BETTER THAN YOU NOW, CHARLIE!

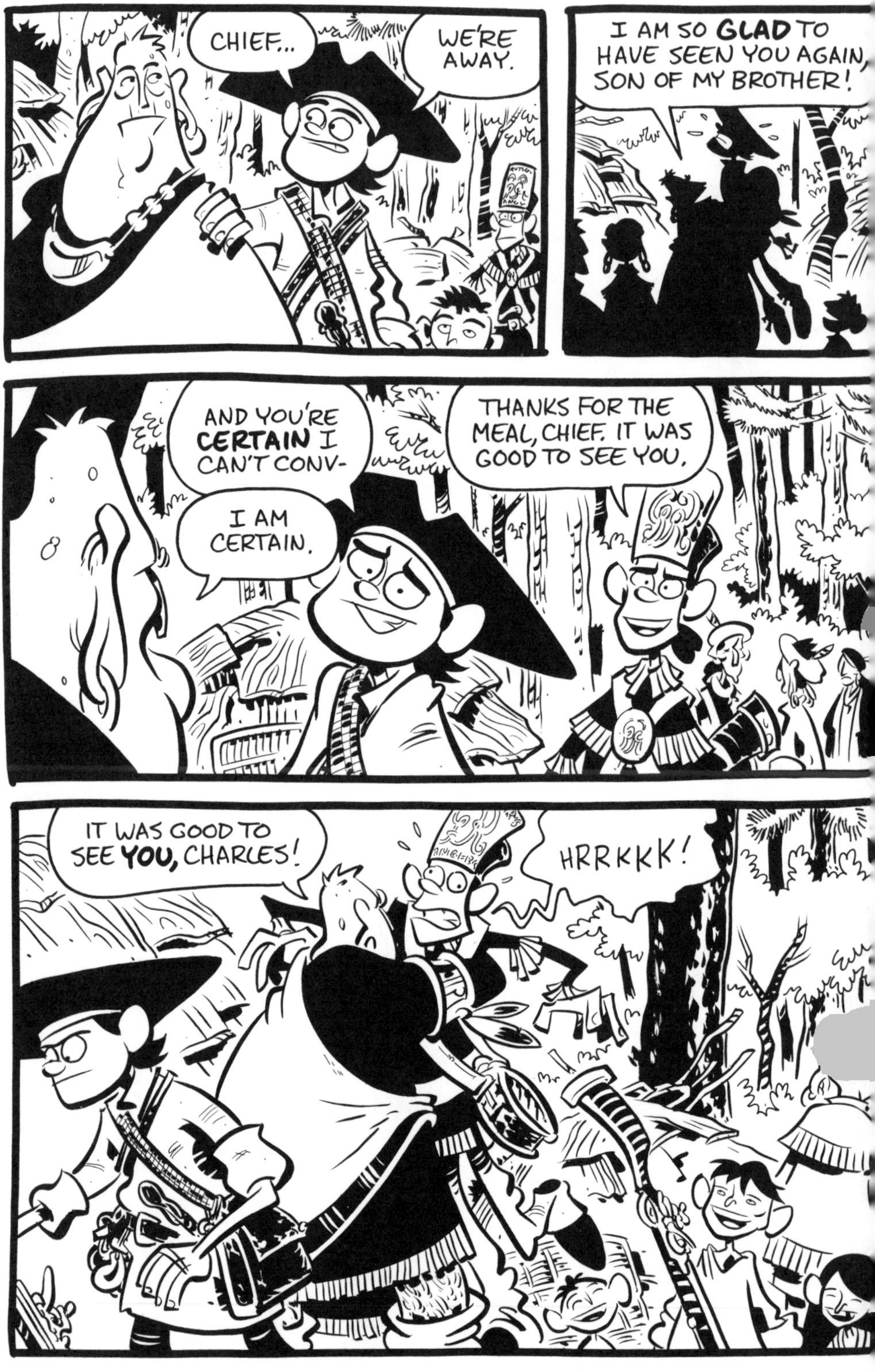
CHIEF...
WE'RE AWAY.
I AM SO **GLAD** TO HAVE SEEN YOU AGAIN, SON OF MY BROTHER!
AND YOU'RE **CERTAIN** I CAN'T CONV-
I AM CERTAIN.
THANKS FOR THE MEAL, CHIEF. IT WAS GOOD TO SEE YOU.
IT WAS GOOD TO SEE **YOU,** CHARLES!
HRRKKK!

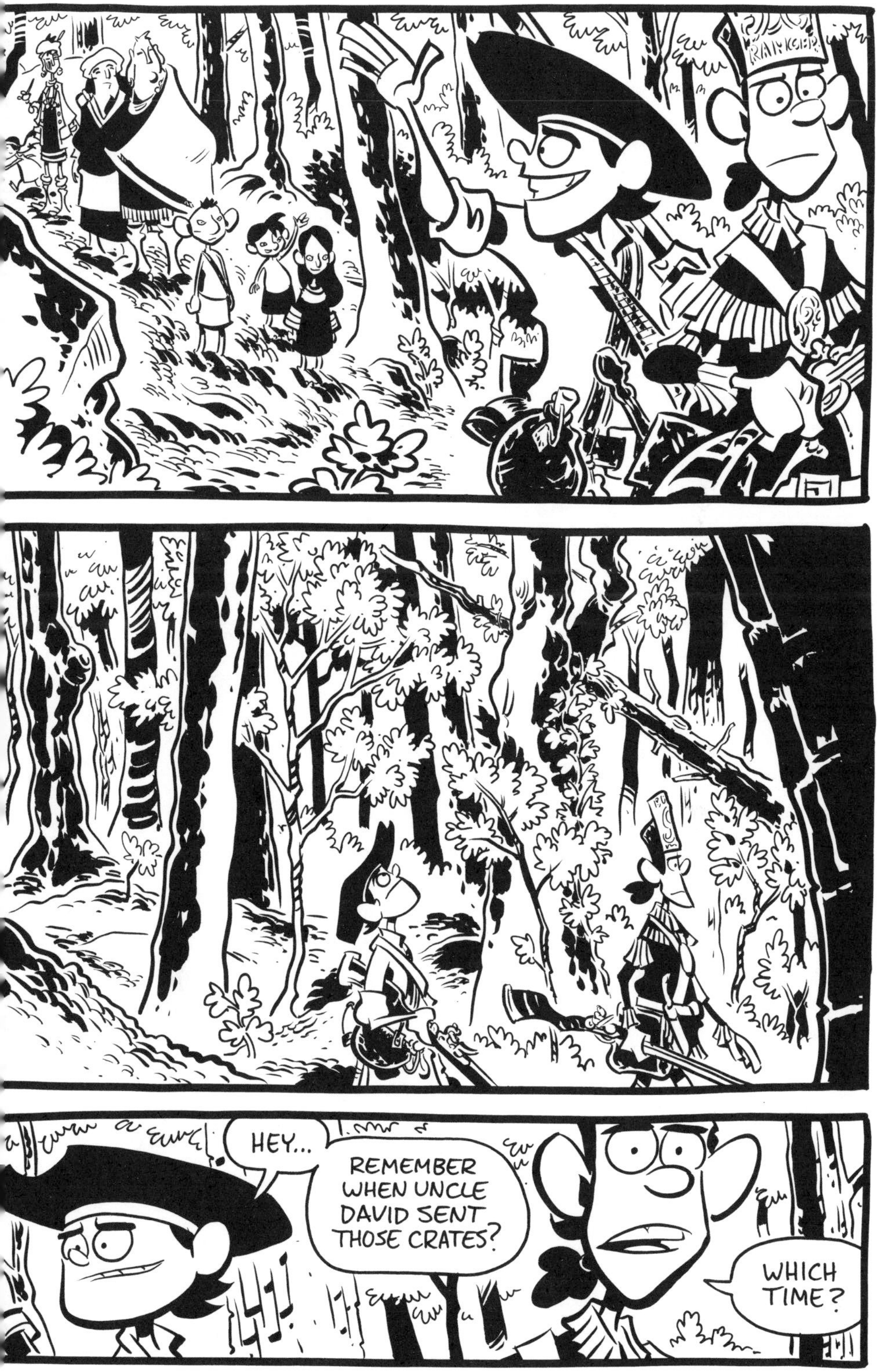
RANGER
HEY...
REMEMBER WHEN UNCLE DAVID SENT THOSE CRATES?
WHICH TIME?

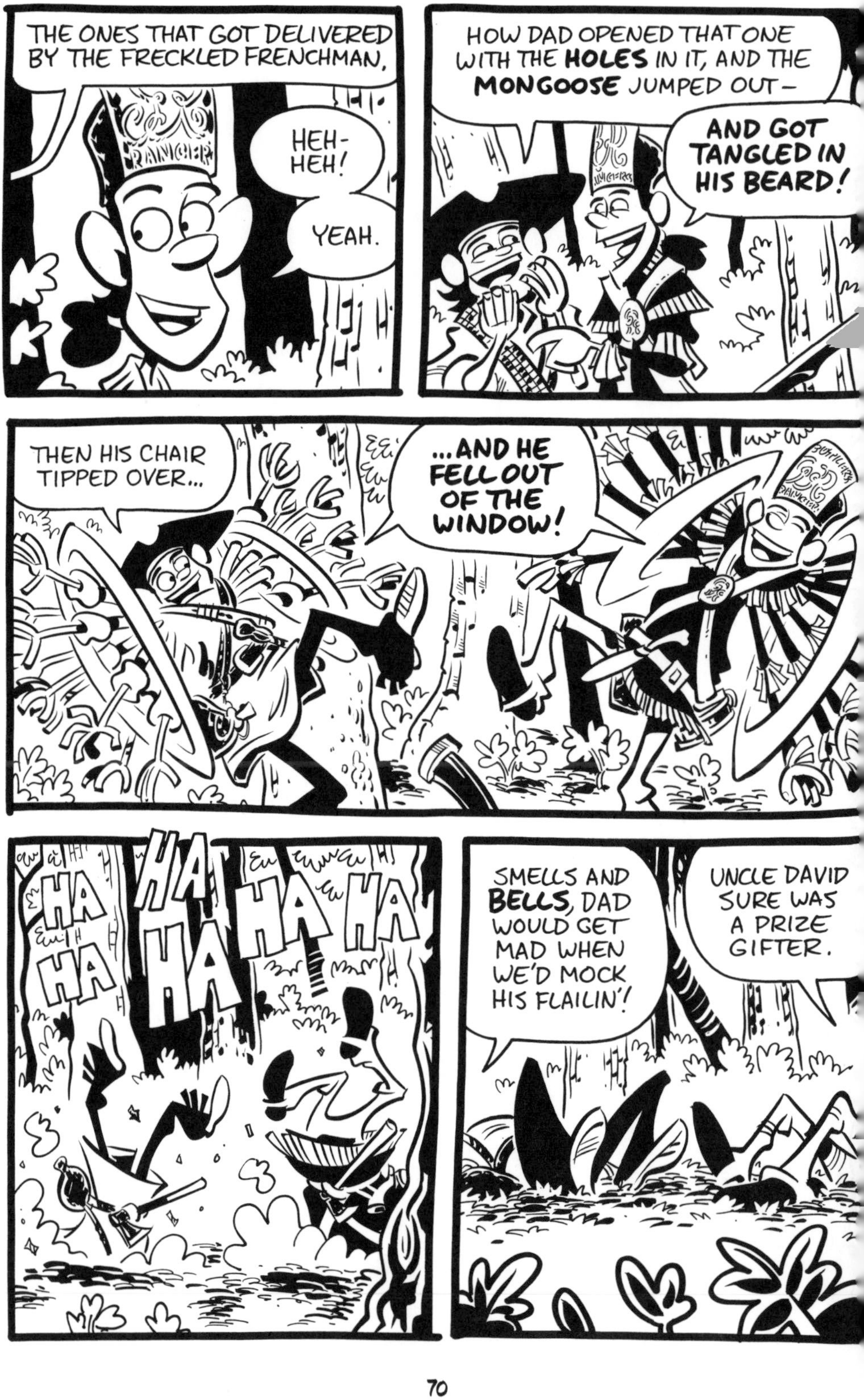
THE ONES THAT GOT DELIVERED BY THE FRECKLED FRENCHMAN,
HEH-HEH!
YEAH.
HOW DAD OPENED THAT ONE WITH THE **HOLES** IN IT, AND THE **MONGOOSE** JUMPED OUT–
AND GOT TANGLED IN HIS BEARD!
THEN HIS CHAIR TIPPED OVER...
...AND HE FELL OUT OF THE WINDOW!
HA HA HA HA HA HA HA HA
SMELLS AND **BELLS**, DAD WOULD GET MAD WHEN WE'D MOCK HIS FLAILIN'!
UNCLE DAVID SURE WAS A PRIZE GIFTER.

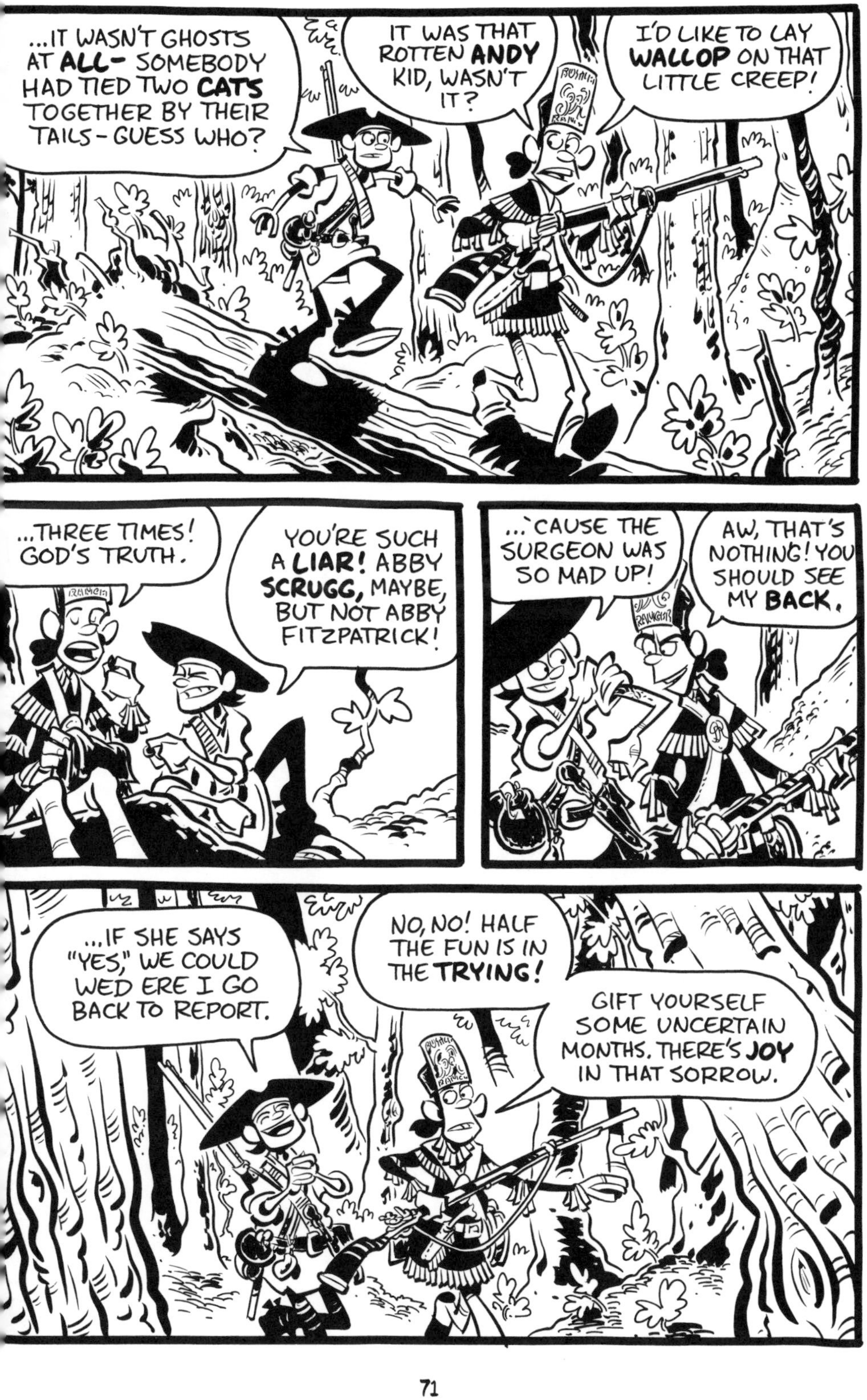
...IT WASN'T GHOSTS AT ALL- SOMEBODY HAD TIED TWO CATS TOGETHER BY THEIR TAILS - GUESS WHO?
IT WAS THAT ROTTEN ANDY KID, WASN'T IT?
I'D LIKE TO LAY WALLOP ON THAT LITTLE CREEP!
...THREE TIMES! GOD'S TRUTH.
YOU'RE SUCH A LIAR! ABBY SCRUGG, MAYBE, BUT NOT ABBY FITZPATRICK!
...'CAUSE THE SURGEON WAS SO MAD UP!
AW, THAT'S NOTHING! YOU SHOULD SEE MY BACK.
...IF SHE SAYS "YES," WE COULD WED ERE I GO BACK TO REPORT.
NO, NO! HALF THE FUN IS IN THE TRYING!
GIFT YOURSELF SOME UNCERTAIN MONTHS. THERE'S JOY IN THAT SORROW.

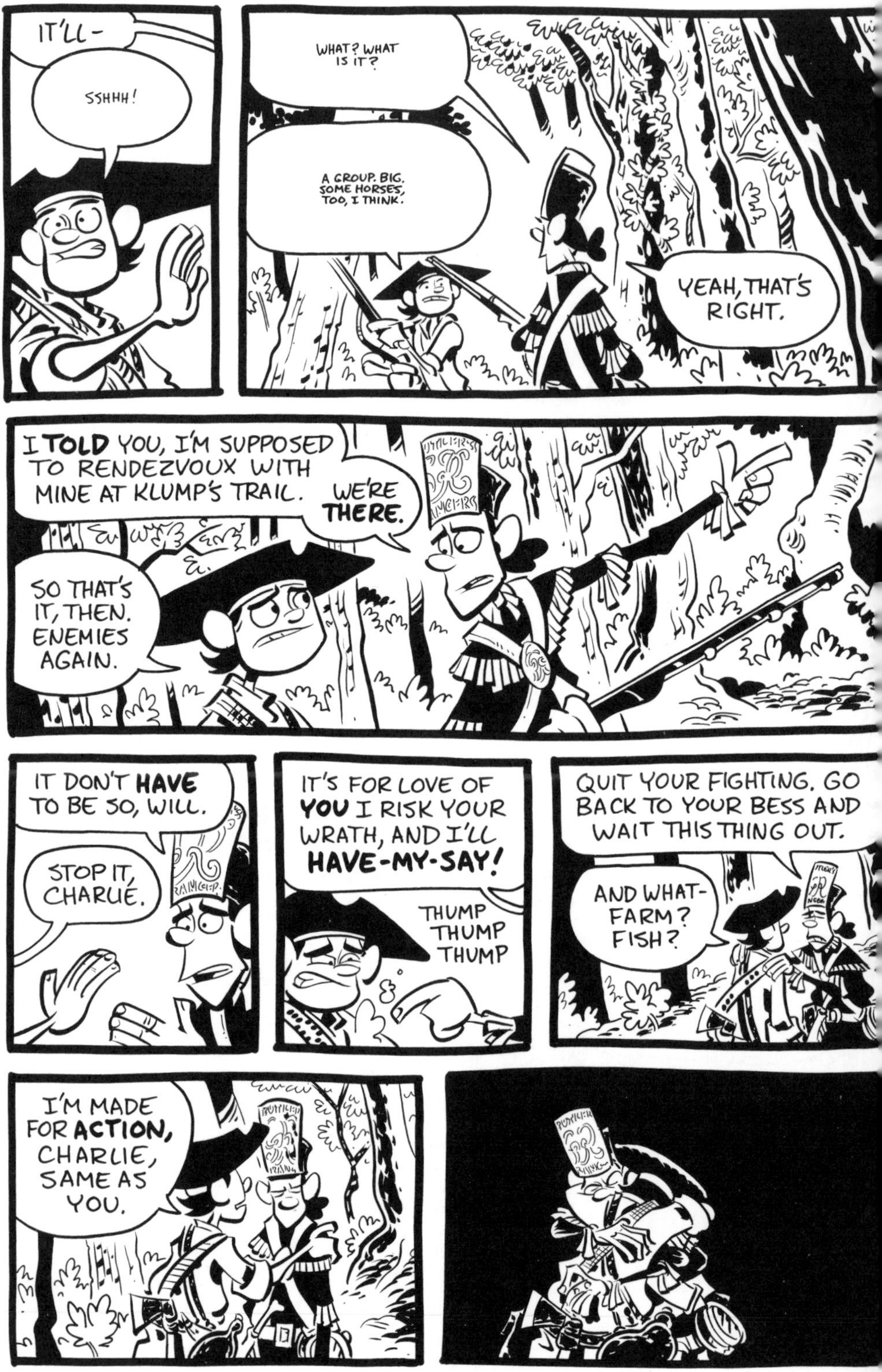
IT'LL-
SSHHH!
WHAT? WHAT IS IT?
A GROUP. BIG. SOME HORSES, TOO, I THINK.
YEAH, THAT'S RIGHT.
I **TOLD** YOU, I'M SUPPOSED TO RENDEZVOUX WITH MINE AT KLUMP'S TRAIL.
WE'RE **THERE.**
SO THAT'S IT, THEN. ENEMIES AGAIN.
IT DON'T **HAVE** TO BE SO, WILL.
STOP IT, CHARLIE.
IT'S FOR LOVE OF **YOU** I RISK YOUR WRATH, AND I'LL **HAVE-MY-SAY!**
THUMP THUMP THUMP
QUIT YOUR FIGHTING. GO BACK TO YOUR BESS AND WAIT THIS THING OUT.
AND WHAT- FARM? FISH?
I'M MADE FOR **ACTION,** CHARLIE, SAME AS YOU.

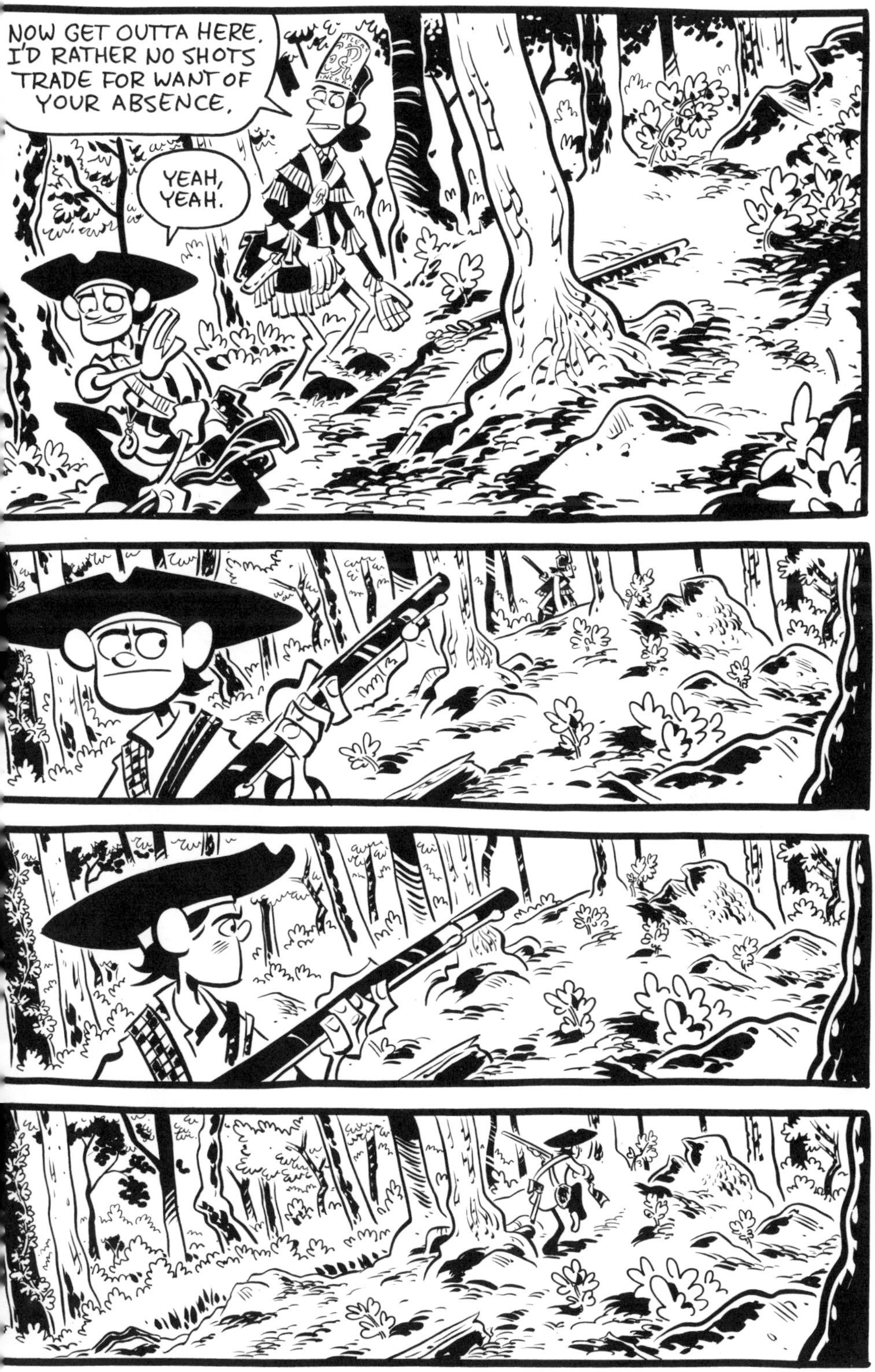
NOW GET OUTTA HERE. I'D RATHER NO SHOTS TRADE FOR WANT OF YOUR ABSENCE.
YEAH, YEAH.

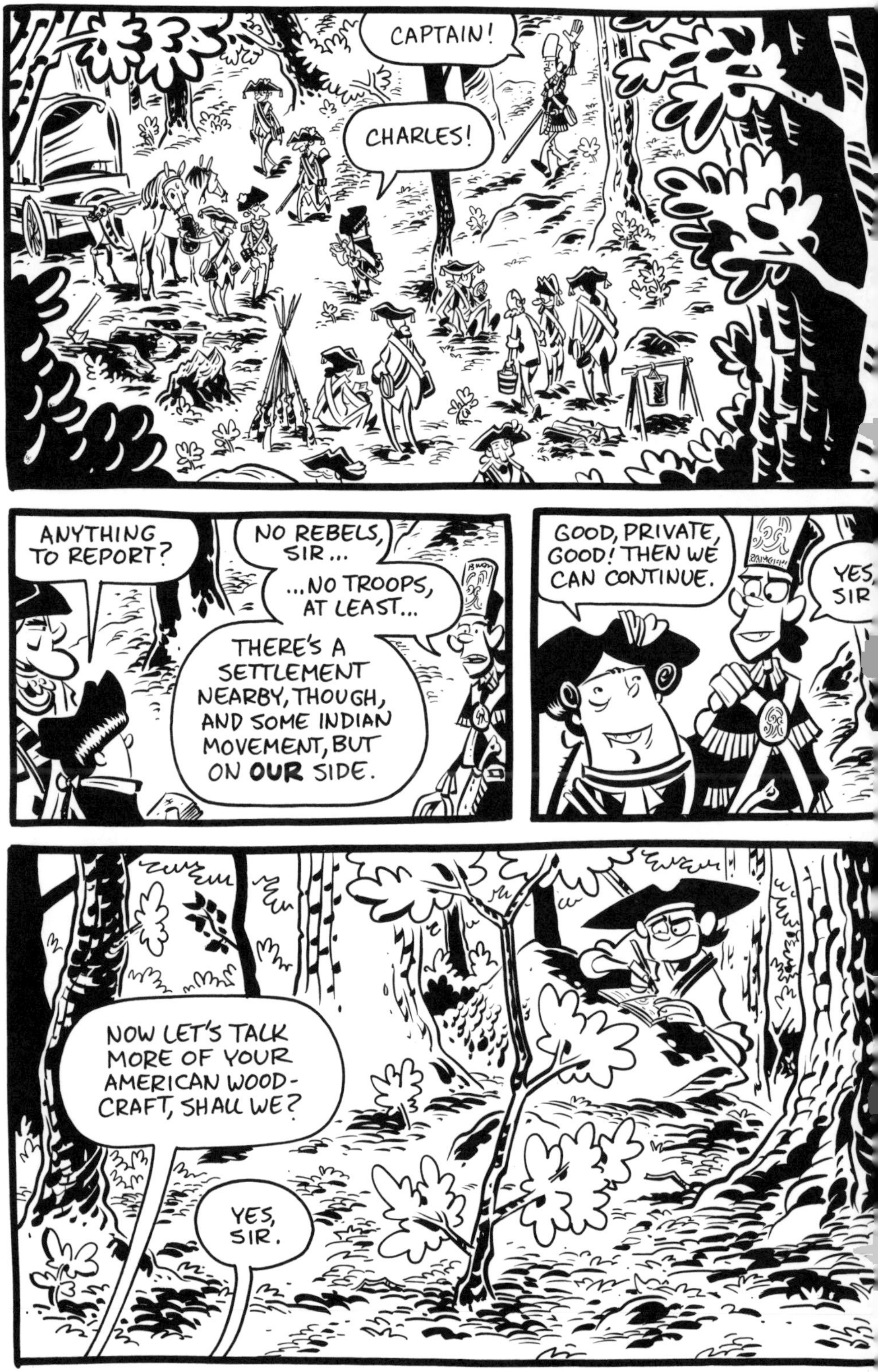
CAPTAIN!
CHARLES!
ANYTHING TO REPORT?
NO REBELS, SIR...
...NO TROOPS, AT LEAST...
THERE'S A SETTLEMENT NEARBY, THOUGH, AND SOME INDIAN MOVEMENT, BUT ON **OUR** SIDE.
GOOD, PRIVATE, GOOD! THEN WE CAN CONTINUE.
YES, SIR
NOW LET'S TALK MORE OF YOUR AMERICAN WOOD-CRAFT, SHALL WE?
YES, SIR.

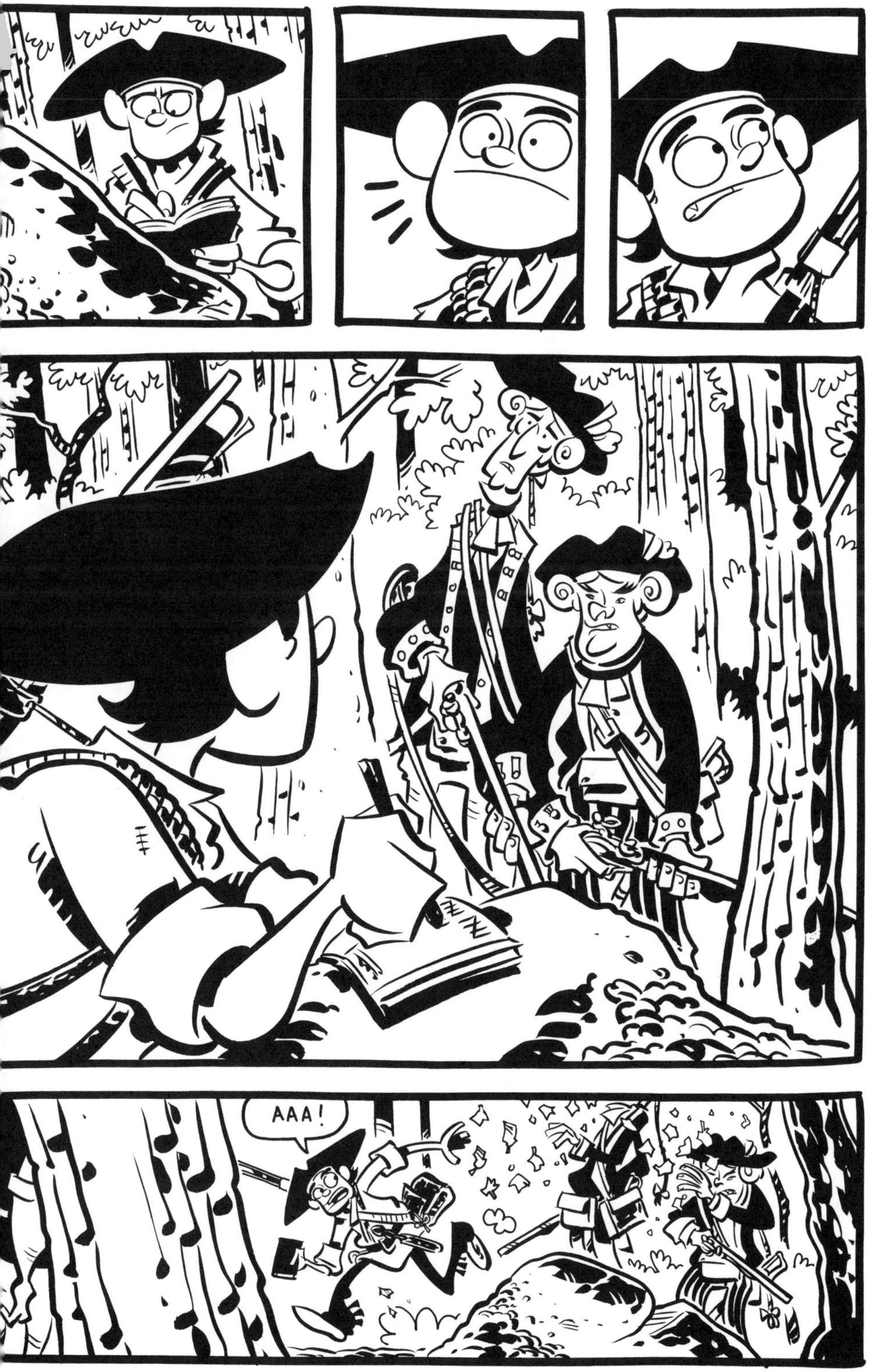
AAA!

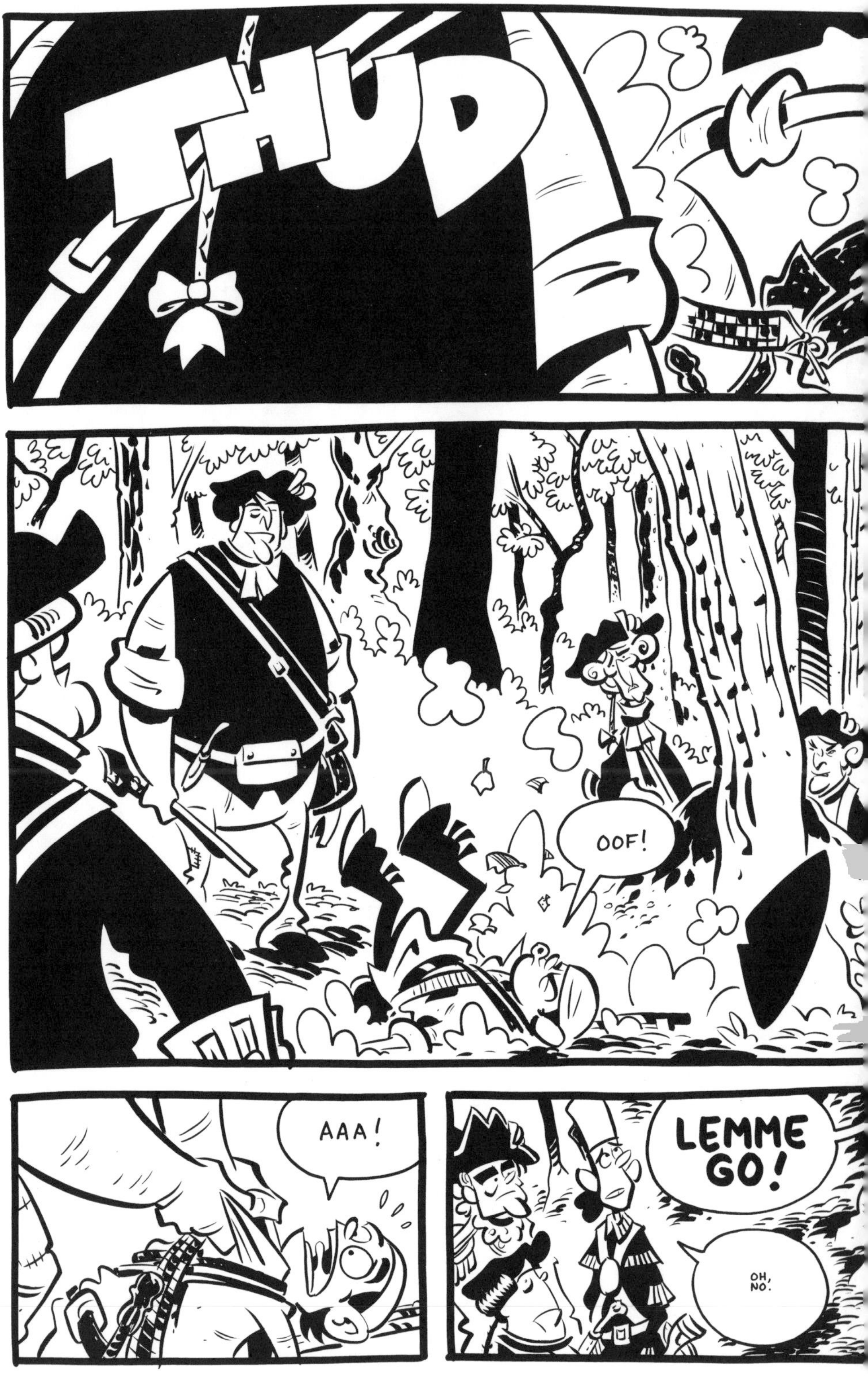
THUD
OOF!
AAA!
LEMME GO!
OH, NO.

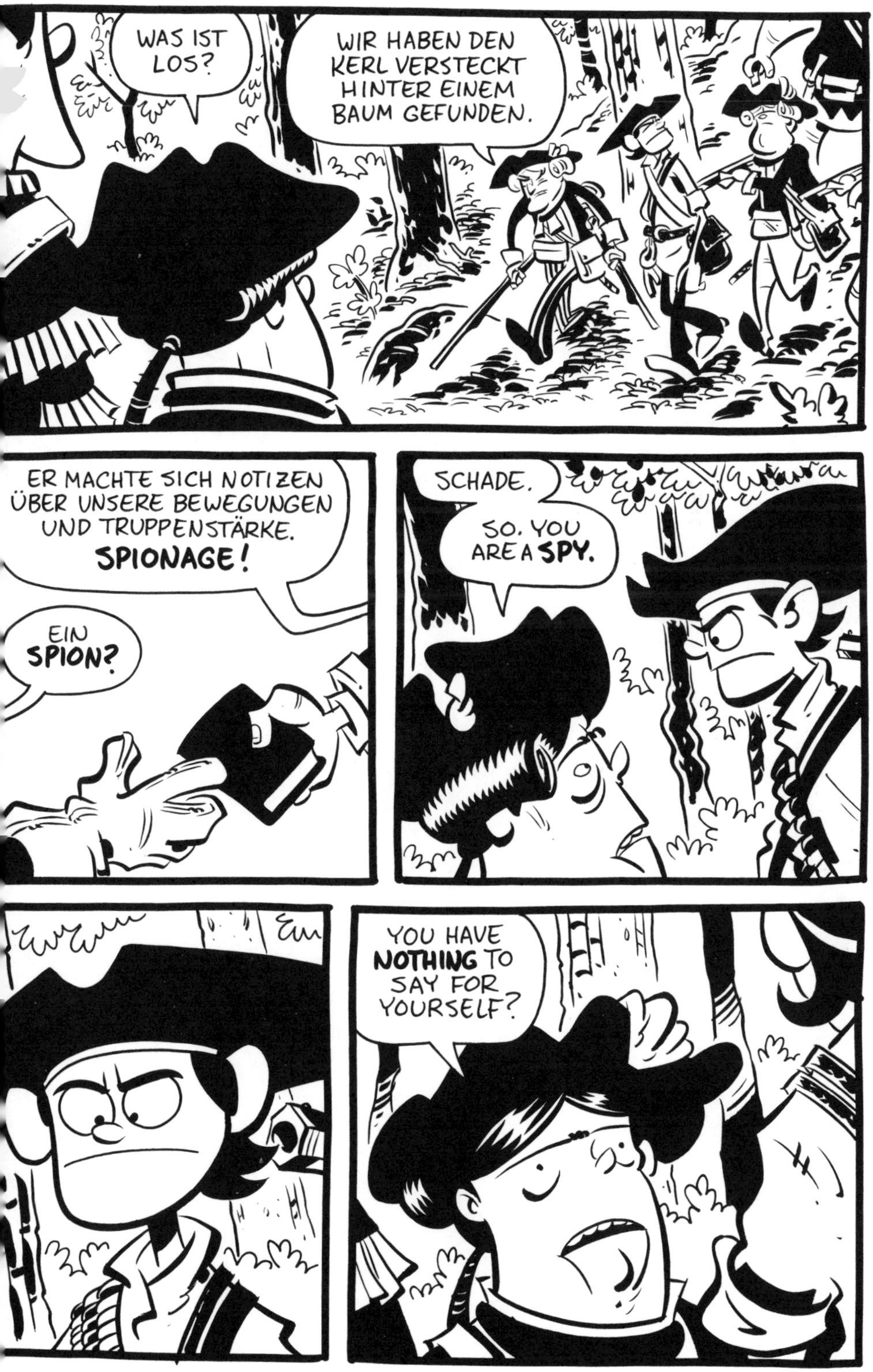
WAS IST LOS?
WIR HABEN DEN KERL VERSTECKT HINTER EINEM BAUM GEFUNDEN.
ER MACHTE SICH NOTIZEN ÜBER UNSERE BEWEGUNGEN UND TRUPPENSTÄRKE. SPIONAGE!
EIN SPION?
SCHADE.
SO, YOU ARE A SPY.
YOU HAVE NOTHING TO SAY FOR YOURSELF?

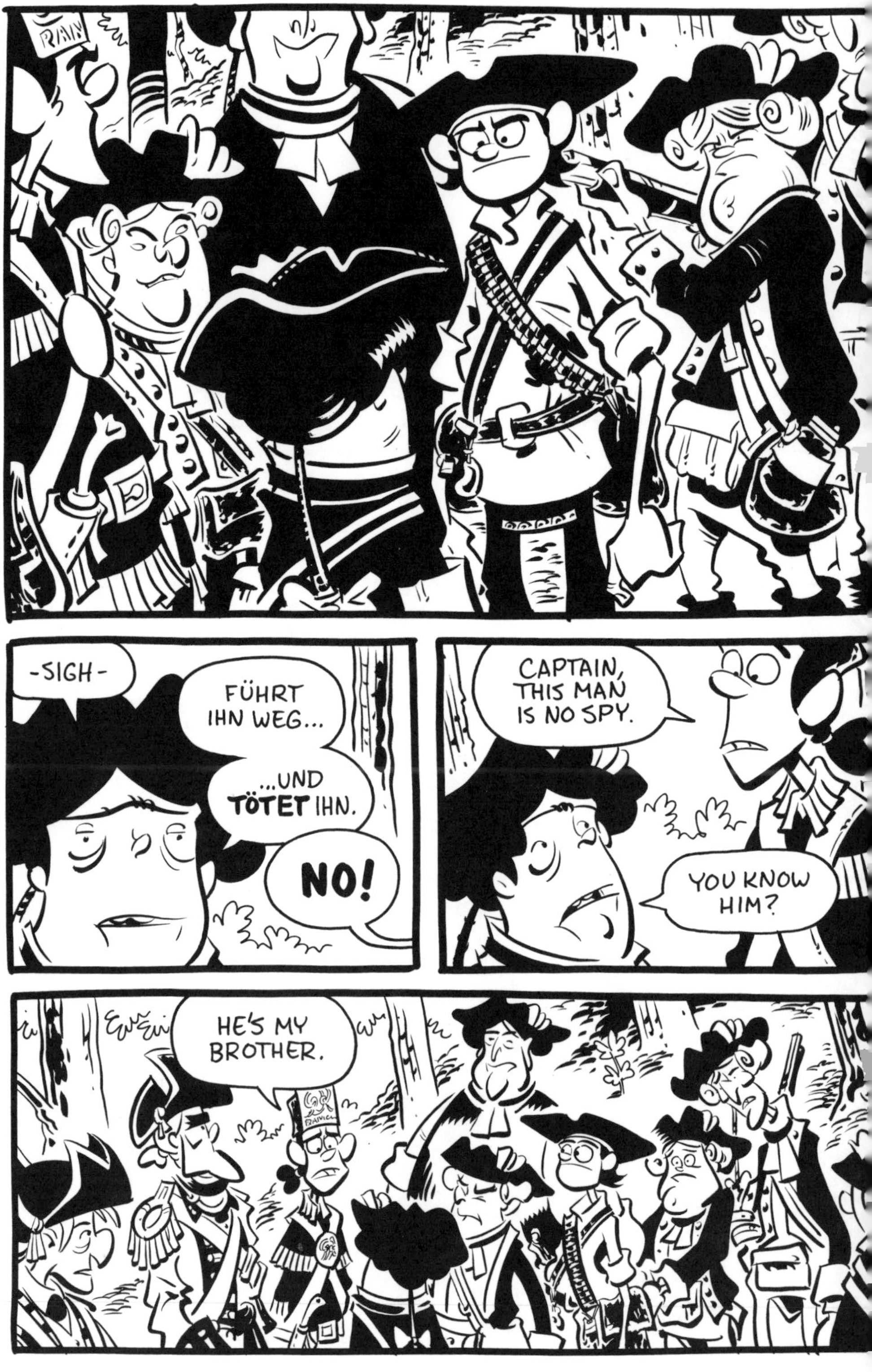
-SIGH-
FÜHRT IHN WEG...
...UND **TÖTET** IHN.
NO!
CAPTAIN, THIS MAN IS NO SPY.
YOU KNOW HIM?
HE'S MY BROTHER.

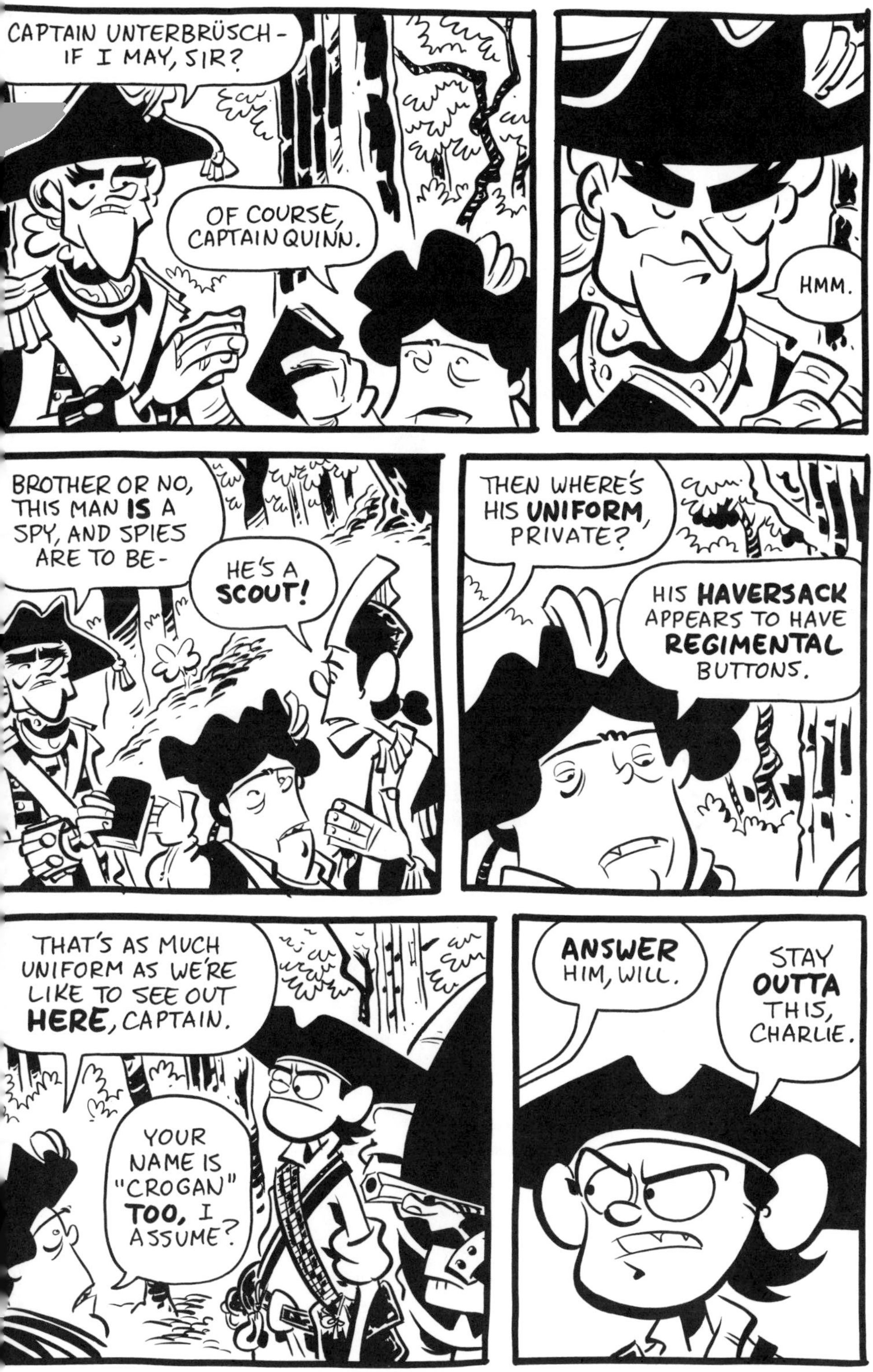
CAPTAIN UNTERBRÜSCH - IF I MAY, SIR?
OF COURSE, CAPTAIN QUINN.
HMM.
BROTHER OR NO, THIS MAN IS A SPY, AND SPIES ARE TO BE-
HE'S A SCOUT!
THEN WHERE'S HIS UNIFORM, PRIVATE?
HIS HAVERSACK APPEARS TO HAVE REGIMENTAL BUTTONS.
THAT'S AS MUCH UNIFORM AS WE'RE LIKE TO SEE OUT HERE, CAPTAIN.
YOUR NAME IS "CROGAN" TOO, I ASSUME?
ANSWER HIM, WILL.
STAY OUTTA THIS, CHARLIE.

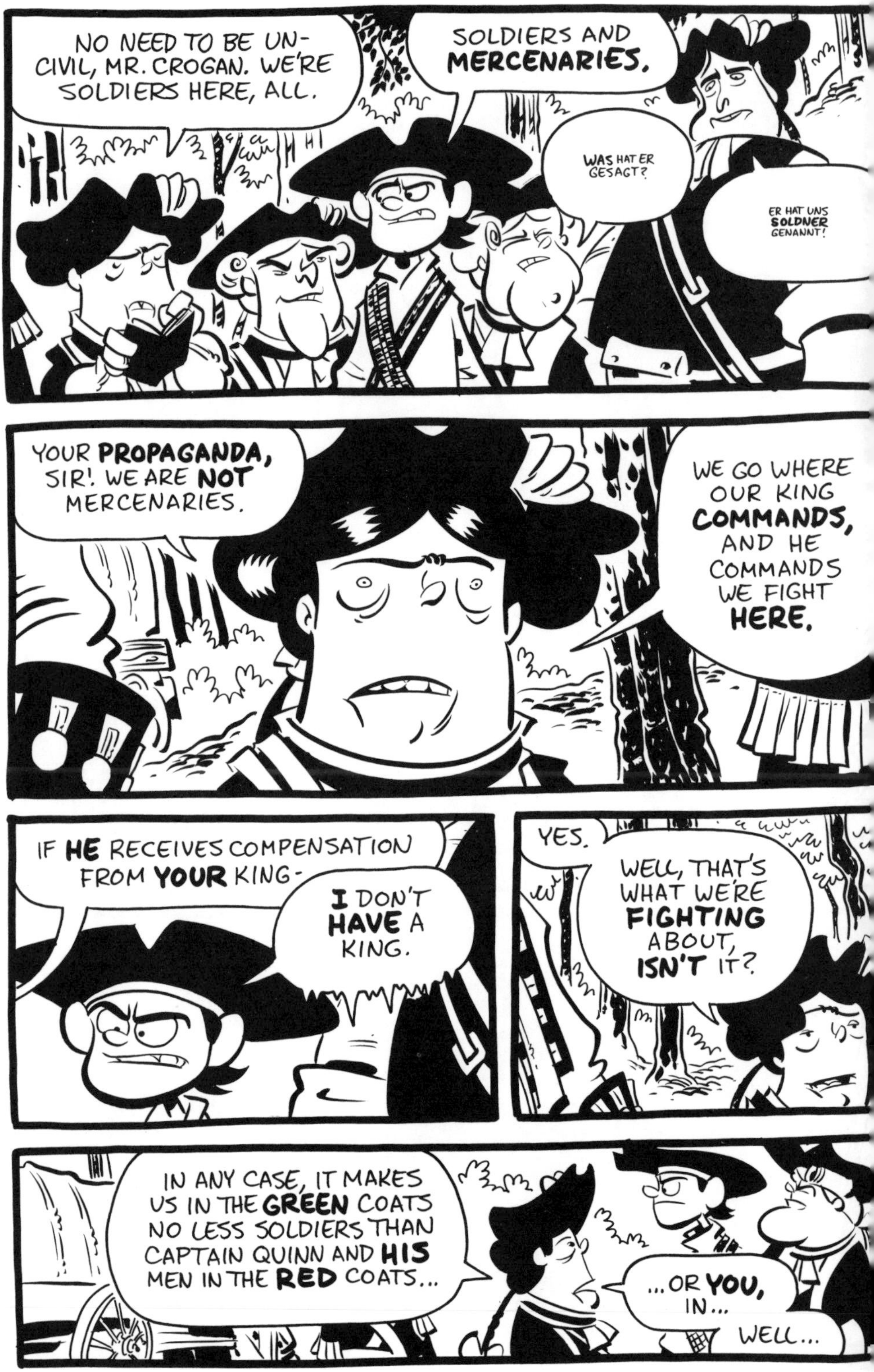
NO NEED TO BE UN-CIVIL, MR. CROGAN. WE'RE SOLDIERS HERE, ALL.
SOLDIERS AND MERCENARIES.
WAS HAT ER GESAGT?
ER HAT UNS SOLDNER GENANNT!
YOUR PROPAGANDA, SIR!. WE ARE NOT MERCENARIES.
WE GO WHERE OUR KING COMMANDS, AND HE COMMANDS WE FIGHT HERE.
IF HE RECEIVES COMPENSATION FROM YOUR KING-
I DON'T HAVE A KING.
YES.
WELL, THAT'S WHAT WE'RE FIGHTING ABOUT, ISN'T IT?
IN ANY CASE, IT MAKES US IN THE GREEN COATS NO LESS SOLDIERS THAN CAPTAIN QUINN AND HIS MEN IN THE RED COATS...
...OR YOU, IN...
WELL...

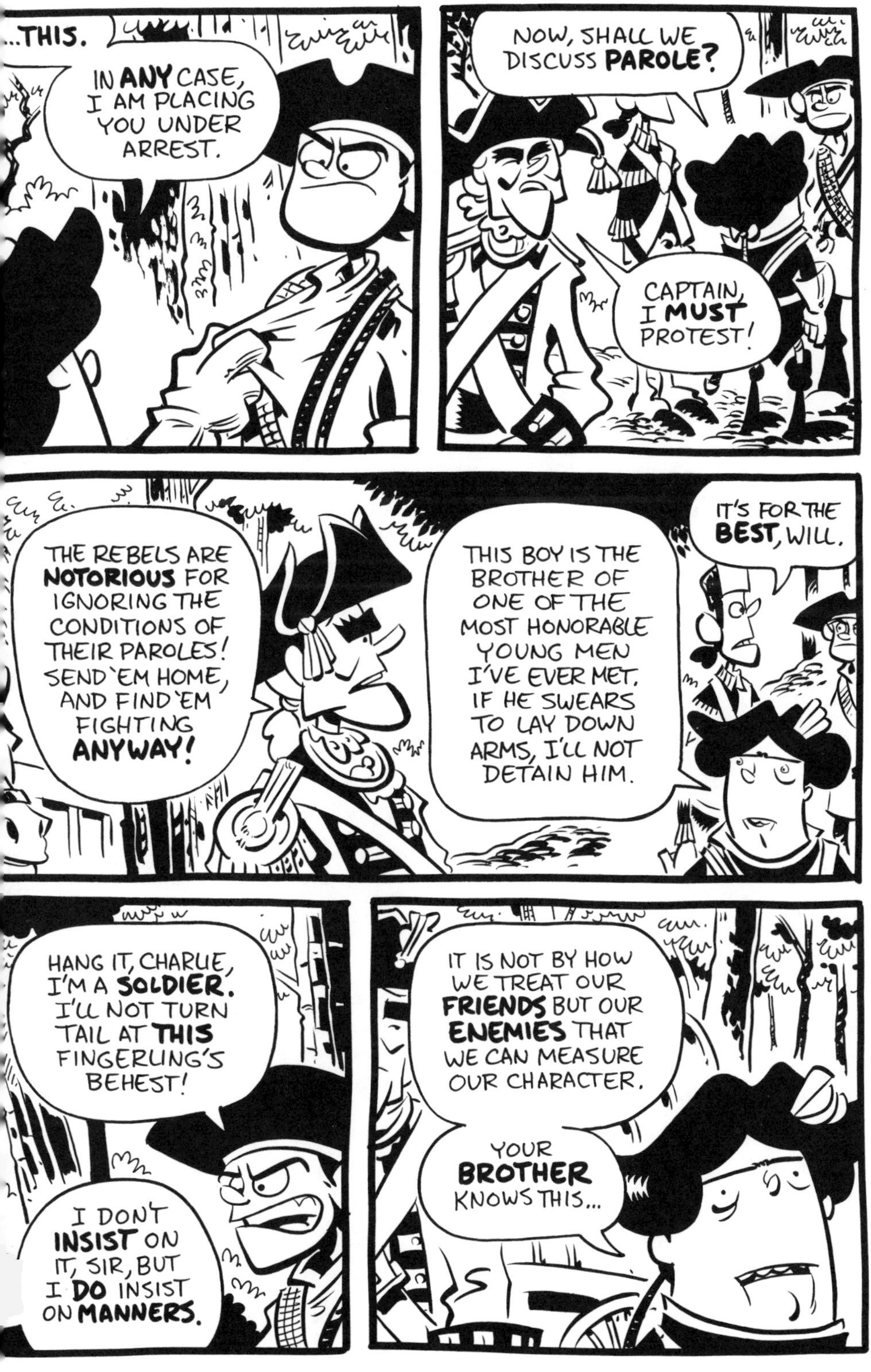
...THIS.
IN ANY CASE, I AM PLACING YOU UNDER ARREST.
NOW, SHALL WE DISCUSS PAROLE?
CAPTAIN, I MUST PROTEST!
THE REBELS ARE NOTORIOUS FOR IGNORING THE CONDITIONS OF THEIR PAROLES! SEND 'EM HOME, AND FIND 'EM FIGHTING ANYWAY!
THIS BOY IS THE BROTHER OF ONE OF THE MOST HONORABLE YOUNG MEN I'VE EVER MET. IF HE SWEARS TO LAY DOWN ARMS, I'LL NOT DETAIN HIM.
IT'S FOR THE BEST, WILL.
HANG IT, CHARLIE, I'M A SOLDIER. I'LL NOT TURN TAIL AT THIS FINGERLING'S BEHEST!
I DON'T INSIST ON IT, SIR, BUT I DO INSIST ON MANNERS.
IT IS NOT BY HOW WE TREAT OUR FRIENDS BUT OUR ENEMIES THAT WE CAN MEASURE OUR CHARACTER.
YOUR BROTHER KNOWS THIS...

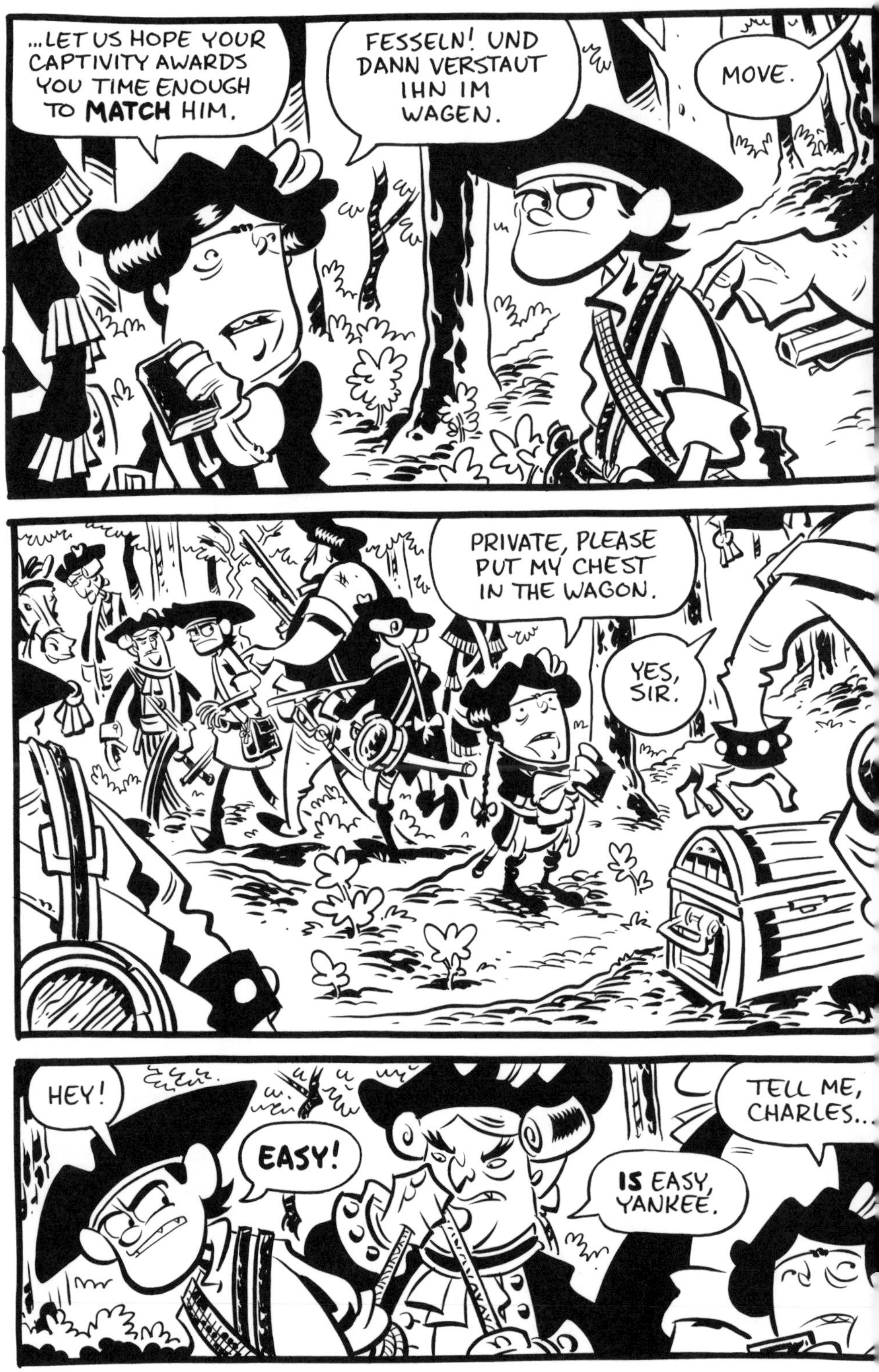
...LET US HOPE YOUR CAPTIVITY AWARDS YOU TIME ENOUGH TO **MATCH** HIM.
FESSELN! UND DANN VERSTAUT IHN IM WAGEN.
MOVE.
PRIVATE, PLEASE PUT MY CHEST IN THE WAGON.
YES, SIR.
HEY!
EASY!
IS EASY, YANKEE.
TELL ME, CHARLES...

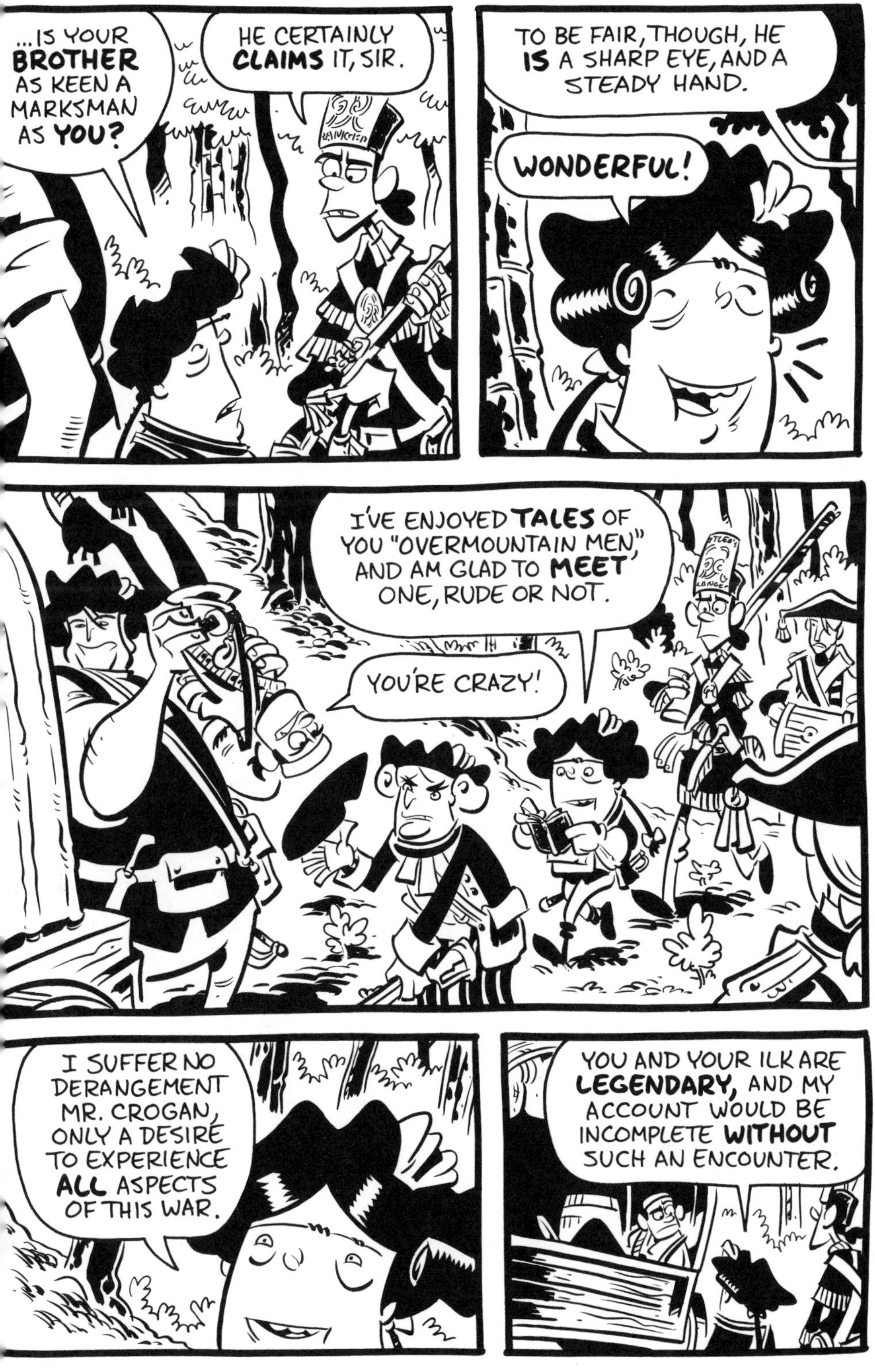
...IS YOUR **BROTHER** AS KEEN A MARKSMAN AS **YOU?**
HE CERTAINLY **CLAIMS** IT, SIR.
TO BE FAIR, THOUGH, HE **IS** A SHARP EYE, AND A STEADY HAND.
WONDERFUL!
I'VE ENJOYED **TALES** OF YOU "OVERMOUNTAIN MEN," AND AM GLAD TO **MEET** ONE, RUDE OR NOT.
YOU'RE CRAZY!
I SUFFER NO DERANGEMENT MR. CROGAN, ONLY A DESIRE TO EXPERIENCE **ALL** ASPECTS OF THIS WAR.
YOU AND YOUR ILK ARE **LEGENDARY,** AND MY ACCOUNT WOULD BE INCOMPLETE **WITHOUT** SUCH AN ENCOUNTER.

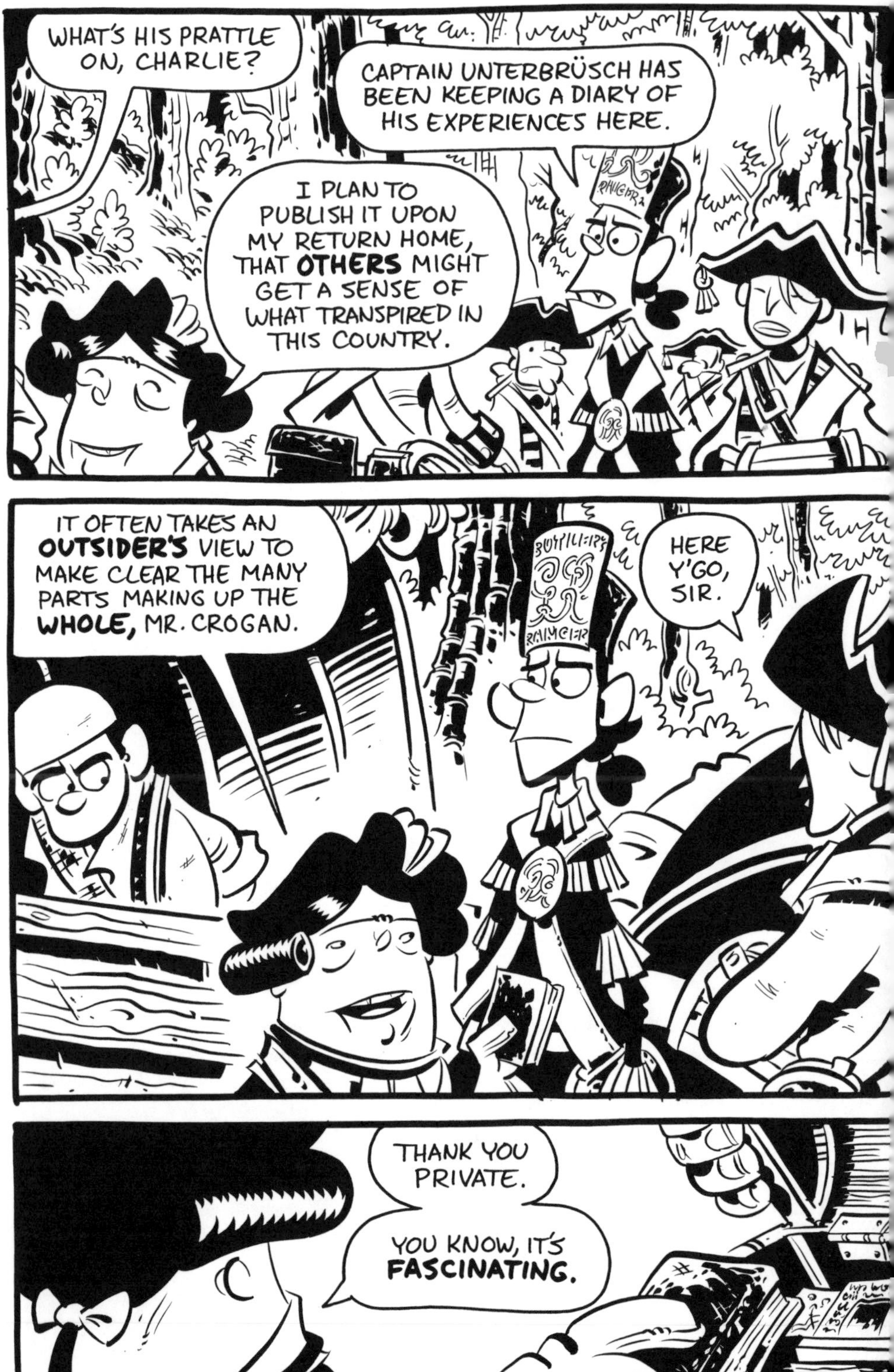
WHAT'S HIS PRATTLE ON, CHARLIE?
CAPTAIN UNTERBRÜSCH HAS BEEN KEEPING A DIARY OF HIS EXPERIENCES HERE.
I PLAN TO PUBLISH IT UPON MY RETURN HOME, THAT **OTHERS** MIGHT GET A SENSE OF WHAT TRANSPIRED IN THIS COUNTRY.
IT OFTEN TAKES AN **OUTSIDER'S** VIEW TO MAKE CLEAR THE MANY PARTS MAKING UP THE **WHOLE,** MR. CROGAN.
HERE Y'GO, SIR.
THANK YOU PRIVATE.
YOU KNOW, IT'S **FASCINATING.**

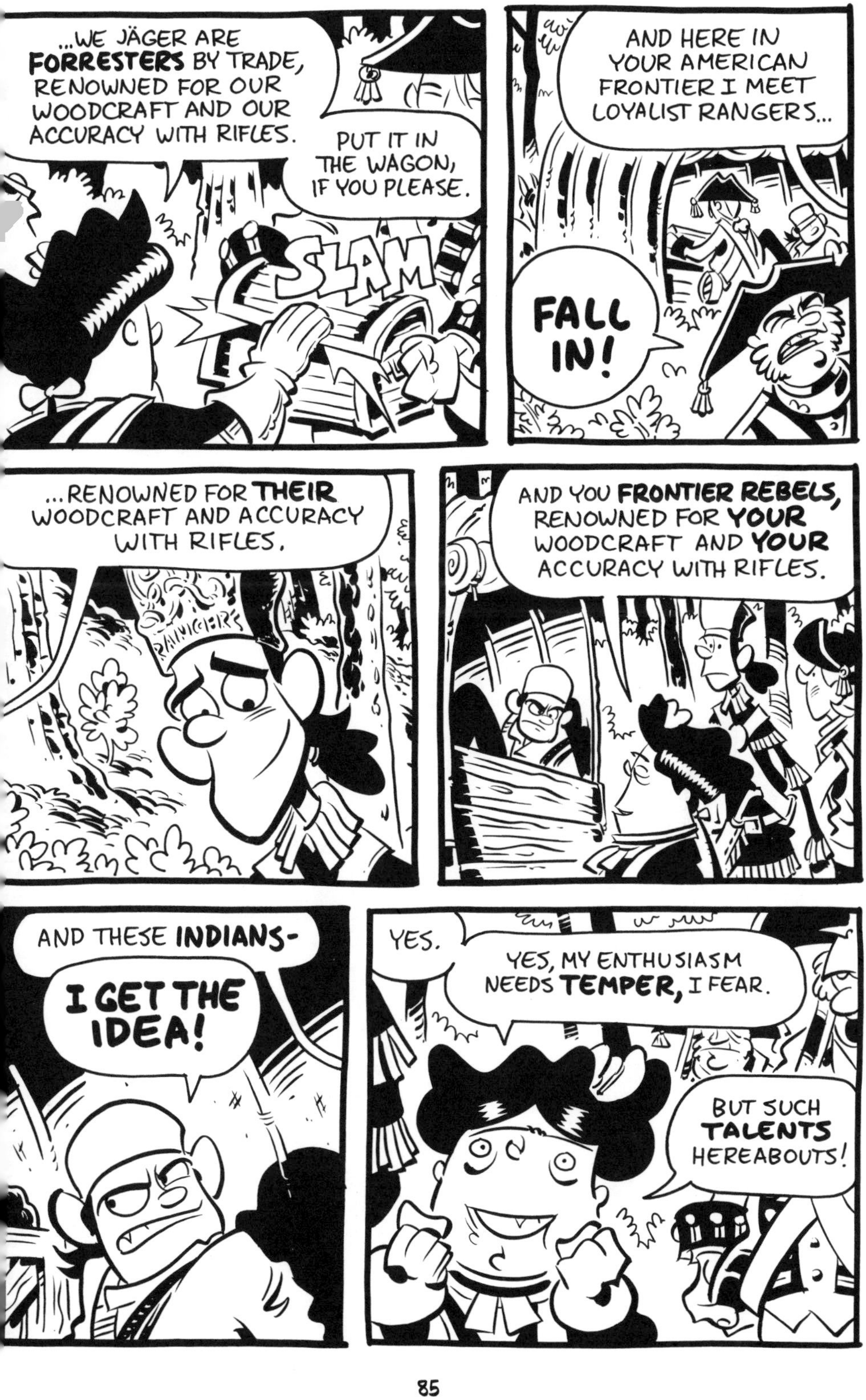
...WE JÄGER ARE FORRESTERS BY TRADE, RENOWNED FOR OUR WOODCRAFT AND OUR ACCURACY WITH RIFLES.
PUT IT IN THE WAGON, IF YOU PLEASE.
SLAM
AND HERE IN YOUR AMERICAN FRONTIER I MEET LOYALIST RANGERS...
FALL IN!
...RENOWNED FOR THEIR WOODCRAFT AND ACCURACY WITH RIFLES.
AND YOU FRONTIER REBELS, RENOWNED FOR YOUR WOODCRAFT AND YOUR ACCURACY WITH RIFLES.
AND THESE INDIANS-
I GET THE IDEA!
YES.
YES, MY ENTHUSIASM NEEDS TEMPER, I FEAR.
BUT SUCH TALENTS HEREABOUTS!

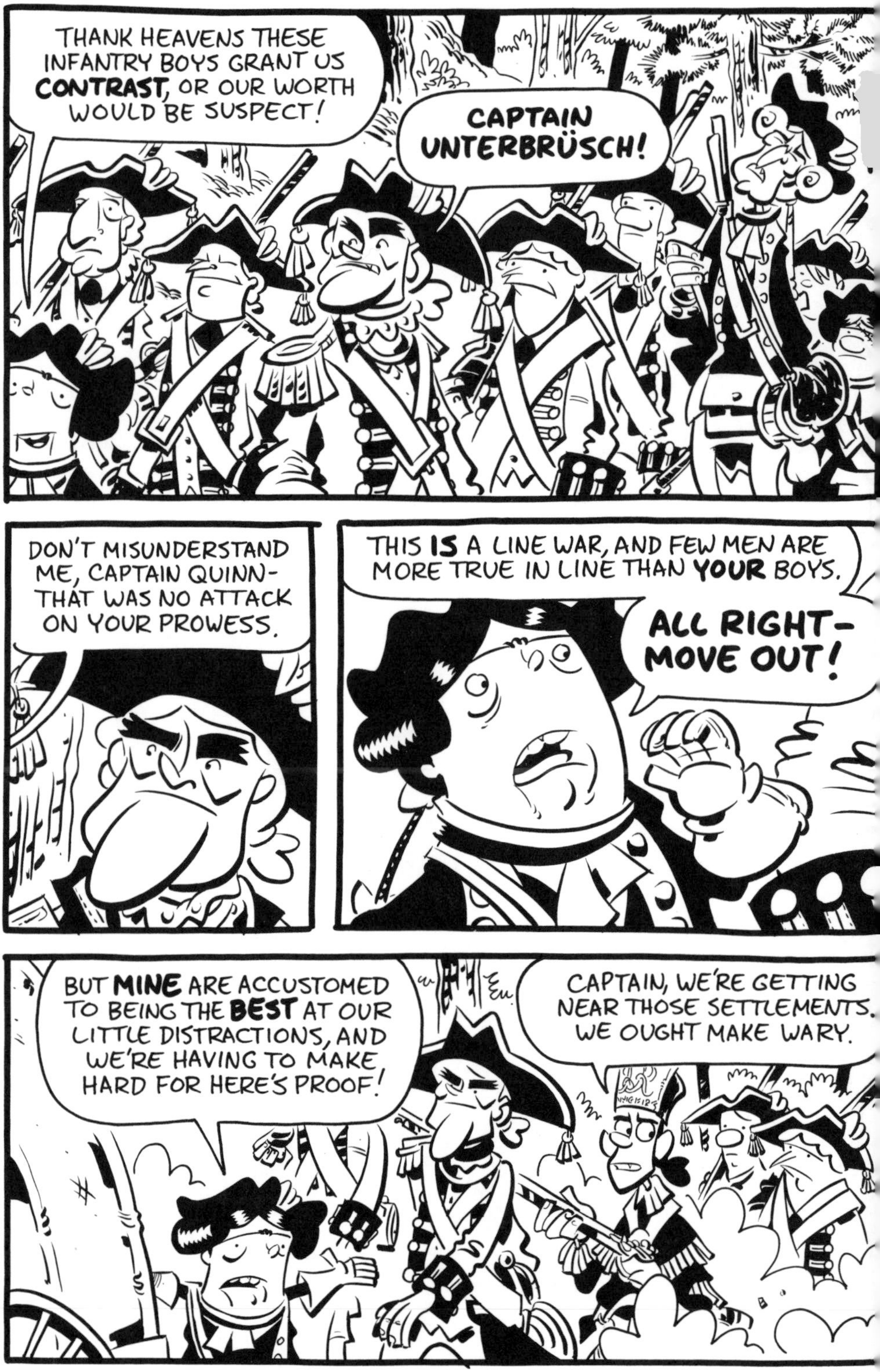
THANK HEAVENS THESE INFANTRY BOYS GRANT US **CONTRAST**, OR OUR WORTH WOULD BE SUSPECT!
CAPTAIN UNTERBRÜSCH!
DON'T MISUNDERSTAND ME, CAPTAIN QUINN- THAT WAS NO ATTACK ON YOUR PROWESS.
THIS **IS** A LINE WAR, AND FEW MEN ARE MORE TRUE IN LINE THAN **YOUR** BOYS.
ALL RIGHT- MOVE OUT!
BUT **MINE** ARE ACCUSTOMED TO BEING THE **BEST** AT OUR LITTLE DISTRACTIONS, AND WE'RE HAVING TO MAKE HARD FOR HERE'S PROOF!
CAPTAIN, WE'RE GETTING NEAR THOSE SETTLEMENTS. WE OUGHT MAKE WARY.

OH, YES?

THE FOLKS HEREABOUTS AREN'T REBELS **PROPER**, BUT THEY **ARE** A HERMITIC LOT, AND **COULD** PROVE THEMSELVES **HOSTILE.**

THEY **MAY NOT** VENTURE **NEAR—**

OH, THEY **HAVE.**

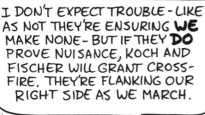

THERE ARE **FOUR** WITHIN FIRING RANGE.

DON'T LOOK.

I DON'T EXPECT TROUBLE—LIKE AS NOT THEY'RE ENSURING **WE** MAKE NONE—BUT IF THEY **DO** PROVE NUISANCE, KOCH AND FISCHER WILL GRANT CROSS-FIRE. THEY'RE FLANKING OUR RIGHT SIDE AS WE MARCH.

CHARLIE!

HEY, CHARLIE!

D'YOU **SMELL** THAT?

AYE.

SOMEONE'S CLEARING **BRUSH,** IS ALL, OR COOKING.

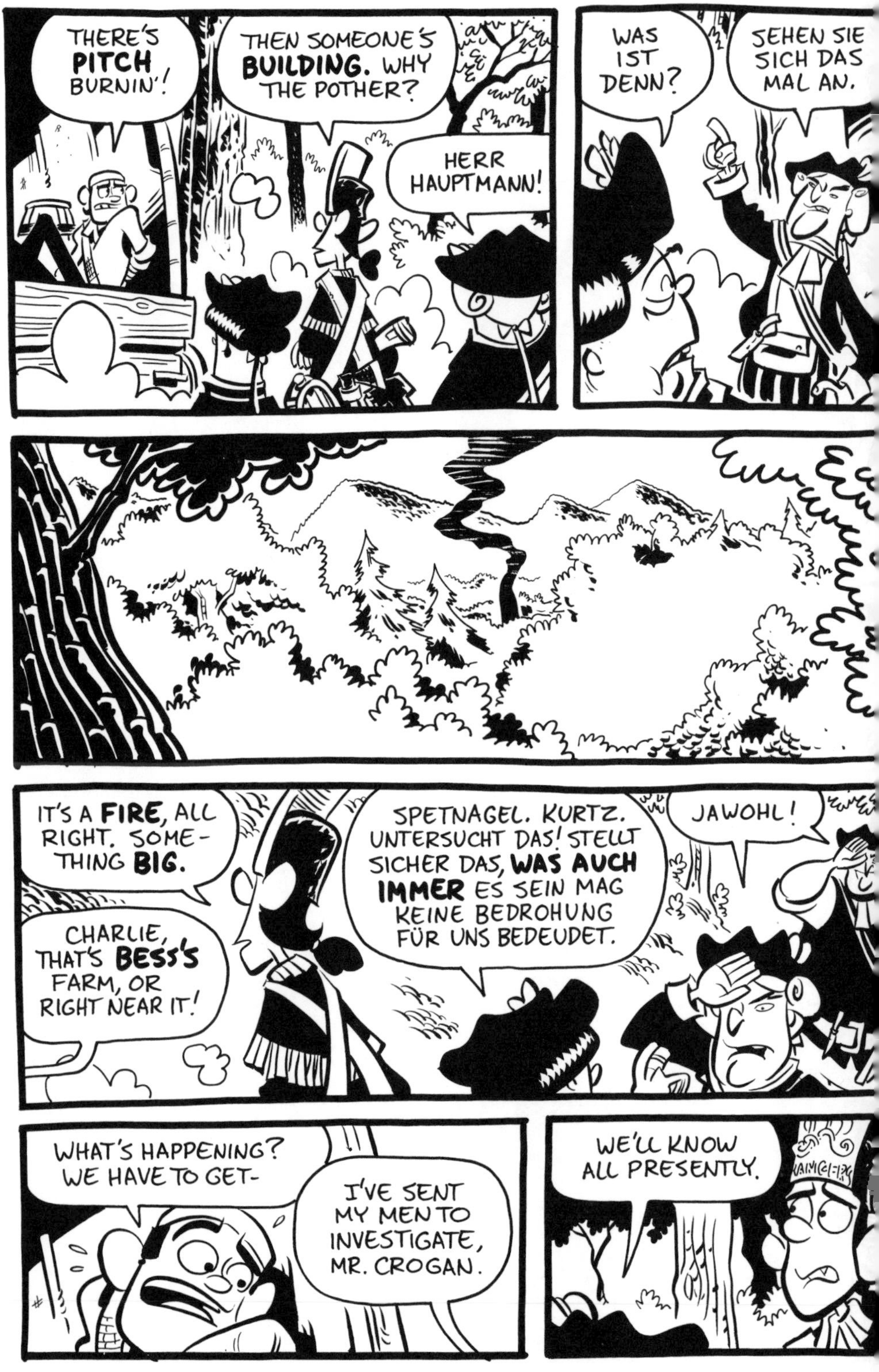
THERE'S PITCH BURNIN'!
THEN SOMEONE'S BUILDING. WHY THE POTHER?
HERR HAUPTMANN!
WAS IST DENN?
SEHEN SIE SICH DAS MAL AN.
IT'S A FIRE, ALL RIGHT. SOMETHING BIG.
CHARLIE, THAT'S BESS'S FARM, OR RIGHT NEAR IT!
SPETNAGEL. KURTZ. UNTERSUCHT DAS! STELLT SICHER DAS, WAS AUCH IMMER ES SEIN MAG KEINE BEDROHUNG FÜR UNS BEDEUDET.
JAWOHL!
WHAT'S HAPPENING? WE HAVE TO GET-
I'VE SENT MY MEN TO INVESTIGATE, MR. CROGAN.
WE'LL KNOW ALL PRESENTLY.

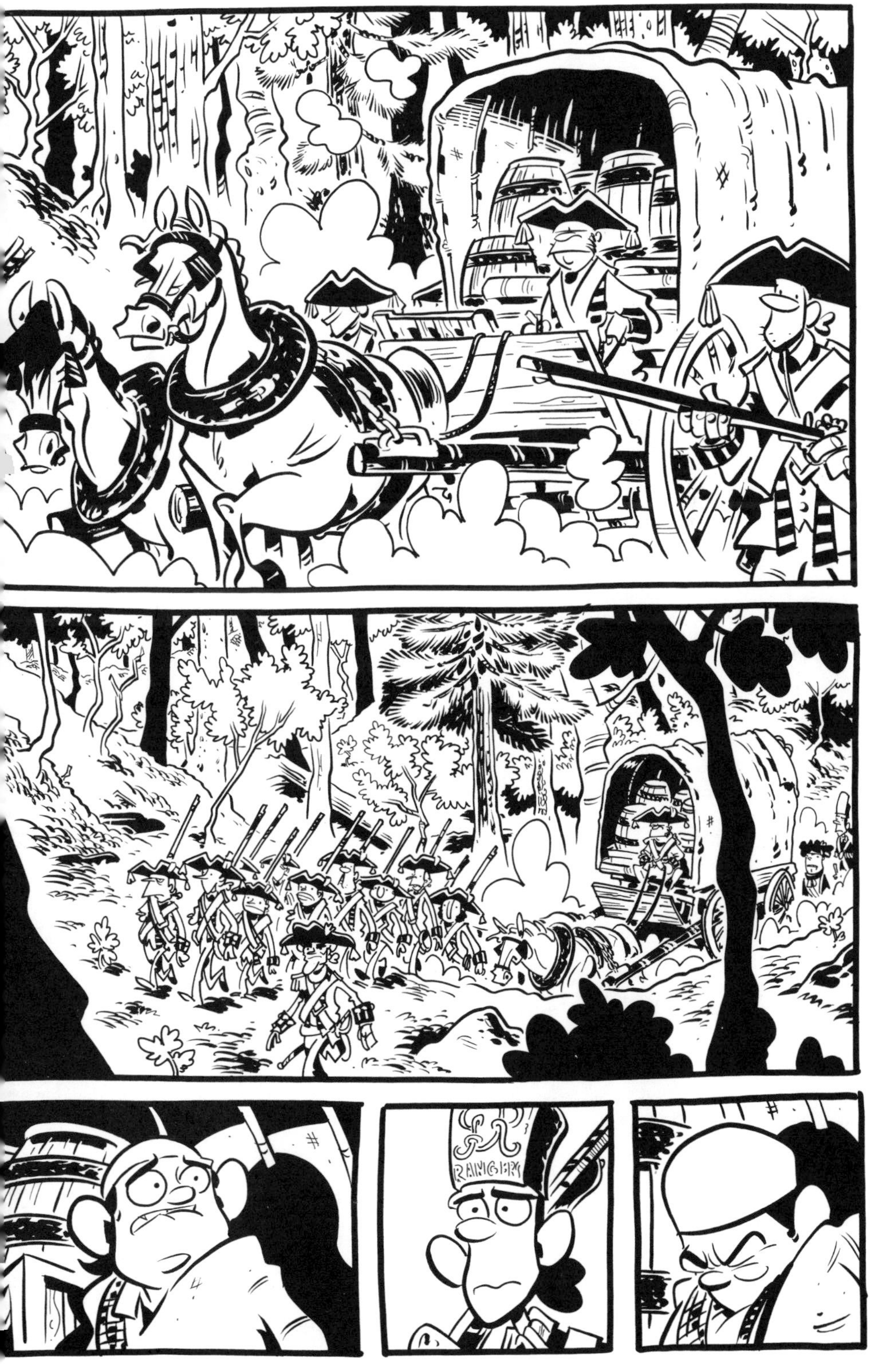
RANGERS

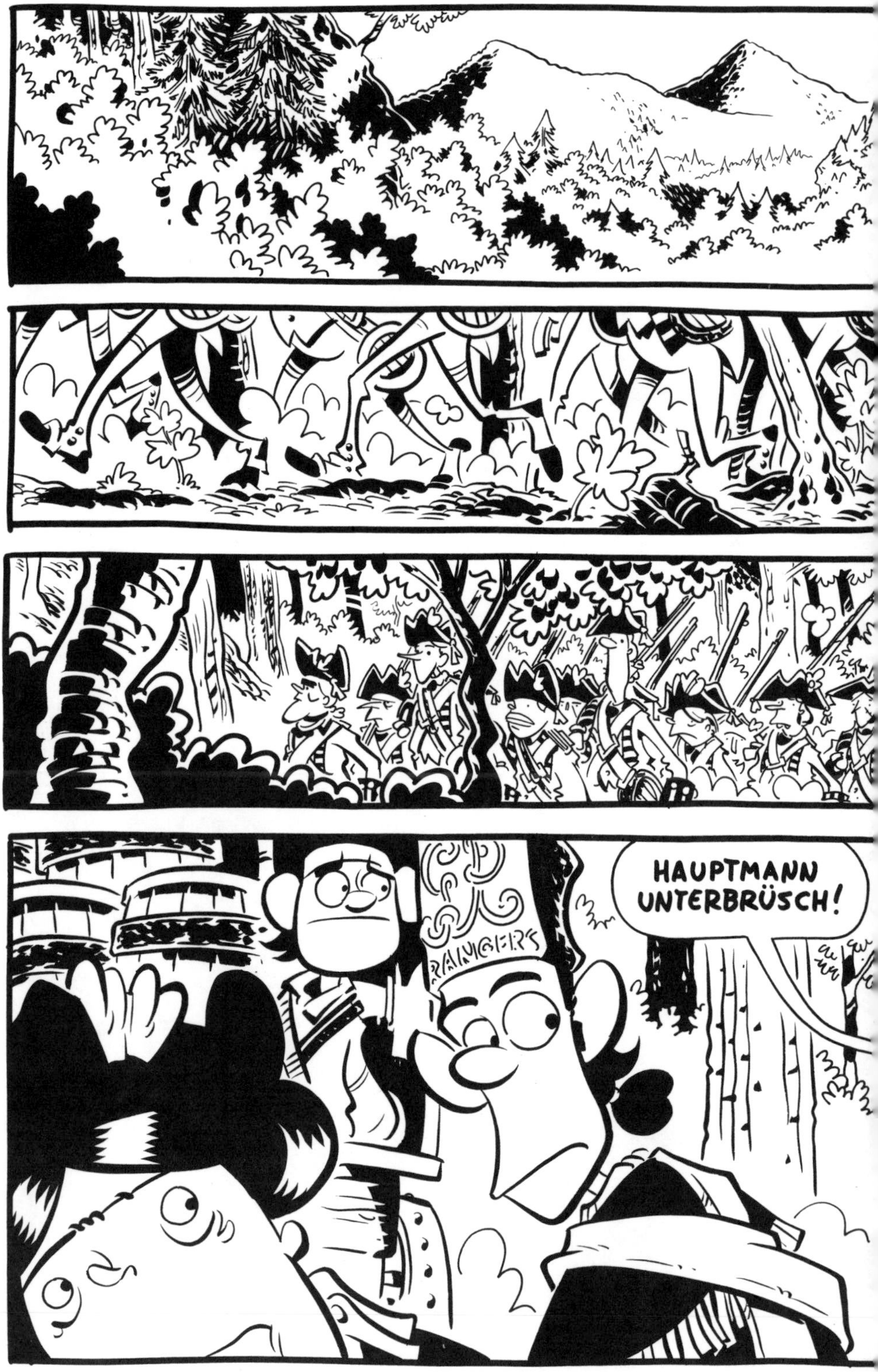
HAUPTMANN UNTERBRÜSCH!
RANGERS

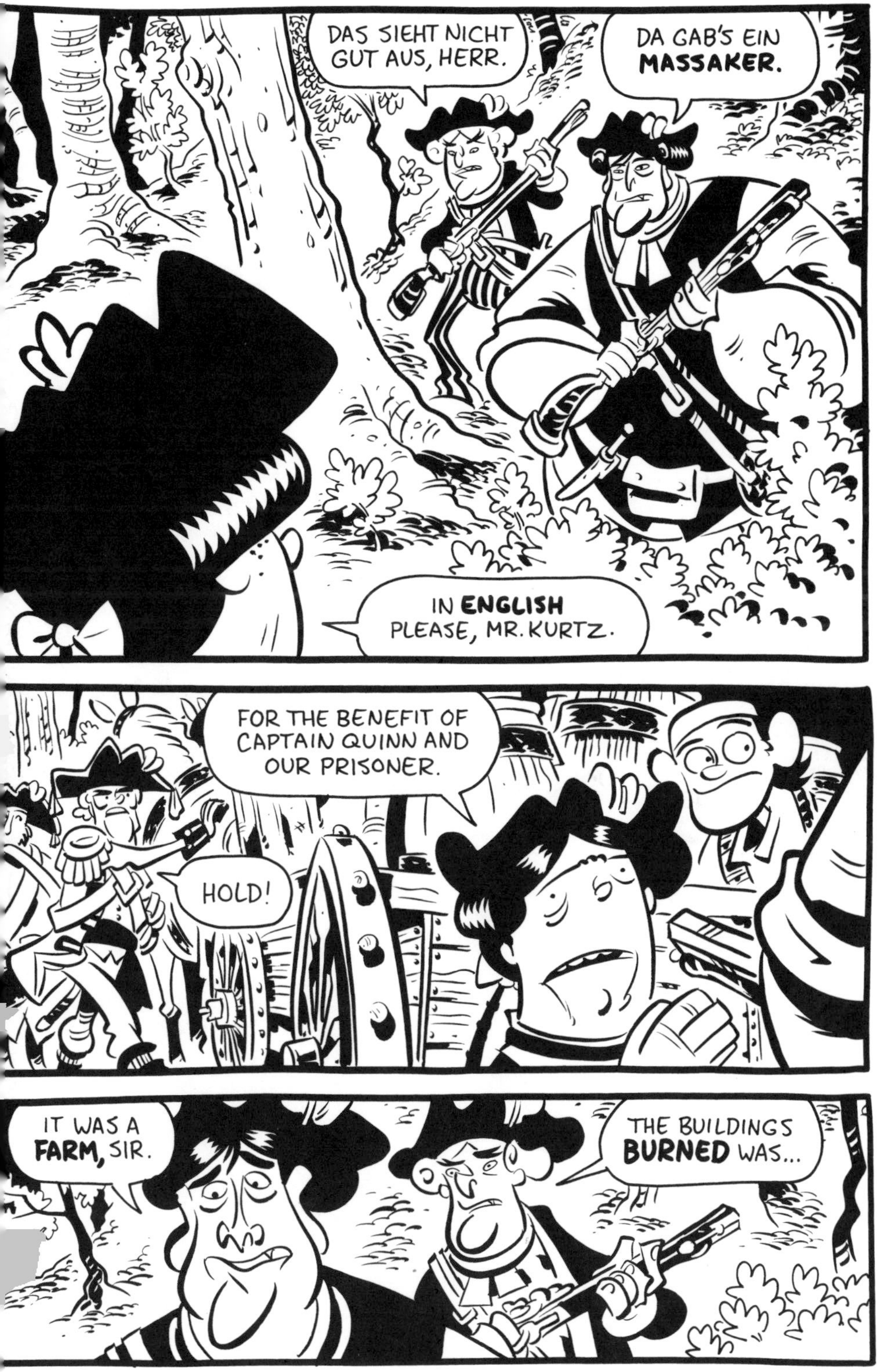
DAS SIEHT NICHT GUT AUS, HERR.
DA GAB'S EIN **MASSAKER.**
IN **ENGLISH** PLEASE, MR. KURTZ.
FOR THE BENEFIT OF CAPTAIN QUINN AND OUR PRISONER.
HOLD!
IT WAS A **FARM,** SIR.
THE BUILDINGS **BURNED** WAS...

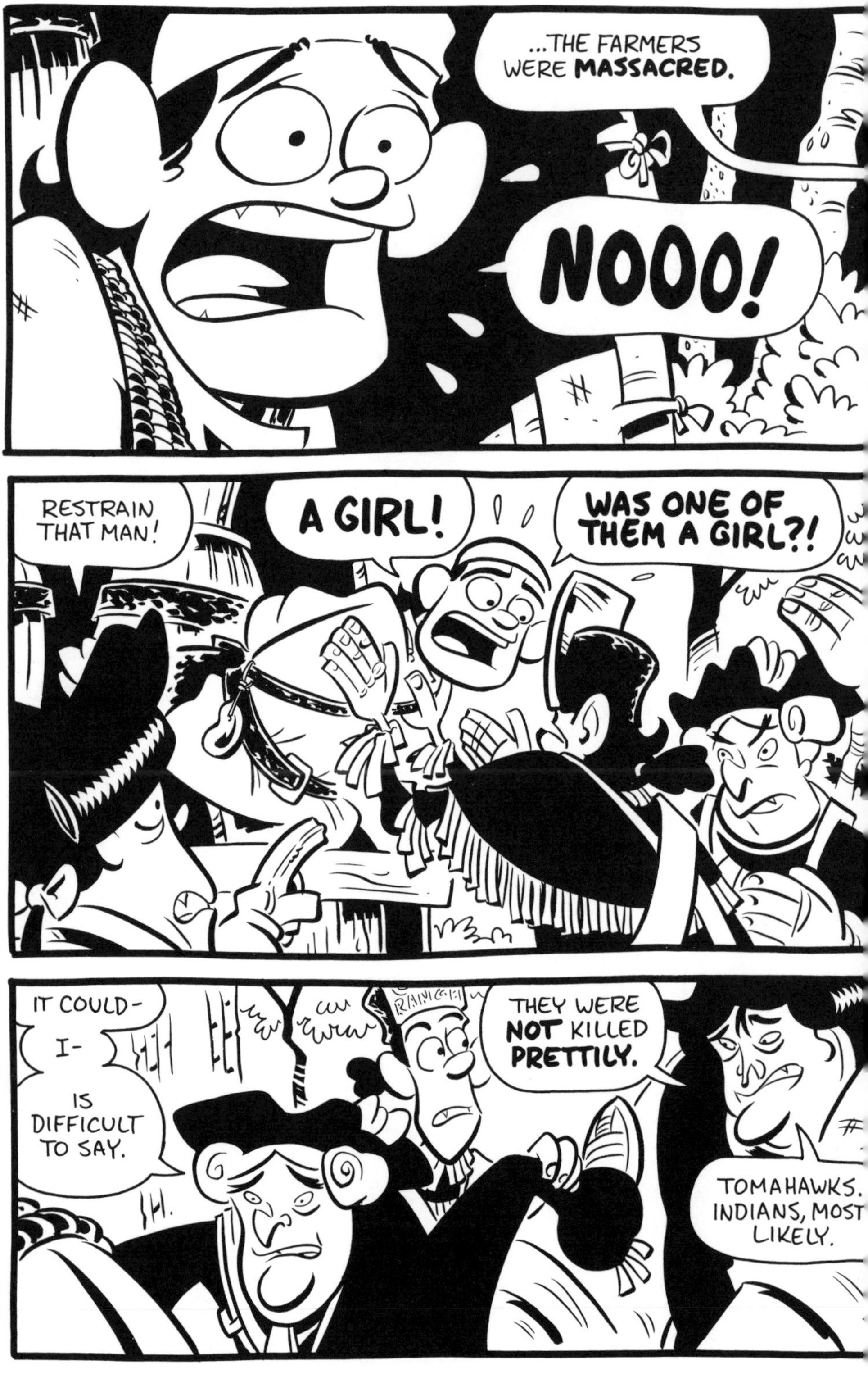
...THE FARMERS WERE **MASSACRED.**
NOOO!
RESTRAIN THAT MAN!
A GIRL!
WAS ONE OF THEM A GIRL?!
IT COULD-
I-
IS DIFFICULT TO SAY.
THEY WERE **NOT** KILLED **PRETTILY.**
TOMAHAWKS. INDIANS, MOST LIKELY.

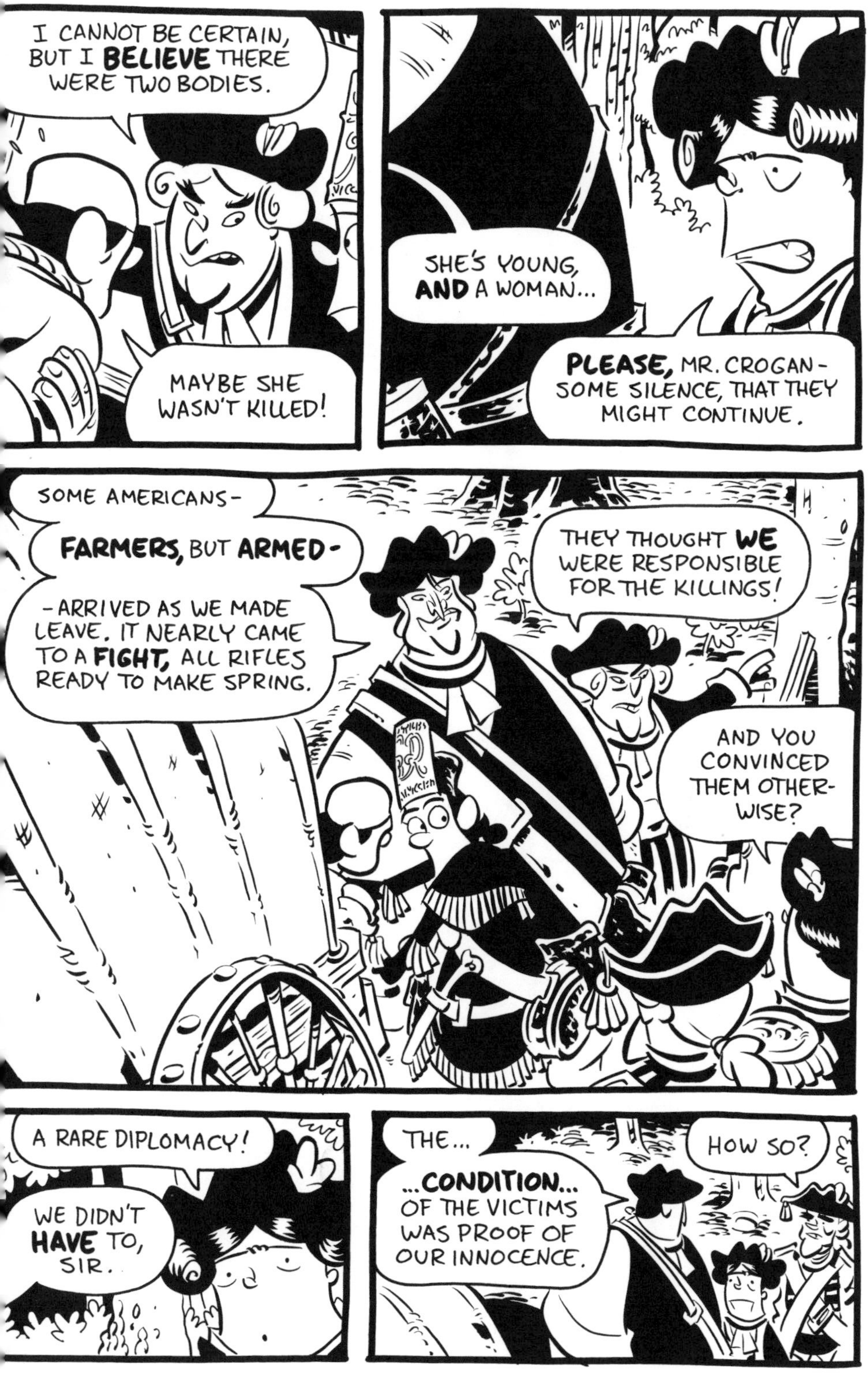
I CANNOT BE CERTAIN, BUT I **BELIEVE** THERE WERE TWO BODIES.
MAYBE SHE WASN'T KILLED!
SHE'S YOUNG, **AND** A WOMAN...
PLEASE, MR. CROGAN - SOME SILENCE, THAT THEY MIGHT CONTINUE.
SOME AMERICANS -
FARMERS, BUT **ARMED** -
- ARRIVED AS WE MADE LEAVE. IT NEARLY CAME TO A **FIGHT,** ALL RIFLES READY TO MAKE SPRING.
THEY THOUGHT **WE** WERE RESPONSIBLE FOR THE KILLINGS!
AND YOU CONVINCED THEM OTHER-WISE?
A RARE DIPLOMACY!
WE DIDN'T **HAVE** TO, SIR.
THE...
...**CONDITION**... OF THE VICTIMS WAS PROOF OF OUR INNOCENCE.
HOW SO?

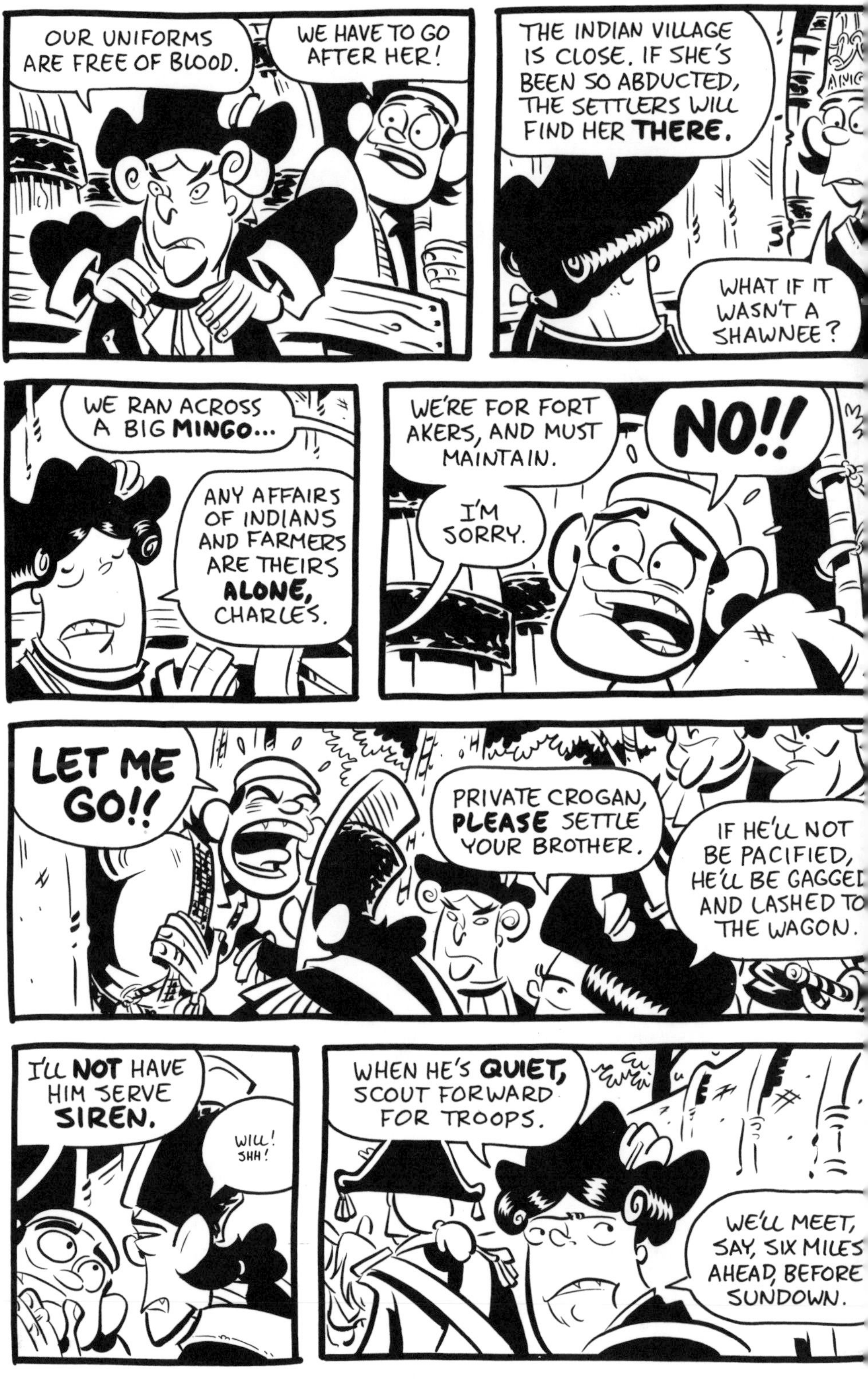
OUR UNIFORMS ARE FREE OF BLOOD.
WE HAVE TO GO AFTER HER!
THE INDIAN VILLAGE IS CLOSE. IF SHE'S BEEN SO ABDUCTED, THE SETTLERS WILL FIND HER THERE.
WHAT IF IT WASN'T A SHAWNEE?
WE RAN ACROSS A BIG MINGO...
ANY AFFAIRS OF INDIANS AND FARMERS ARE THEIRS ALONE, CHARLES.
WE'RE FOR FORT AKERS, AND MUST MAINTAIN.
I'M SORRY.
NO!!
LET ME GO!!
PRIVATE CROGAN, PLEASE SETTLE YOUR BROTHER.
IF HE'LL NOT BE PACIFIED, HE'LL BE GAGGED AND LASHED TO THE WAGON.
I'LL NOT HAVE HIM SERVE SIREN.
WILL! SHH!
WHEN HE'S QUIET, SCOUT FORWARD FOR TROOPS.
WE'LL MEET, SAY, SIX MILES AHEAD, BEFORE SUNDOWN.

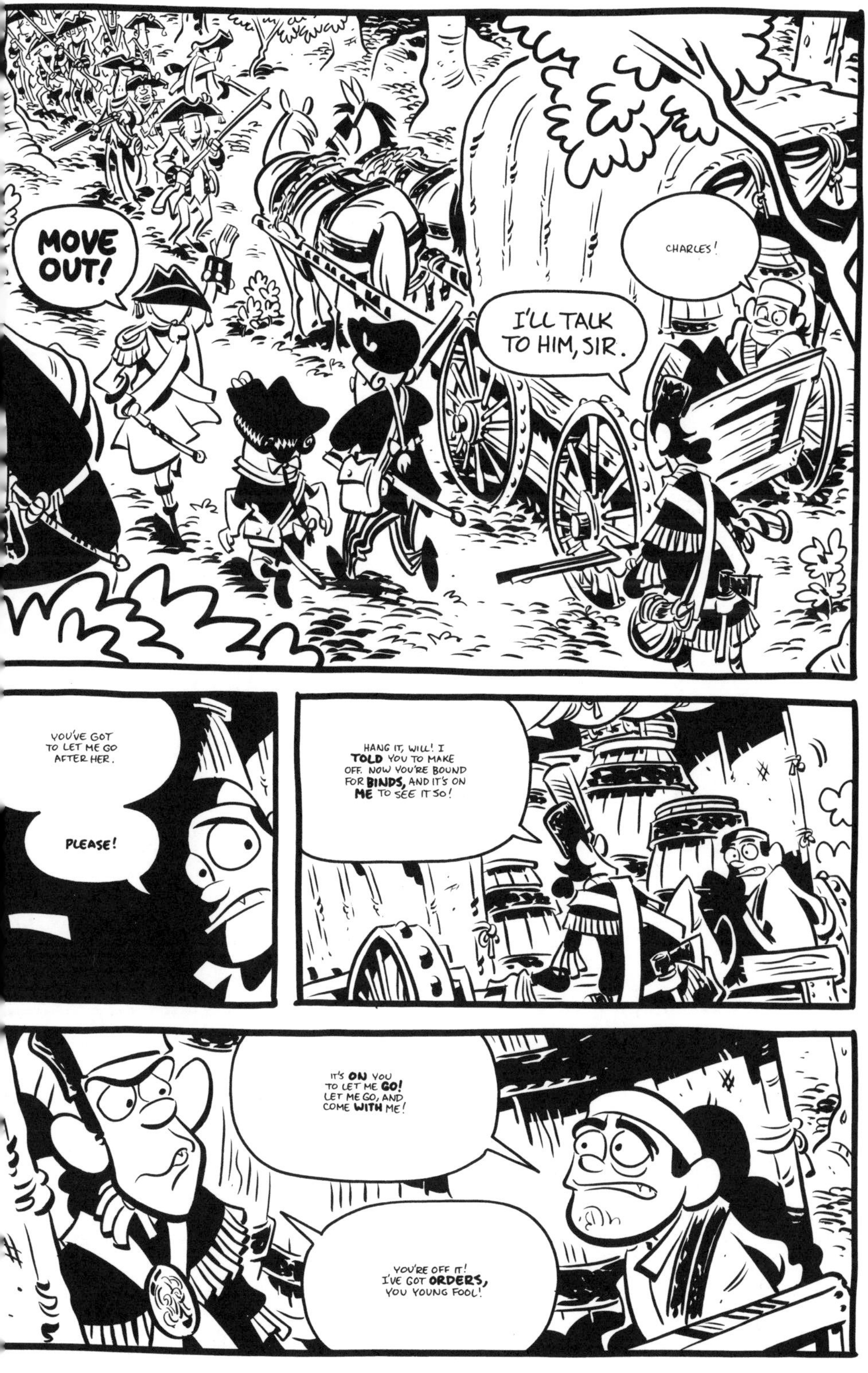
MOVE OUT!
CHARLES!
I'LL TALK TO HIM, SIR.
YOU'VE GOT TO LET ME GO AFTER HER.
PLEASE!
HANG IT, WILL! I TOLD YOU TO MAKE OFF. NOW YOU'RE BOUND FOR BINDS, AND IT'S ON ME TO SEE IT SO!
IT'S ON YOU TO LET ME GO! LET ME GO, AND COME WITH ME!
YOU'RE OFF IT! I'VE GOT ORDERS, YOU YOUNG FOOL!

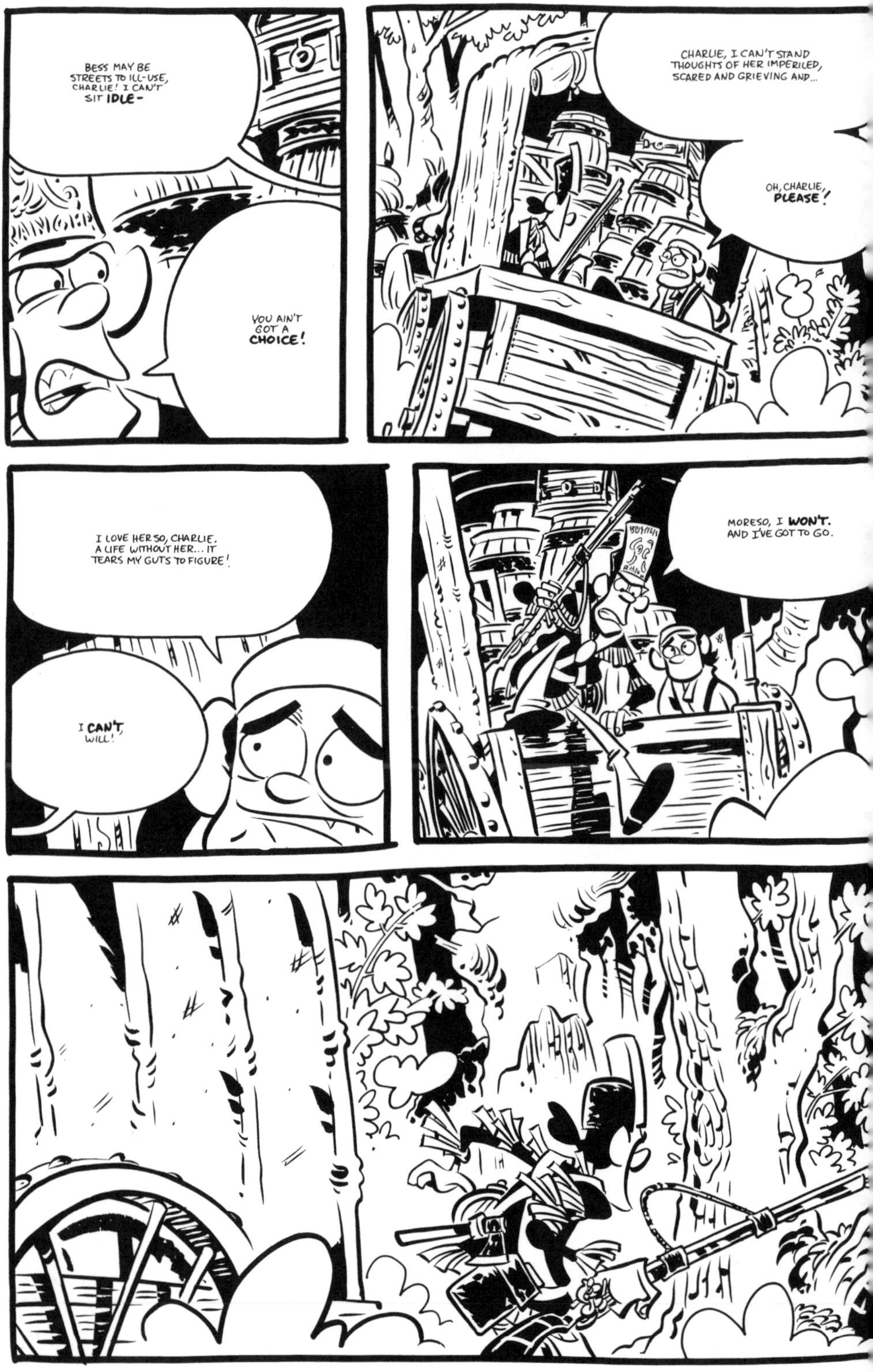
BESS MAY BE STREETS TO ILL-USE, CHARLIE! I CAN'T SIT IDLE-
YOU AIN'T GOT A CHOICE!
CHARLIE, I CAN'T STAND THOUGHTS OF HER IMPERILED, SCARED AND GRIEVING AND...
OH, CHARLIE, PLEASE!
I LOVE HER SO, CHARLIE. A LIFE WITHOUT HER... IT TEARS MY GUTS TO FIGURE!
I CAN'T, WILL!
MORESO, I WON'T. AND I'VE GOT TO GO.

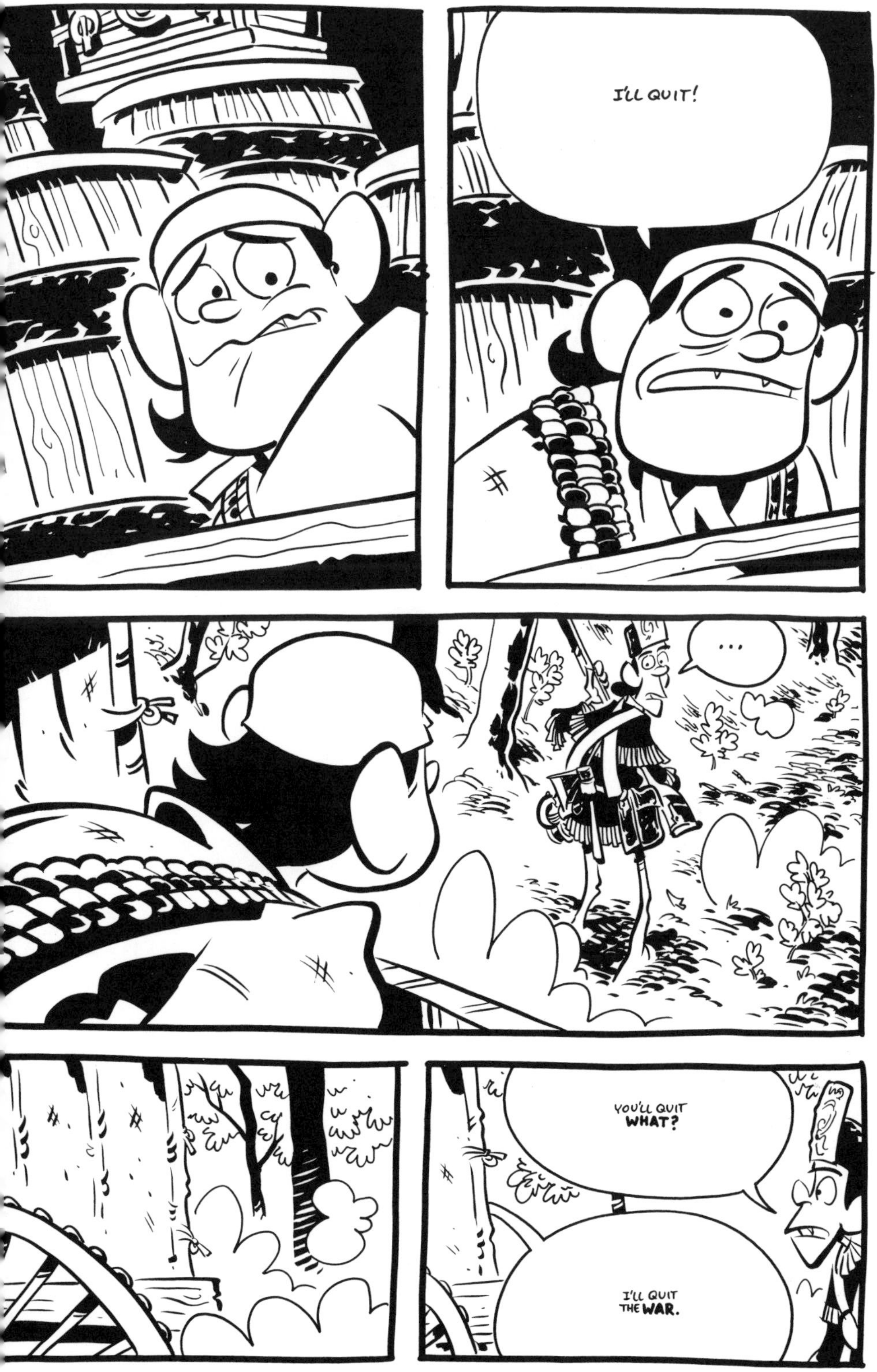
I'LL QUIT!
...
YOU'LL QUIT WHAT?
I'LL QUIT THE WAR.

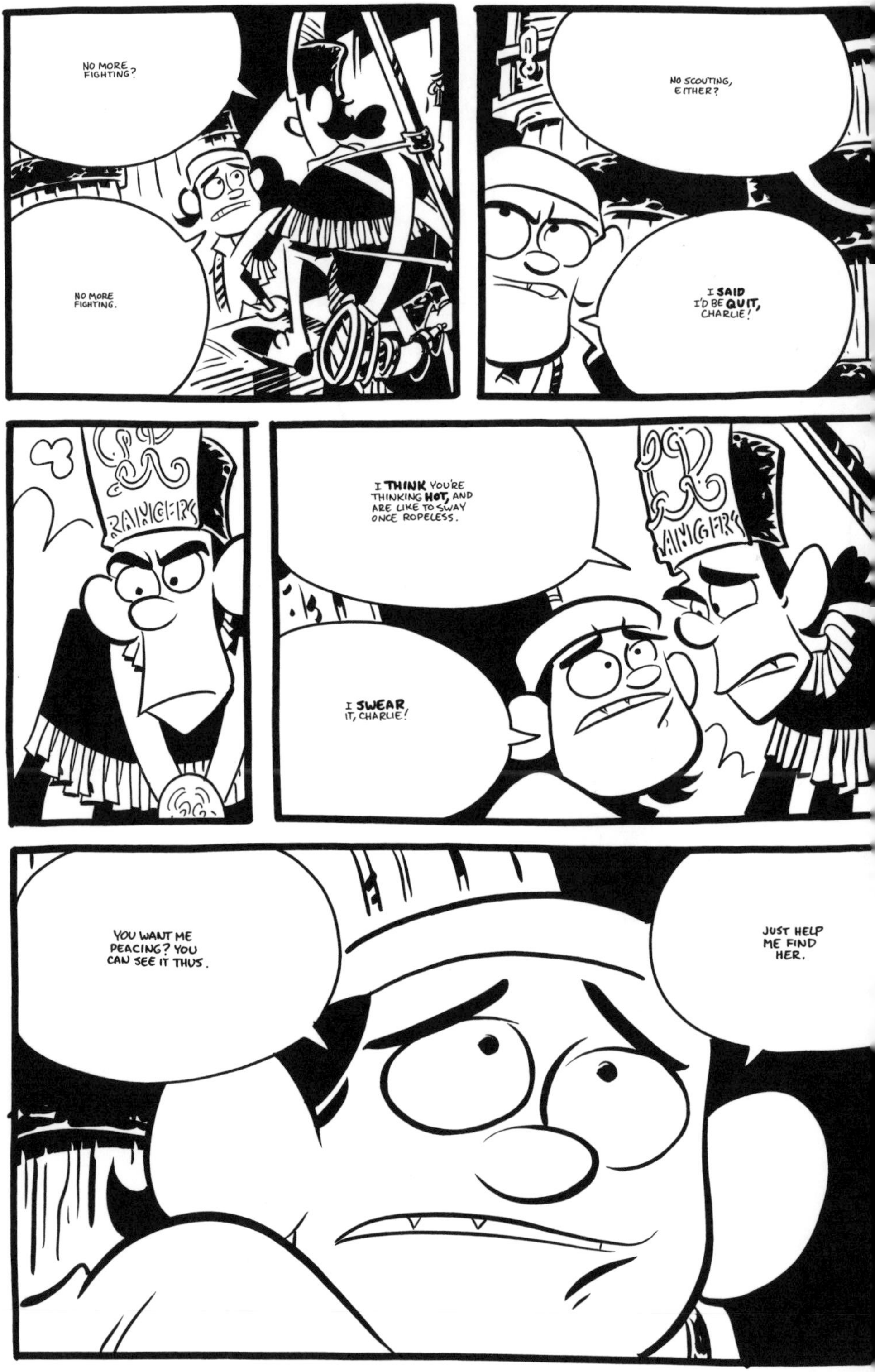
NO MORE FIGHTING?
NO MORE FIGHTING.
NO SCOUTING, EITHER?
I SAID I'D BE QUIT, CHARLIE!
I THINK YOU'RE THINKING HOT, AND ARE LIKE TO SWAY ONCE ROPELESS.
I SWEAR IT, CHARLIE!
YOU WANT ME PEACING? YOU CAN SEE IT THUS.
JUST HELP ME FIND HER.

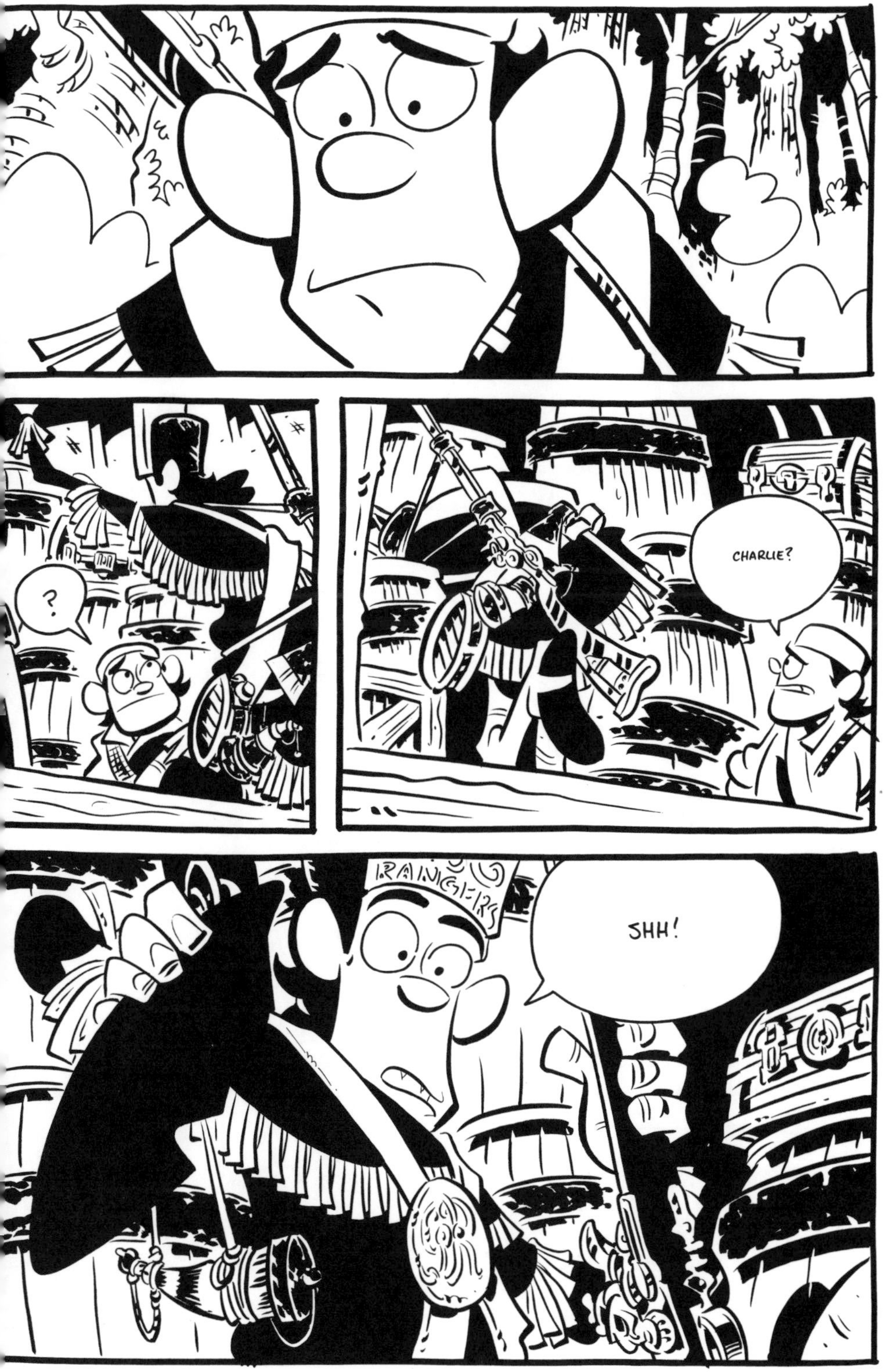
?
CHARLIE?
RANGERS
SHH!

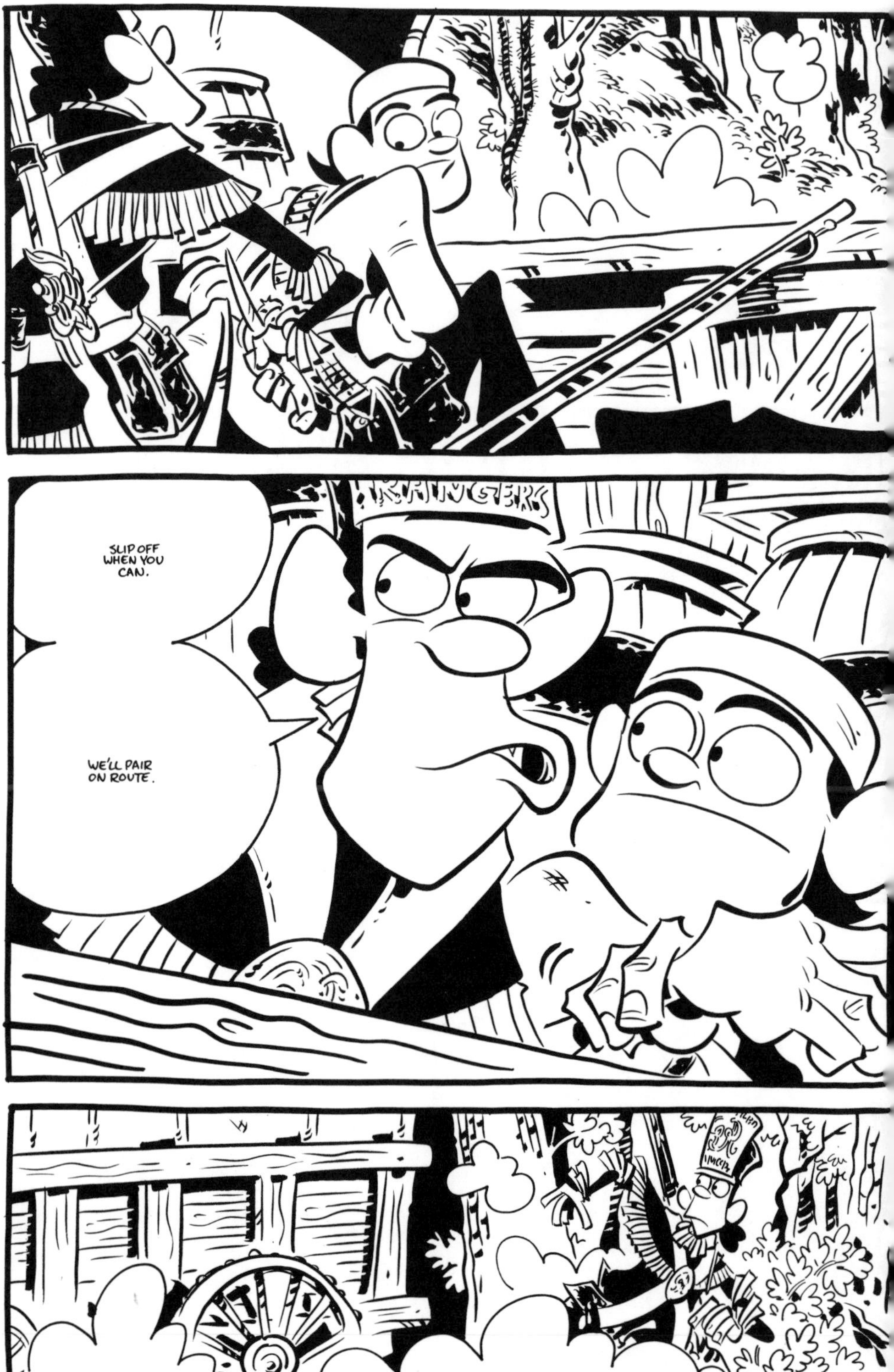
RANGERS
SLIP OFF WHEN YOU CAN.
WE'LL PAIR ON ROUTE.

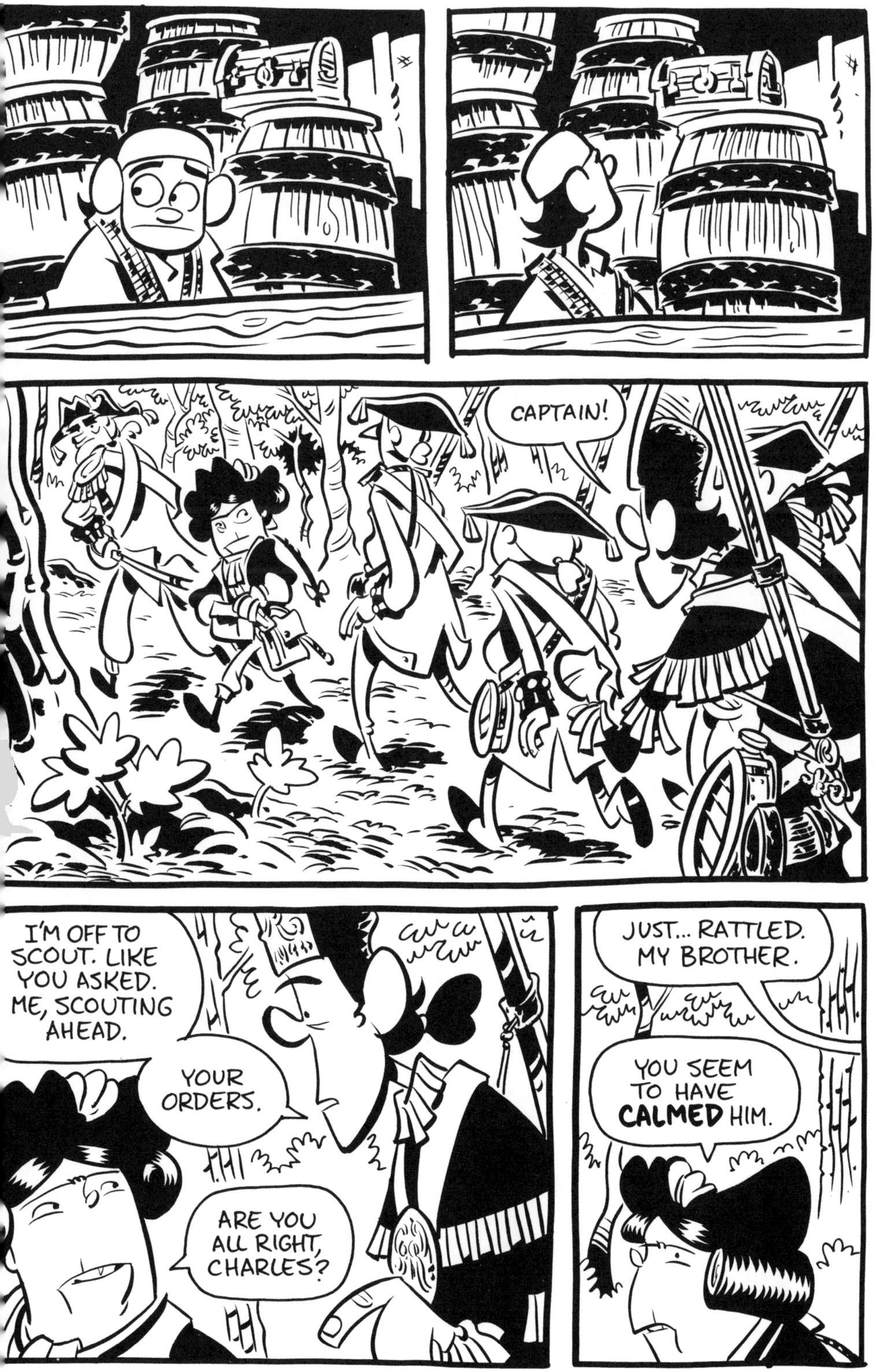
CAPTAIN!
I'M OFF TO SCOUT. LIKE YOU ASKED. ME, SCOUTING AHEAD.
YOUR ORDERS.
ARE YOU ALL RIGHT, CHARLES?
JUST... RATTLED. MY BROTHER.
YOU SEEM TO HAVE CALMED HIM.

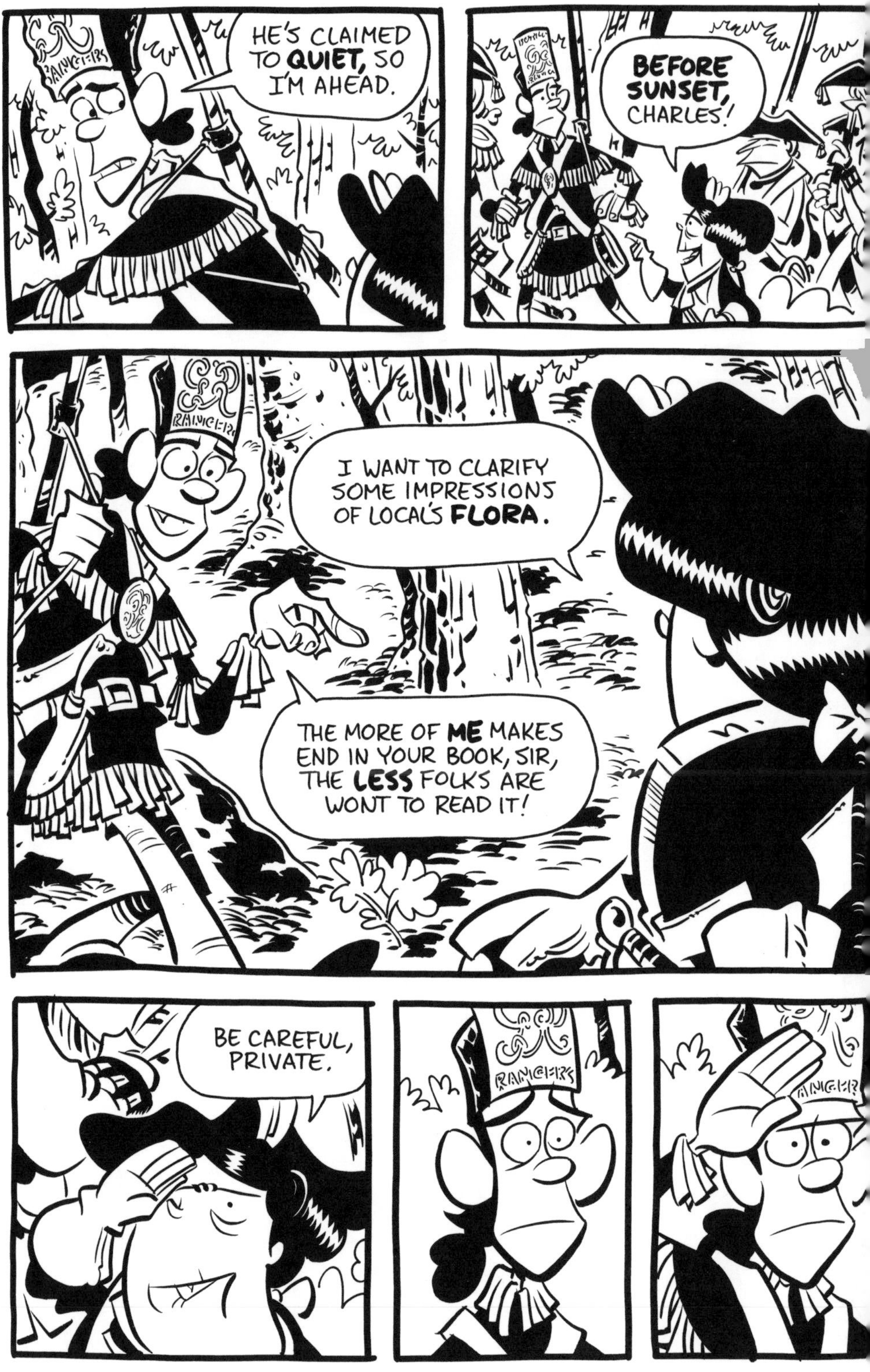
HE'S CLAIMED TO QUIET, SO I'M AHEAD.
BEFORE SUNSET, CHARLES!
I WANT TO CLARIFY SOME IMPRESSIONS OF LOCAL'S FLORA.
THE MORE OF ME MAKES END IN YOUR BOOK, SIR, THE LESS FOLKS ARE WONT TO READ IT!
BE CAREFUL, PRIVATE.

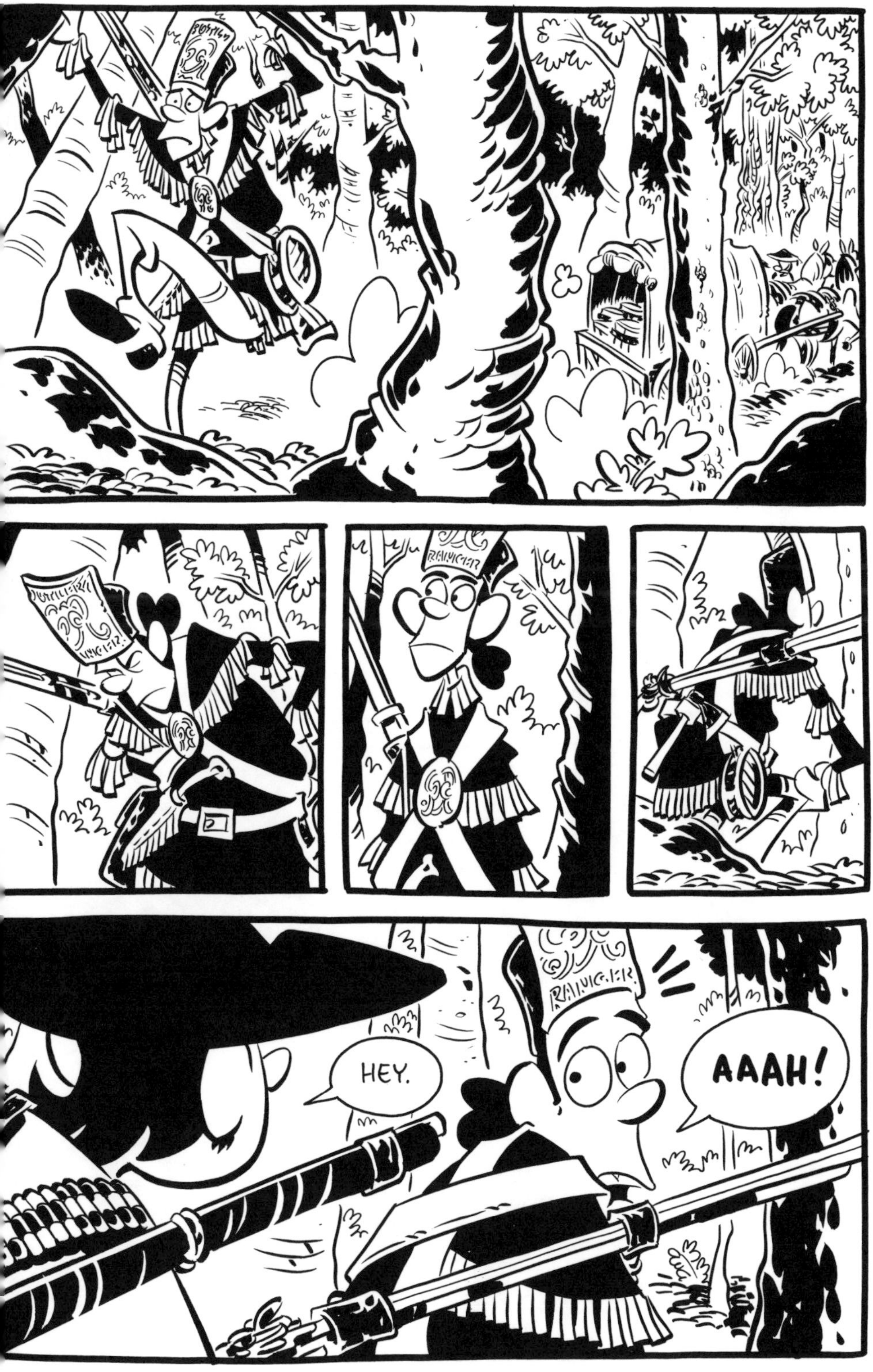
HEY.
AAAH!

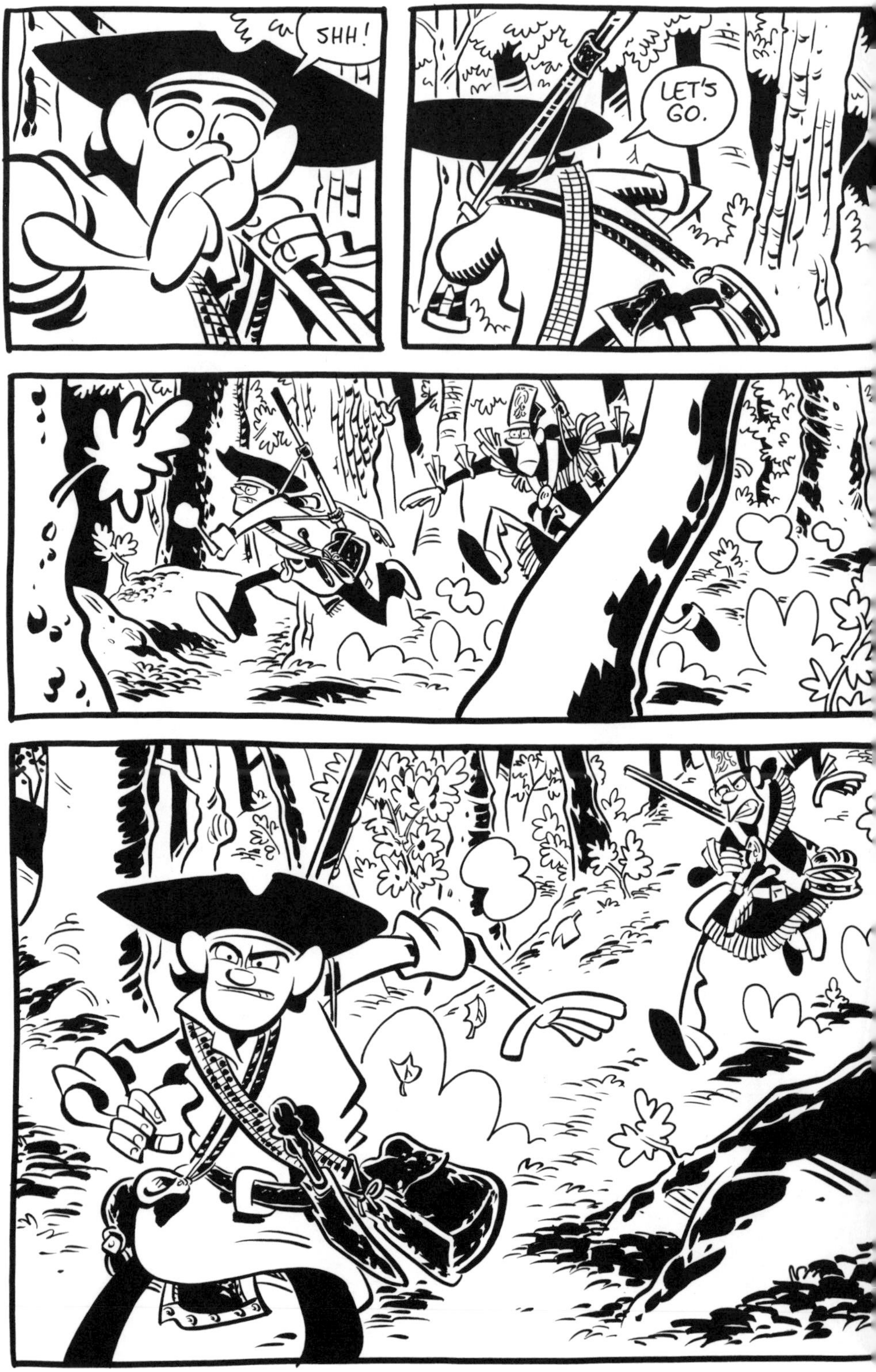
SHH!
LET'S GO.

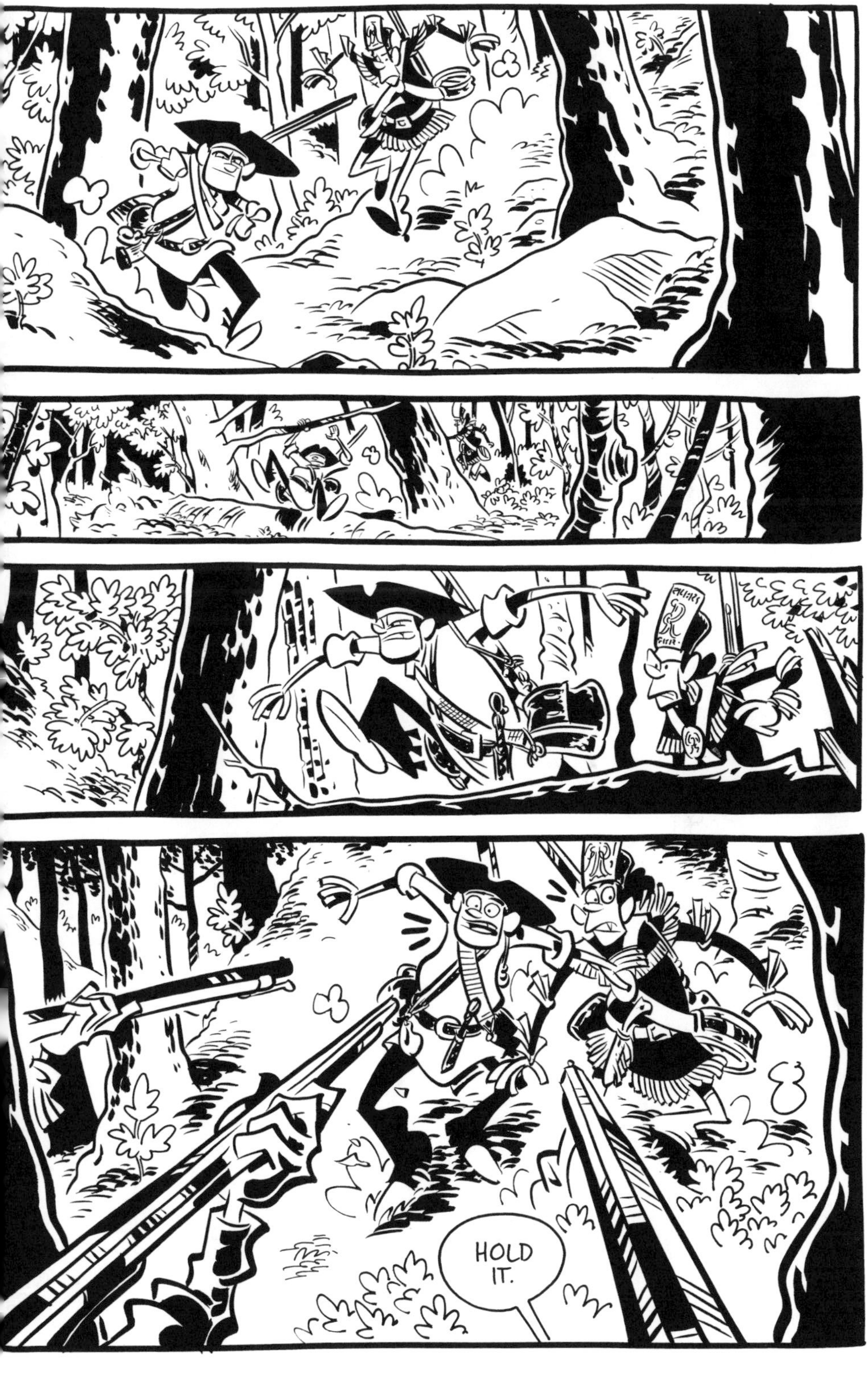
HOLD IT.

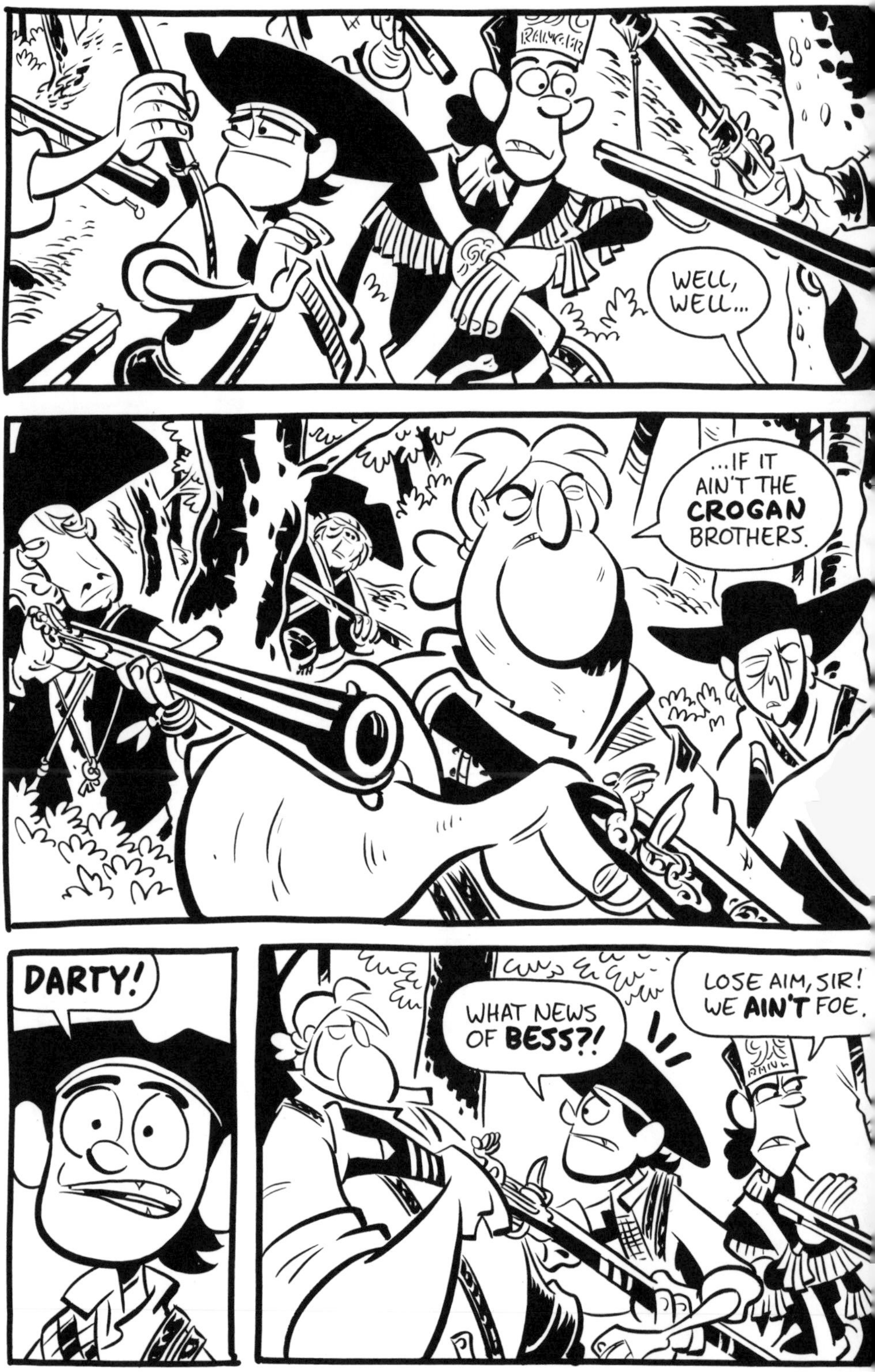
WELL, WELL...
...IF IT AIN'T THE CROGAN BROTHERS.
DARTY!
WHAT NEWS OF BESS?!
LOSE AIM, SIR! WE AIN'T FOE.

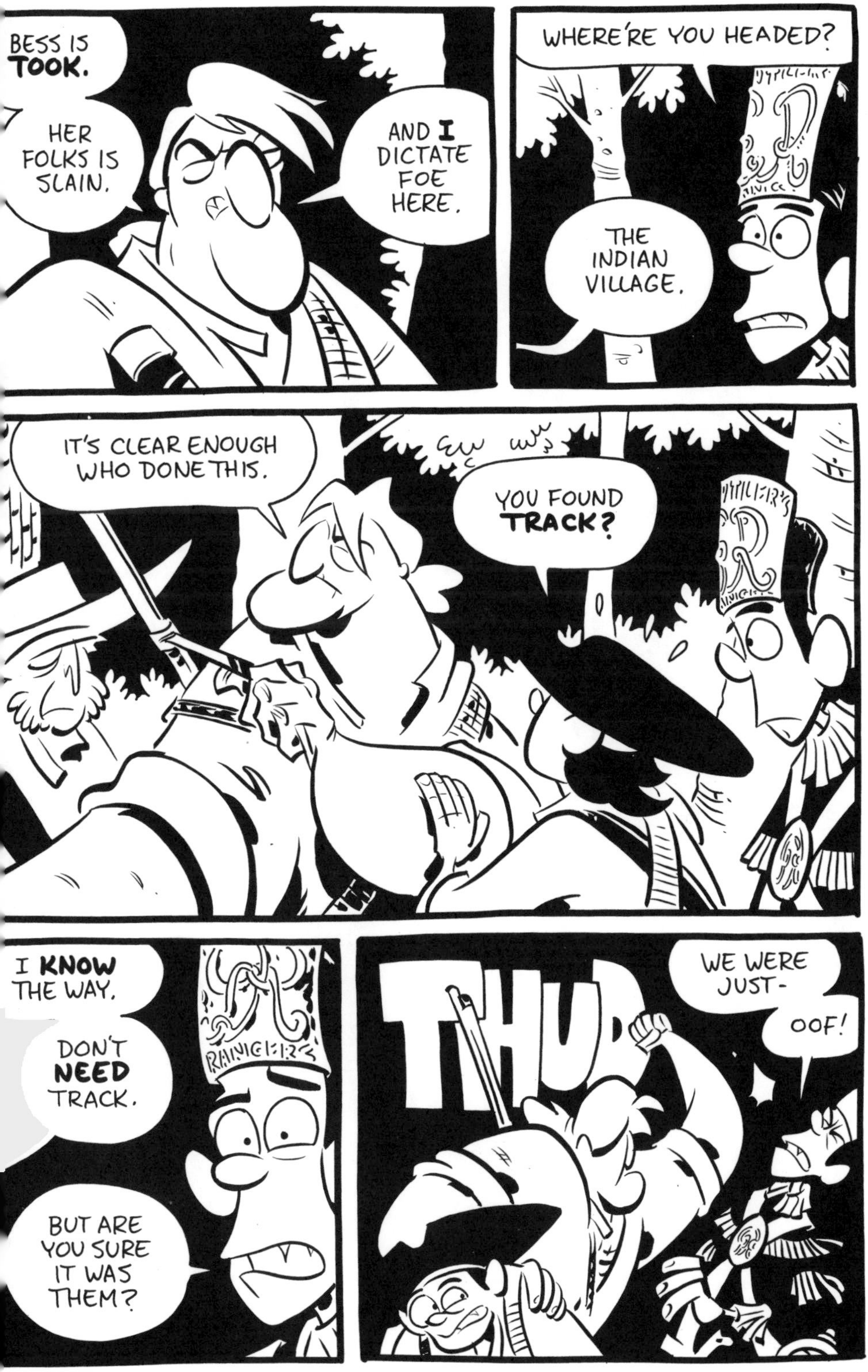
BESS IS **TOOK.**
HER FOLKS IS SLAIN.
AND **I** DICTATE FOE HERE.
WHERE'RE YOU HEADED?
THE INDIAN VILLAGE.
IT'S CLEAR ENOUGH WHO DONE THIS.
YOU FOUND **TRACK?**
I **KNOW** THE WAY.
DON'T **NEED** TRACK.
BUT ARE YOU SURE IT WAS THEM?
THUD
WE WERE JUST-
OOF!

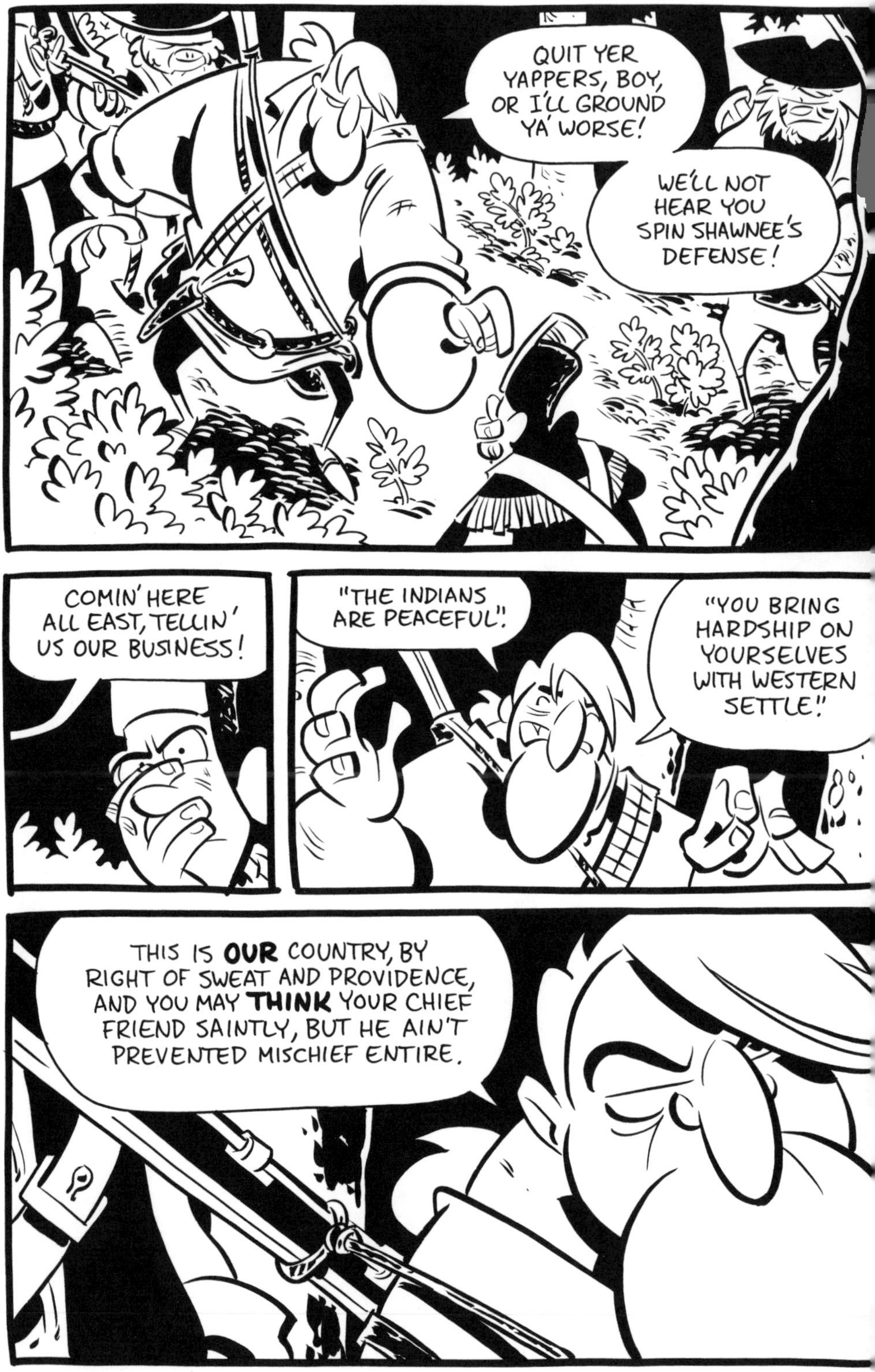
QUIT YER YAPPERS, BOY, OR I'LL GROUND YA' WORSE!
WE'LL NOT HEAR YOU SPIN SHAWNEE'S DEFENSE!
COMIN' HERE ALL EAST, TELLIN' US OUR BUSINESS!
"THE INDIANS ARE PEACEFUL".
"YOU BRING HARDSHIP ON YOURSELVES WITH WESTERN SETTLE".
THIS IS **OUR** COUNTRY, BY RIGHT OF SWEAT AND PROVIDENCE, AND YOU MAY **THINK** YOUR CHIEF FRIEND SAINTLY, BUT HE AIN'T PREVENTED MISCHIEF ENTIRE.

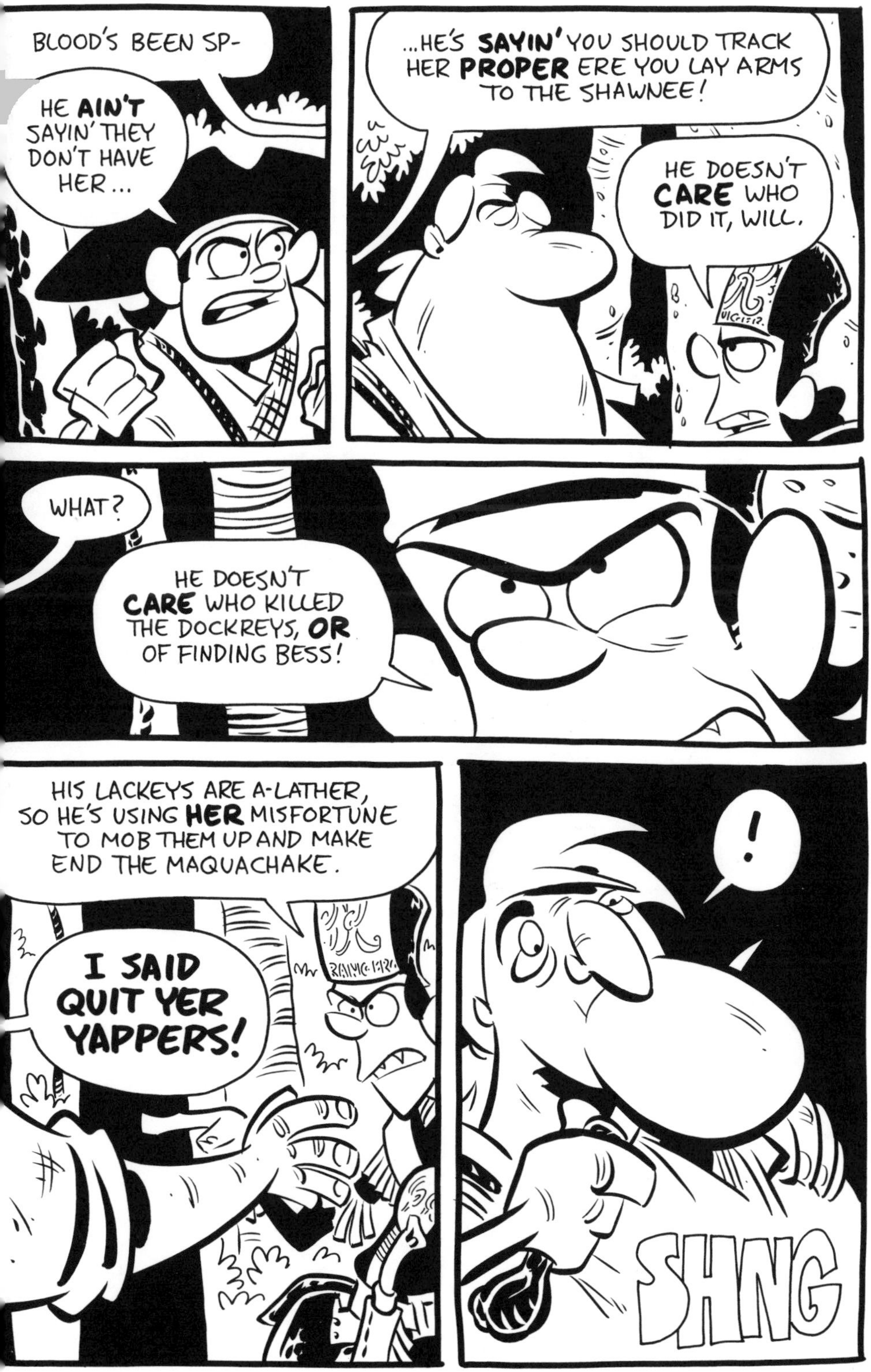
BLOOD'S BEEN SP-
HE **AIN'T** SAYIN' THEY DON'T HAVE HER...
...HE'S **SAYIN'** YOU SHOULD TRACK HER **PROPER** ERE YOU LAY ARMS TO THE SHAWNEE!
HE DOESN'T **CARE** WHO DID IT, WILL.
WHAT?
HE DOESN'T **CARE** WHO KILLED THE DOCKREYS, **OR** OF FINDING BESS!
HIS LACKEYS ARE A-LATHER, SO HE'S USING **HER** MISFORTUNE TO MOB THEM UP AND MAKE END THE MAQUACHAKE.
I SAID QUIT YER YAPPERS!
!
SHNG

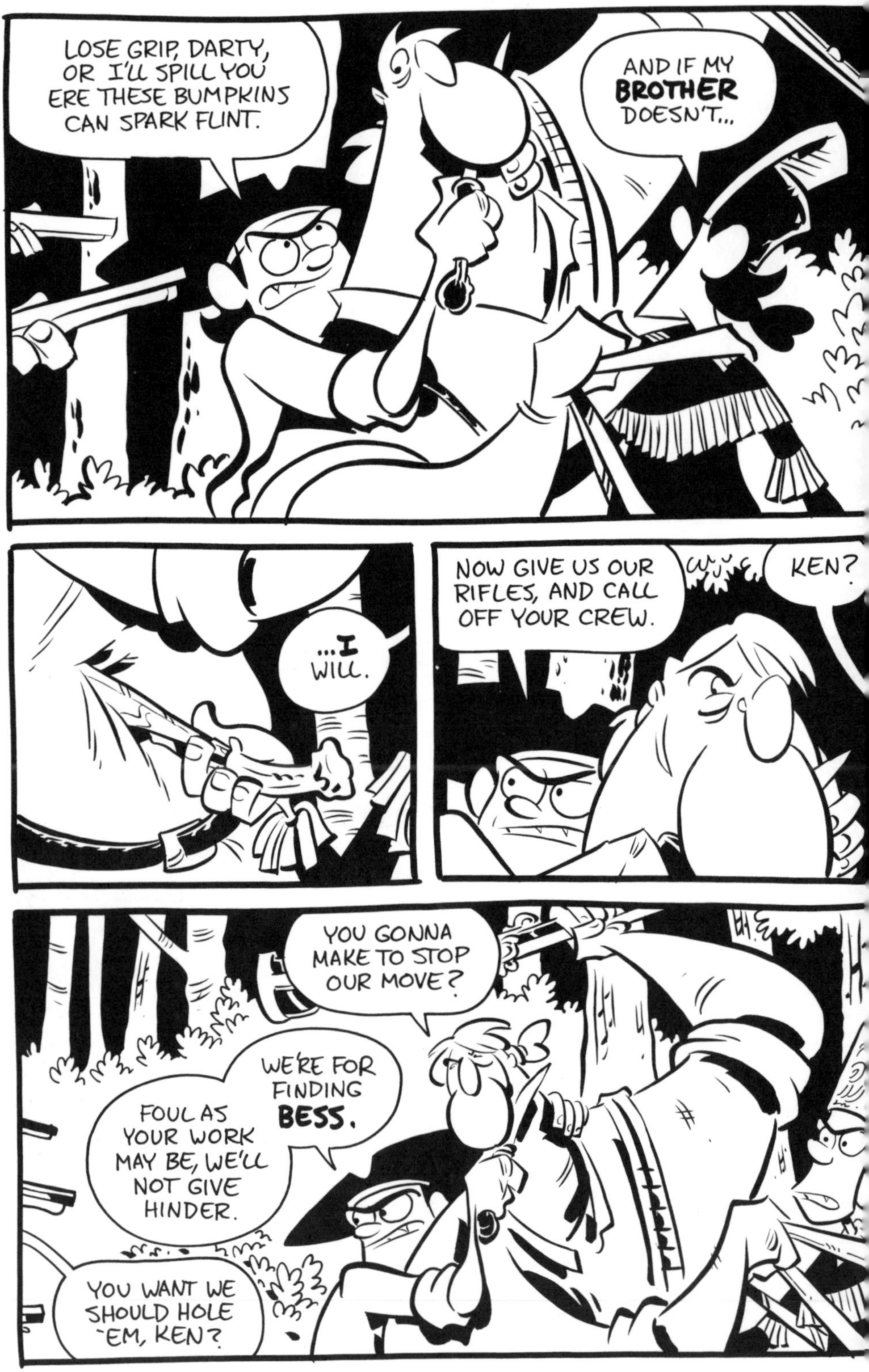
LOSE GRIP, DARTY, OR I'LL SPILL YOU ERE THESE BUMPKINS CAN SPARK FLINT.
AND IF MY **BROTHER** DOESN'T...
...I WILL.
NOW GIVE US OUR RIFLES, AND CALL OFF YOUR CREW.
KEN?
YOU GONNA MAKE TO STOP OUR MOVE?
WE'RE FOR FINDING **BESS.**
FOUL AS YOUR WORK MAY BE, WE'LL NOT GIVE HINDER.
YOU WANT WE SHOULD HOLE 'EM, KEN?

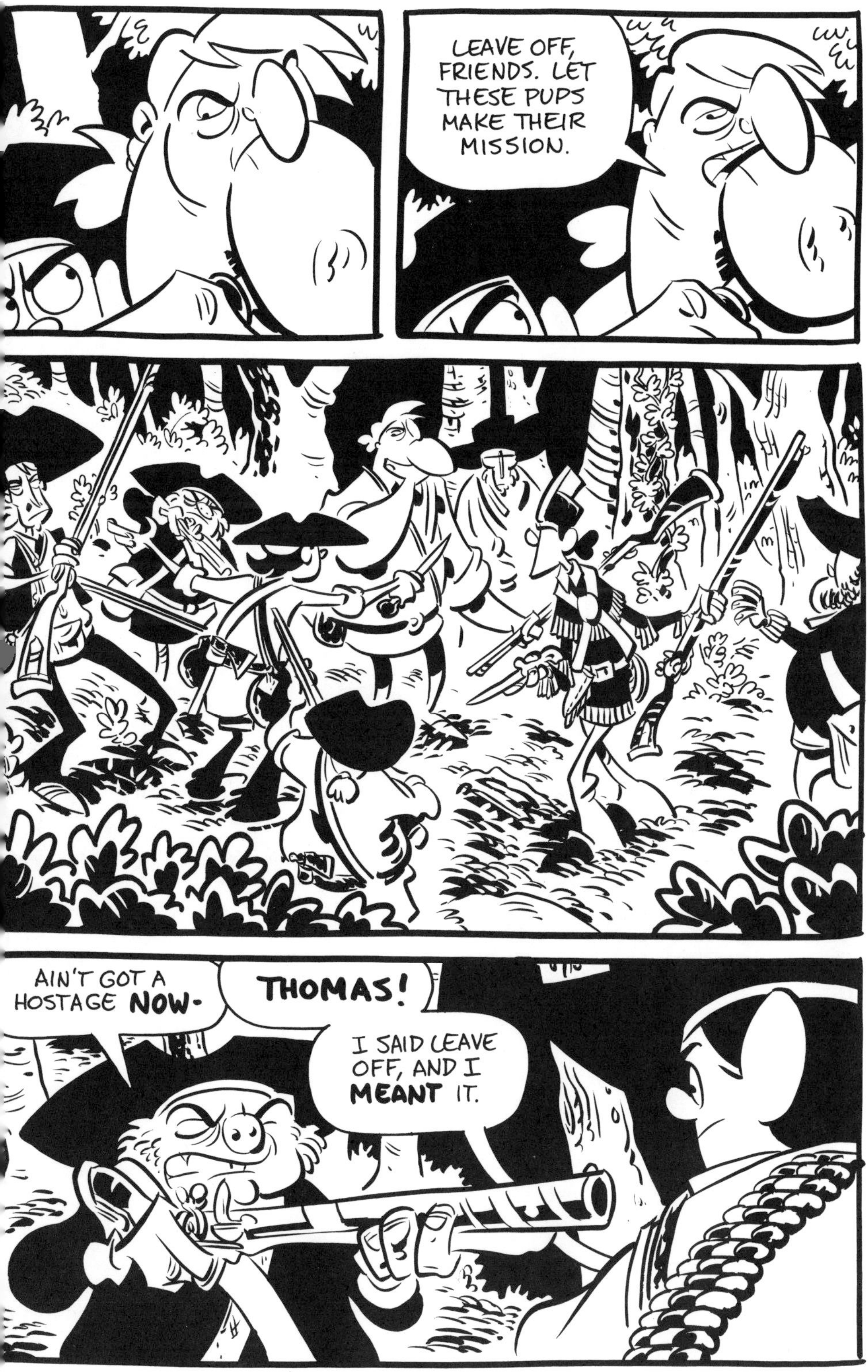
LEAVE OFF, FRIENDS. LET THESE PUPS MAKE THEIR MISSION.
AIN'T GOT A HOSTAGE **NOW**-
THOMAS!
I SAID LEAVE OFF, AND I **MEANT** IT.

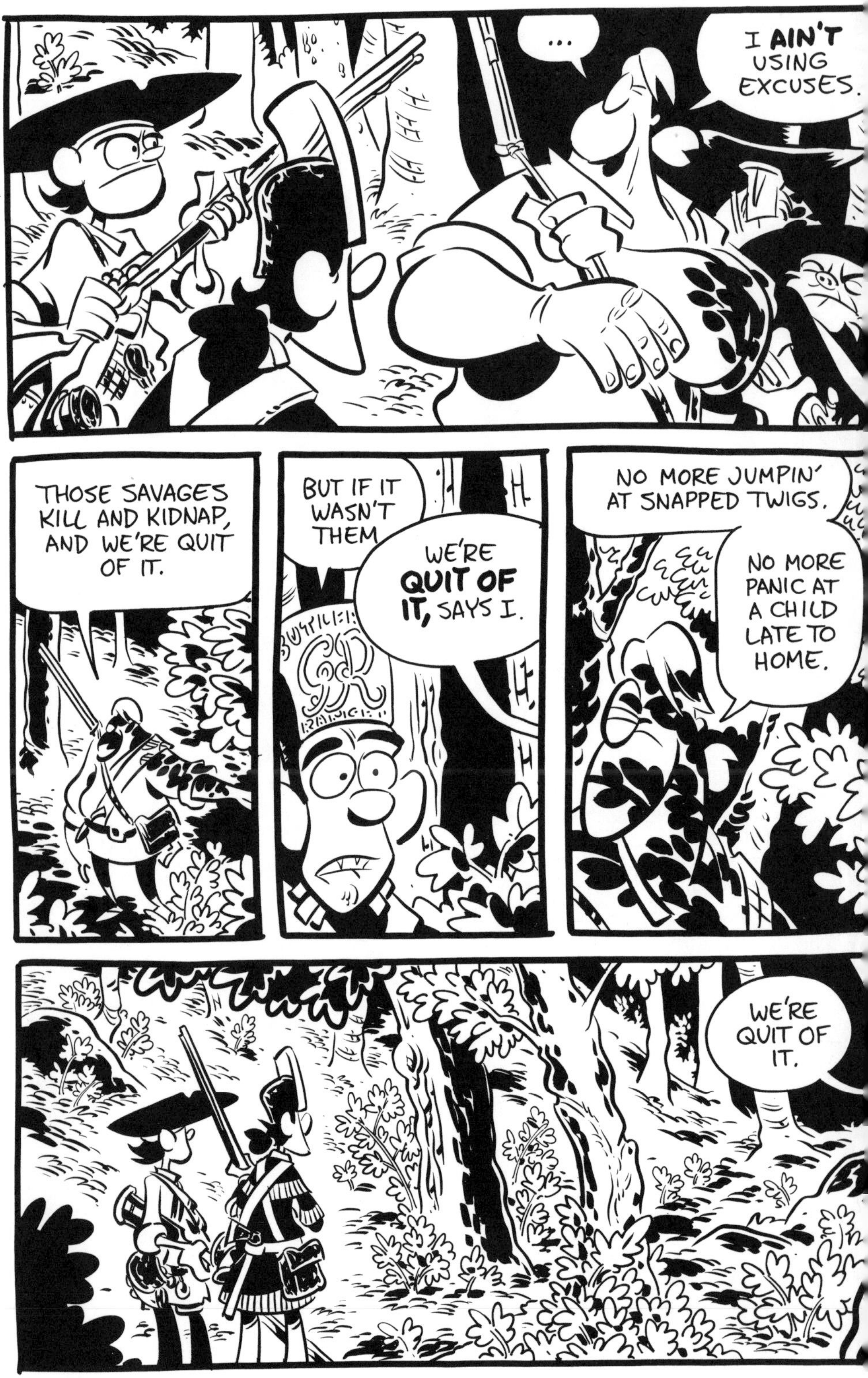
...
I AIN'T USING EXCUSES.
THOSE SAVAGES KILL AND KIDNAP, AND WE'RE QUIT OF IT.
BUT IF IT WASN'T THEM
WE'RE QUIT OF IT, SAYS I.
NO MORE JUMPIN' AT SNAPPED TWIGS.
NO MORE PANIC AT A CHILD LATE TO HOME.
WE'RE QUIT OF IT.

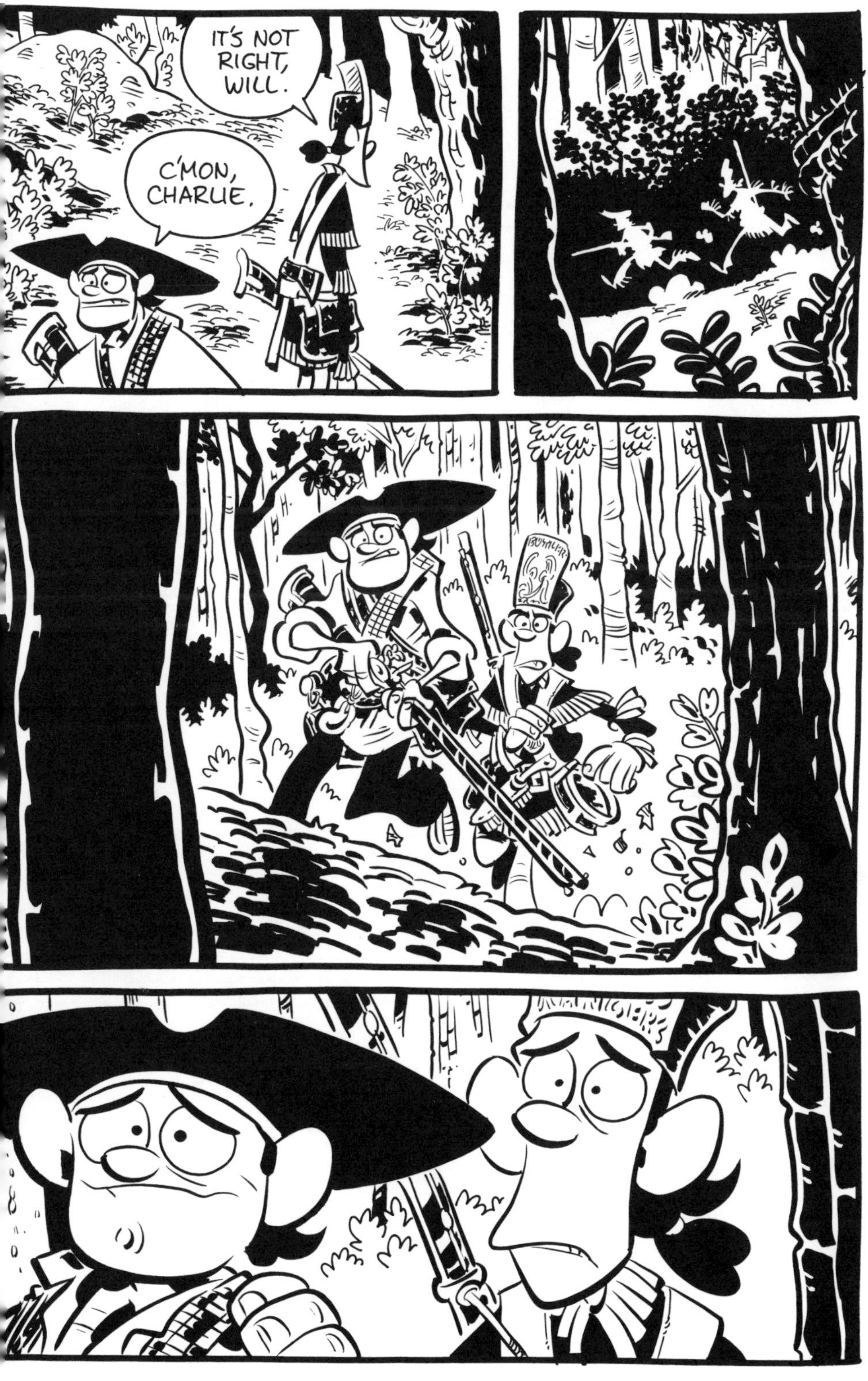
IT'S NOT RIGHT, WILL.
C'MON, CHARLIE.

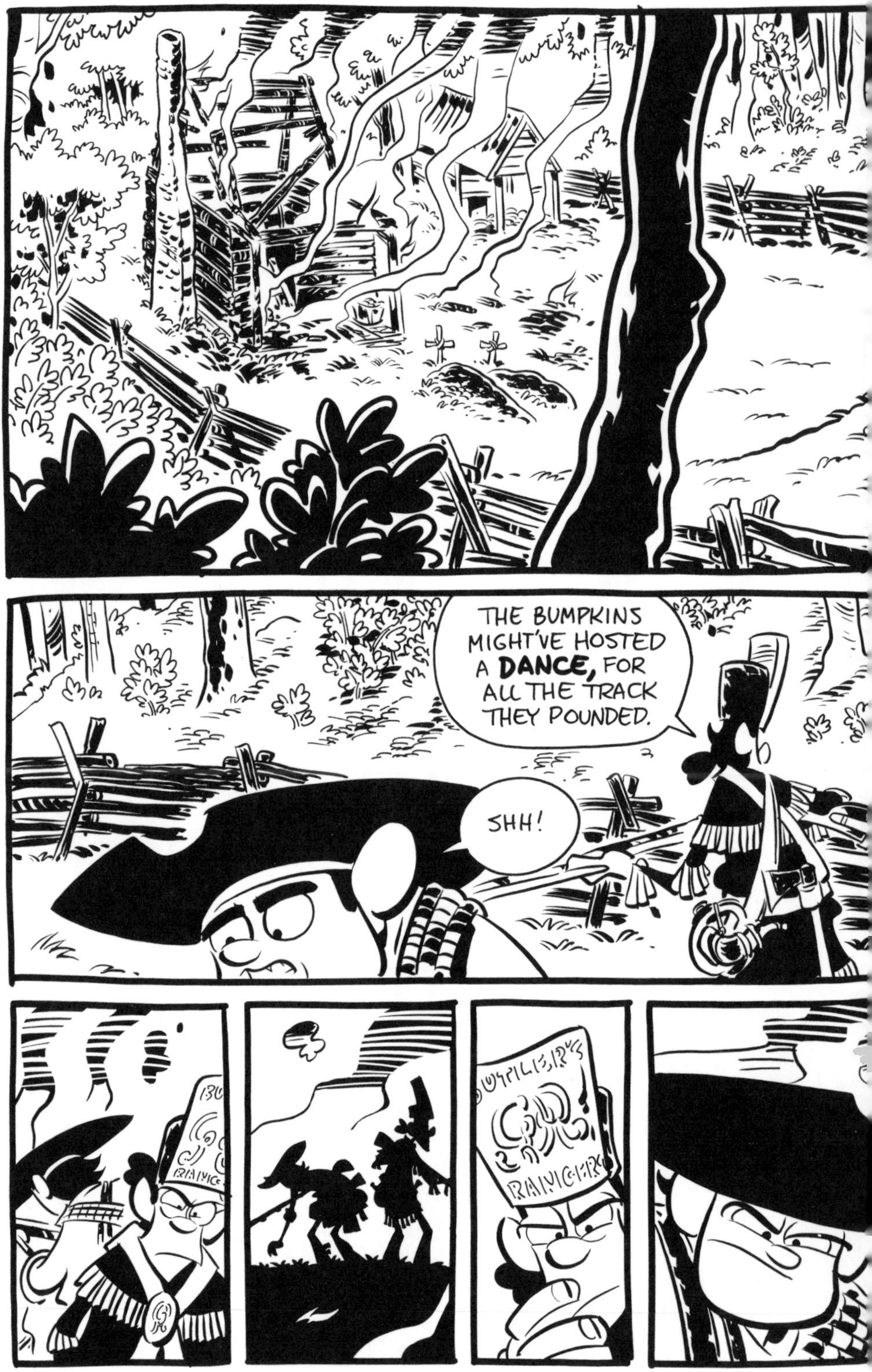
THE BUMPKINS MIGHT'VE HOSTED A **DANCE,** FOR ALL THE TRACK THEY POUNDED.
SHH!

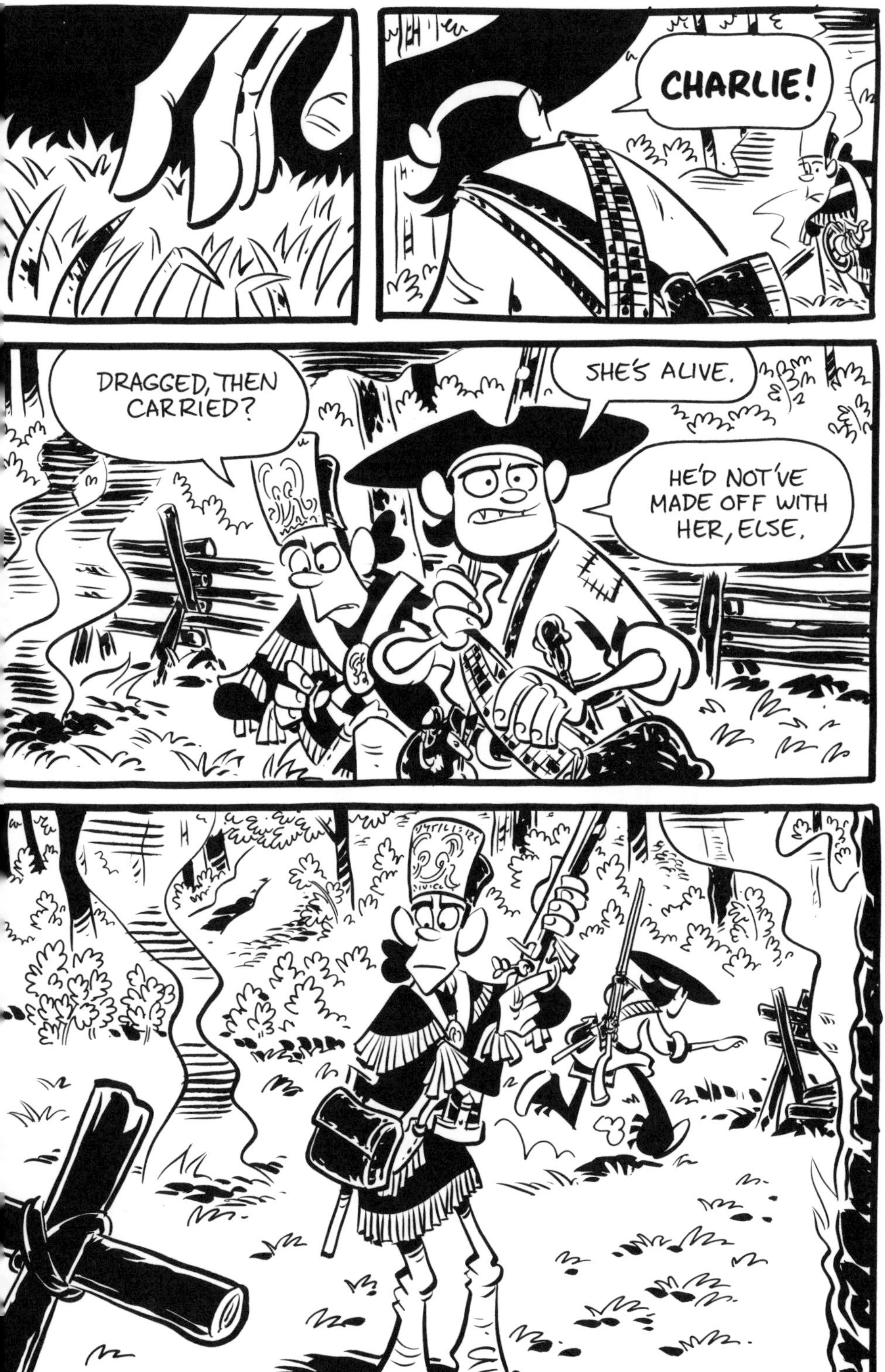
CHARLIE!
DRAGGED, THEN CARRIED?
SHE'S ALIVE.
HE'D NOT'VE MADE OFF WITH HER, ELSE.

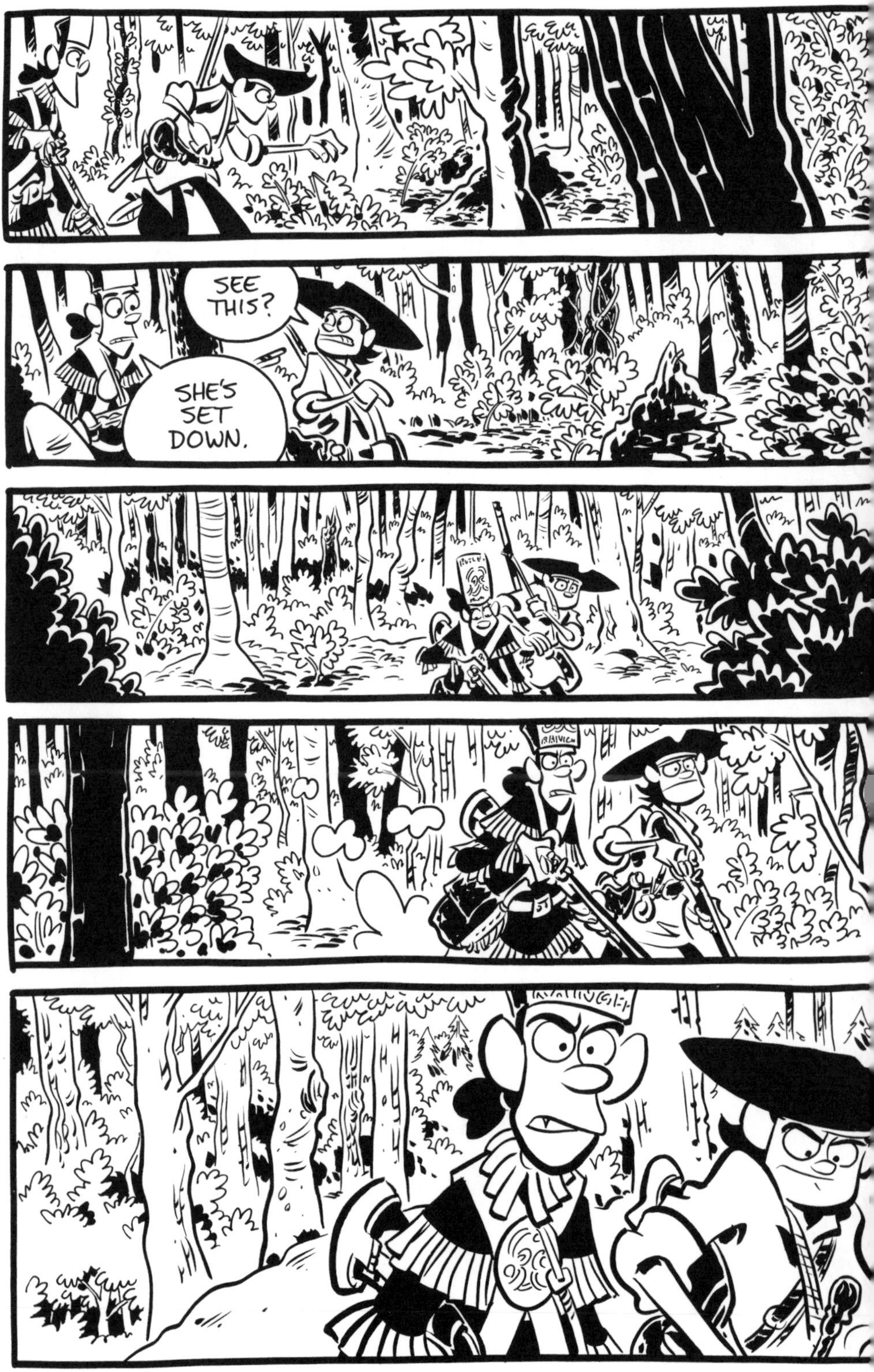
SEE THIS?
SHE'S SET DOWN.

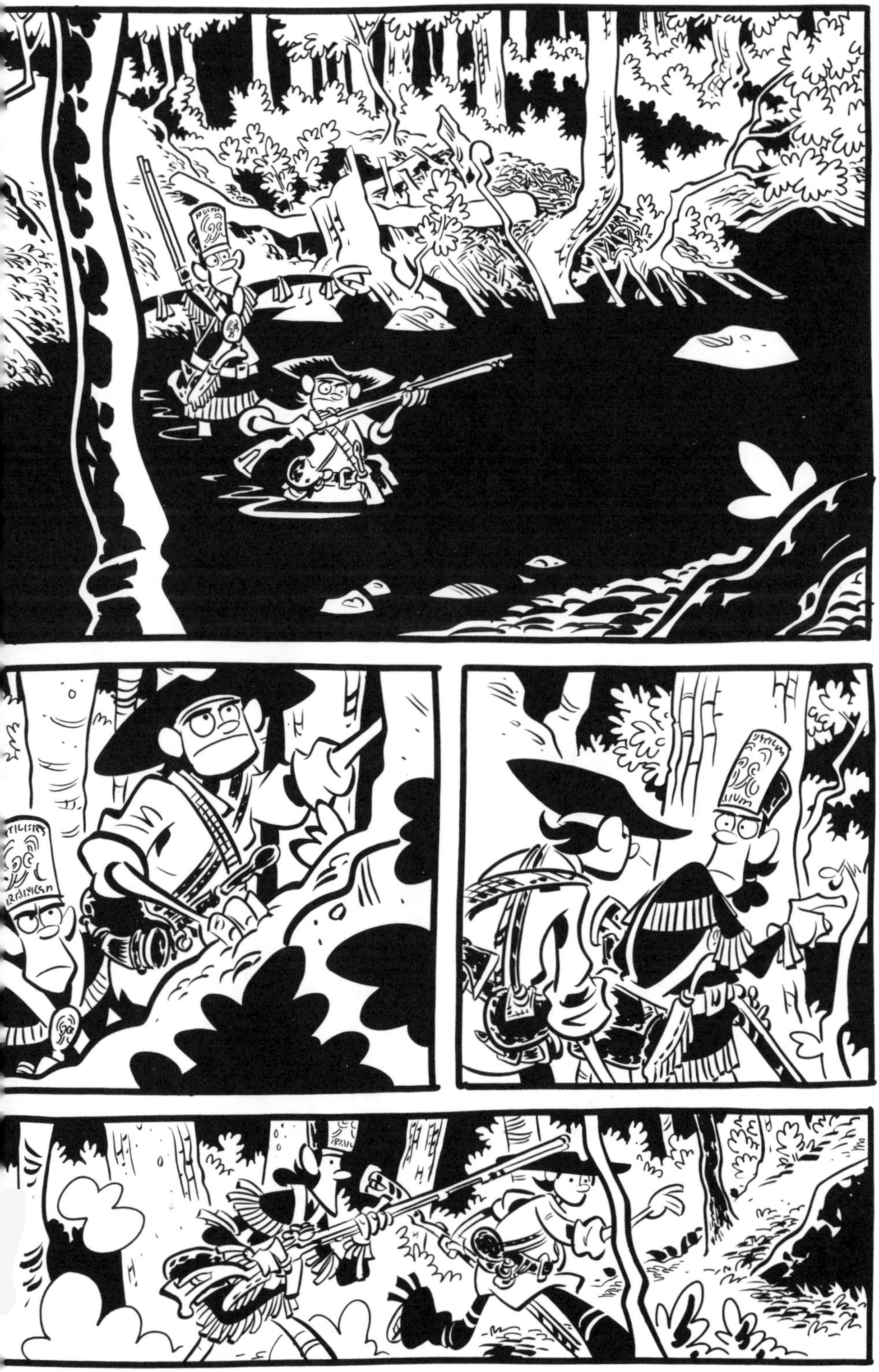

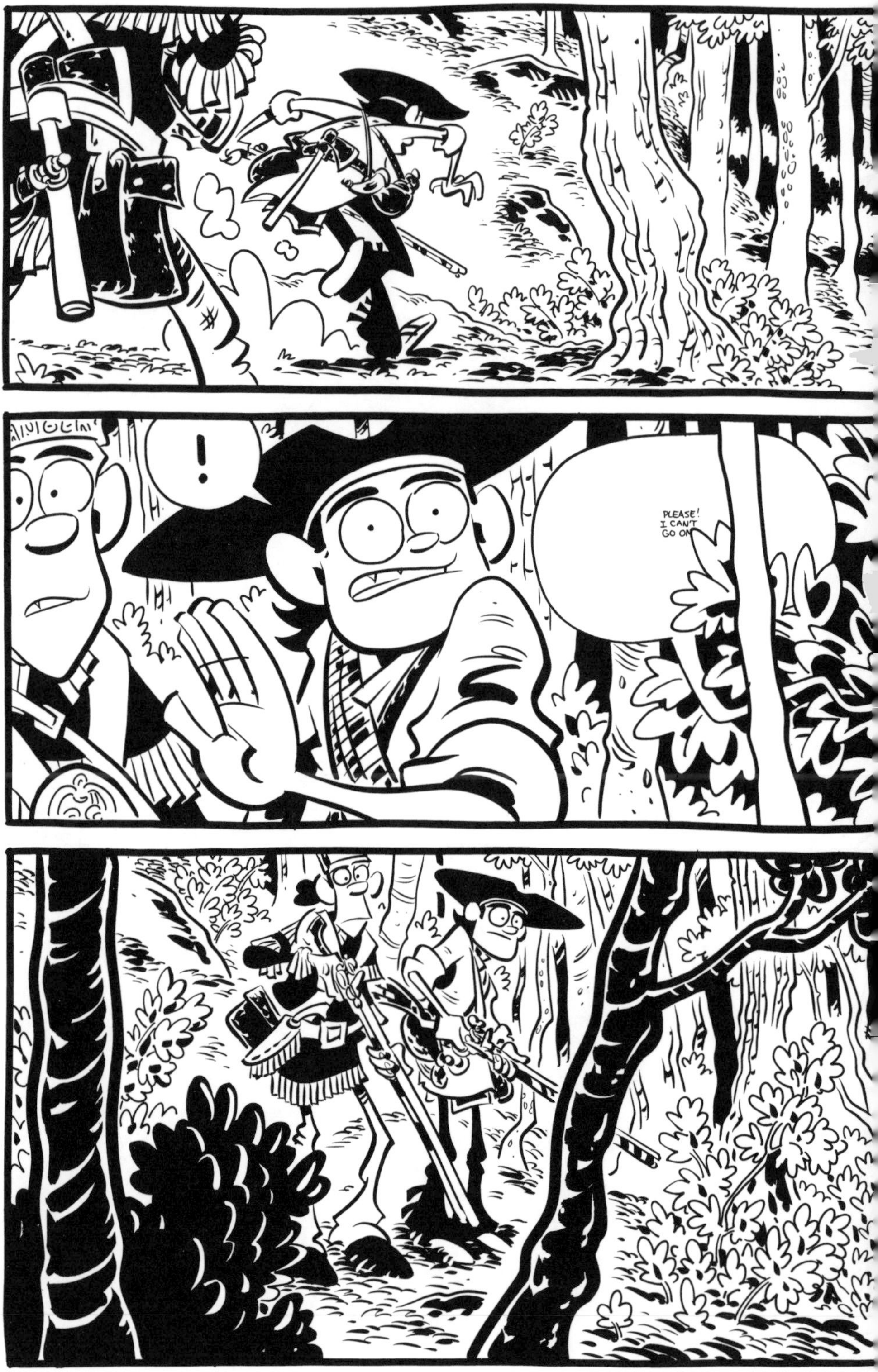
!
PLEASE!
I CAN'T
GO ON

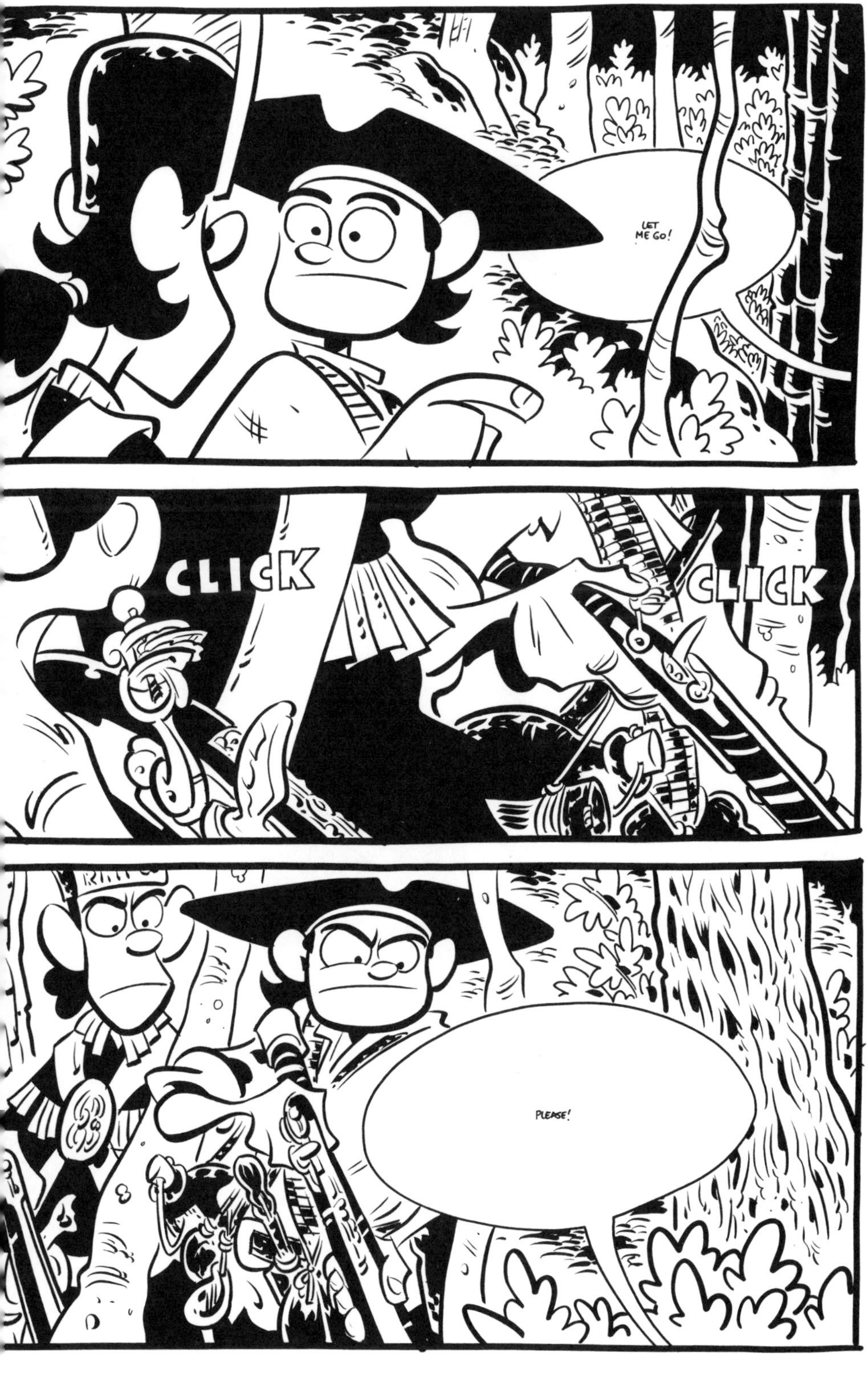
LET ME GO!
CLICK
CLICK
PLEASE!

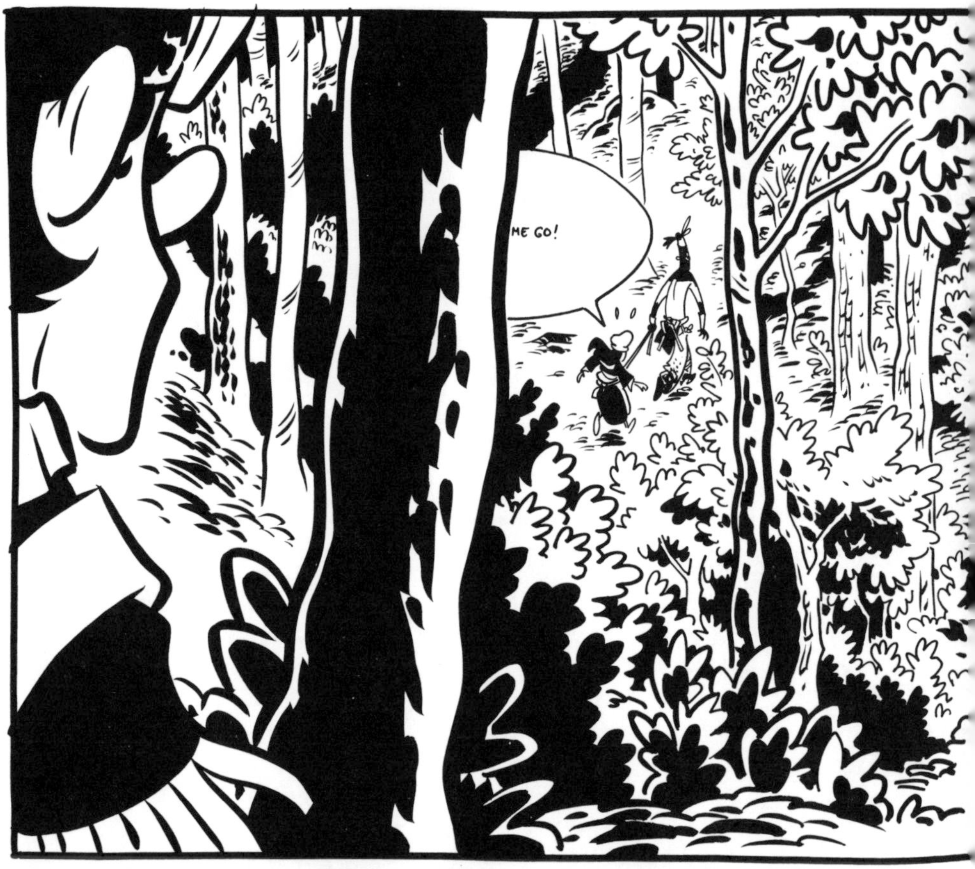
ME GO!

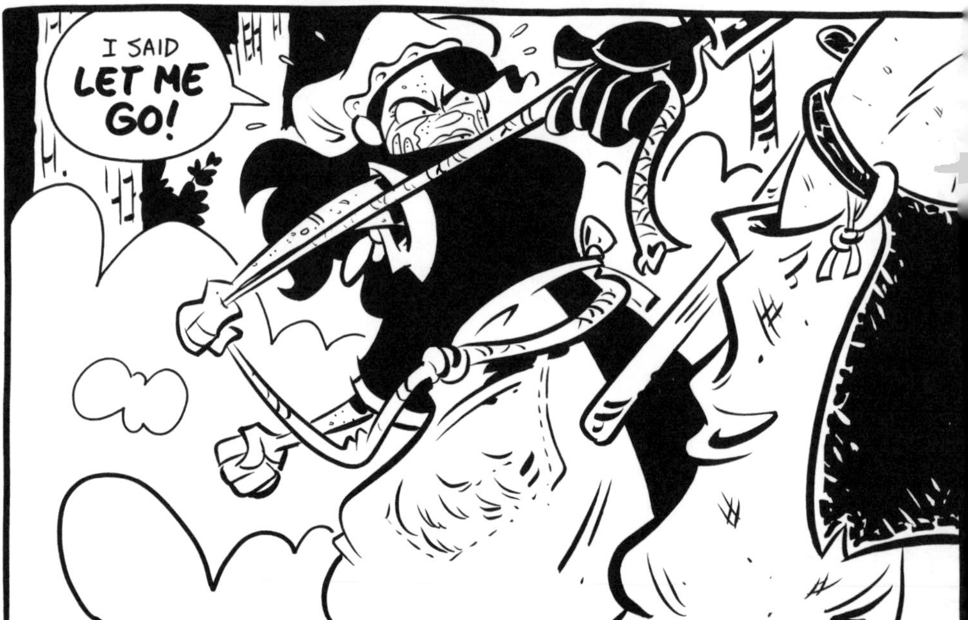
I SAID LET ME GO!

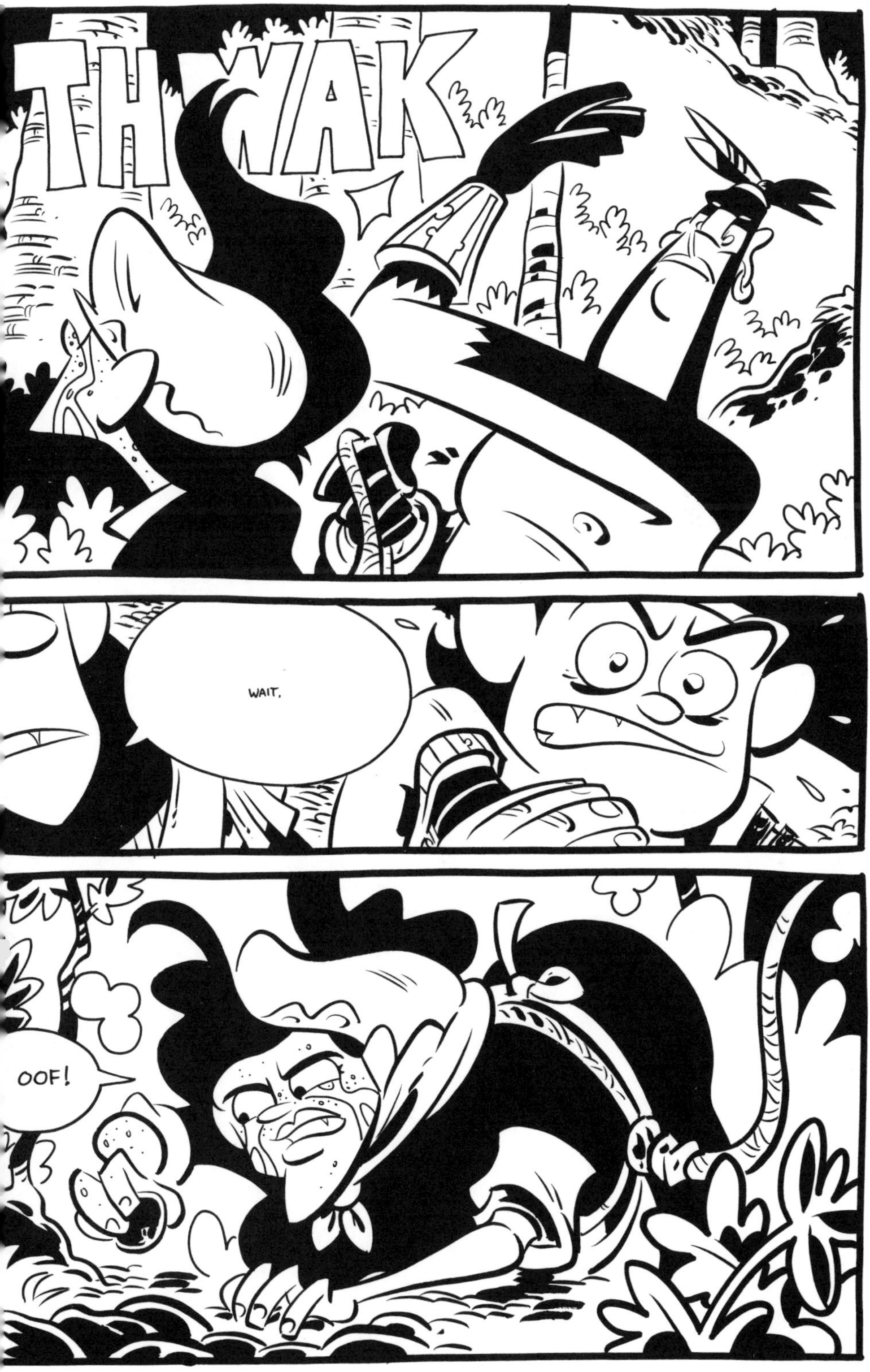
THWAK
WAIT.
OOF!

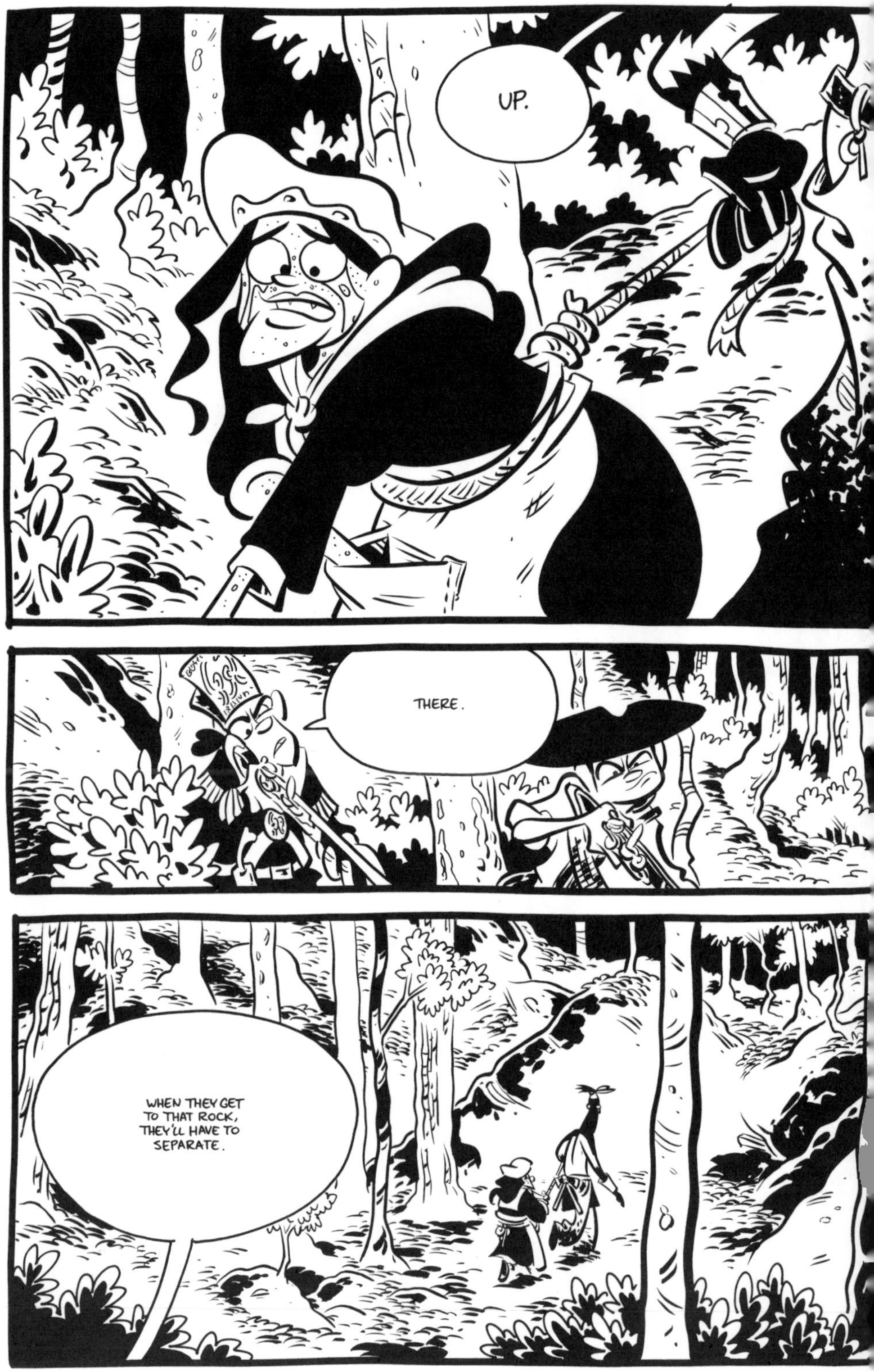
UP.
THERE.
WHEN THEY GET TO THAT ROCK, THEY'LL HAVE TO SEPARATE.

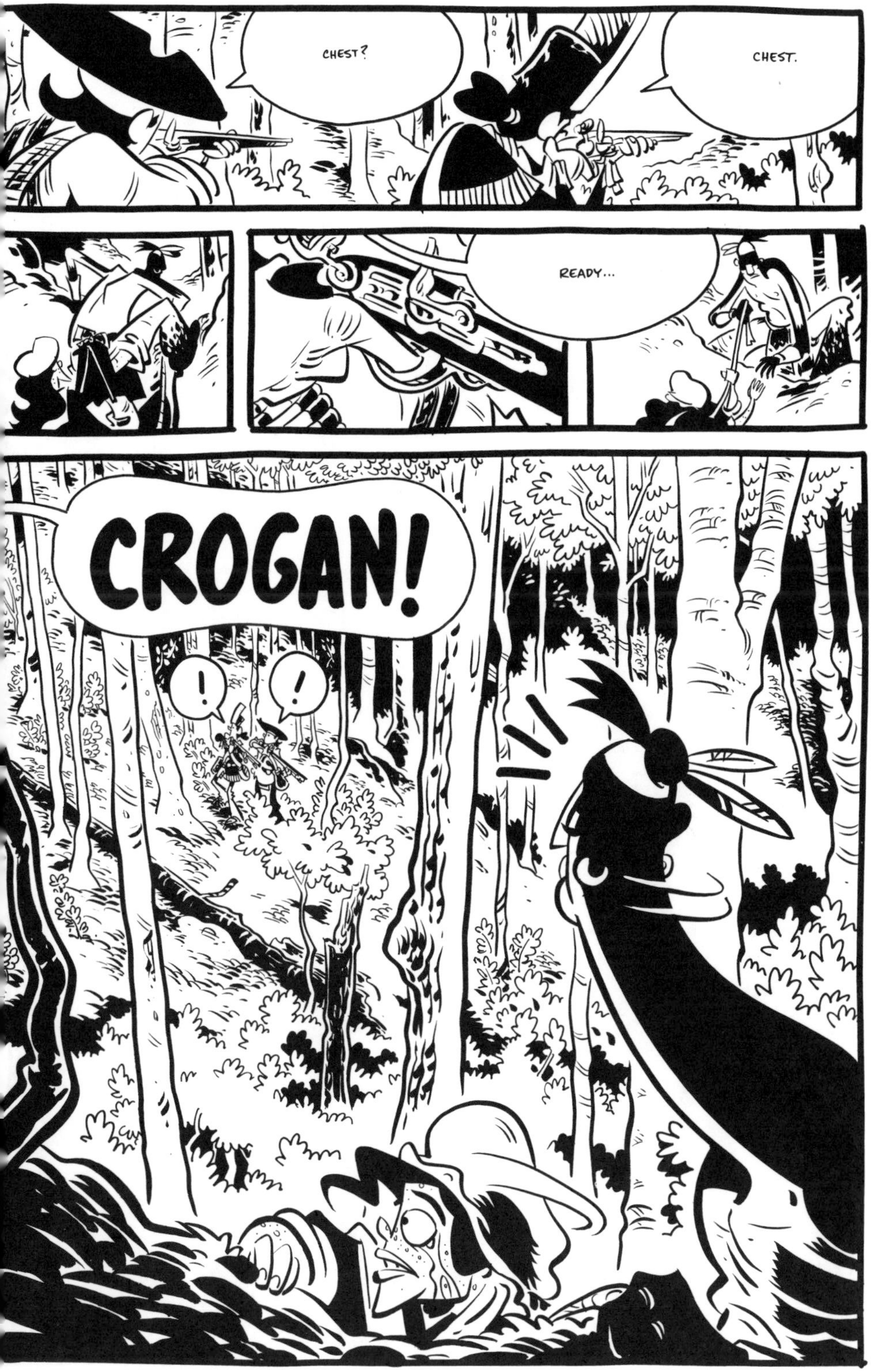
CHEST?
CHEST.
READY...
CROGAN!
!
!

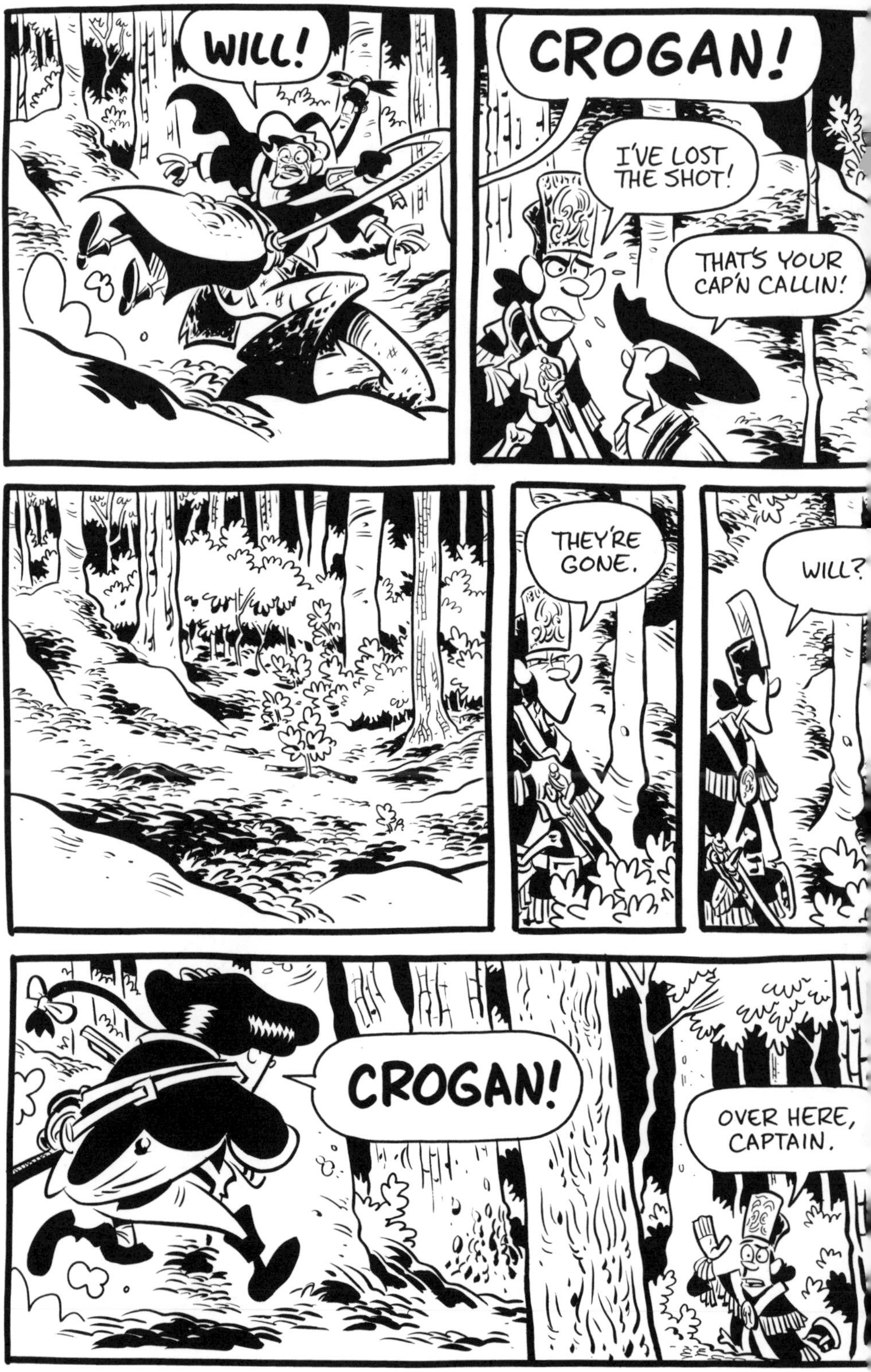
WILL!
CROGAN!
I'VE LOST THE SHOT!
THAT'S YOUR CAP'N CALLIN'!
THEY'RE GONE.
WILL?
CROGAN!
OVER HERE, CAPTAIN.

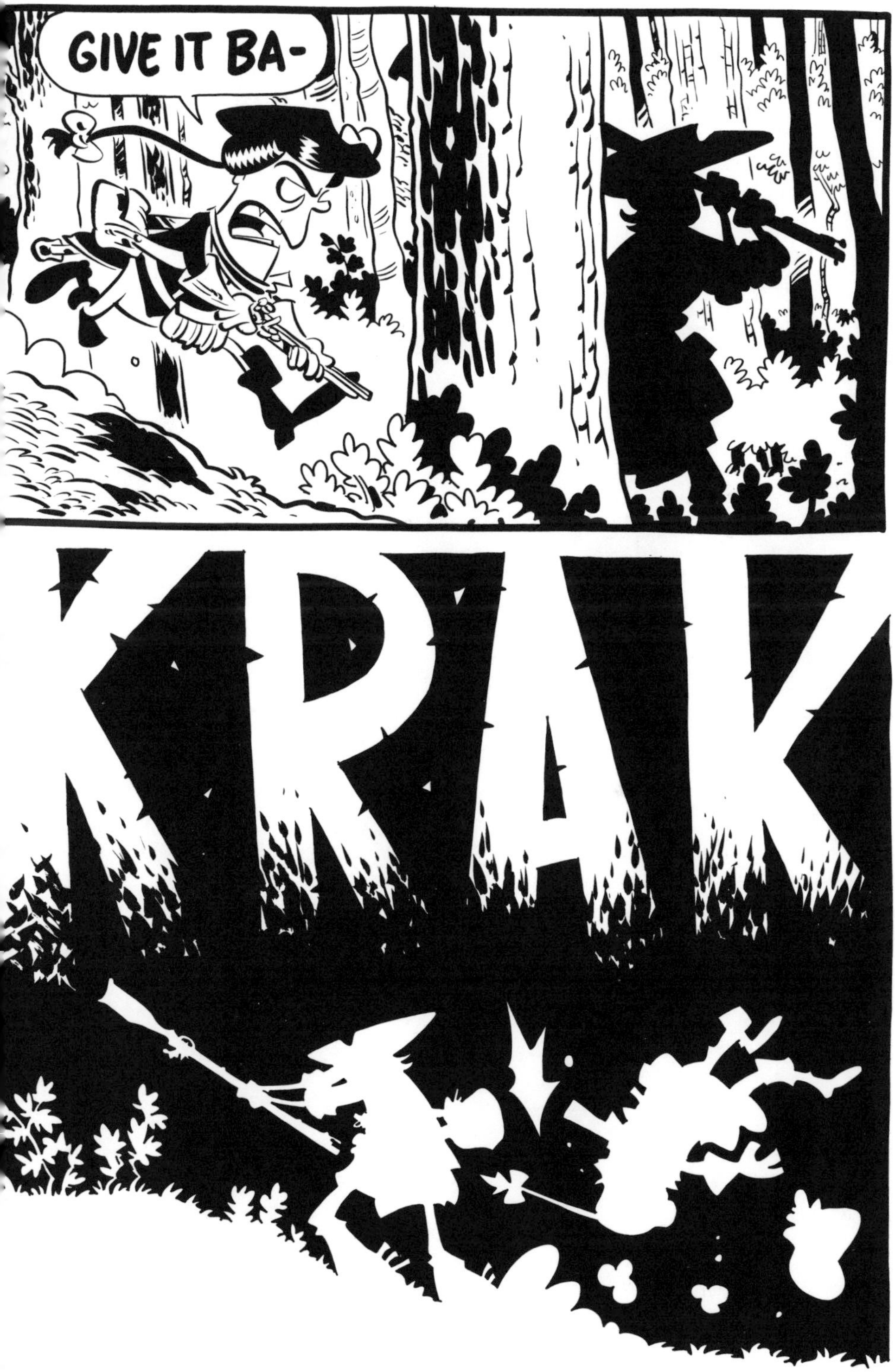
GIVE IT BA-
KRAK

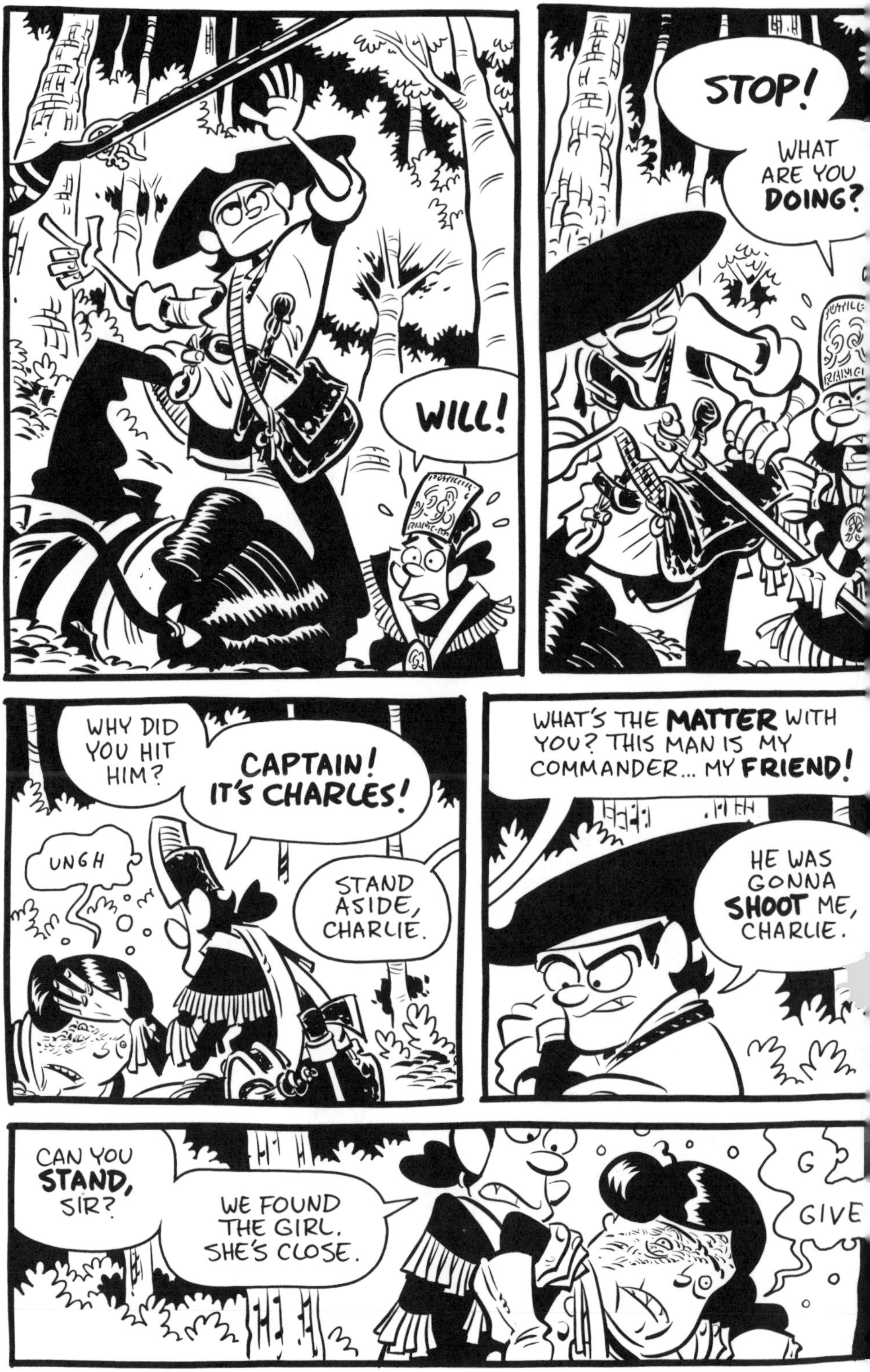
WILL!
STOP!
WHAT ARE YOU DOING?
WHY DID YOU HIT HIM?
CAPTAIN! IT'S CHARLES!
UNGH
STAND ASIDE, CHARLIE.
WHAT'S THE MATTER WITH YOU? THIS MAN IS MY COMMANDER... MY FRIEND!
HE WAS GONNA SHOOT ME, CHARLIE.
CAN YOU STAND, SIR?
WE FOUND THE GIRL. SHE'S CLOSE.
G
GIVE

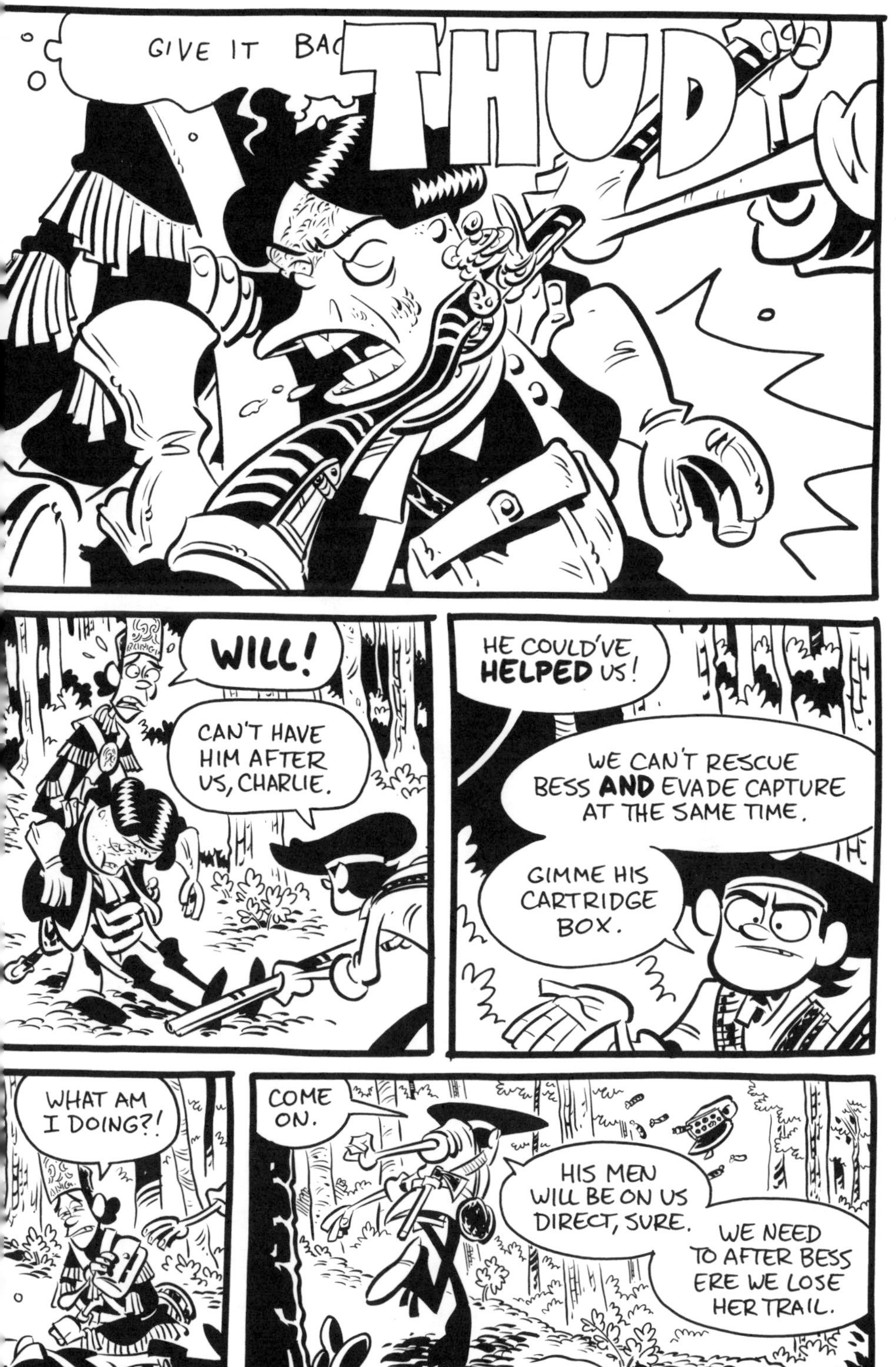
GIVE IT BAC
THUD
WILL!
CAN'T HAVE HIM AFTER US, CHARLIE.
HE COULD'VE HELPED US!
WE CAN'T RESCUE BESS AND EVADE CAPTURE AT THE SAME TIME.
GIMME HIS CARTRIDGE BOX.
WHAT AM I DOING?!
COME ON.
HIS MEN WILL BE ON US DIRECT, SURE.
WE NEED TO AFTER BESS ERE WE LOSE HER TRAIL.

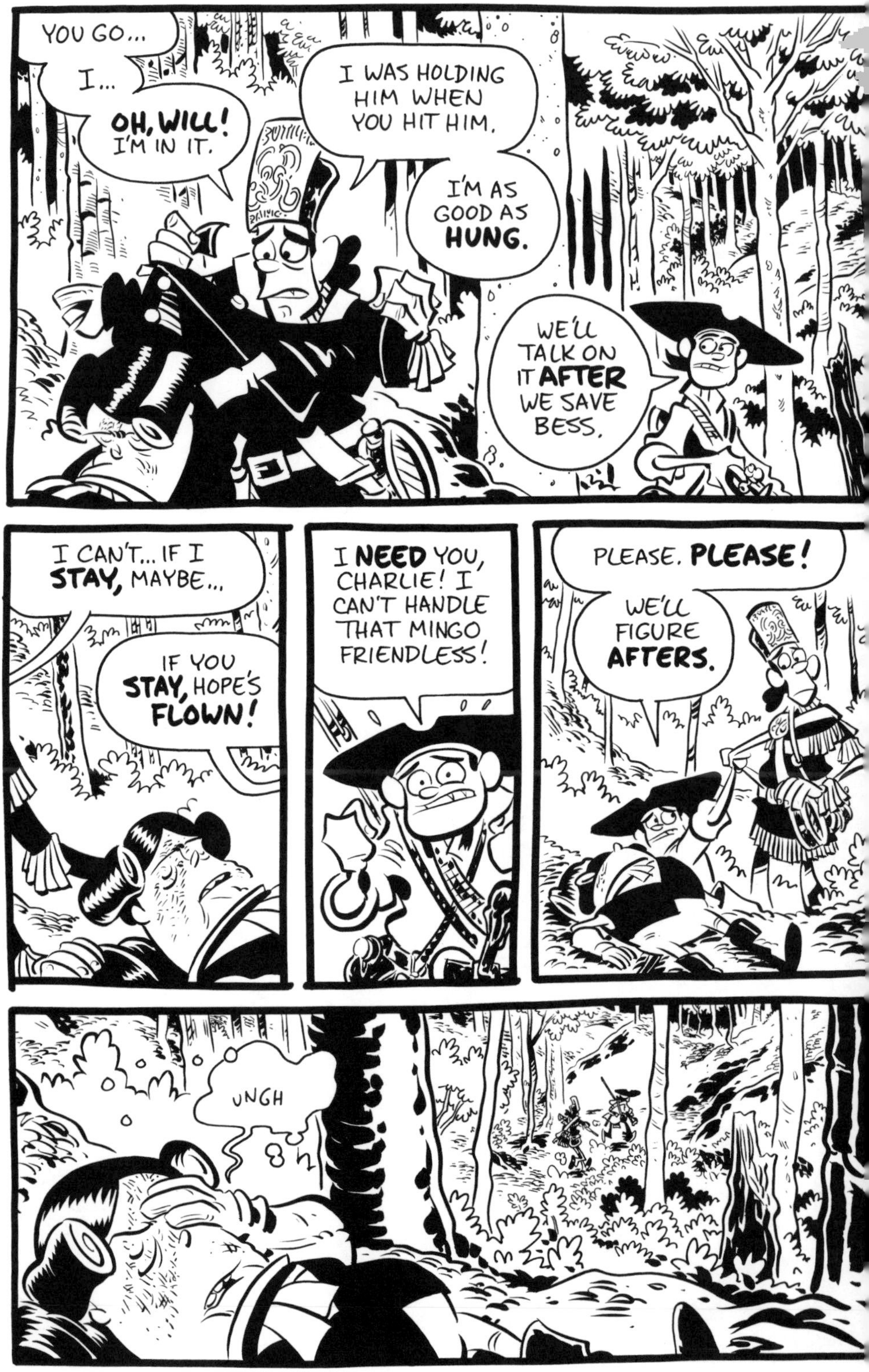
YOU GO...
I...
OH, WILL! I'M IN IT.
I WAS HOLDING HIM WHEN YOU HIT HIM.
I'M AS GOOD AS HUNG.
WE'LL TALK ON IT AFTER WE SAVE BESS.
I CAN'T... IF I STAY, MAYBE...
IF YOU STAY, HOPE'S FLOWN!
I NEED YOU, CHARLIE! I CAN'T HANDLE THAT MINGO FRIENDLESS!
PLEASE. PLEASE!
WE'LL FIGURE AFTERS.
UNGH

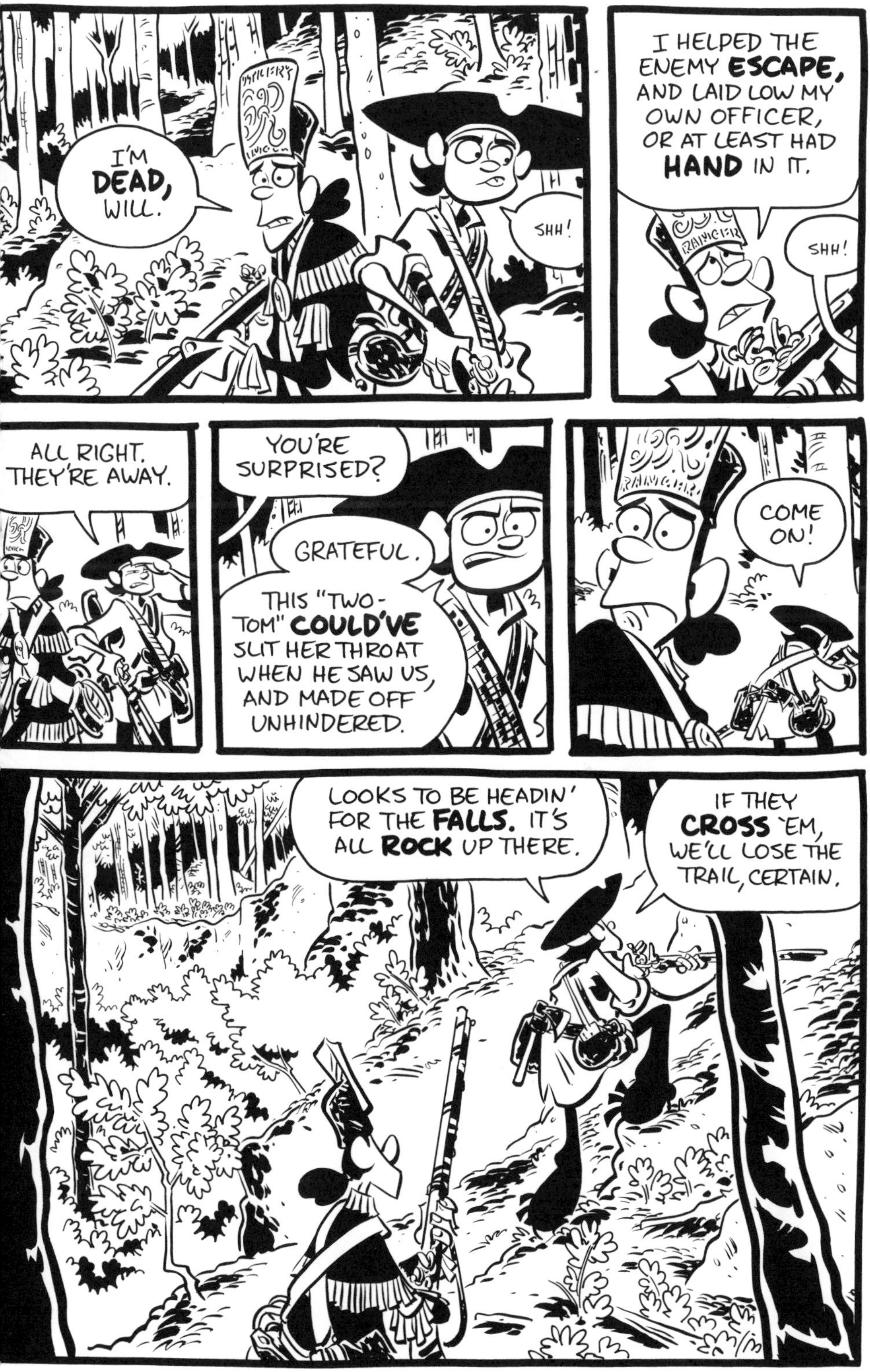
I'M DEAD, WILL.
SHH!
I HELPED THE ENEMY ESCAPE, AND LAID LOW MY OWN OFFICER, OR AT LEAST HAD HAND IN IT.
SHH!
ALL RIGHT. THEY'RE AWAY.
YOU'RE SURPRISED?
GRATEFUL.
THIS "TWO-TOM" COULD'VE SLIT HER THROAT WHEN HE SAW US, AND MADE OFF UNHINDERED.
COME ON!
LOOKS TO BE HEADIN' FOR THE FALLS. IT'S ALL ROCK UP THERE.
IF THEY CROSS 'EM, WE'LL LOSE THE TRAIL, CERTAIN.

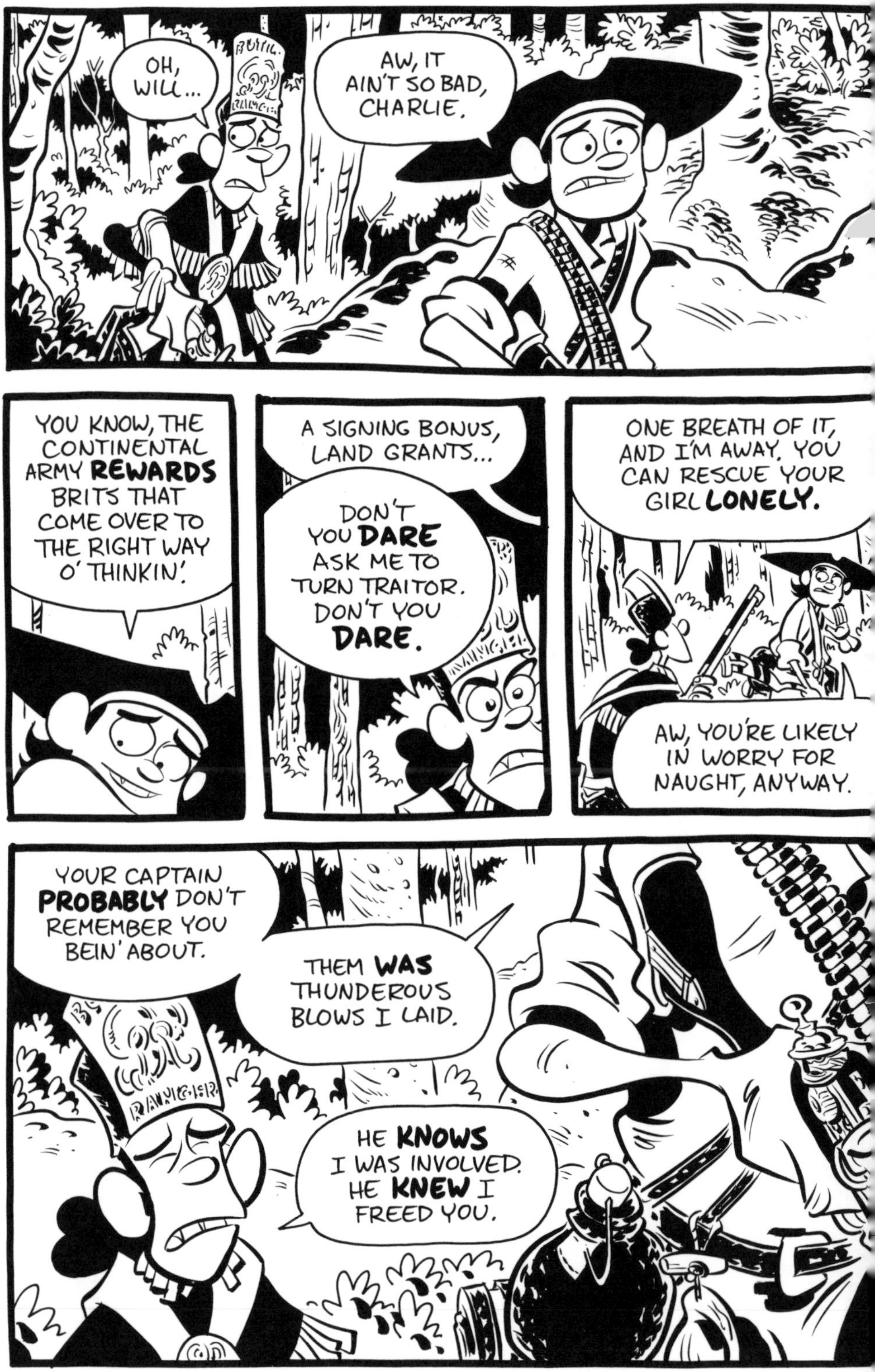
OH, WILL...
AW, IT AIN'T SO BAD, CHARLIE.
YOU KNOW, THE CONTINENTAL ARMY **REWARDS** BRITS THAT COME OVER TO THE RIGHT WAY O' THINKIN'.
A SIGNING BONUS, LAND GRANTS...
DON'T YOU **DARE** ASK ME TO TURN TRAITOR. DON'T YOU **DARE**.
ONE BREATH OF IT, AND I'M AWAY. YOU CAN RESCUE YOUR GIRL **LONELY**.
AW, YOU'RE LIKELY IN WORRY FOR NAUGHT, ANYWAY.
YOUR CAPTAIN **PROBABLY** DON'T REMEMBER YOU BEIN' ABOUT.
THEM **WAS** THUNDEROUS BLOWS I LAID.
HE **KNOWS** I WAS INVOLVED. HE **KNEW** I FREED YOU.

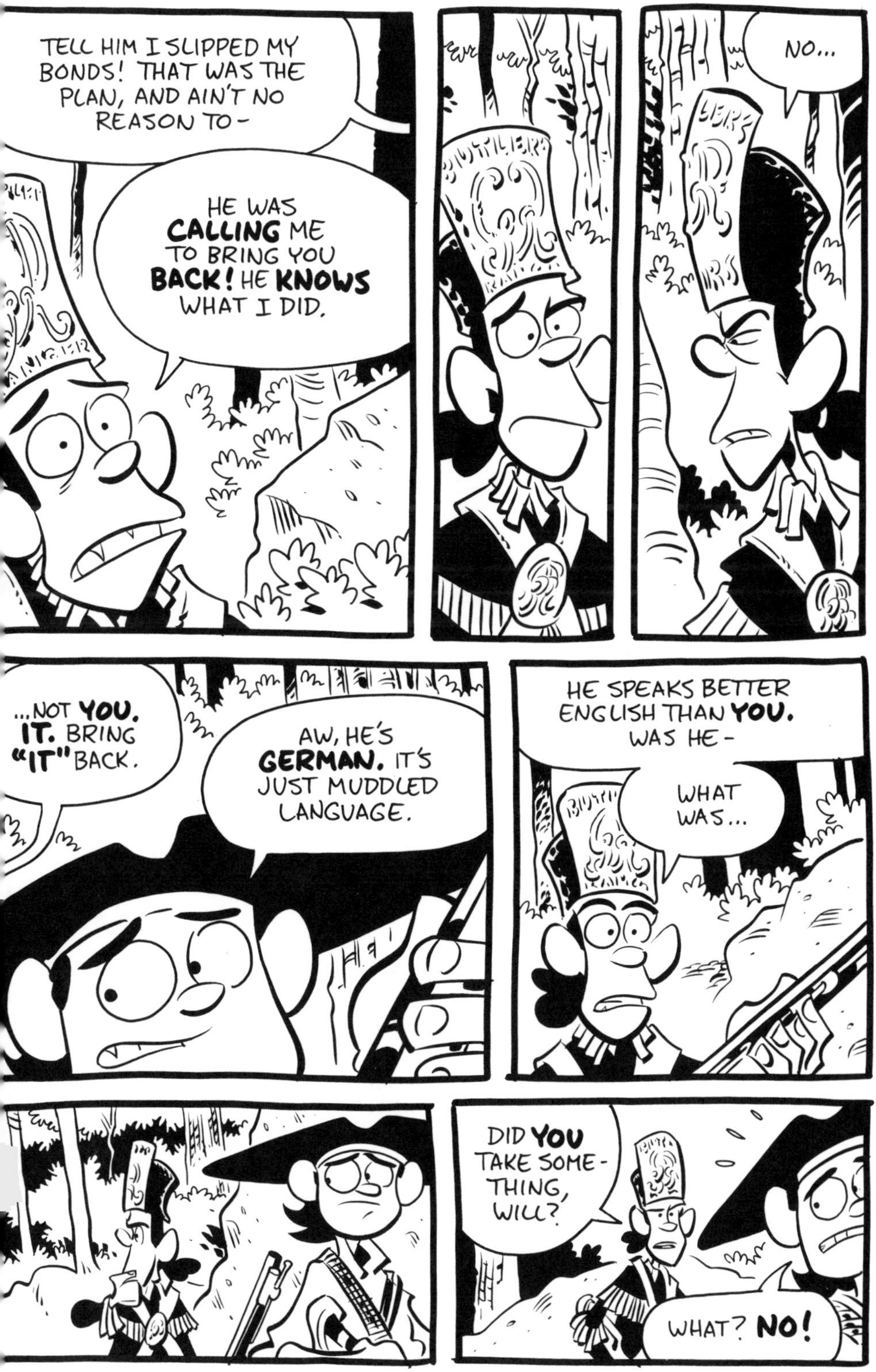
TELL HIM I SLIPPED MY BONDS! THAT WAS THE PLAN, AND AIN'T NO REASON TO-
HE WAS **CALLING** ME TO BRING YOU **BACK!** HE **KNOWS** WHAT I DID.
NO...
...NOT **YOU. IT.** BRING **"IT"** BACK.
AW, HE'S **GERMAN.** IT'S JUST MUDDLED LANGUAGE.
HE SPEAKS BETTER ENGLISH THAN **YOU.** WAS HE-
WHAT WAS...
DID **YOU** TAKE SOME-THING, WILL?
WHAT? **NO!**

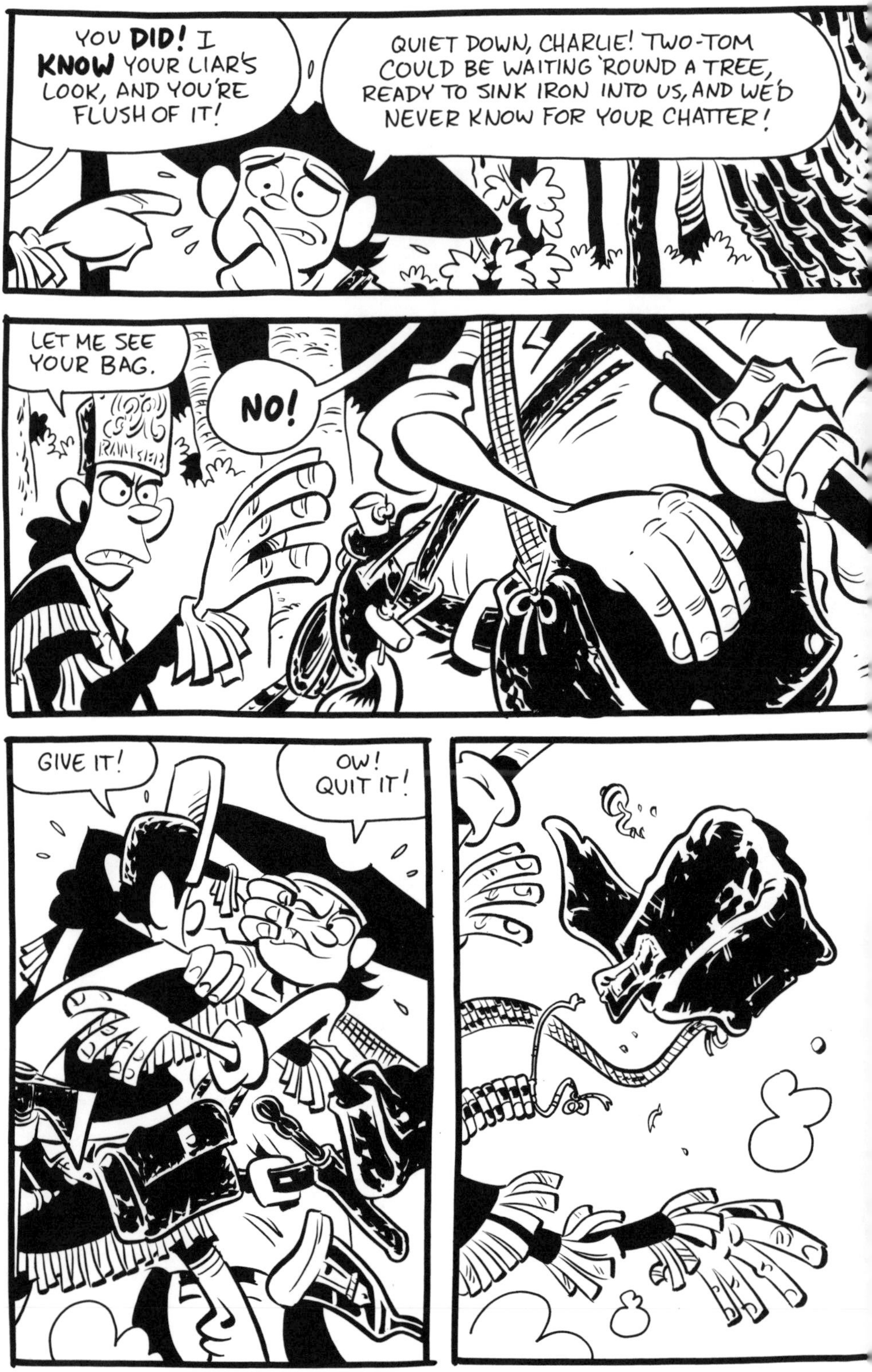

YOU **DID!** I **KNOW** YOUR LIAR'S LOOK, AND YOU'RE FLUSH OF IT!
QUIET DOWN, CHARLIE! TWO-TOM COULD BE WAITING 'ROUND A TREE, READY TO SINK IRON INTO US, AND WE'D NEVER KNOW FOR YOUR CHATTER!
LET ME SEE YOUR BAG.
NO!
GIVE IT!
OW! QUIT IT!

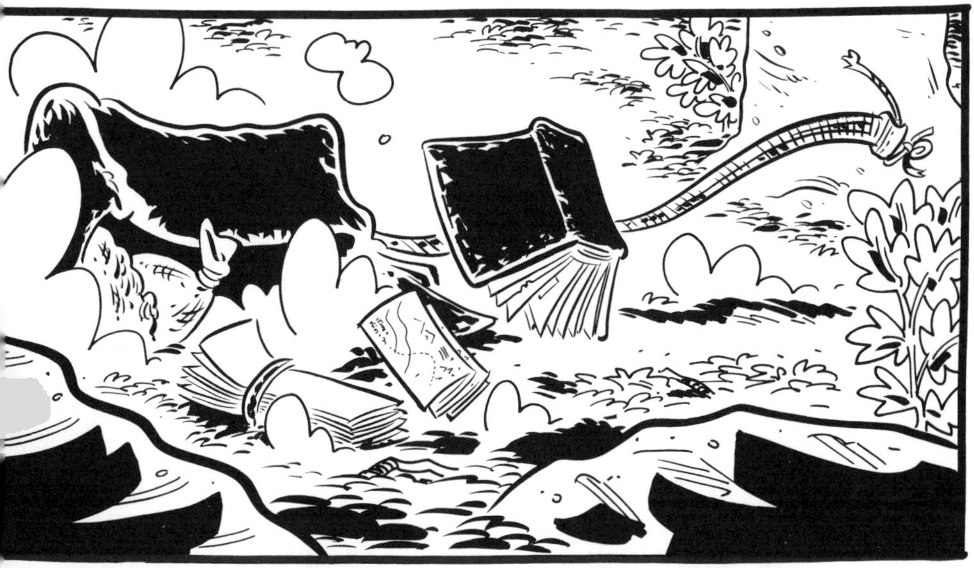

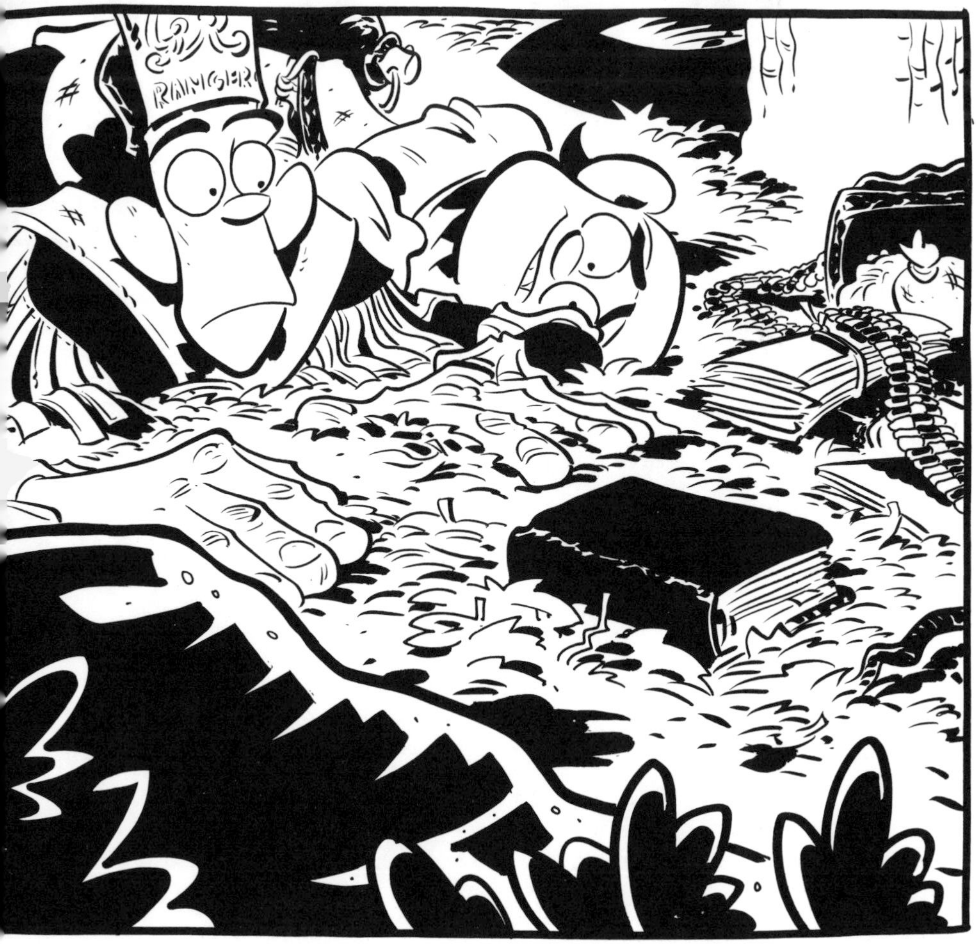
RANGER

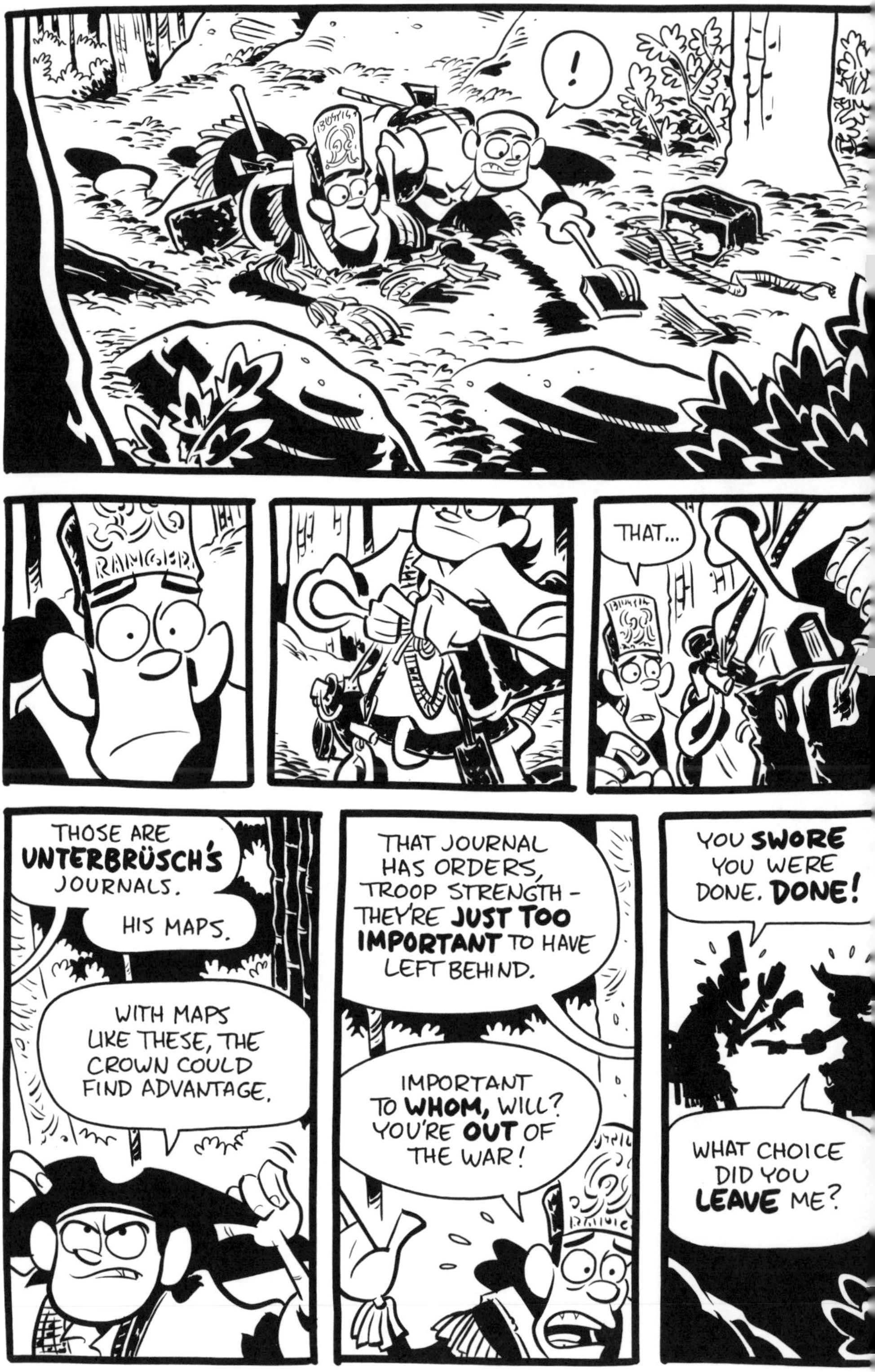
!
THAT...
THOSE ARE UNTERBRÜSCH'S JOURNALS.
HIS MAPS.
WITH MAPS LIKE THESE, THE CROWN COULD FIND ADVANTAGE.
THAT JOURNAL HAS ORDERS, TROOP STRENGTH - THEY'RE JUST TOO IMPORTANT TO HAVE LEFT BEHIND.
IMPORTANT TO WHOM, WILL? YOU'RE OUT OF THE WAR!
YOU SWORE YOU WERE DONE. DONE!
WHAT CHOICE DID YOU LEAVE ME?

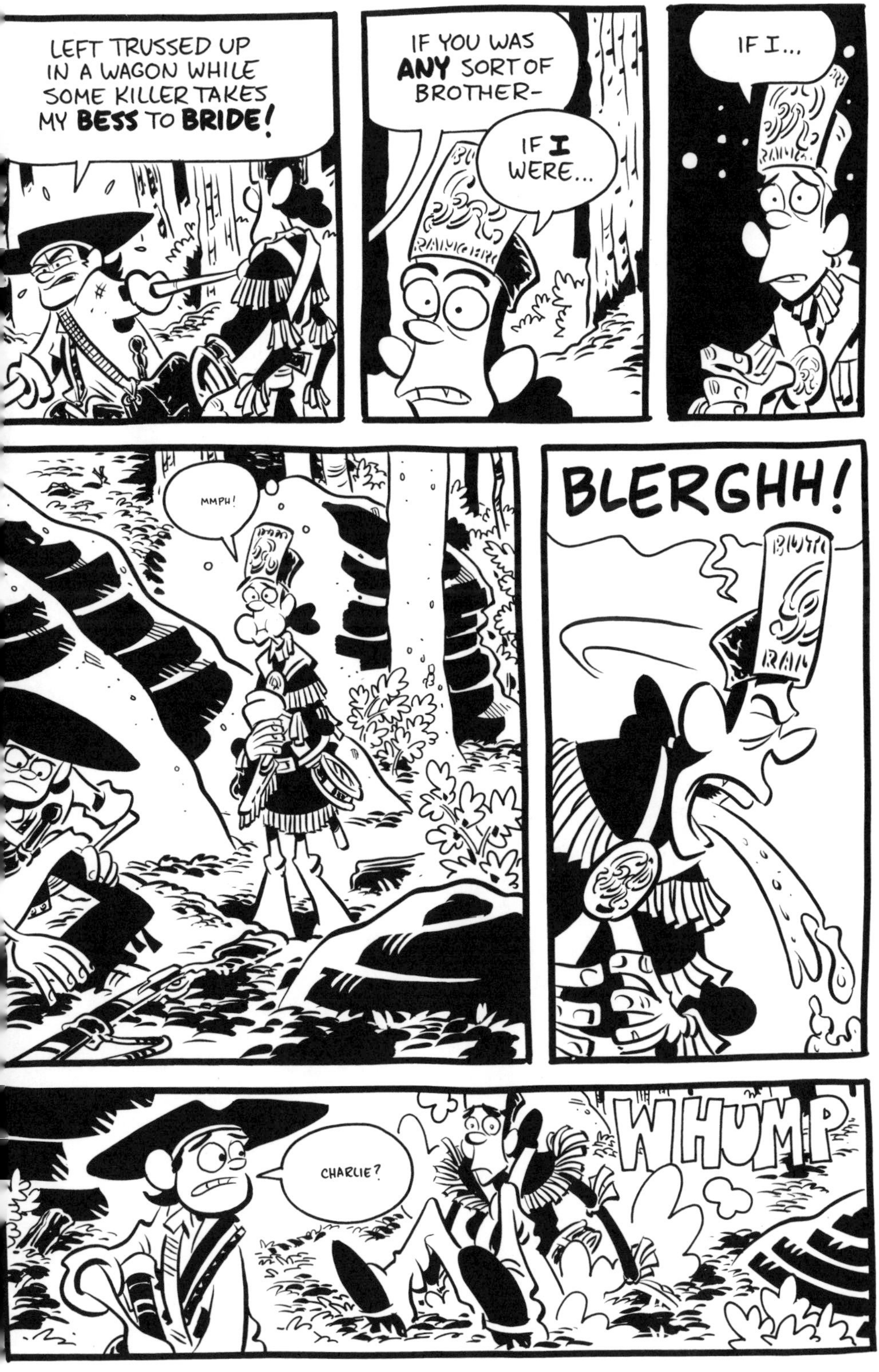
LEFT TRUSSED UP IN A WAGON WHILE SOME KILLER TAKES MY BESS TO BRIDE!
IF YOU WAS ANY SORT OF BROTHER-
IF I WERE...
IF I...
MMPH!
BLERGHH!
CHARLIE?
WHUMP

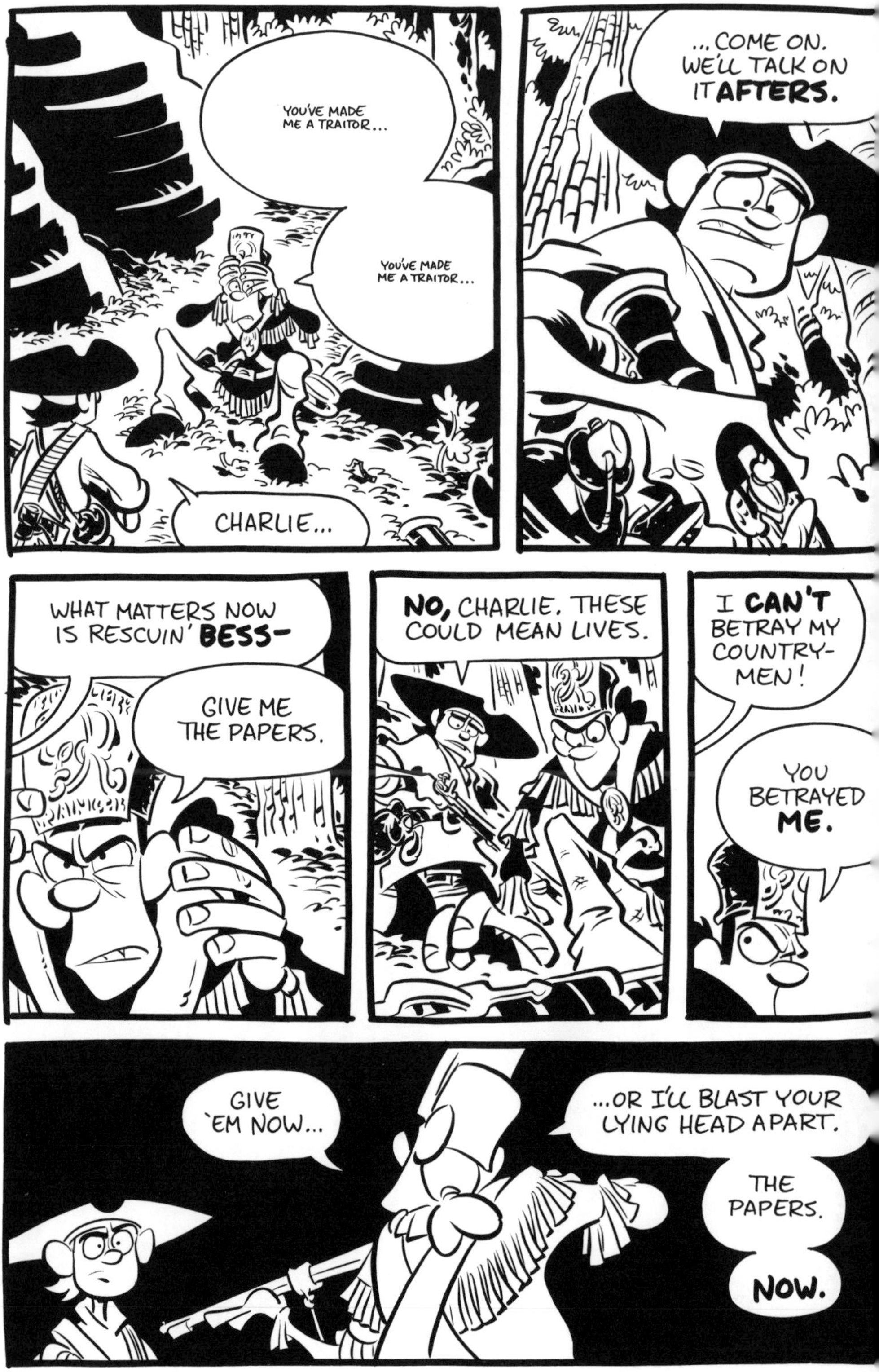
YOU'VE MADE ME A TRAITOR...
YOU'VE MADE ME A TRAITOR...
CHARLIE...
...COME ON. WE'LL TALK ON IT AFTERS.
WHAT MATTERS NOW IS RESCUIN' BESS-
GIVE ME THE PAPERS.
NO, CHARLIE. THESE COULD MEAN LIVES.
I CAN'T BETRAY MY COUNTRYMEN!
YOU BETRAYED ME.
GIVE 'EM NOW...
...OR I'LL BLAST YOUR LYING HEAD APART.
THE PAPERS.
NOW.

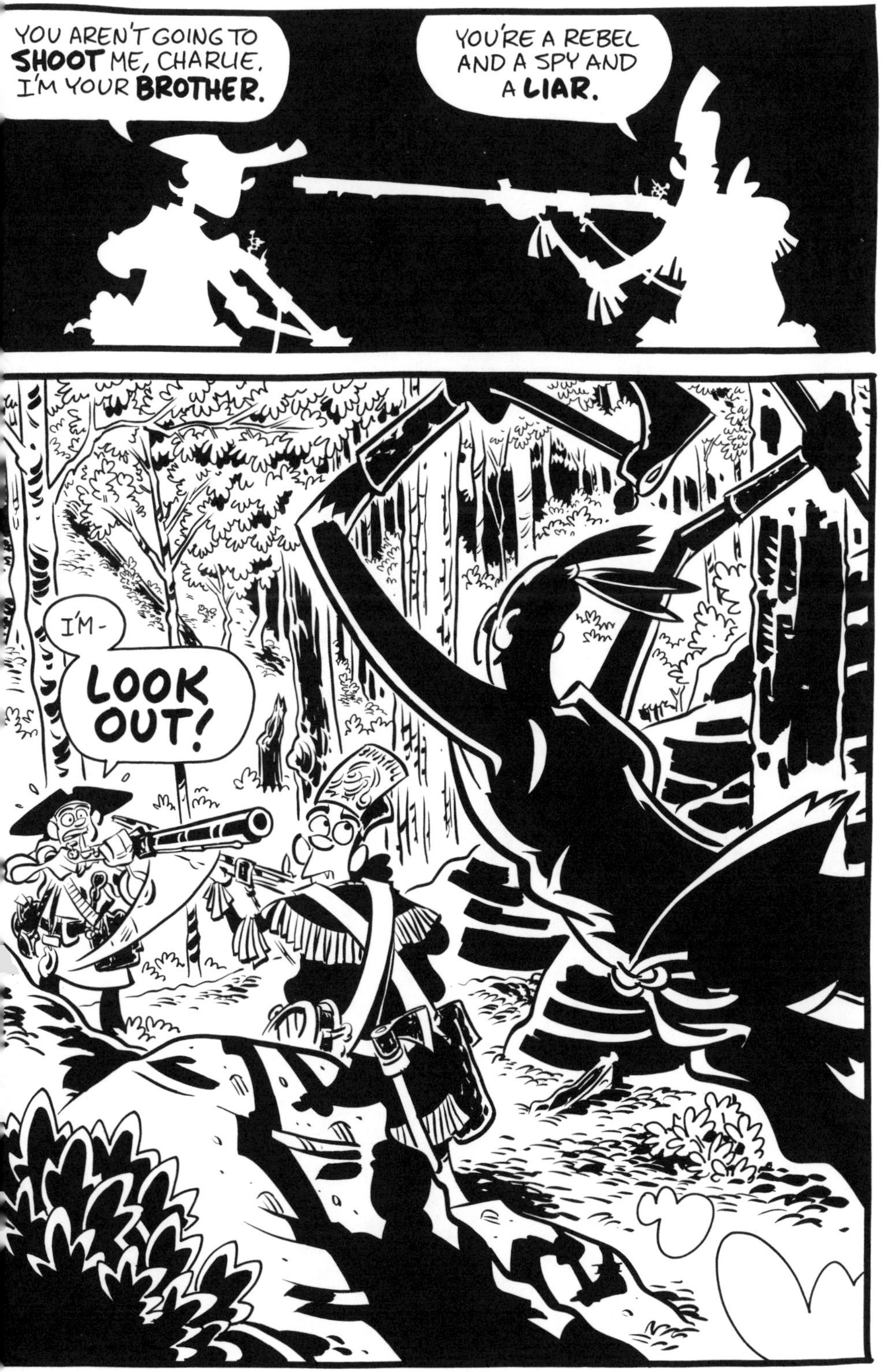
YOU AREN'T GOING TO SHOOT ME, CHARLIE. I'M YOUR BROTHER.
YOU'RE A REBEL AND A SPY AND A LIAR.
I'M-
LOOK OUT!

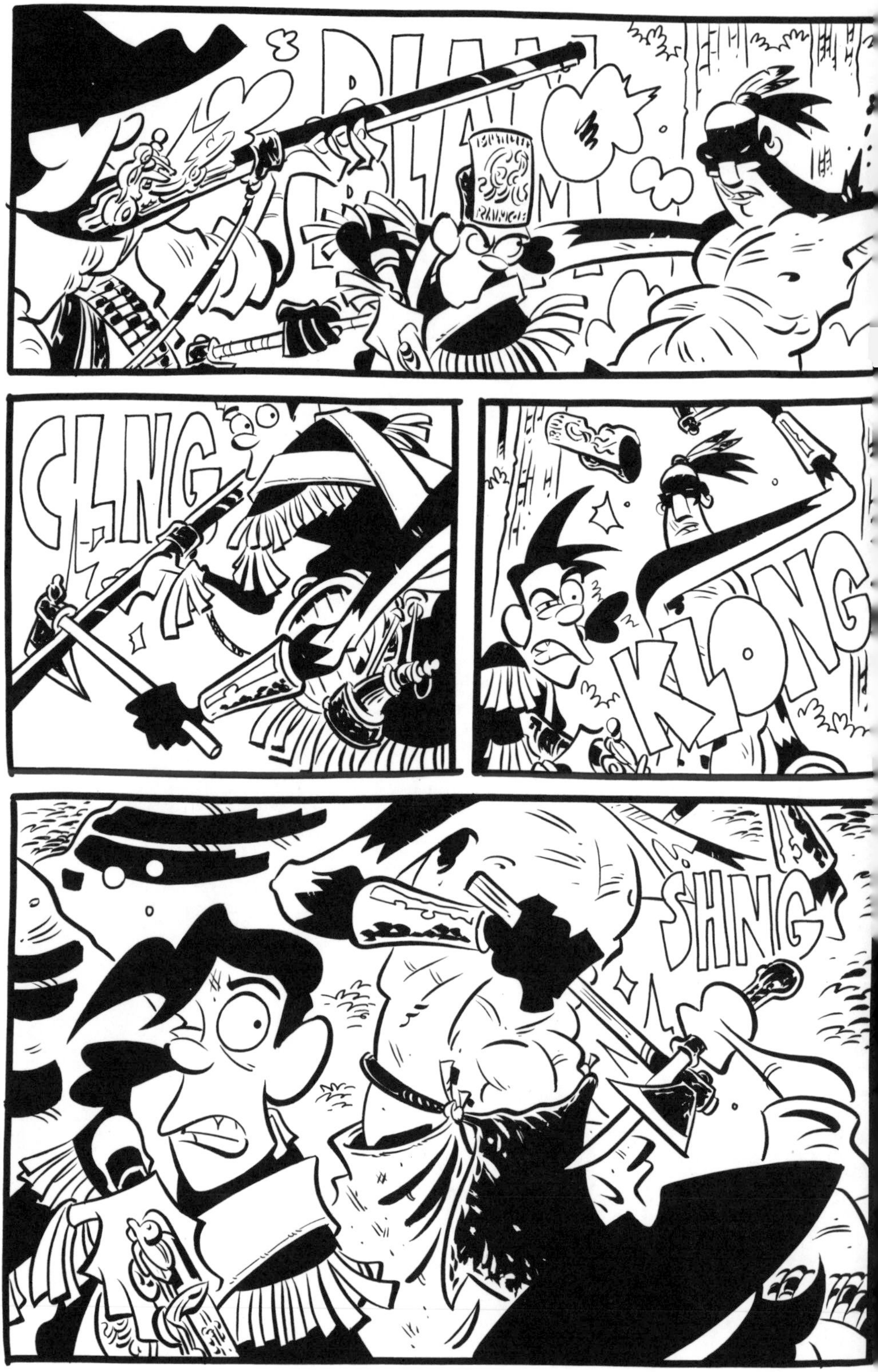
BLAM
CLNG
KLONG
SHNG

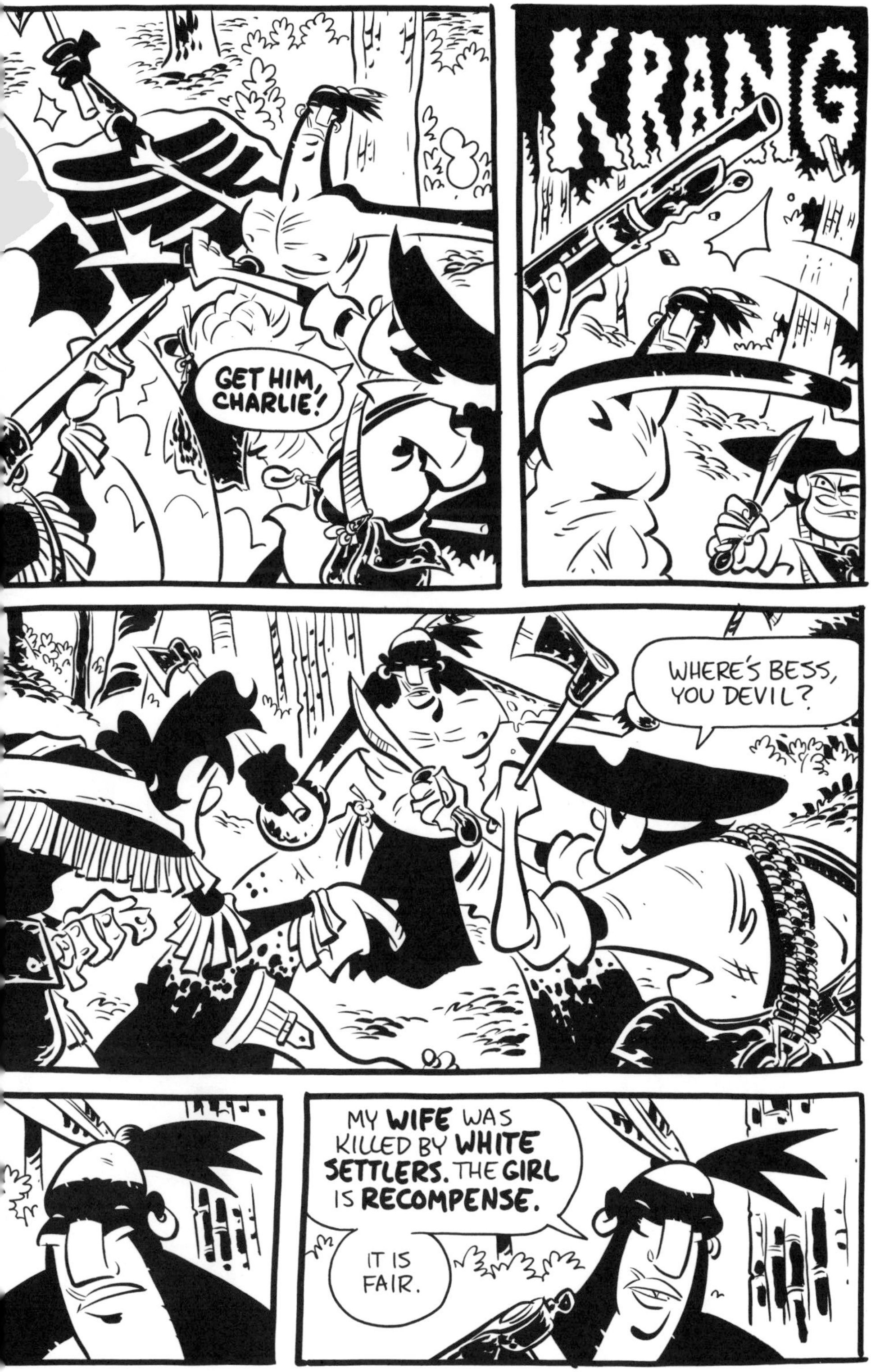
GET HIM, CHARLIE!
KRANG
WHERE'S BESS, YOU DEVIL?
MY WIFE WAS KILLED BY WHITE SETTLERS. THE GIRL IS RECOMPENSE.
IT IS FAIR.

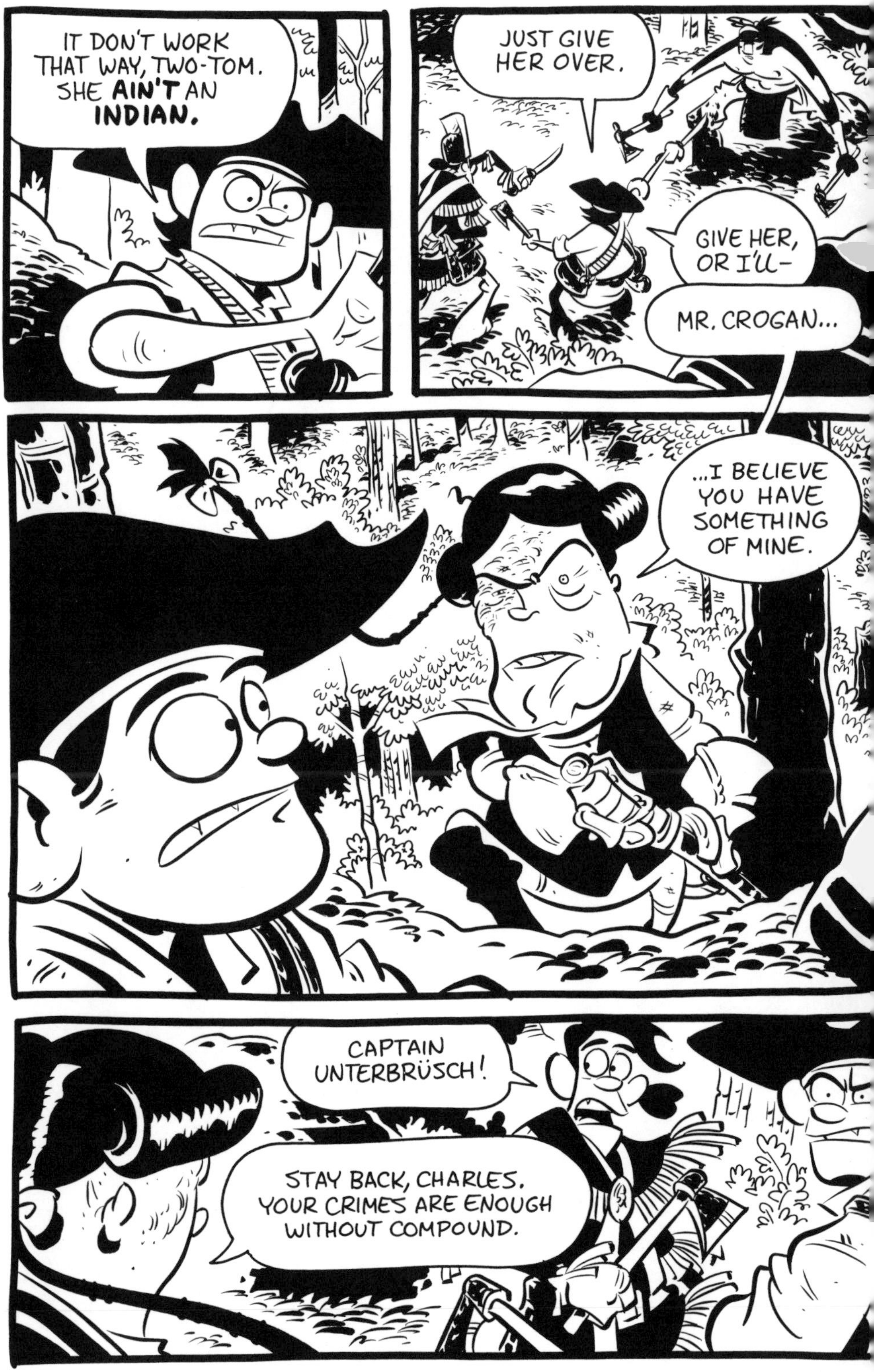
IT DON'T WORK THAT WAY, TWO-TOM. SHE **AIN'T** AN **INDIAN.**
JUST GIVE HER OVER.
GIVE HER, OR I'LL-
MR. CROGAN...
...I BELIEVE YOU HAVE SOMETHING OF MINE.
CAPTAIN UNTERBRÜSCH!
STAY BACK, CHARLES. YOUR CRIMES ARE ENOUGH WITHOUT COMPOUND.

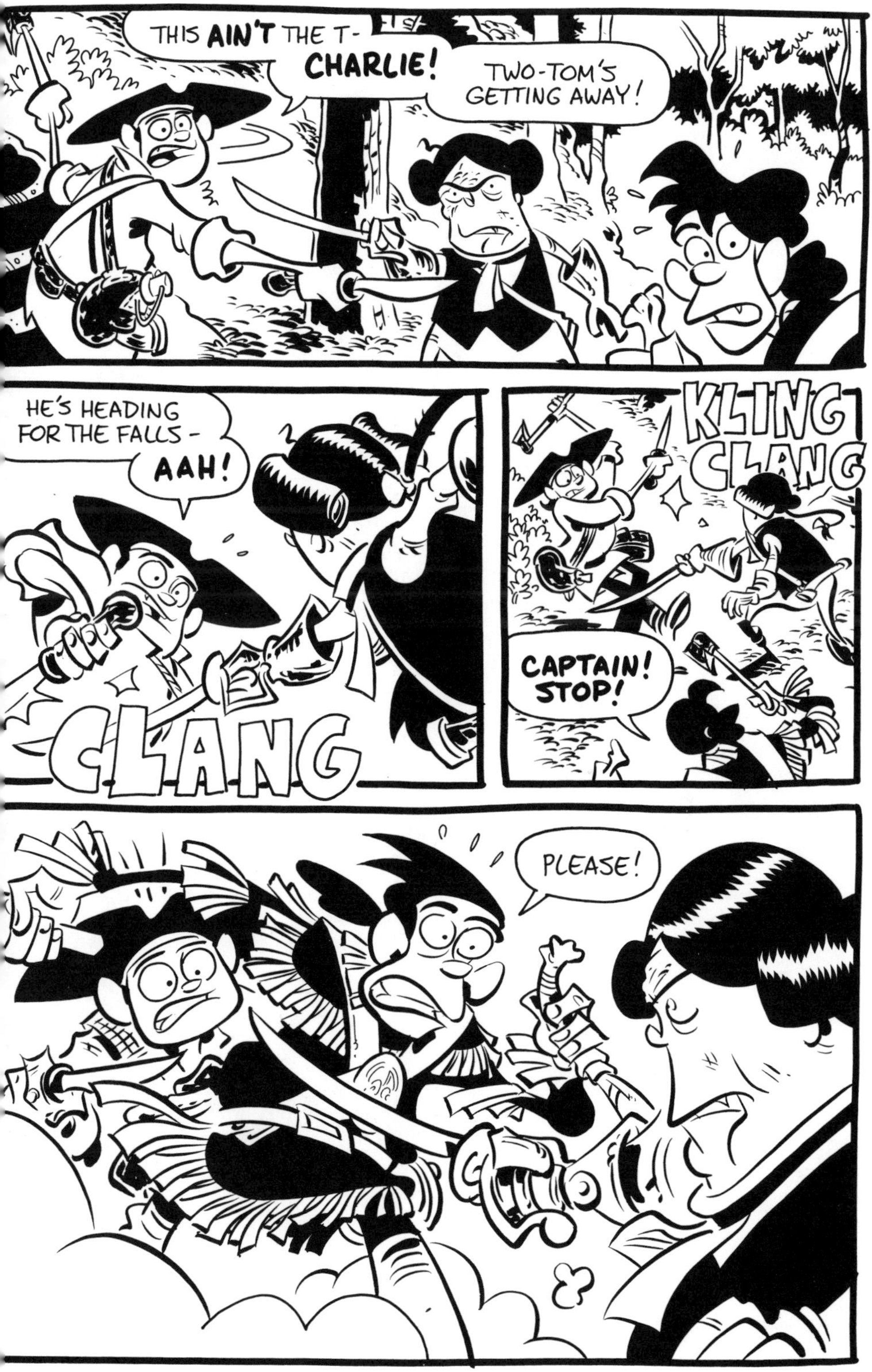
THIS AIN'T THE T-
CHARLIE!
TWO-TOM'S GETTING AWAY!
HE'S HEADING FOR THE FALLS -
AAH!
CLANG
KLING CLANG
CAPTAIN! STOP!
PLEASE!

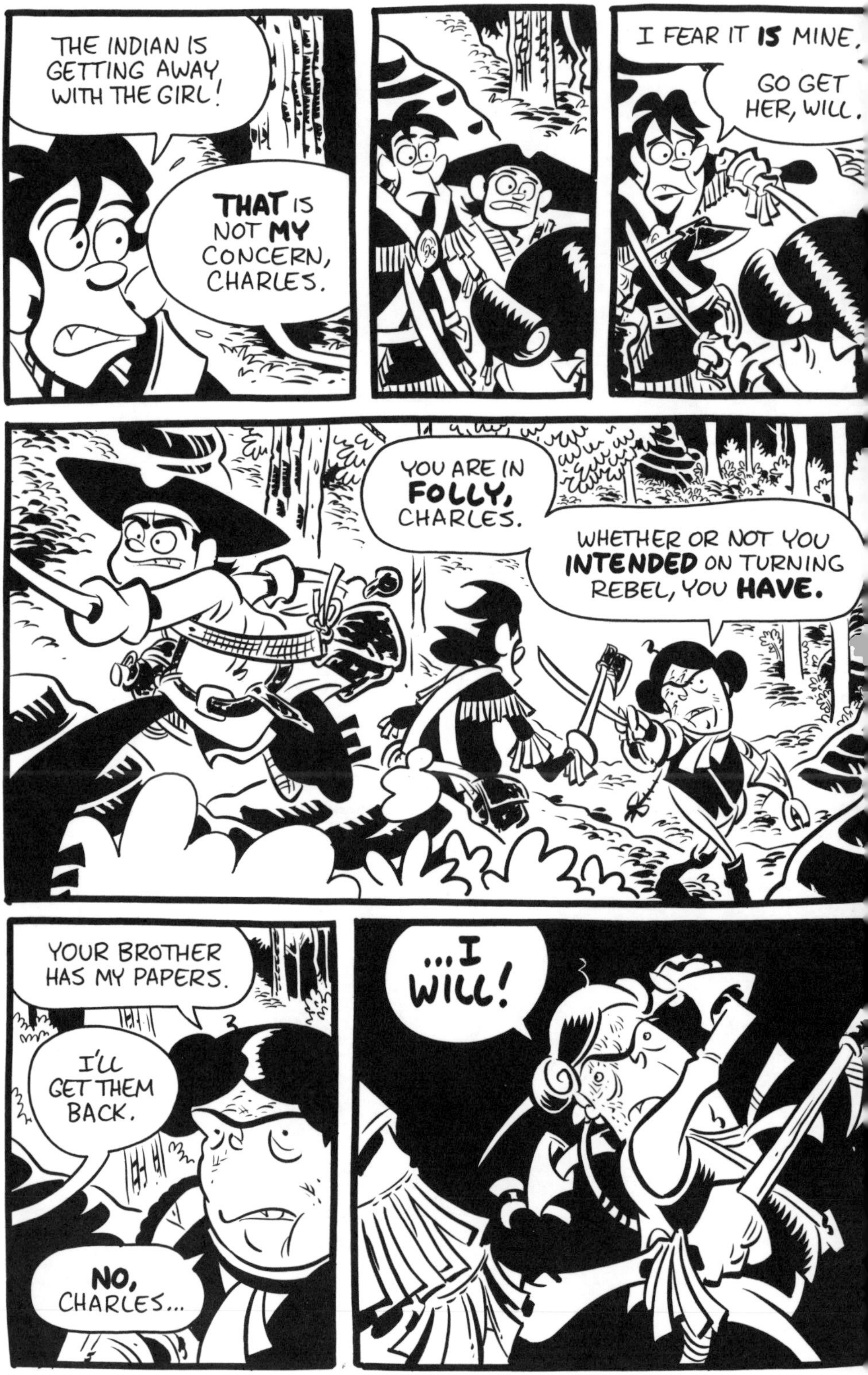
THE INDIAN IS GETTING AWAY WITH THE GIRL!
THAT IS NOT MY CONCERN, CHARLES.
I FEAR IT IS MINE.
GO GET HER, WILL.
YOU ARE IN FOLLY, CHARLES.
WHETHER OR NOT YOU INTENDED ON TURNING REBEL, YOU HAVE.
YOUR BROTHER HAS MY PAPERS.
I'LL GET THEM BACK.
NO, CHARLES...
...I WILL!

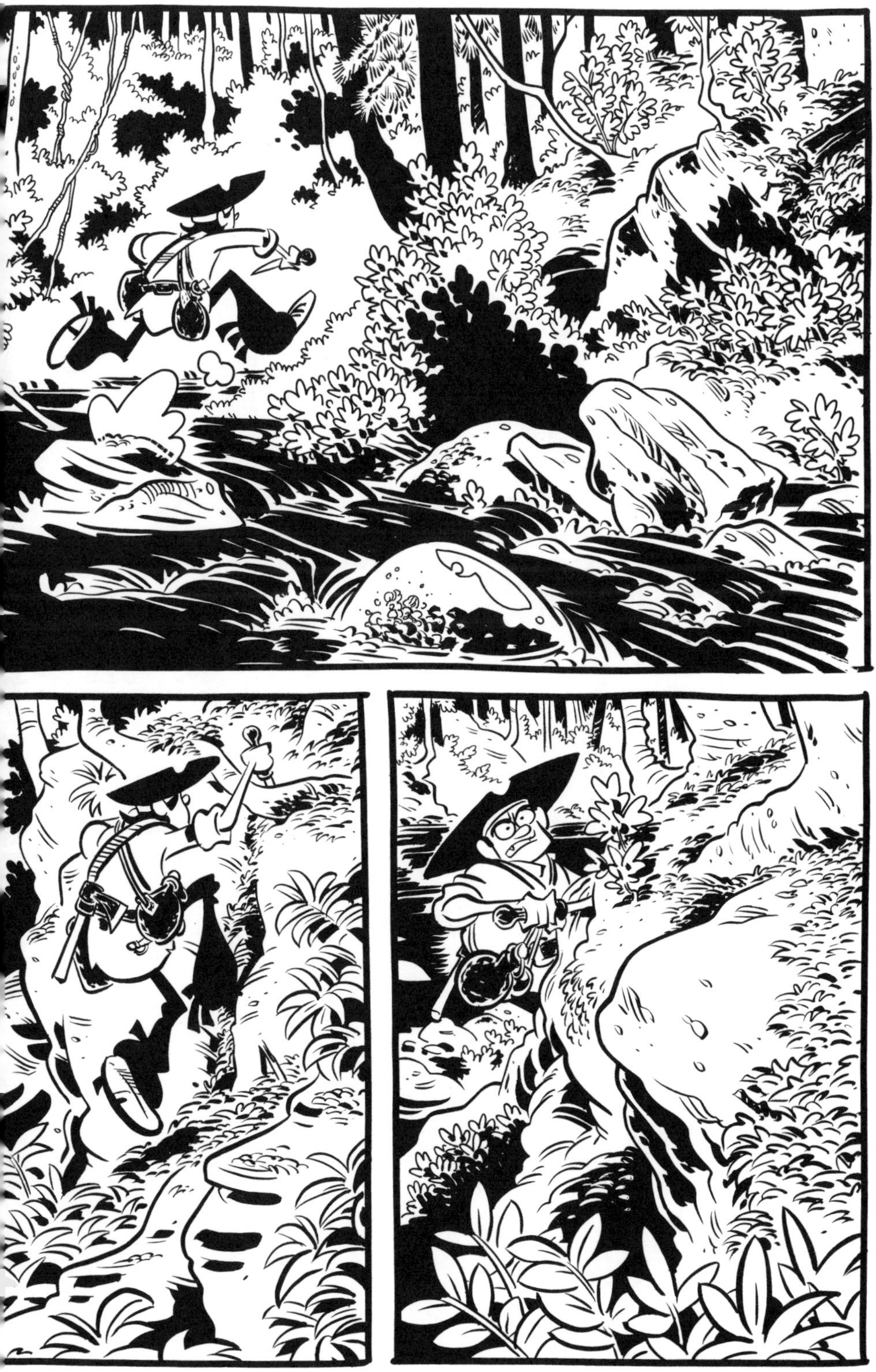

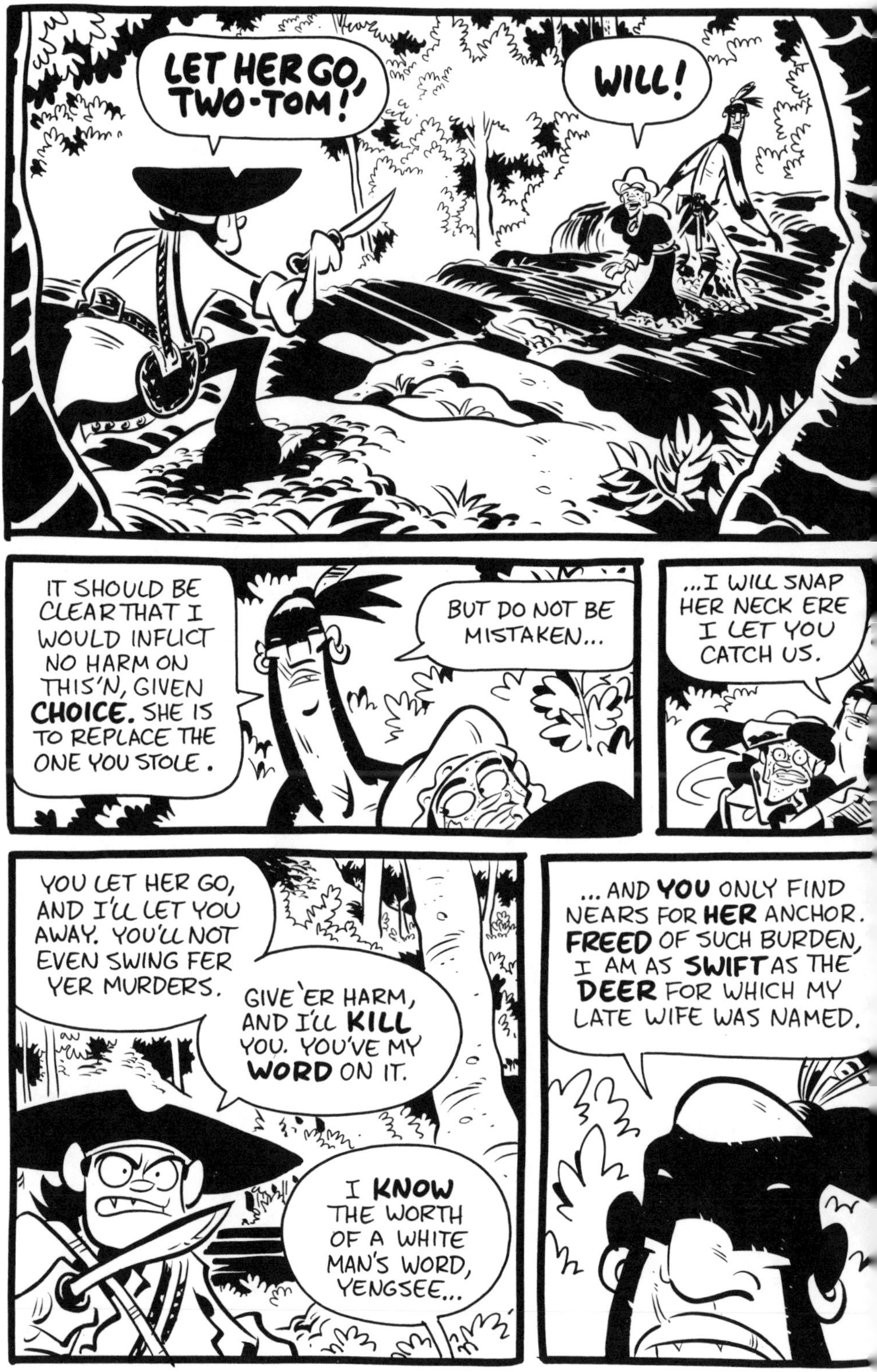
LET HER GO, TWO-TOM!
WILL!
IT SHOULD BE CLEAR THAT I WOULD INFLICT NO HARM ON THIS'N, GIVEN CHOICE. SHE IS TO REPLACE THE ONE YOU STOLE.
BUT DO NOT BE MISTAKEN...
...I WILL SNAP HER NECK ERE I LET YOU CATCH US.
YOU LET HER GO, AND I'LL LET YOU AWAY. YOU'LL NOT EVEN SWING FER YER MURDERS.
GIVE 'ER HARM, AND I'LL KILL YOU. YOU'VE MY WORD ON IT.
I KNOW THE WORTH OF A WHITE MAN'S WORD, YENGSEE...
... AND YOU ONLY FIND NEARS FOR HER ANCHOR. FREED OF SUCH BURDEN, I AM AS SWIFT AS THE DEER FOR WHICH MY LATE WIFE WAS NAMED.

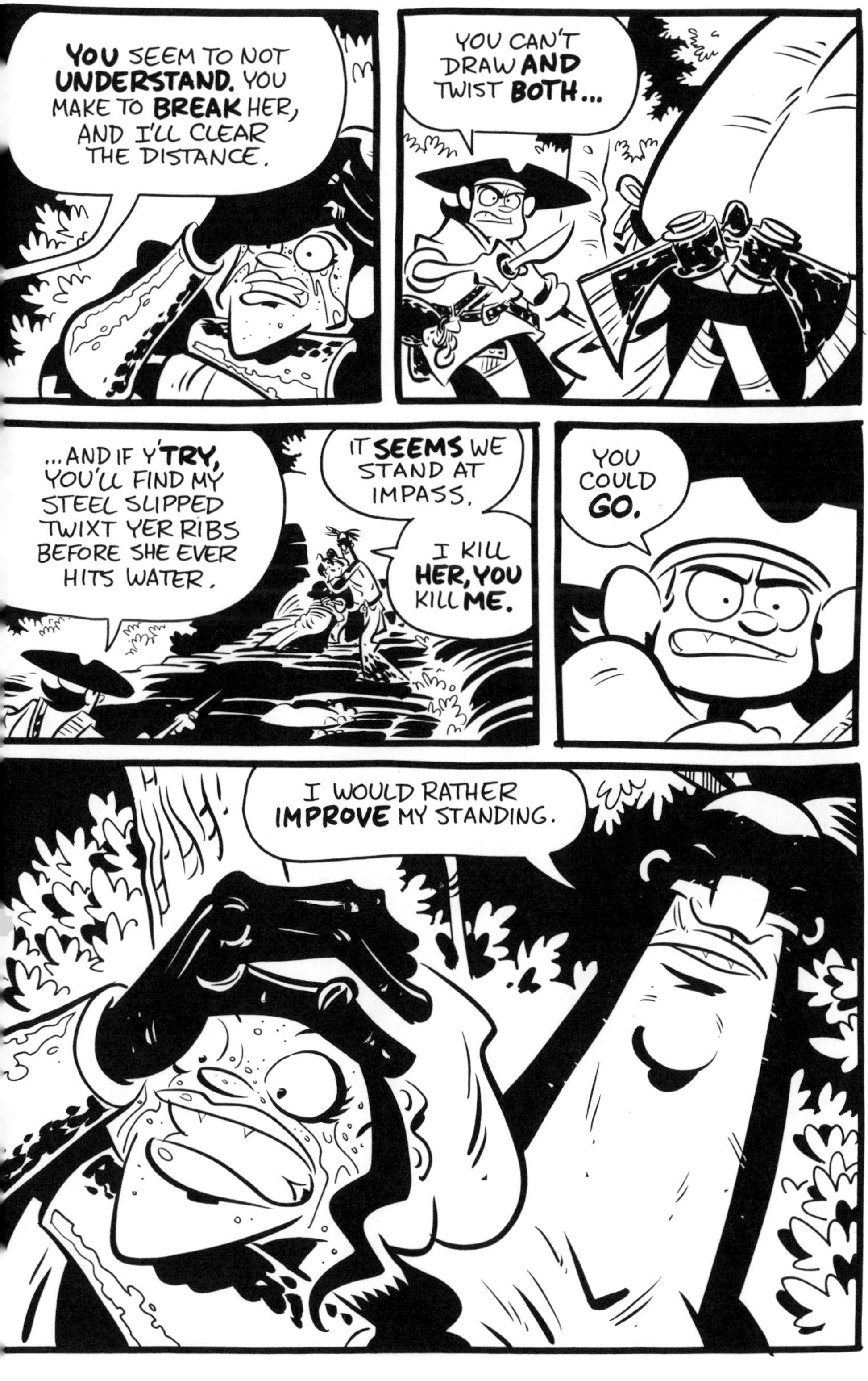
YOU SEEM TO NOT UNDERSTAND. YOU MAKE TO BREAK HER, AND I'LL CLEAR THE DISTANCE.
YOU CAN'T DRAW AND TWIST BOTH...
...AND IF Y'TRY, YOU'LL FIND MY STEEL SLIPPED TWIXT YER RIBS BEFORE SHE EVER HITS WATER.
IT SEEMS WE STAND AT IMPASS.
I KILL HER, YOU KILL ME.
YOU COULD GO.
I WOULD RATHER IMPROVE MY STANDING.

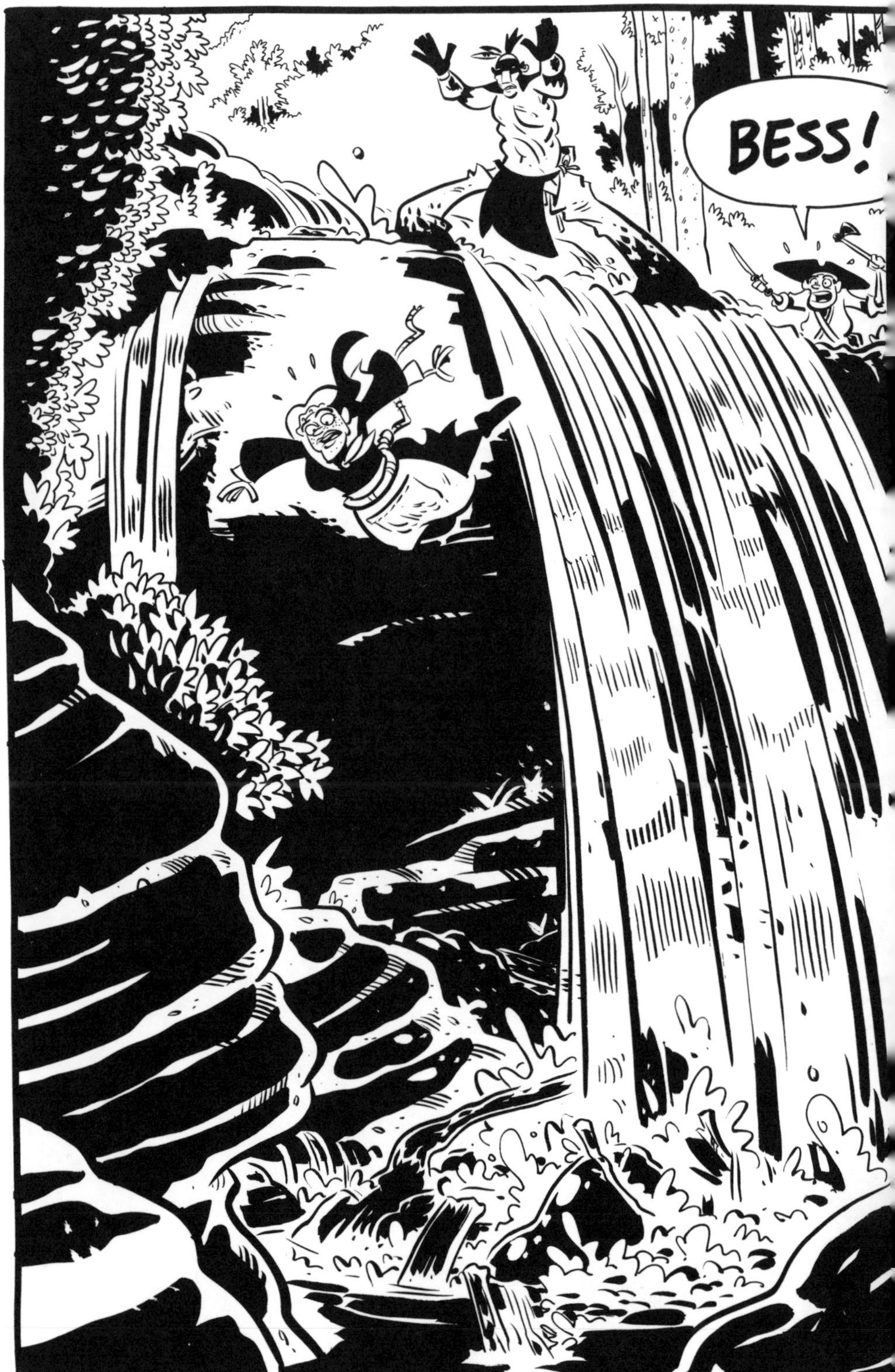
BESS!

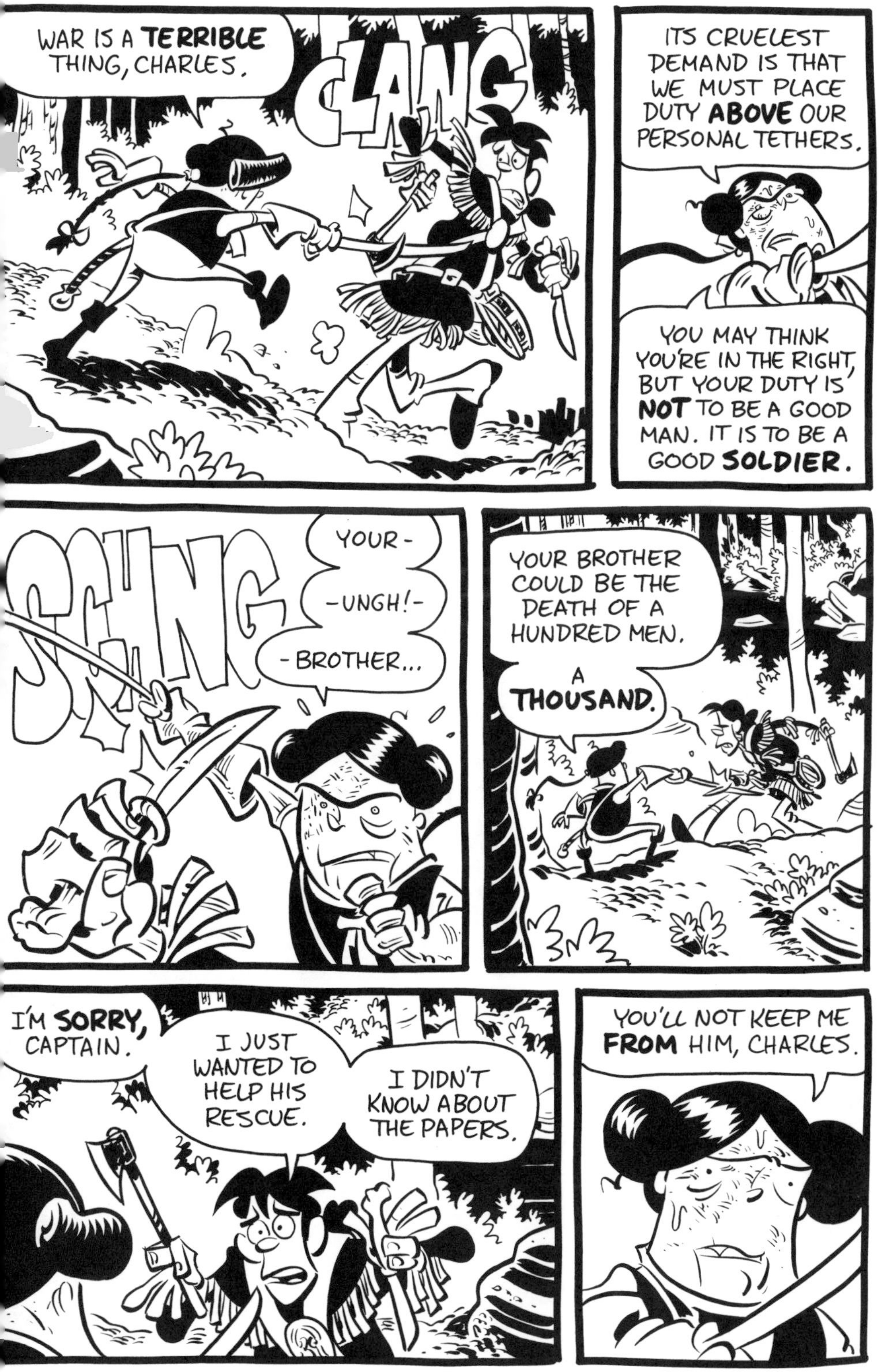
WAR IS A TERRIBLE THING, CHARLES.
CLANG
ITS CRUELEST DEMAND IS THAT WE MUST PLACE DUTY ABOVE OUR PERSONAL TETHERS.
YOU MAY THINK YOU'RE IN THE RIGHT, BUT YOUR DUTY IS NOT TO BE A GOOD MAN. IT IS TO BE A GOOD SOLDIER.
SCHING
YOUR-
-UNGH!-
-BROTHER...
YOUR BROTHER COULD BE THE DEATH OF A HUNDRED MEN.
A THOUSAND.
I'M SORRY, CAPTAIN.
I JUST WANTED TO HELP HIS RESCUE.
I DIDN'T KNOW ABOUT THE PAPERS.
YOU'LL NOT KEEP ME FROM HIM, CHARLES.

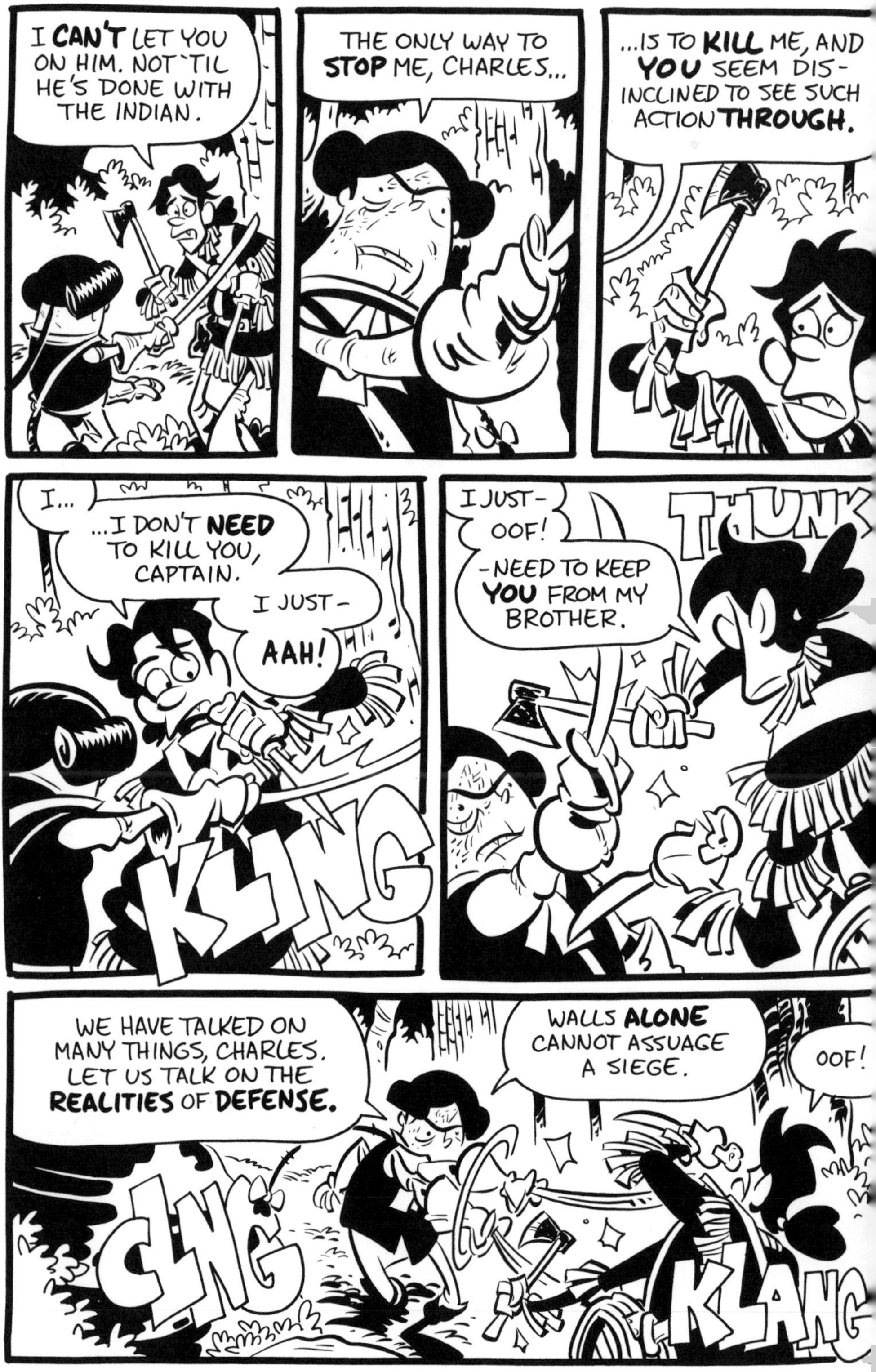
I **CAN'T** LET YOU ON HIM. NOT 'TIL HE'S DONE WITH THE INDIAN.
THE ONLY WAY TO **STOP** ME, CHARLES...
...IS TO **KILL** ME, AND **YOU** SEEM DIS-INCLINED TO SEE SUCH ACTION **THROUGH.**
I...
...I DON'T **NEED** TO KILL YOU, CAPTAIN.
I JUST-
AAH!
KLING
I JUST-
OOF!
-NEED TO KEEP **YOU** FROM MY BROTHER.
THUNK
WE HAVE TALKED ON MANY THINGS, CHARLES. LET US TALK ON THE **REALITIES** OF **DEFENSE.**
WALLS **ALONE** CANNOT ASSUAGE A SIEGE.
OOF!
CLNG
KLANG

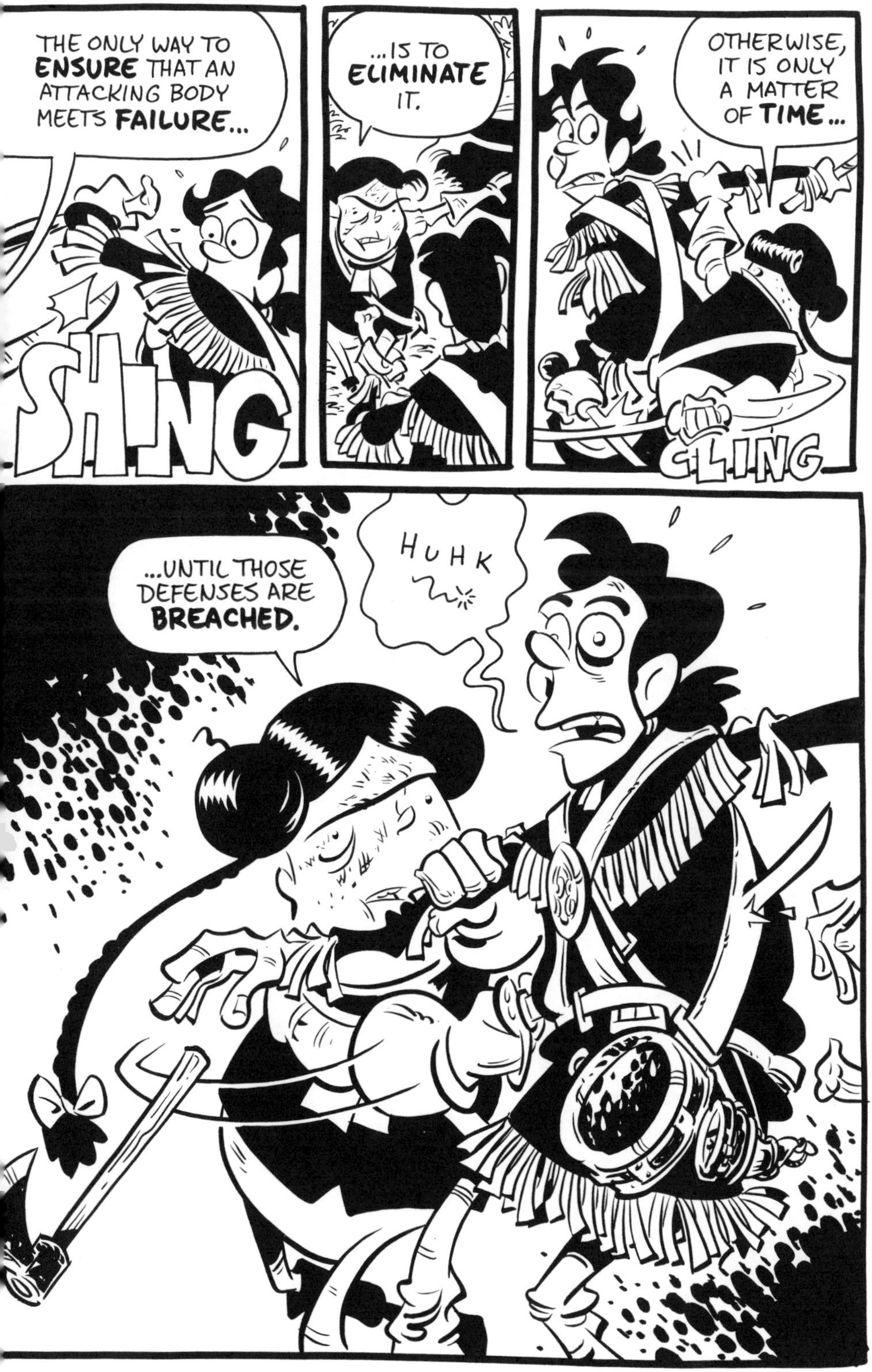
THE ONLY WAY TO **ENSURE** THAT AN ATTACKING BODY MEETS **FAILURE**...
SHING
...IS TO **ELIMINATE** IT.
OTHERWISE, IT IS ONLY A MATTER OF **TIME**...
CLING
...UNTIL THOSE DEFENSES ARE **BREACHED.**
HUHK

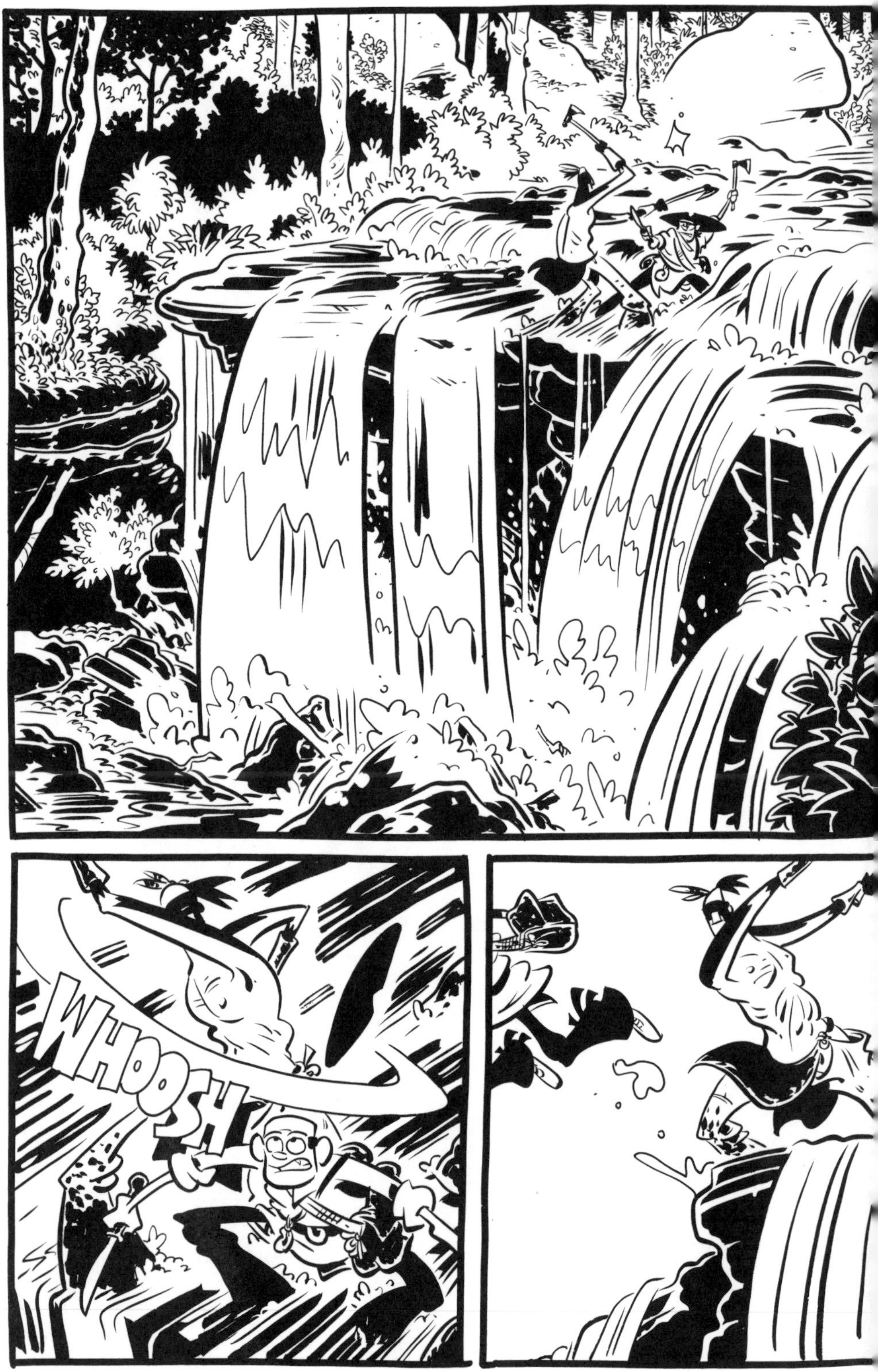
WHOOSH

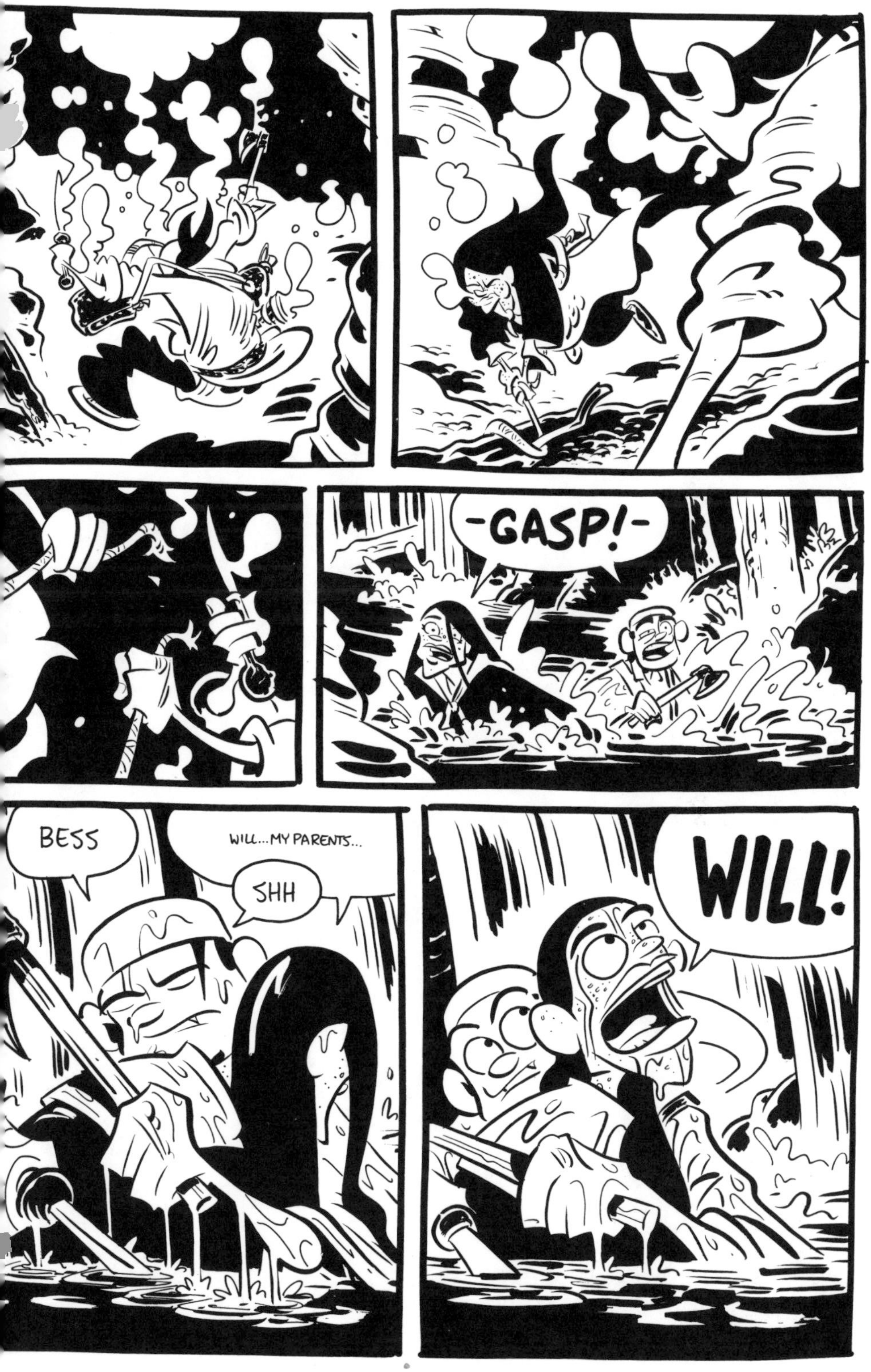
-GASP!-
BESS
WILL... MY PARENTS...
SHH
WILL!

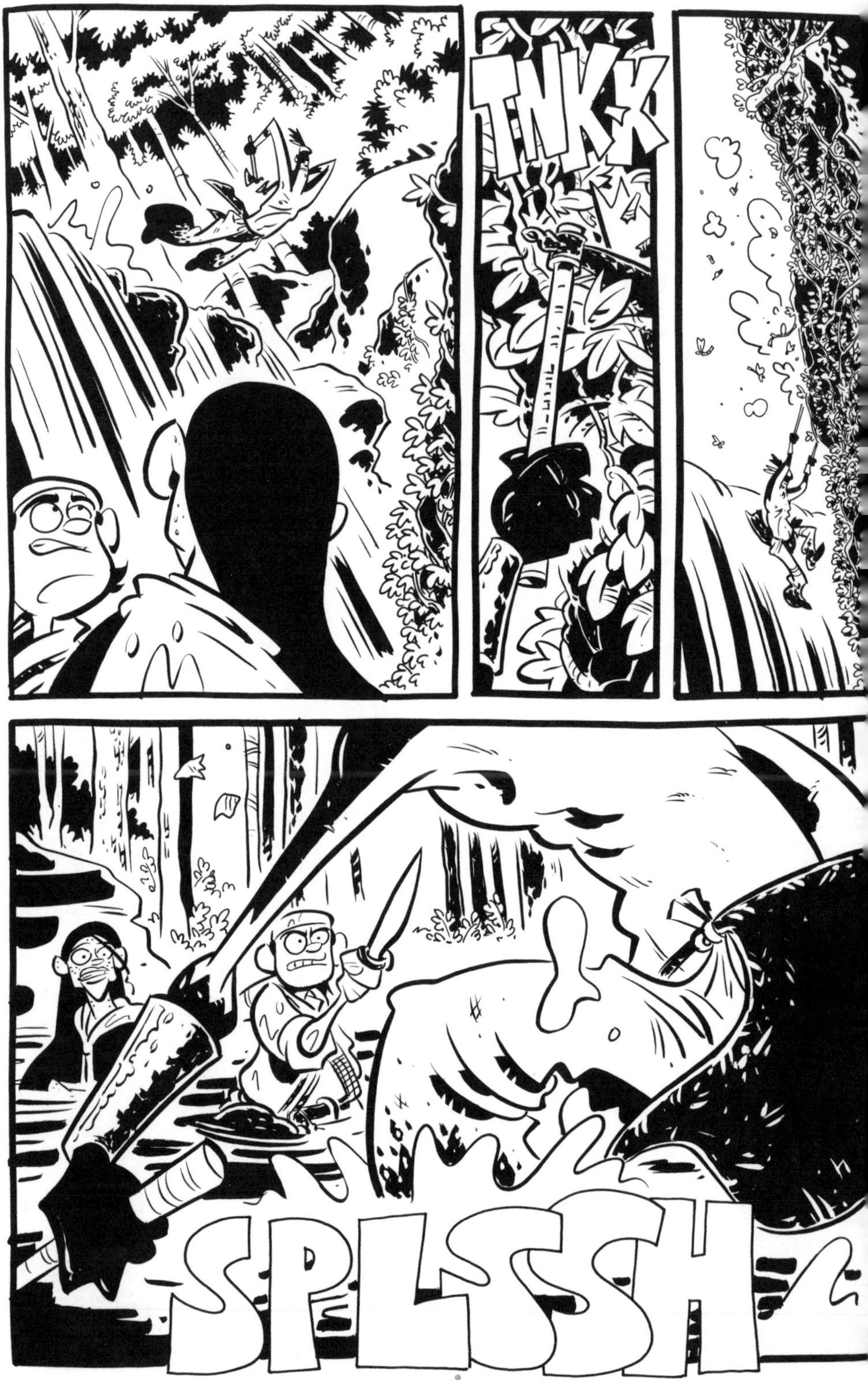
TNK-K
SPLSSH

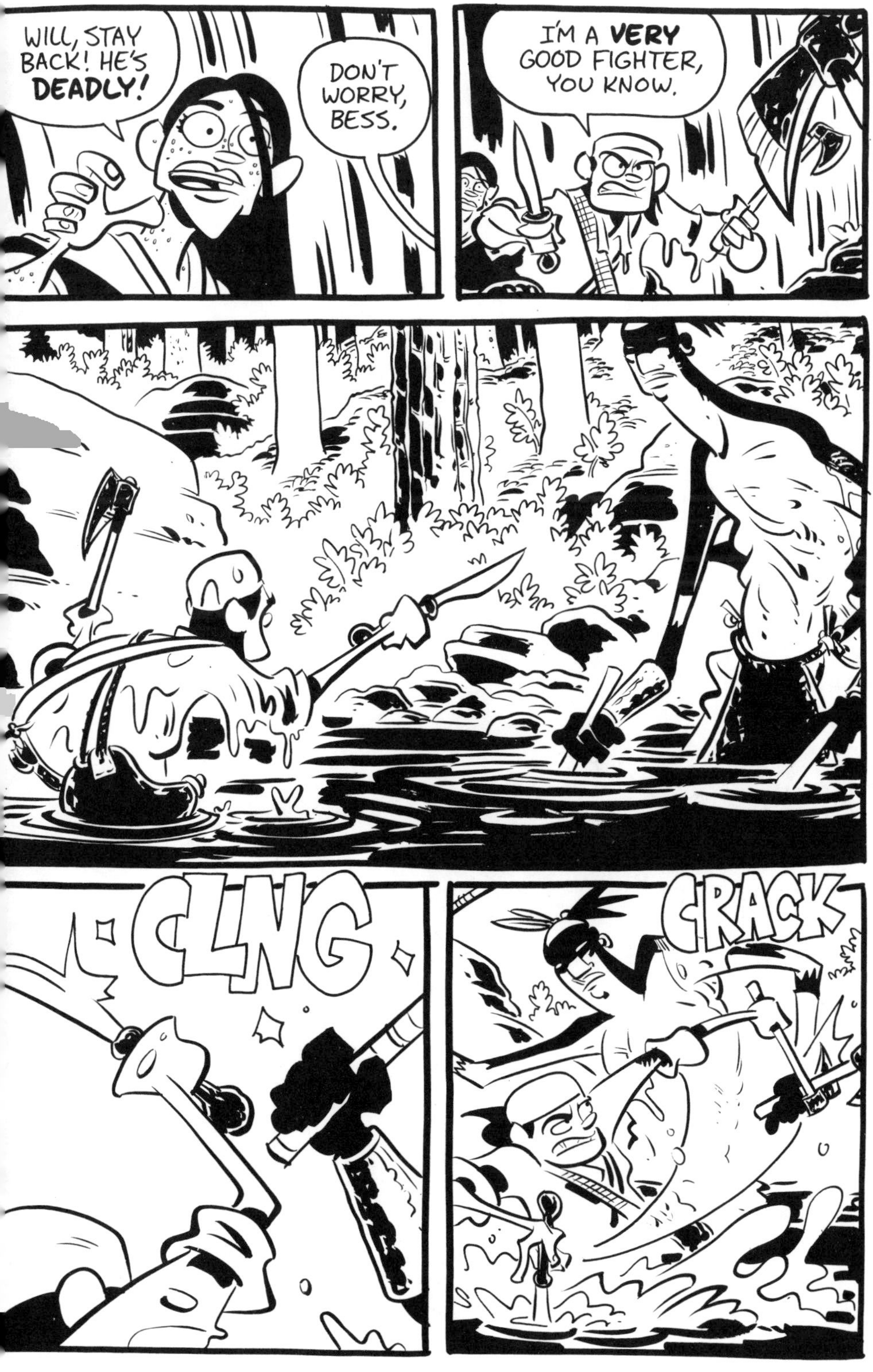
WILL, STAY BACK! HE'S DEADLY!
DON'T WORRY, BESS.
I'M A VERY GOOD FIGHTER, YOU KNOW.
CLNG
CRACK

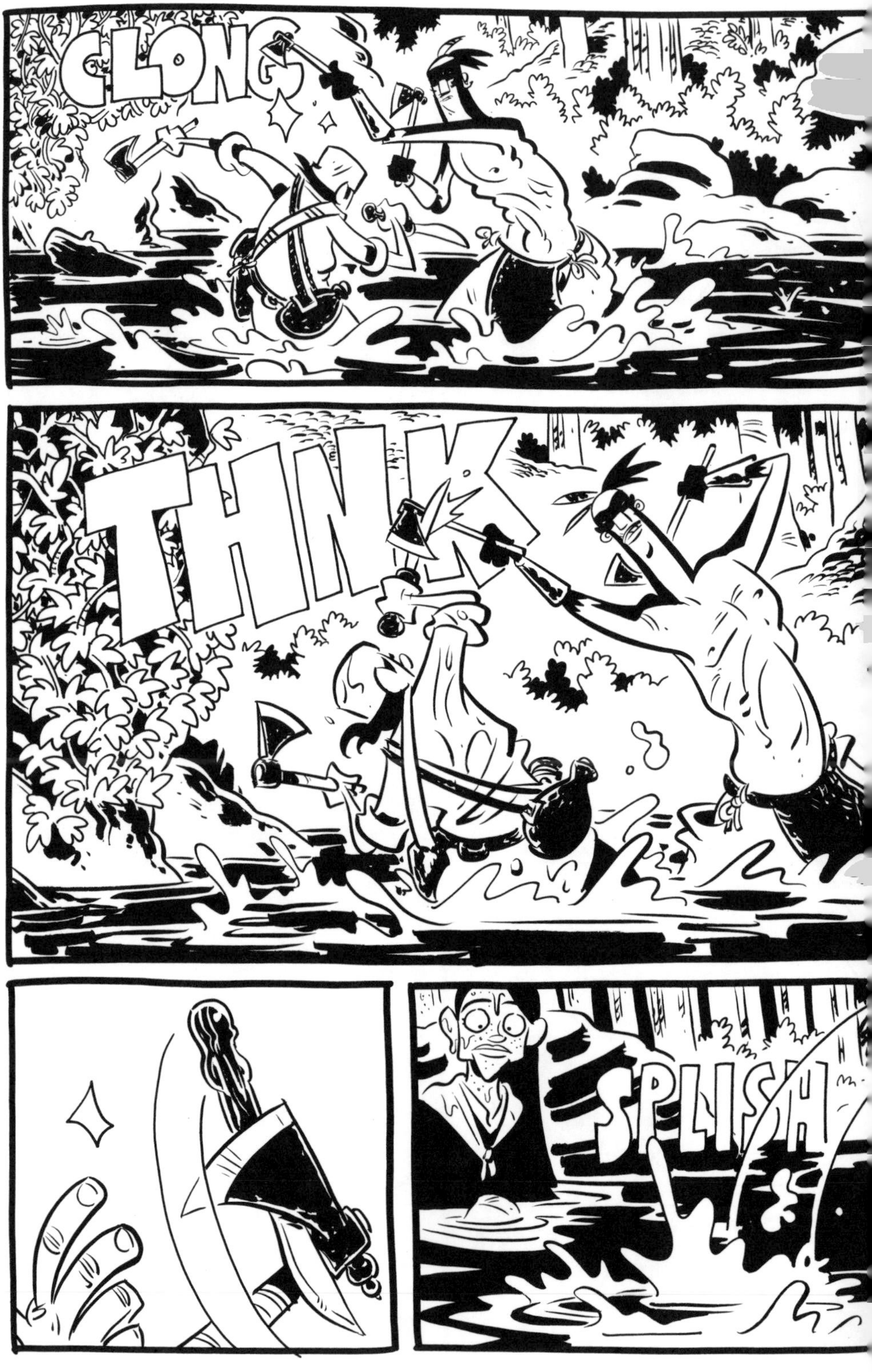
CLONG
THINK
SPLISH

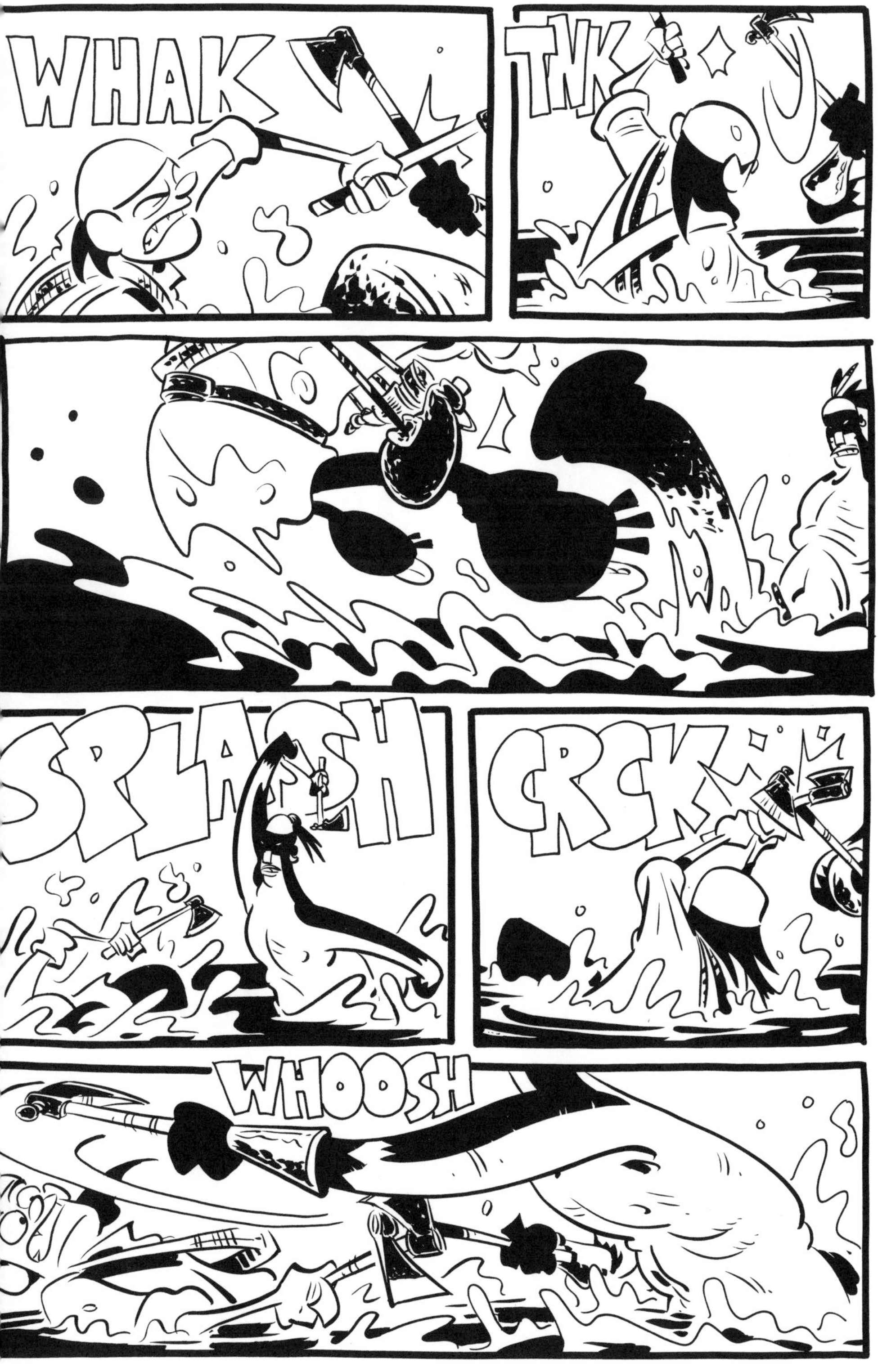
WHAK
TNK
SPLASH
CRCK
WHOOSH

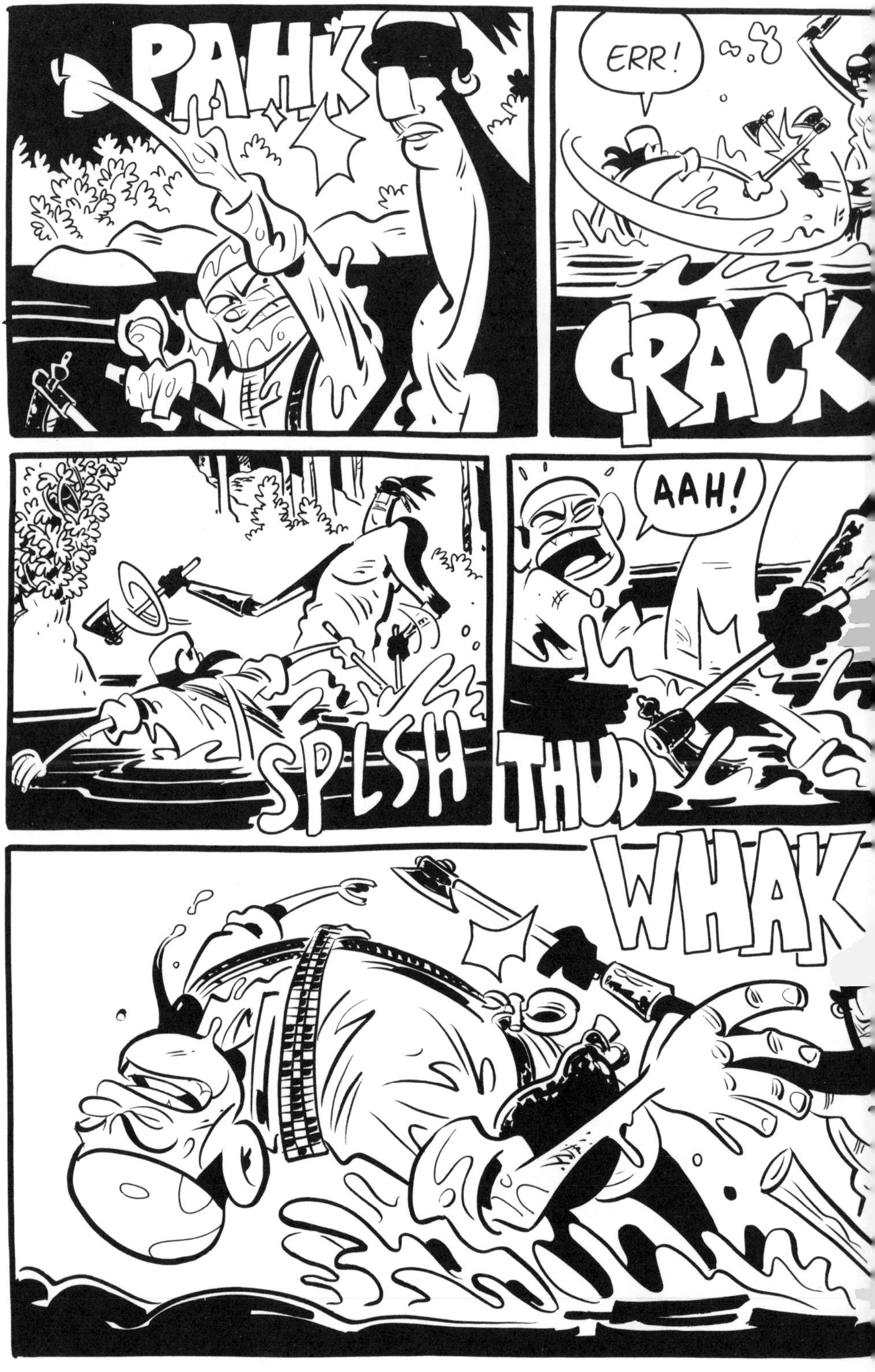
PAHK
ERR!
CRACK
AAH!
SPLSH
THUD
WHAK

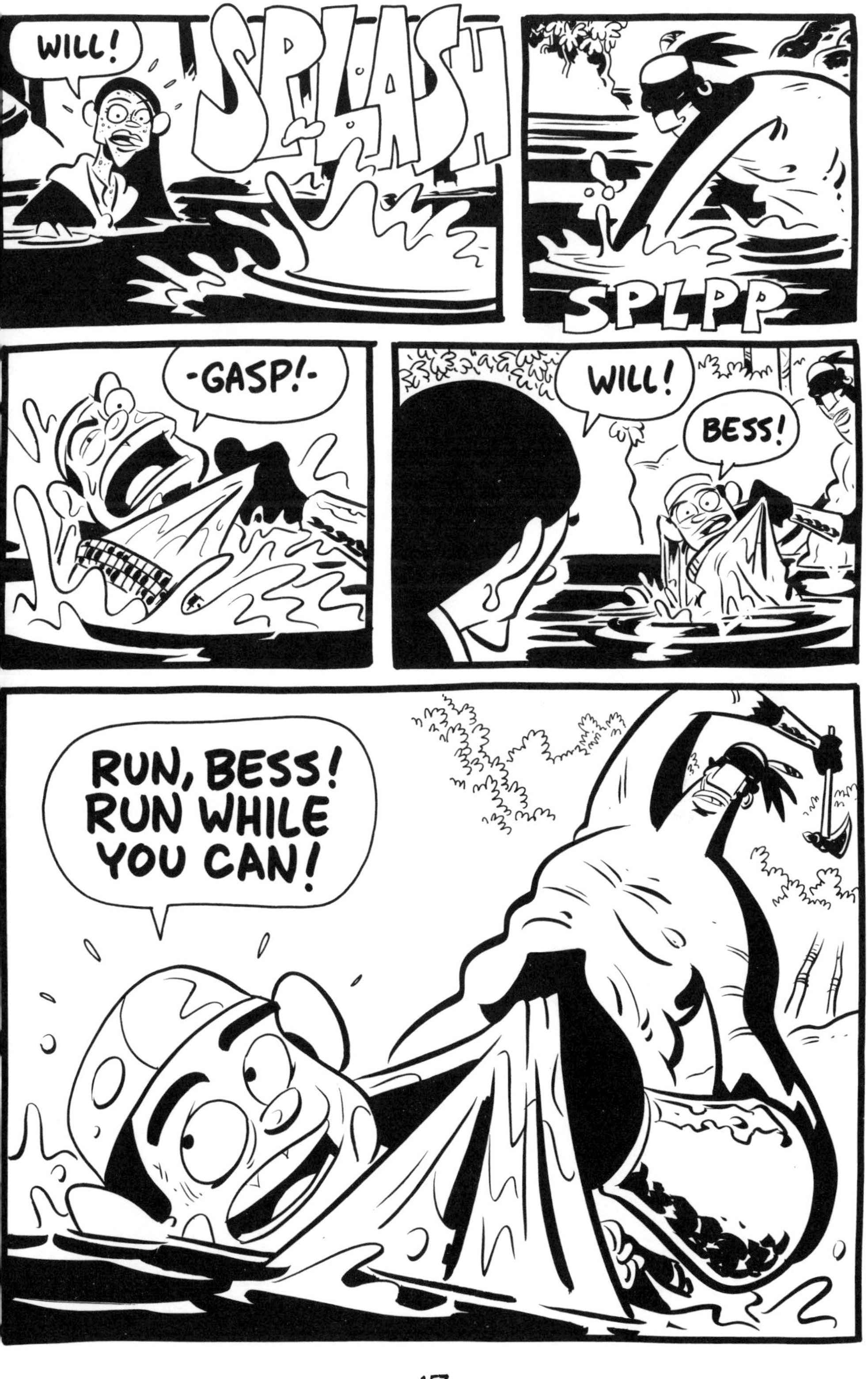
WILL!
SPLASH
SPLPP
-GASP!-
WILL!
BESS!
RUN, BESS! RUN WHILE YOU CAN!

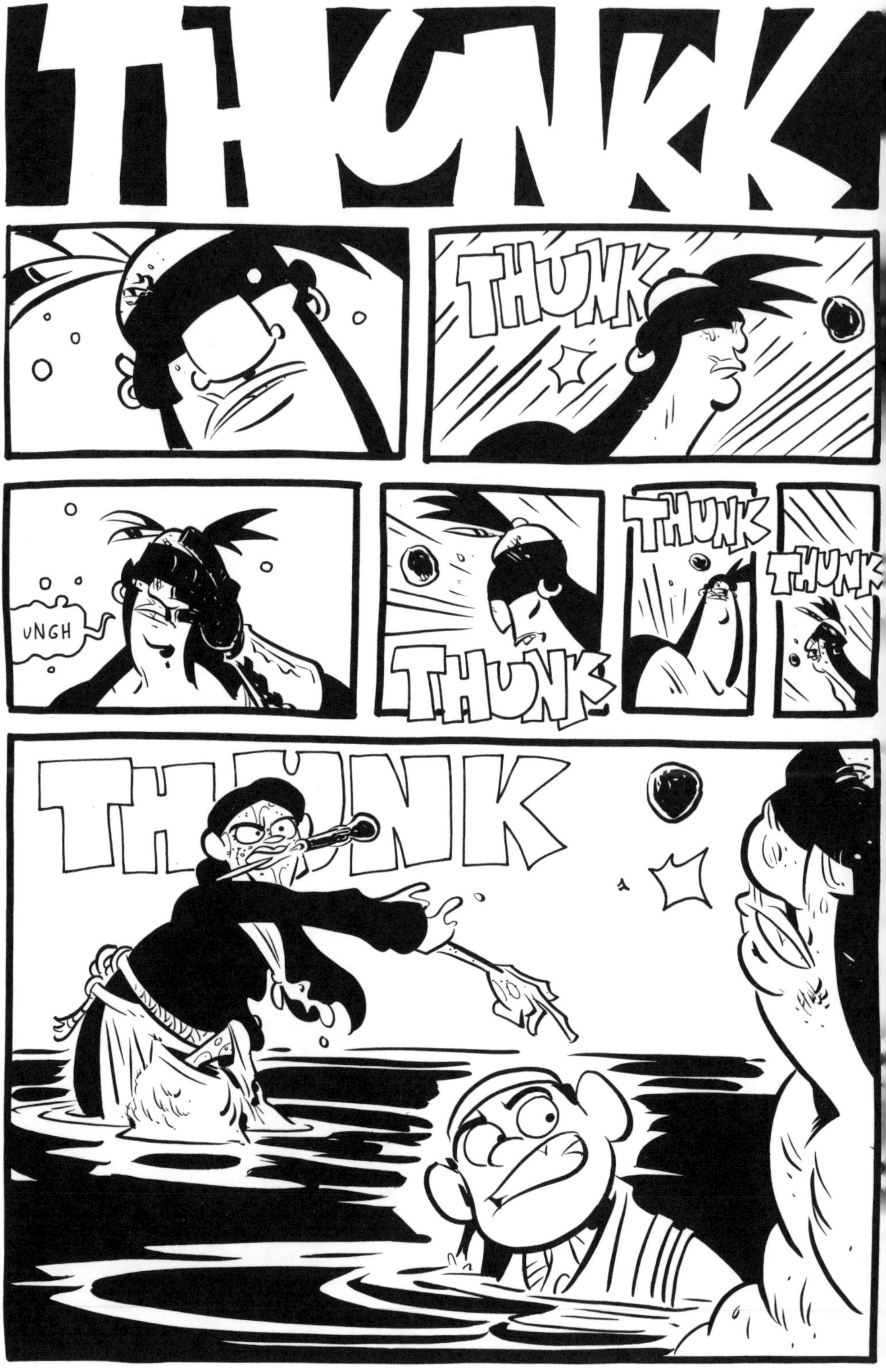
THUNK
THUNK
UNGH
THUNK
THUNK
THUNK
THUNK

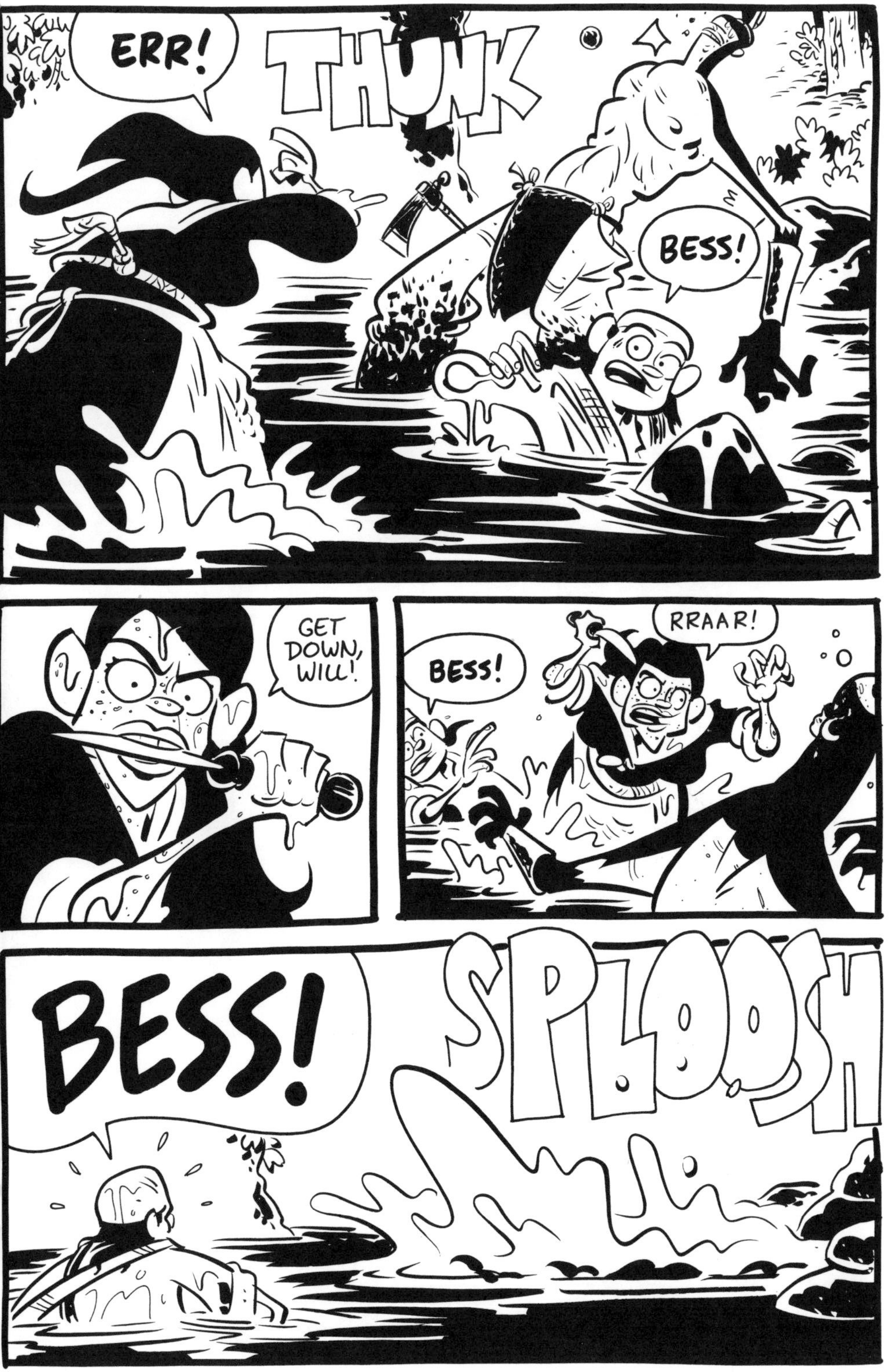
ERR!
THUNK
BESS!
GET DOWN, WILL!
BESS!
RRAAR!
BESS!
SPLOOSH

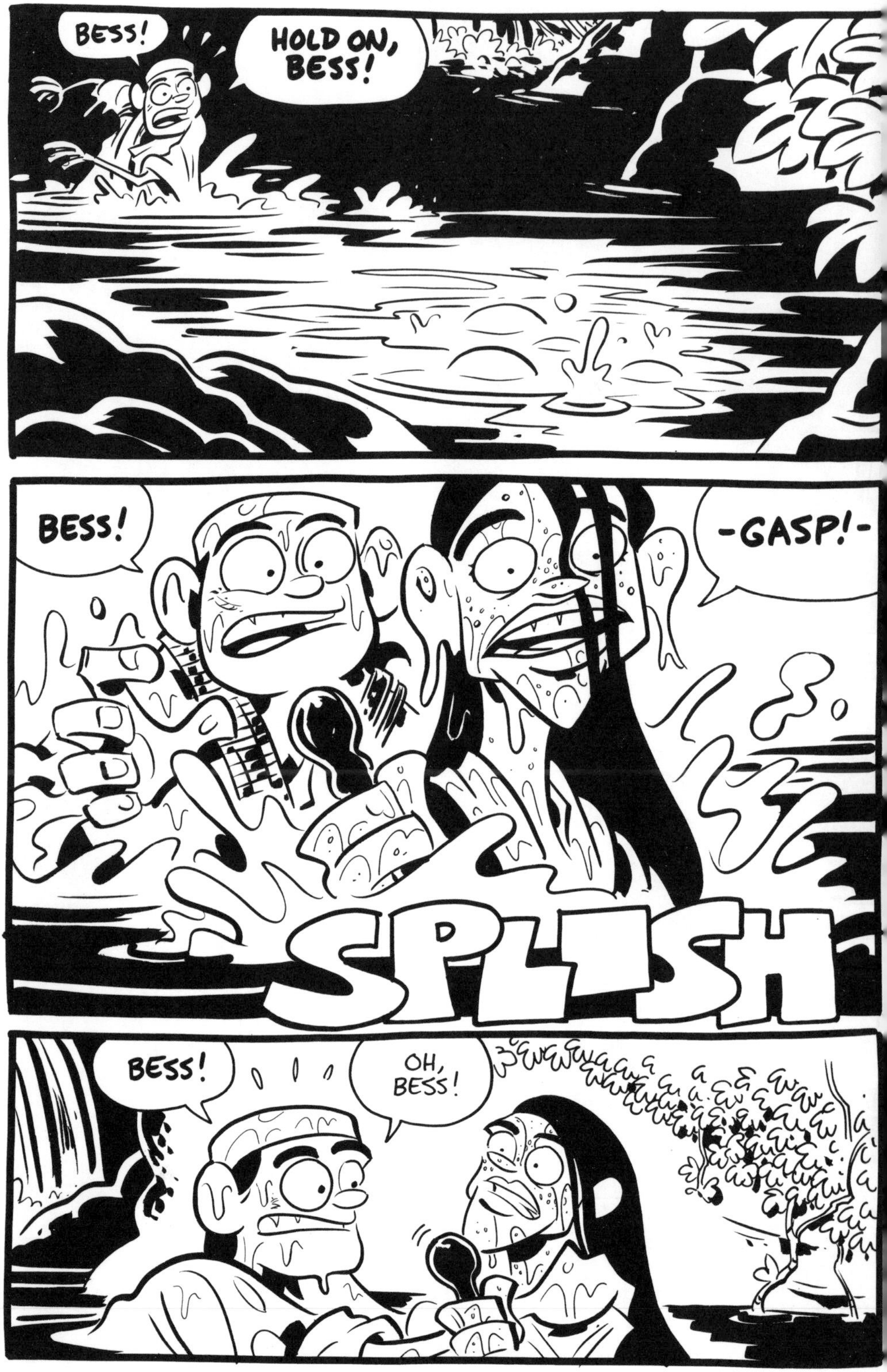
BESS!
HOLD ON, BESS!
BESS!
-GASP!-
SPLISH
BESS!
OH, BESS!

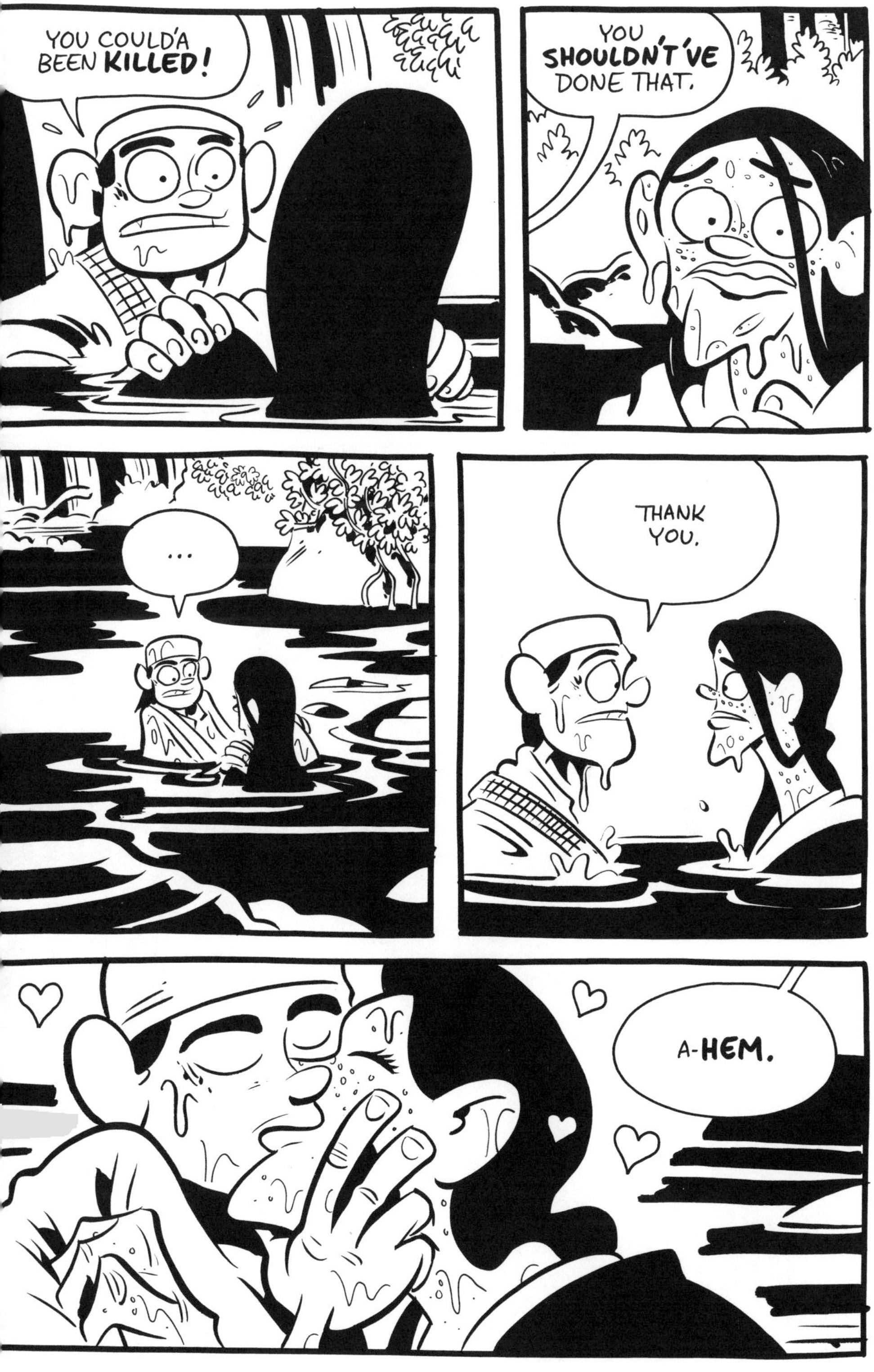
YOU COULD'A BEEN KILLED!
YOU SHOULDN'T'VE DONE THAT.
...
THANK YOU.
A-HEM.

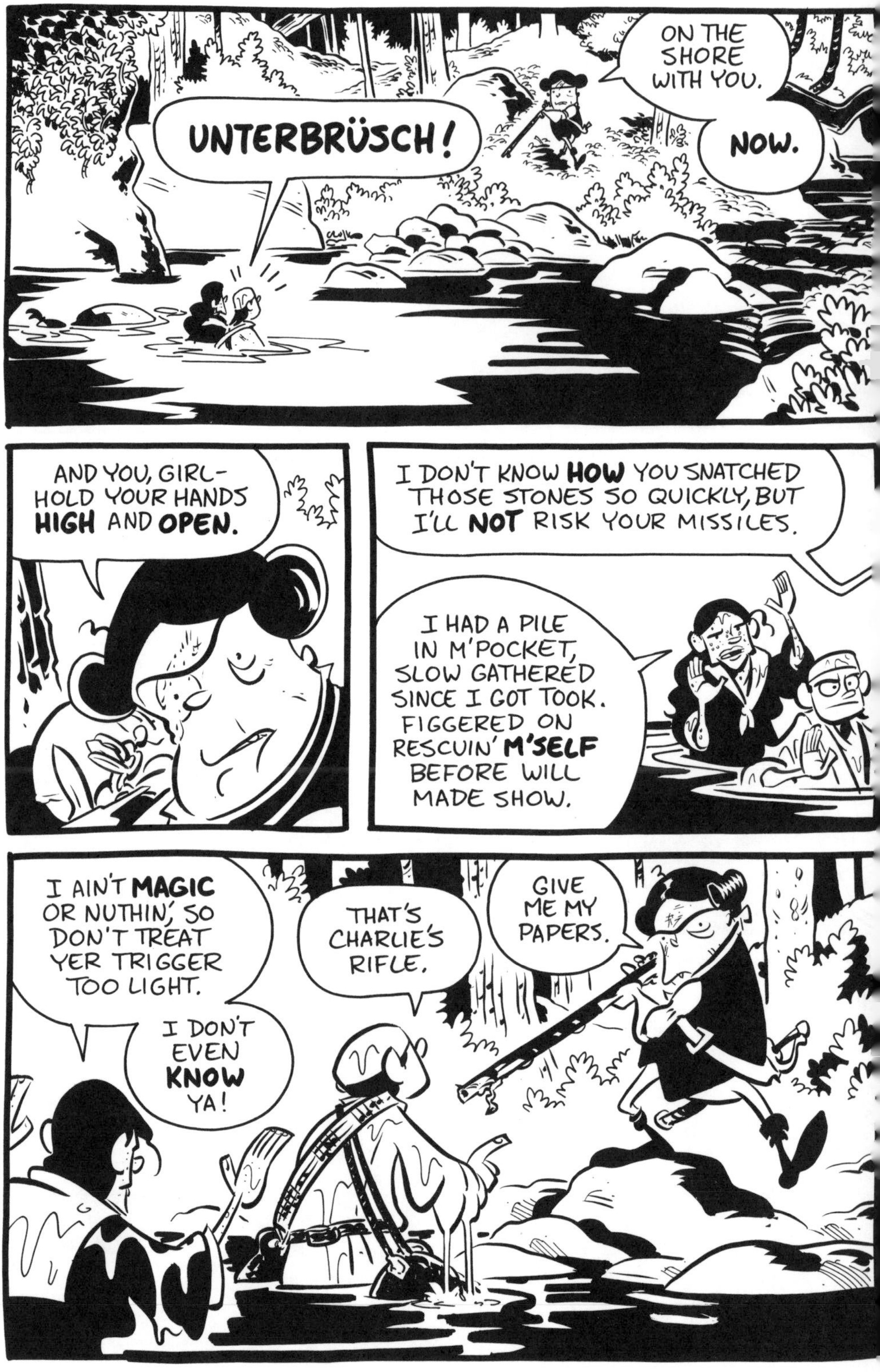
UNTERBRÜSCH!
ON THE SHORE WITH YOU.
NOW.
AND YOU, GIRL- HOLD YOUR HANDS HIGH AND OPEN.
I DON'T KNOW HOW YOU SNATCHED THOSE STONES SO QUICKLY, BUT I'LL NOT RISK YOUR MISSILES.
I HAD A PILE IN M'POCKET, SLOW GATHERED SINCE I GOT TOOK. FIGGERED ON RESCUIN' M'SELF BEFORE WILL MADE SHOW.
I AIN'T MAGIC OR NUTHIN', SO DON'T TREAT YER TRIGGER TOO LIGHT.
I DON'T EVEN KNOW YA!
THAT'S CHARLIE'S RIFLE.
GIVE ME MY PAPERS.

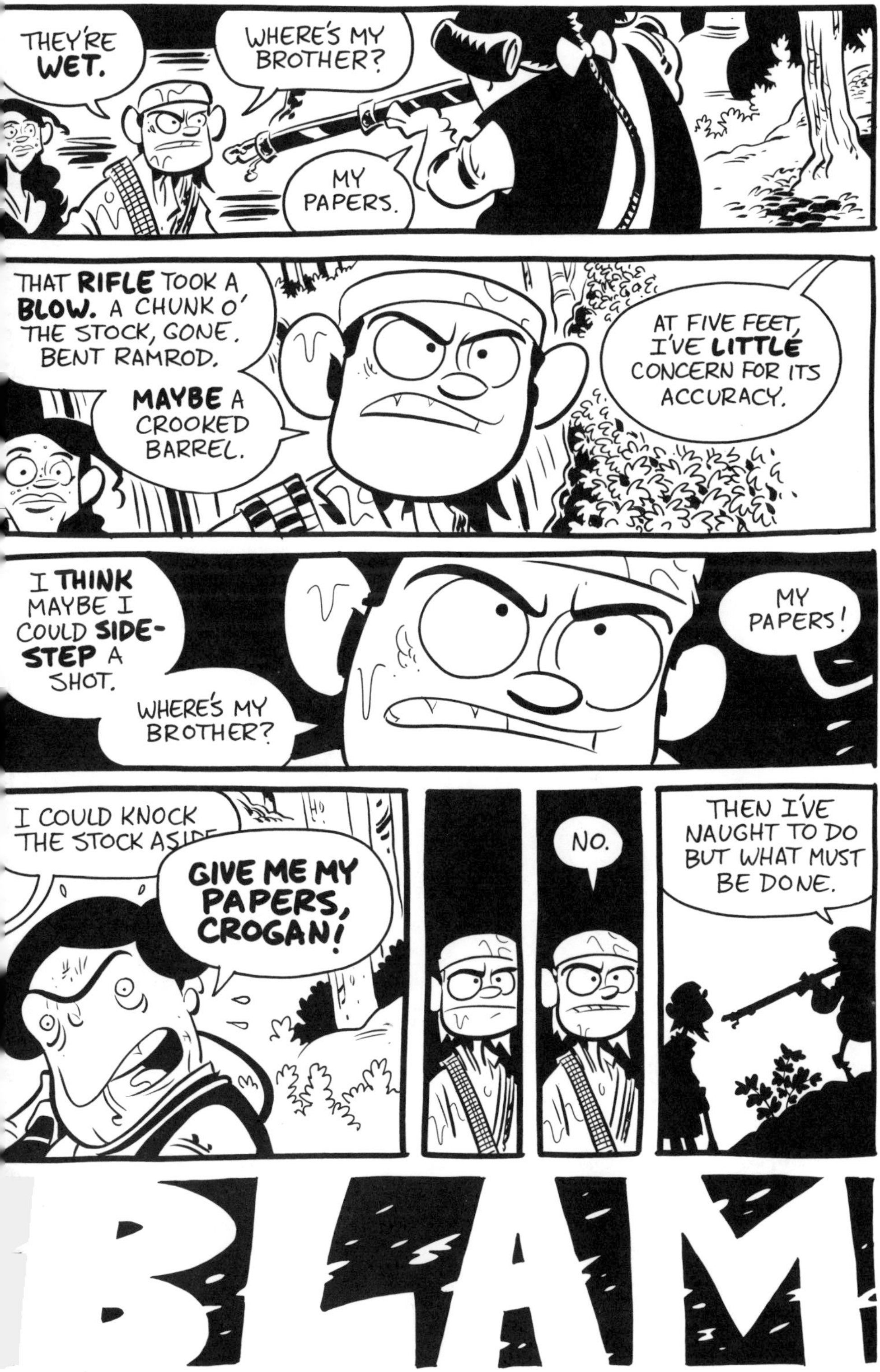
THEY'RE WET.
WHERE'S MY BROTHER?
MY PAPERS.
THAT RIFLE TOOK A BLOW. A CHUNK O' THE STOCK, GONE. BENT RAMROD.
MAYBE A CROOKED BARREL.
AT FIVE FEET, I'VE LITTLE CONCERN FOR ITS ACCURACY.
I THINK MAYBE I COULD SIDE-STEP A SHOT.
WHERE'S MY BROTHER?
MY PAPERS!
I COULD KNOCK THE STOCK ASIDE
GIVE ME MY PAPERS, CROGAN!
NO.
THEN I'VE NAUGHT TO DO BUT WHAT MUST BE DONE.
BLAM!

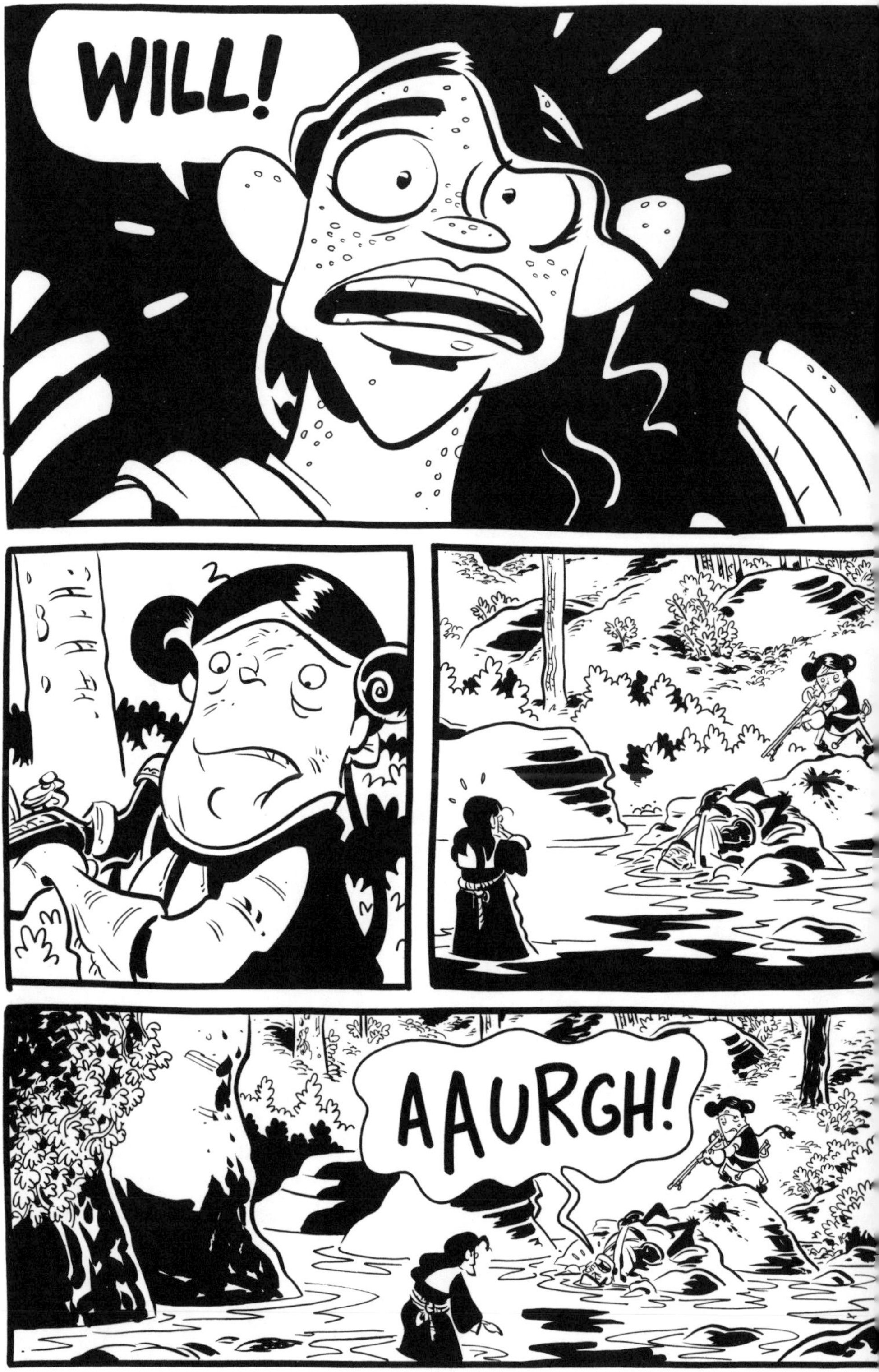
WILL!
AAURGH!

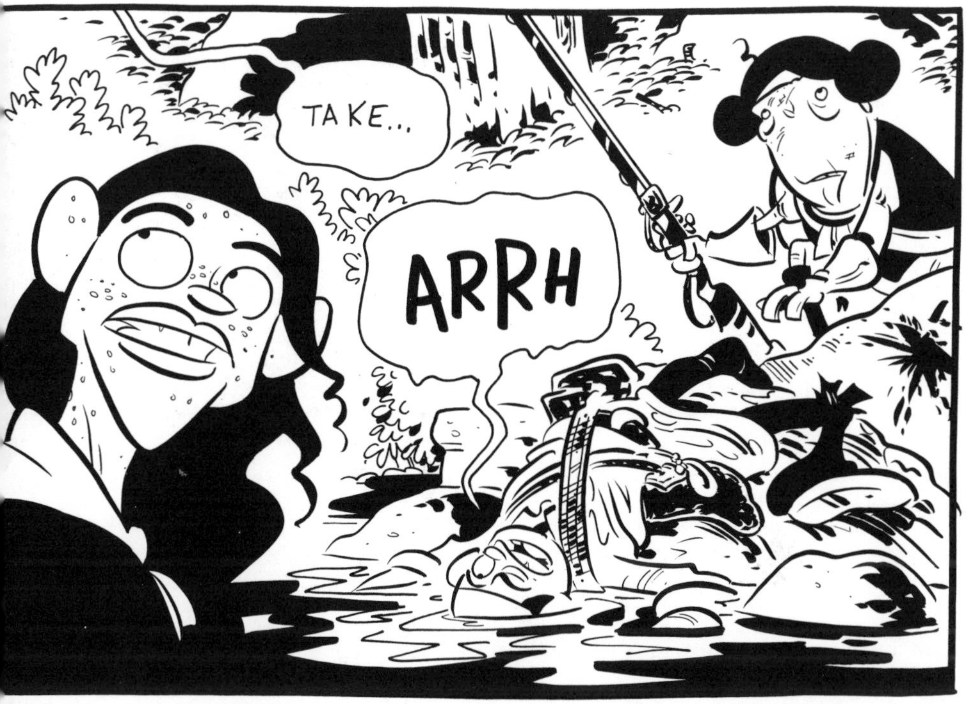
TAKE...
ARRH

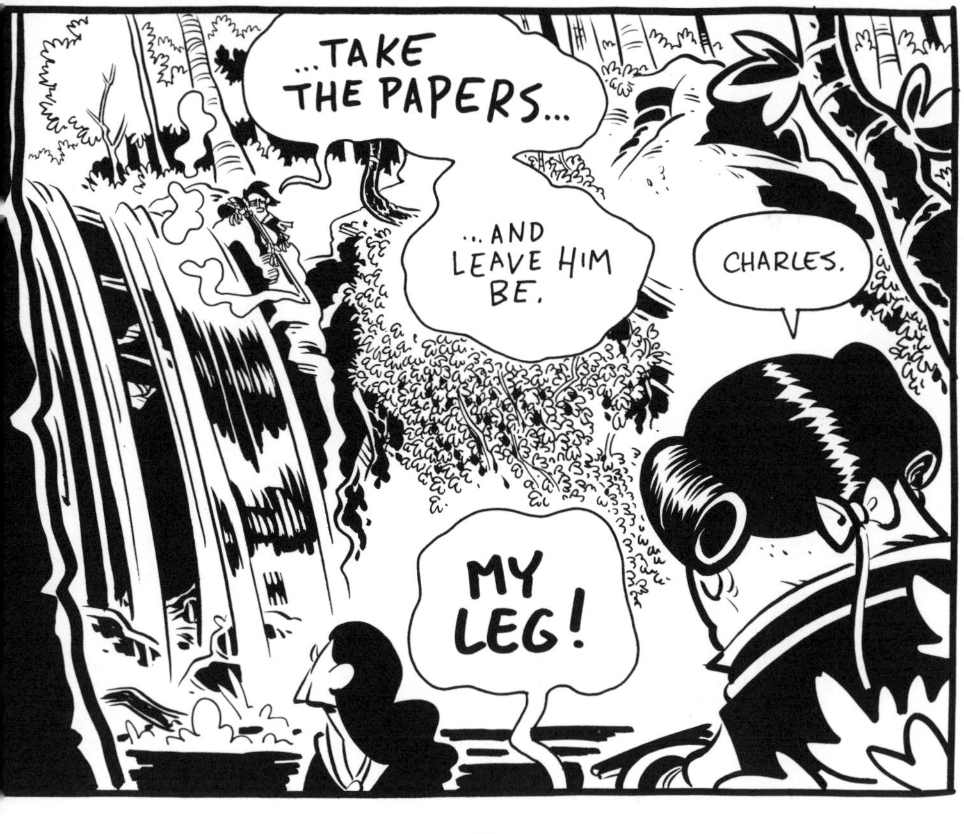
...TAKE THE PAPERS...
...AND LEAVE HIM BE.
CHARLES.
MY LEG!

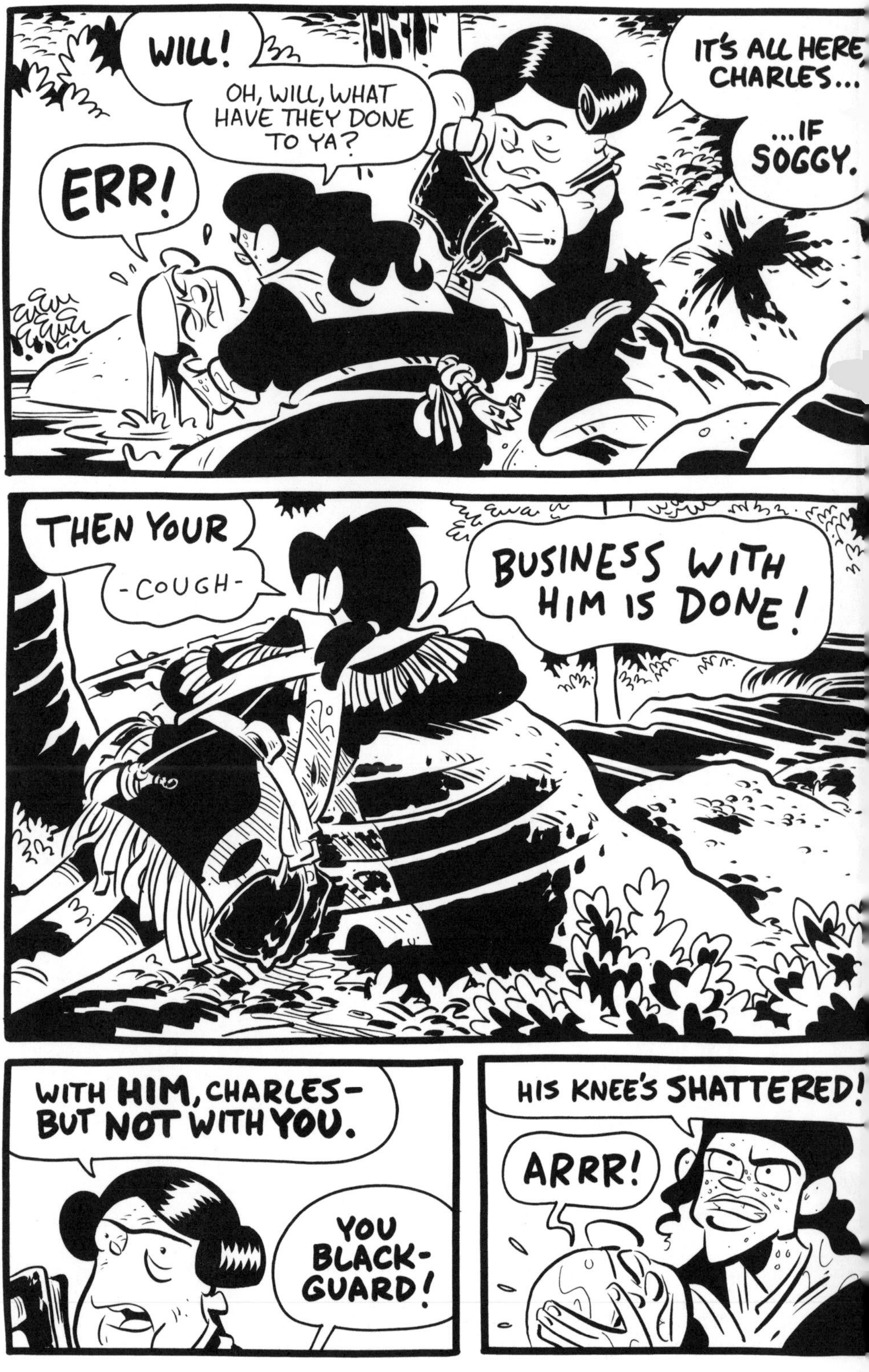
WILL!
OH, WILL, WHAT HAVE THEY DONE TO YA?
ERR!
IT'S ALL HERE, CHARLES...
...IF SOGGY.
THEN YOUR
-COUGH-
BUSINESS WITH HIM IS DONE!
WITH HIM, CHARLES- BUT NOT WITH YOU.
YOU BLACK-GUARD!
HIS KNEE'S SHATTERED!
ARRR!

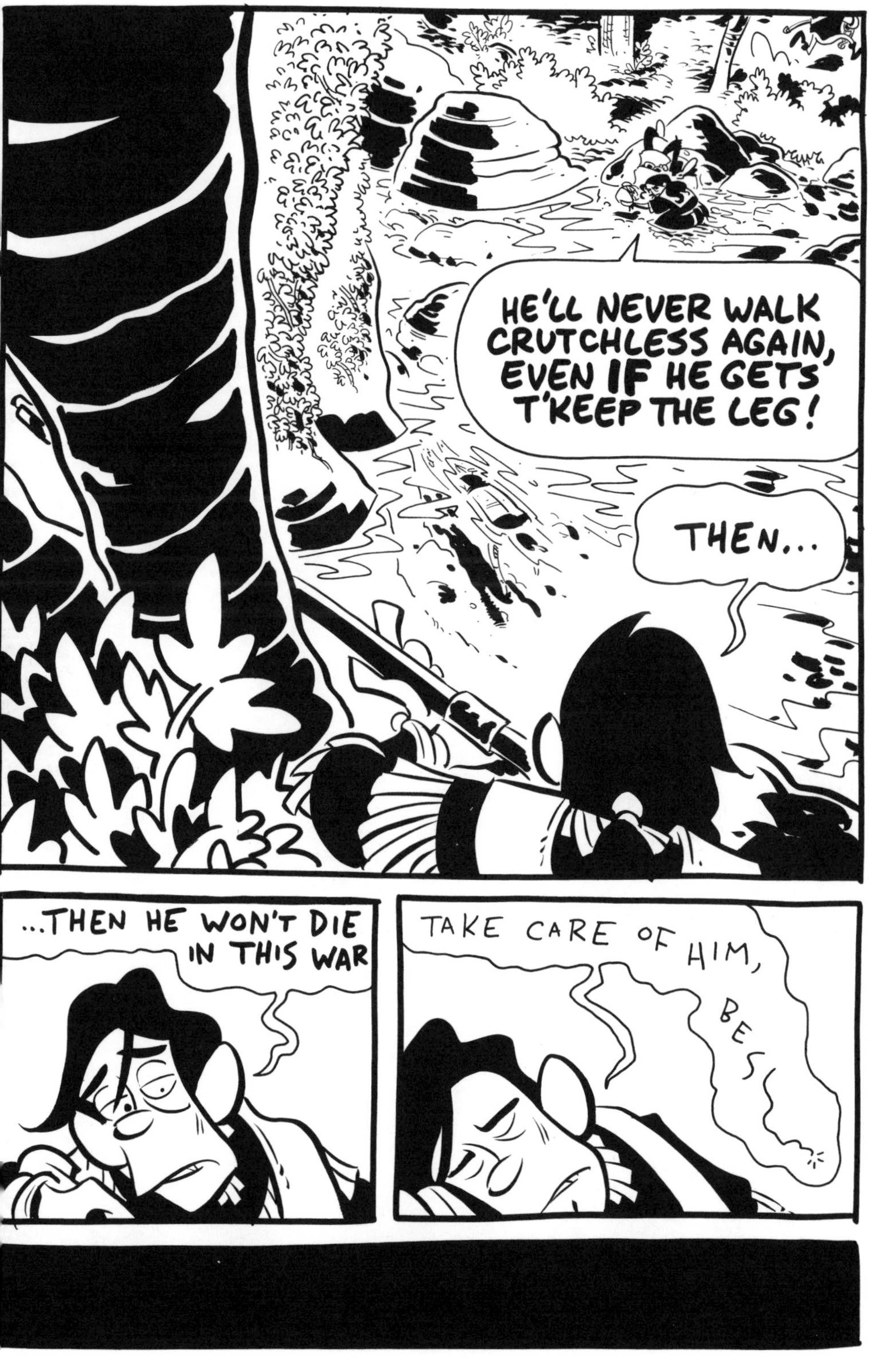
HE'LL NEVER WALK CRUTCHLESS AGAIN, EVEN IF HE GETS T'KEEP THE LEG!
THEN...
...THEN HE WON'T DIE IN THIS WAR
TAKE CARE OF HIM, BES

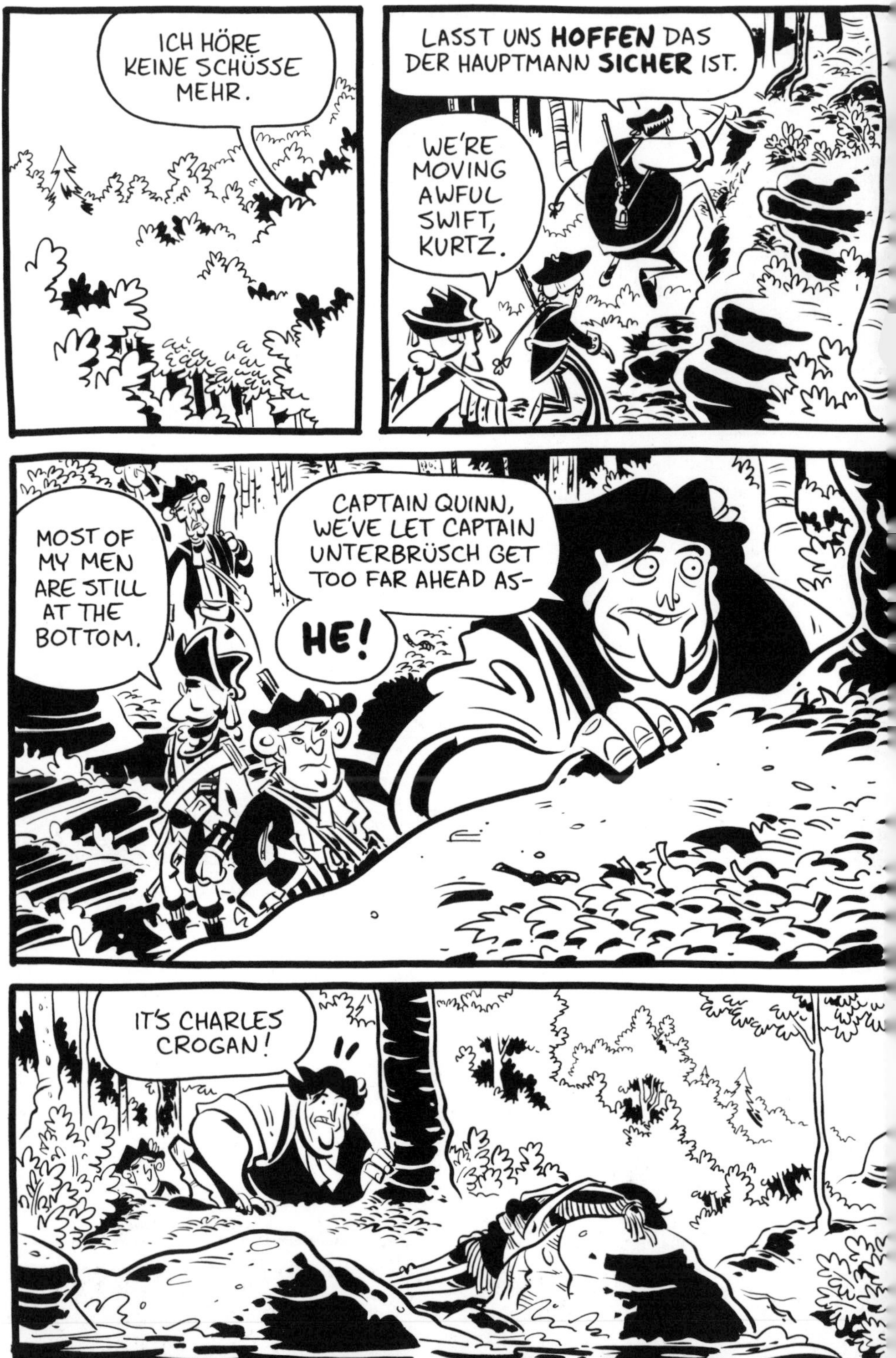
ICH HÖRE KEINE SCHÜSSE MEHR.
LASST UNS **HOFFEN** DAS DER HAUPTMANN **SICHER** IST.
WE'RE MOVING AWFUL SWIFT, KURTZ.
MOST OF MY MEN ARE STILL AT THE BOTTOM.
CAPTAIN QUINN, WE'VE LET CAPTAIN UNTERBRÜSCH GET TOO FAR AHEAD AS-
HE!
IT'S CHARLES CROGAN!

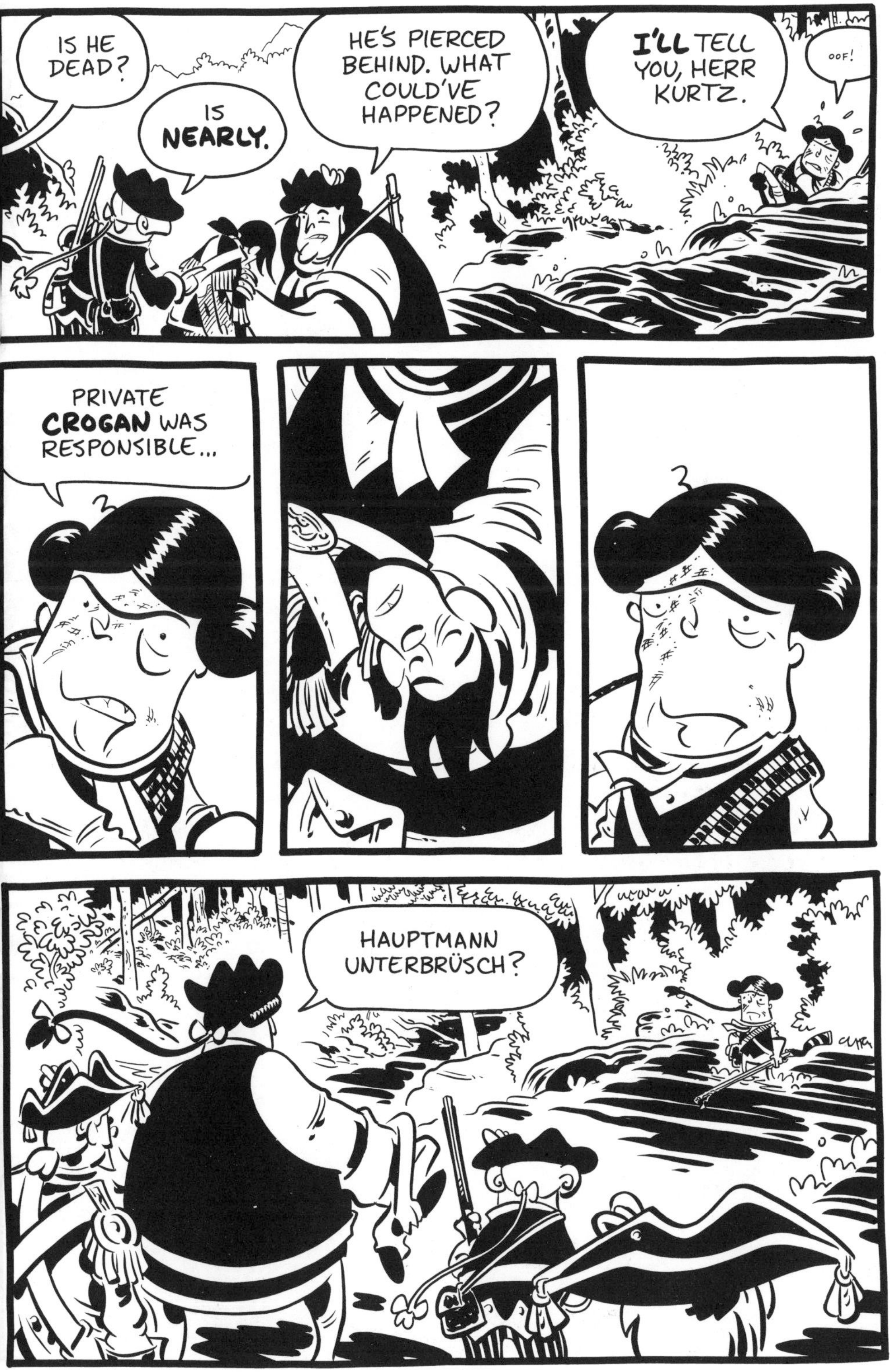
IS HE DEAD?
IS **NEARLY.**
HE'S PIERCED BEHIND. WHAT COULD'VE HAPPENED?
I'LL TELL YOU, HERR KURTZ.
OOF!
PRIVATE **CROGAN** WAS RESPONSIBLE...
HAUPTMANN UNTERBRÜSCH?

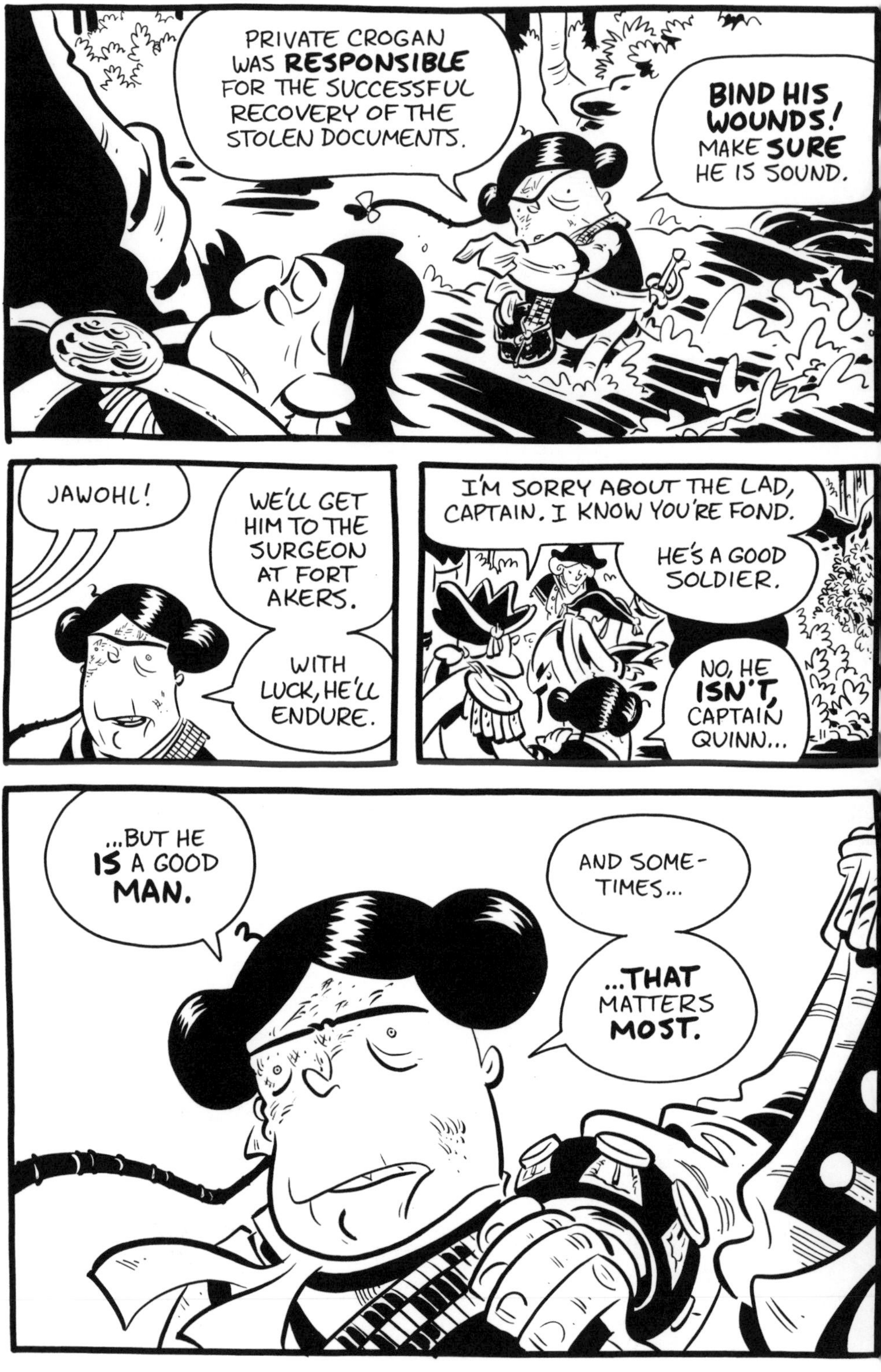
PRIVATE CROGAN WAS RESPONSIBLE FOR THE SUCCESSFUL RECOVERY OF THE STOLEN DOCUMENTS.
BIND HIS WOUNDS! MAKE SURE HE IS SOUND.
JAWOHL!
WE'LL GET HIM TO THE SURGEON AT FORT AKERS.
WITH LUCK, HE'LL ENDURE.
I'M SORRY ABOUT THE LAD, CAPTAIN. I KNOW YOU'RE FOND.
HE'S A GOOD SOLDIER.
NO, HE ISN'T, CAPTAIN QUINN...
...BUT HE IS A GOOD MAN.
AND SOME-TIMES...
...THAT MATTERS MOST.

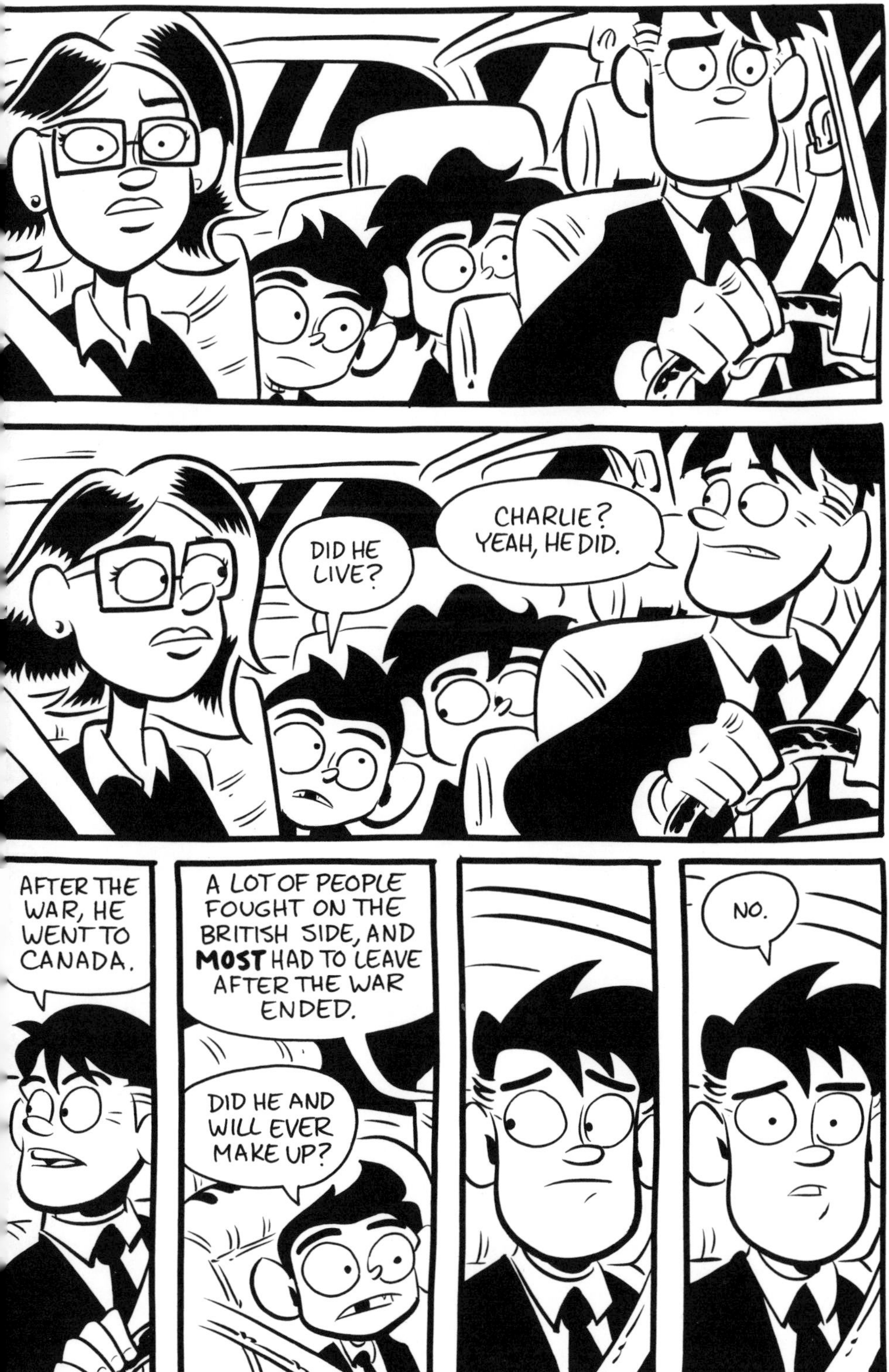
DID HE LIVE?
CHARLIE? YEAH, HE DID.
AFTER THE WAR, HE WENT TO CANADA.
A LOT OF PEOPLE FOUGHT ON THE BRITISH SIDE, AND **MOST** HAD TO LEAVE AFTER THE WAR ENDED.
DID HE AND WILL EVER MAKE UP?
NO.

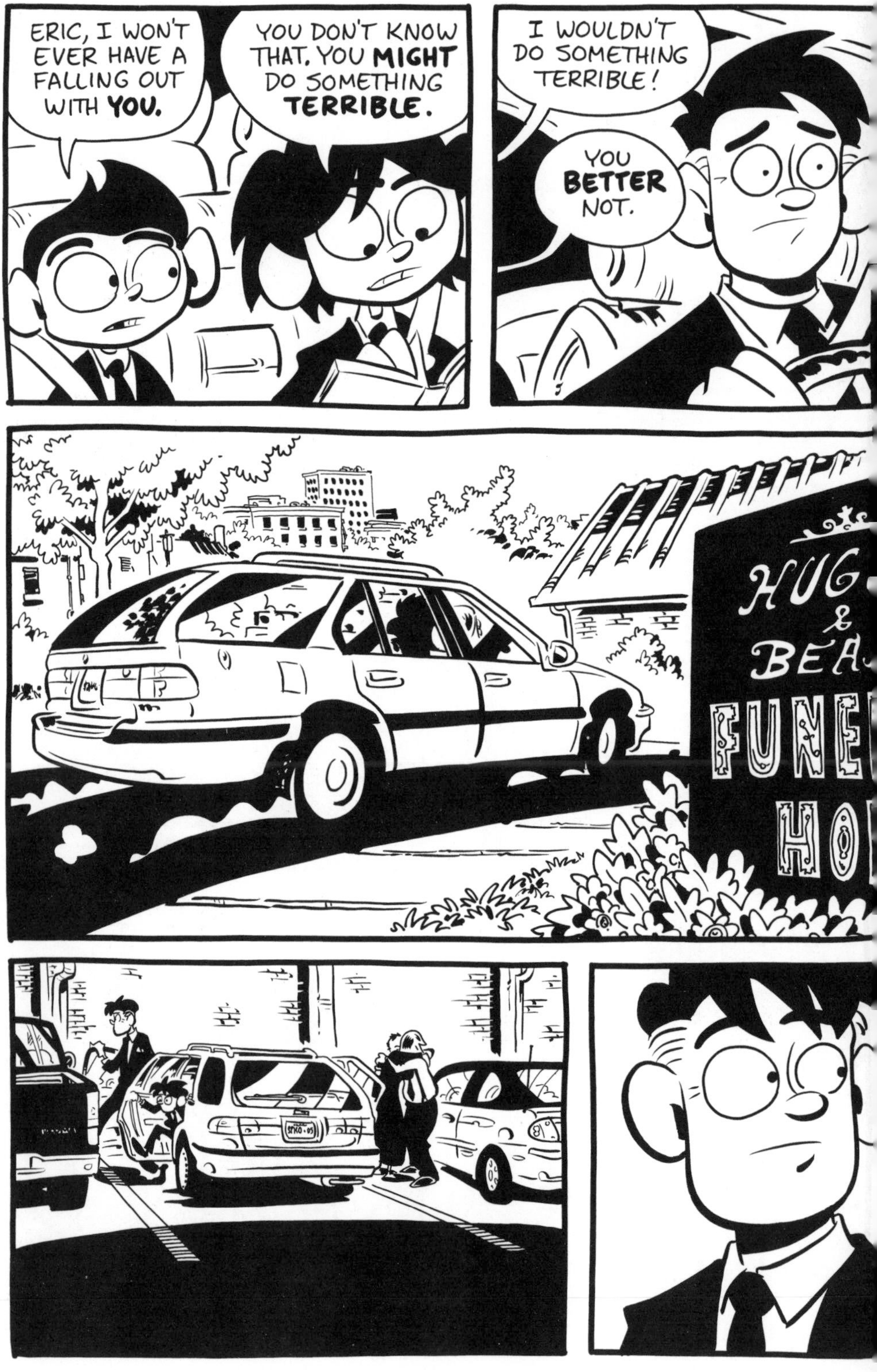
ERIC, I WON'T EVER HAVE A FALLING OUT WITH **YOU.**
YOU DON'T KNOW THAT. YOU **MIGHT** DO SOMETHING **TERRIBLE.**
I WOULDN'T DO SOMETHING TERRIBLE!
YOU **BETTER** NOT.

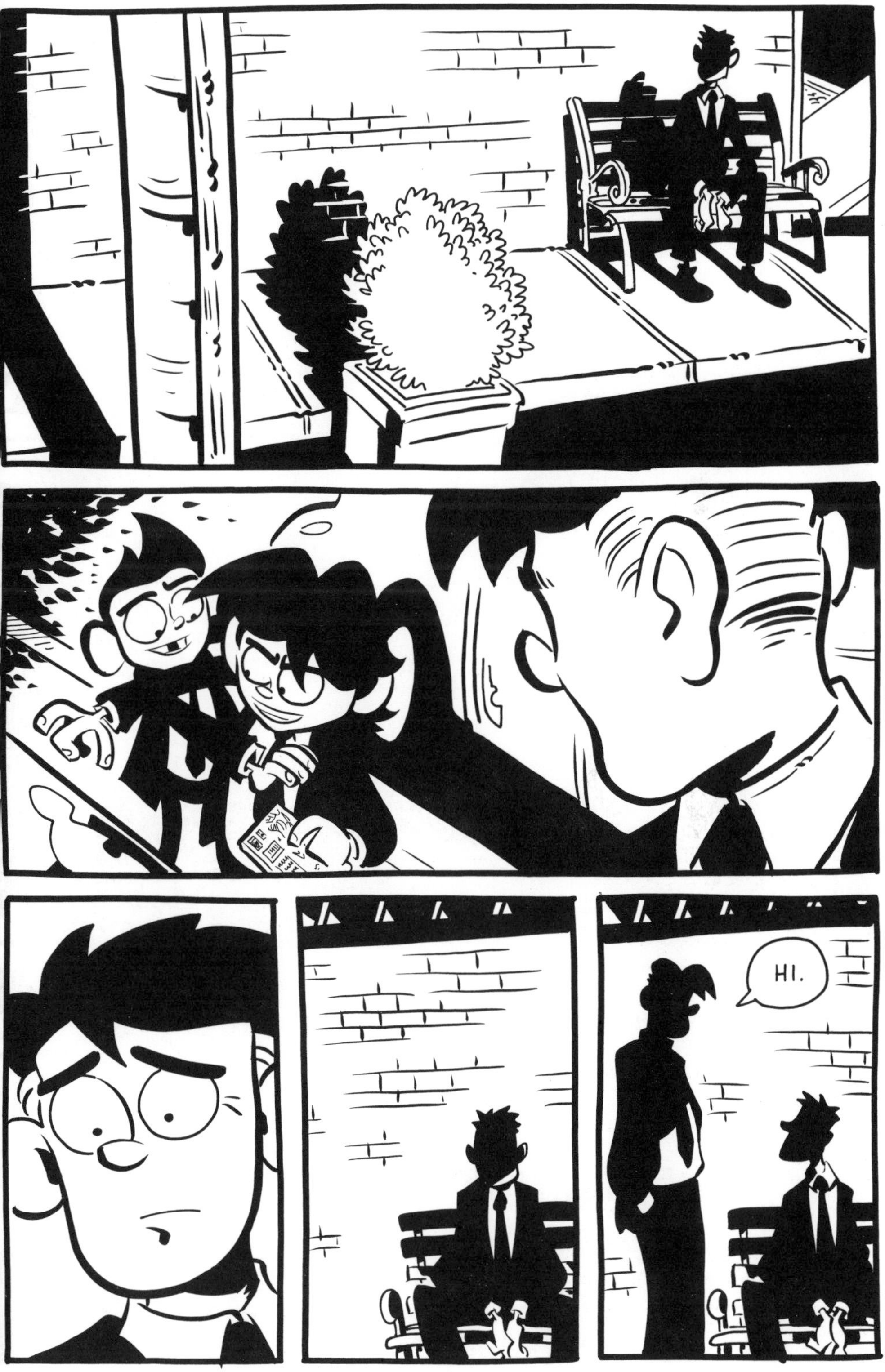
HI.

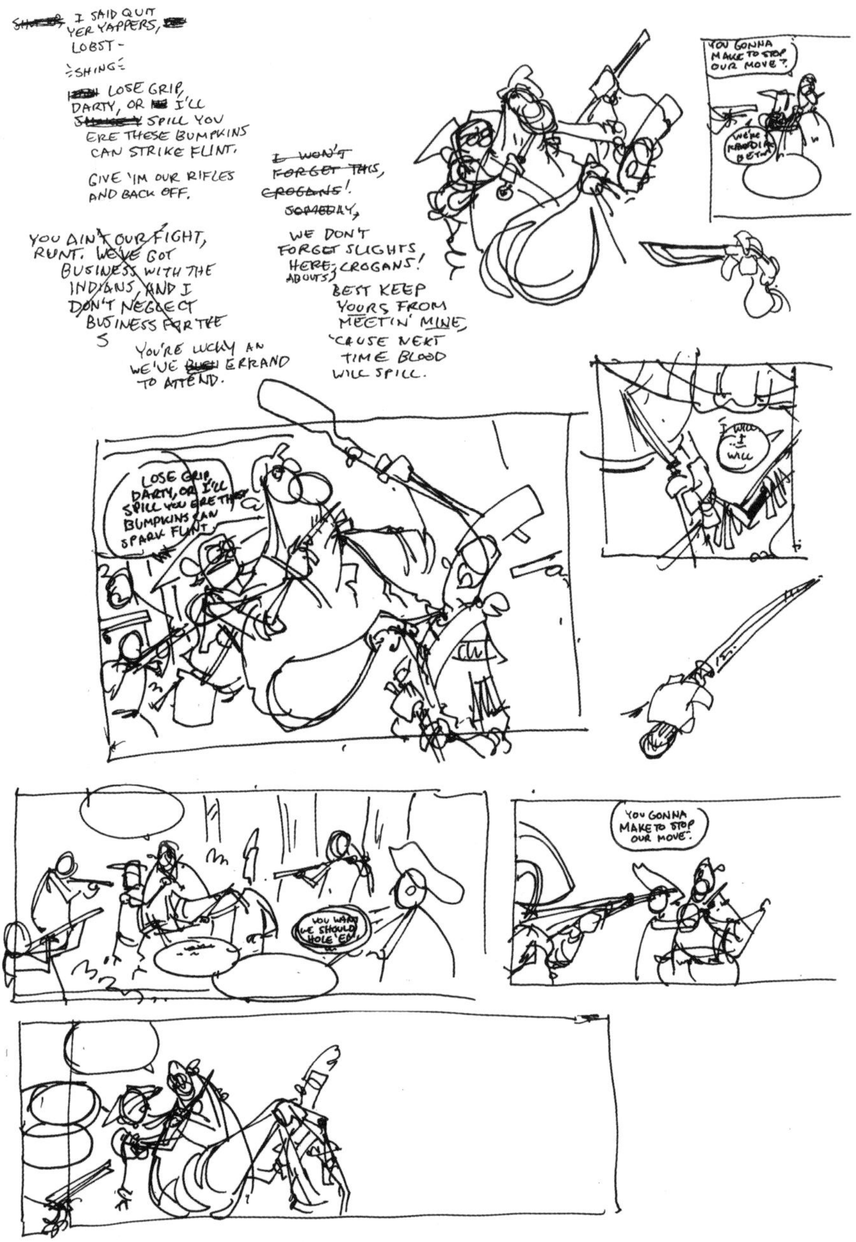
I SAID QUIT YER YAPPERS, LOBST-
SHING
LOSE GRIP, DARTY, OR I'LL SPILL YOU ERE THESE BUMPKINS CAN STRIKE FLINT.
GIVE 'IM OUR RIFLES AND BACK OFF.
YOU AIN'T OUR FIGHT, RUNT. WE'VE GOT BUSINESS WITH THE INDIANS, AND I DON'T NEGLECT BUSINESS FOR THE S
YOU'RE LUCKY AN WE'VE ERRAND TO ATTEND.
I WON'T FORGET THIS, CROGANS! SOMEDAY,
WE DON'T FORGET SLIGHTS HERE, CROGANS!
BEST KEEP YOURS FROM MEETIN' MINE, 'CAUSE NEXT TIME BLOOD WILL SPILL.
YOU GONNA MAKE TO STOP OUR MOVE?
LOSE GRIP DARTY, OR I'LL SPILL YOU ERE THESE BUMPKINS CAN SPARK FLINT
I WILL
YOU WANT WE SHOULD HOLE 'EM?
YOU GONNA MAKE TO STOP OUR MOVE.

Crogan's Loyalty Process...

My comics are made in stages. I write an outline first, and with *Loyalty* I developed the dialogue as I thumbnailed. A thumbnail is a preparatory drawing meant to help the artist determine the best possible composition for the panels. As you can see, I go through a lot for each page!

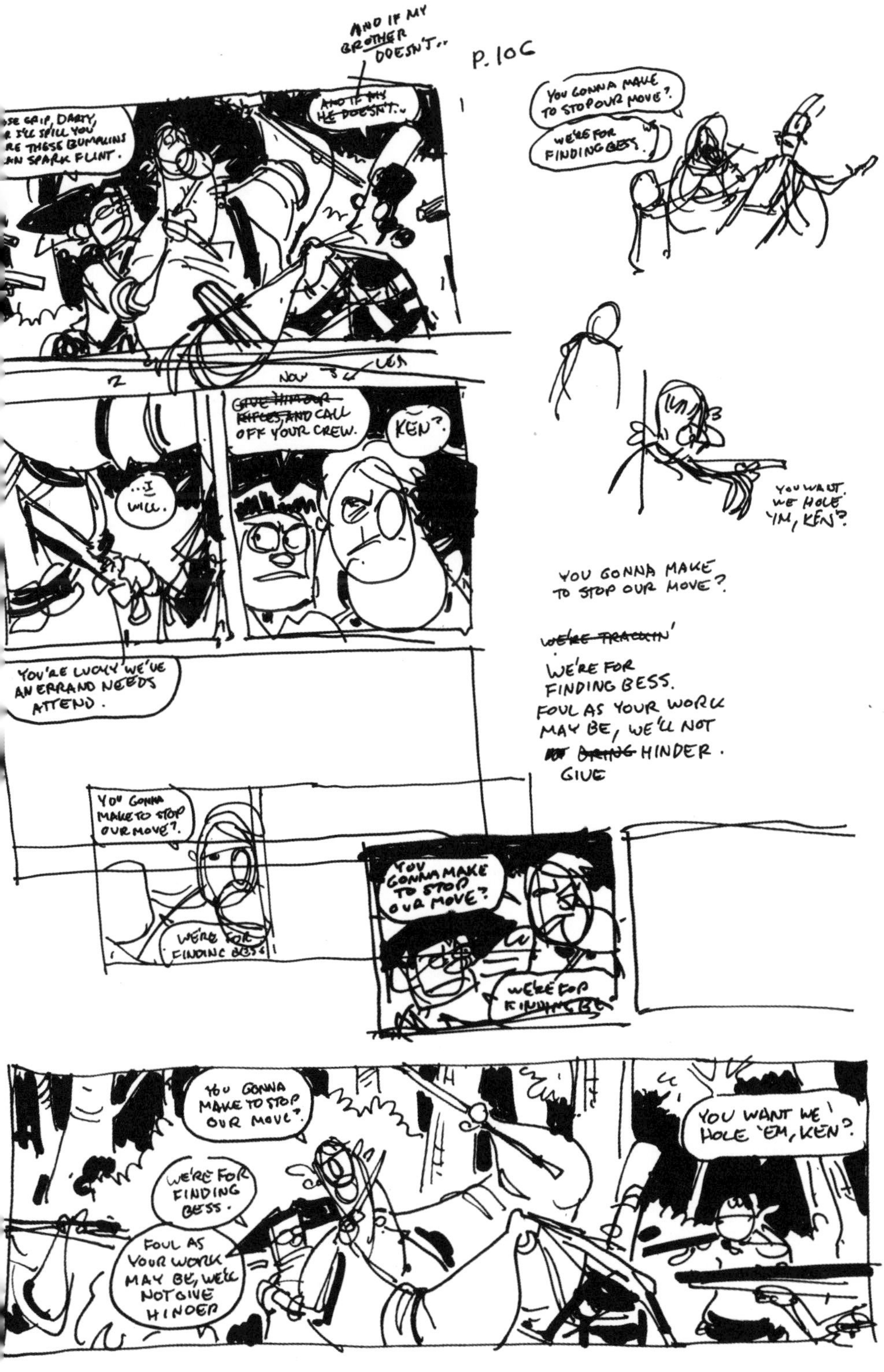
AND IF MY BROTHER DOESN'T..
P. 10C
YOU GONNA MAKE TO STOP OUR MOVE?
WE'RE FOR FINDING BESS.
NOW
CALL OFF YOUR CREW.
KEN?
...I WILL.
YOU WANT WE HOLE 'IM, KEN?
YOU GONNA MAKE TO STOP OUR MOVE?
WE'RE FOR FINDING BESS.
FOUL AS YOUR WORK MAY BE, WE'LL NOT HINDER.
GIVE
YOU'RE LUCKY WE'VE AN ERRAND NEEDS ATTEND.
YOU GONNA MAKE TO STOP OUR MOVE?
WE'RE FOR FINDING BESS
YOU GONNA MAKE TO STOP OUR MOVE?
WE'RE FOR
YOU GONNA MAKE TO STOP OUR MOVE?
WE'RE FOR FINDING BESS.
FOUL AS YOUR WORK MAY BE, WE'LL NOT GIVE HINDER
YOU WANT WE HOLE 'EM, KEN?

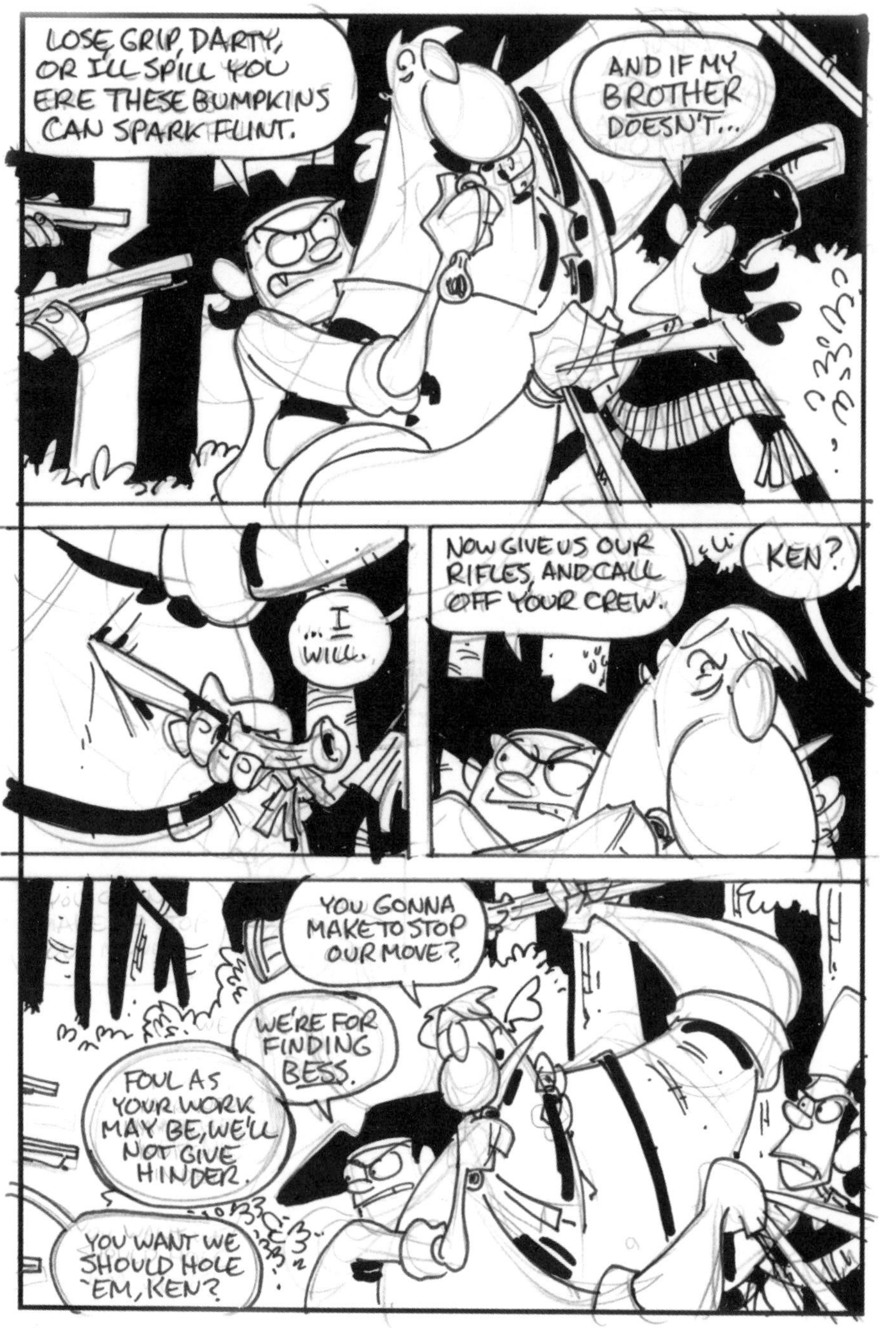
LOSE GRIP, DARTY, OR I'LL SPILL YOU ERE THESE BUMPKINS CAN SPARK FLINT.
AND IF MY BROTHER DOESN'T...
...I WILL.
NOW GIVE US OUR RIFLES, AND CALL OFF YOUR CREW.
KEN?
YOU GONNA MAKE TO STOP OUR MOVE?
WE'RE FOR FINDING BESS.
FOUL AS YOUR WORK MAY BE, WE'LL NOT GIVE HINDER.
YOU WANT WE SHOULD HOLE 'EM, KEN?

Once I'm satisfied with my thumbnails, I move to what are traditionally called "pencils." Pencils are the underdrawing for the final page. I do mine in a mix of pencil and pen. When I'm finished, I scan this in to the computer and print it out in very light blue ink. Then I ink on top of it with a brush. The final art can be seen on page 110.

Thanks to...

My thanks go out first and foremost to Liz, who offered her customary patience and support during the book's undertaking. These same thanks go to my daughter Penny, who is still too young to fully understand why her father has to hole up in the studio every day.

I would also like to thank Shawn Crystal and Pat Quinn, who do all they can to shield me from anything that would be detrimental to my work as a professor. I hear horror stories about the difficulties and politics of academia, and it is due to their tenacity and character that I've never had to suffer such things. They, along with my colleagues Nolan Woodard, Doug Dabbs, and June Bridgeman, consistently challenge and inspire me.

I'd like to thank my editors James Lucas Jones and Jill Beaton for their guidance – Jill for her attention to detail, and James for insisting on a different working method than what I'd used to produce the previous two *Crogan* books. It was not an approach that I enjoyed, but it definitely resulted in a better final piece than if I'd worked according to my inclinations. Thank you, James, for making me hate you for a little while.

Lastly, my thanks go to my students, for whom I must daily articulate my reasons for each principle of cartooning that I espouse. It is because of them that I constantly reexamine my thoughts on what we do, and I think my work is better for it.

Acknowledgments

The German dialogue in the book was initially translated by cartoonist Allen Spetnagel. I subsequently sent the pages on to Joachim Wenzel, who made a number of changes to ensure that the phrasing was properly suited to the military situation and social hierarchy of the characters. To both of these gentlemen, I offer my sincerest thanks.

One of my graduate students, Jay Peteranetz, suggested a funeral as the setting for the framing sequence. I thought this was an excellent idea, and I am indebted to him for it.

I attended the annual reenactment of the Battle of Guilford Courthouse in 2010. All of the reenactors were kind enough to answer my questions, especially the members of the 84th Royal Highland Emmigrants and the Hesse-Kassel Jager Korps. Both groups permitted me to examine their equipment, make sketches, and pick their brains. I'd have felt far less comfortable undertaking the art of this book had it not been for their help.

Quite a few books were referenced when writing this story, but I make significant use of Colin G. Calloway's *The American Revolution in Indian Country*, Patrick Griffin's *American Leviathon*, Christopher Hibbert's *Redcoats and Rebels*, Ray Raphael's *A People's History of the American Revolution*, and Stanley Weintraub's *Iron Tears*. On the art side of things, few books have ever proved more valuable to me than C. Keith Wilbur's *The Revolutionary Soldier 1775-1783*, without which I would have greatly struggled when trying to depict certain accoutrements and how they worked.

Charlie's uniform is based off of a painting in *An Illustrated Encyclopedia of Uniforms from 1775–1783: The American Revolutionary War*. The illustrations are not specifically credited to the artists, however, so I am unsure as to who painted it.

About the author...

CHRIS SCHWEIZER was born in 1980, and received his BFA from Murray State University, where he studied art and English, and his MFA from SCAD-Atlanta, where he is now teaches comics as a professor of Sequential Art. He is a member of the National Cartoonist Society, and lives in Marietta, Georgia with his wife Liz and daughter Penelope.

Like Will and Charlie, Chris spent most of his formative years playing in and exploring the woods, but he didn't have a brother. He did have a sister whose nose he accidentally broke with a pool ball the day before her prom. She, however, once burned down the house and in doing so destroyed an original Walt Kelly *Pogo* strip that would certainly have become his one day, so they're probably even.

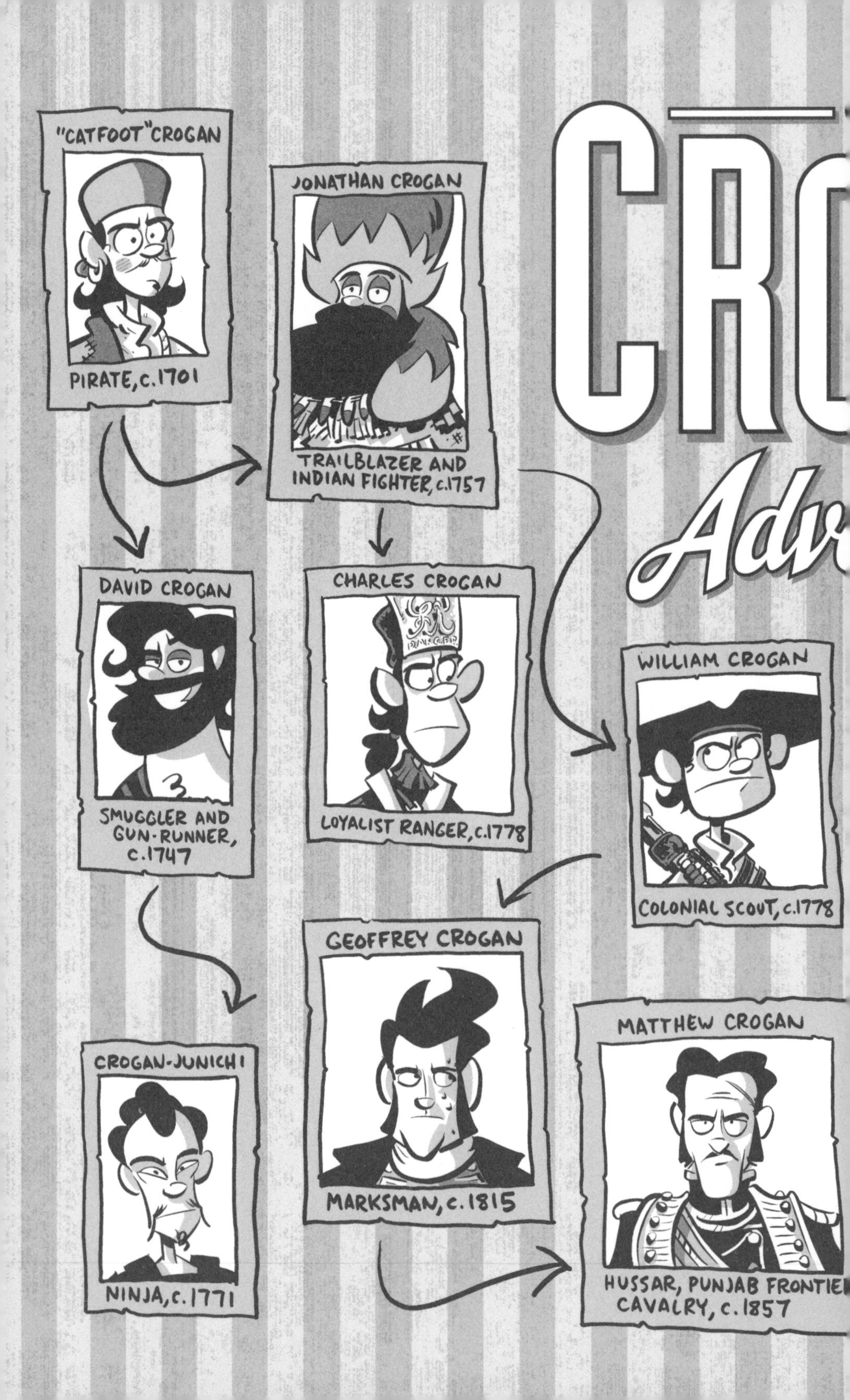
"CATFOOT" CROGAN
PIRATE, c.1701
JONATHAN CROGAN
TRAILBLAZER AND INDIAN FIGHTER, c.1757
DAVID CROGAN
SMUGGLER AND GUN-RUNNER, c.1747
CHARLES CROGAN
LOYALIST RANGER, c.1778
WILLIAM CROGAN
COLONIAL SCOUT, c.1778
CROGAN-JUNICHI
NINJA, c.1771
GEOFFREY CROGAN
MARKSMAN, c.1815
MATTHEW CROGAN
HUSSAR, PUNJAB FRONTIE
CAVALRY, c.1857